The
Dog Who
Saved Me

SUSAN WILSON

ST. MARTIN'S PRESS

NEW YORK

This is a work of fiction. All of the characters, organizations, and events portrayed in this novel are either products of the author's imagination or are used fictitiously.

www.stmartins.com

LIBRARY OF CONGRESS CATALOGING-IN-PUBLICATION DATA

Wilson, Susan, 1951–
   The dog who saved me / Susan Wilson.—1st Ed.
     p. cm.
   ISBN 978-1-250-01434-4 (hardcover)
   ISBN 978-1-250-01435-1 (e-book)
   1. Human-animal relationships—Fiction.   2. Dog owners—Fiction.
3. Grief—Fiction. I. Title.
   PS3573.I47533D65 2015
   813'.54—dc23

                  2014035535

St. Martin's Press books may be purchased for educational, business, or promotional use. For information on bulk purchases, please contact the Macmillan Corporate and Premium Sales Department at 1-800-221-7945, extension 5442, or write to specialmarkets@macmillan.com.

First Edition: March 2015

10 9 8 7 6 5 4 3 2 1

To my daughters, Elizabeth and Alison.
You are still my best creations.

The
Dog Who
Saved Me

Prologue

W hen Lev Parker, Harmony Farms' chief of police, called me the first time about the job as animal control officer, I was insulted—there was no way I was going to return to Harmony Farms, and certainly not to wear the uniform of a dog officer. I'd escaped from there long ago. The first in my family to go to college, I'd lived in an overcrowded and rowdy apartment, attending a community college with a tuition I could afford on my own with the help of a part-time job that filled every hour I wasn't in class or studying. I majored in criminal justice. That path led to acceptance in the Police Academy and, finally, the fulfillment of a dream, a position on the Boston police force. I'd found my place, my niche, a purpose. I wore that blue uniform with pride. I had outgrown my past, my family history. On my rare trips back to Harmony Farms, I imagined that now people looked at me with a new respect.

Three times Lev called with the offer, each time modifying it with pot sweetening—a little more money squeezed out of the finance committee, an almost new town vehicle, an assistant. I'd be a dynamic part of his team.

Lev's clumsy "I need a good man" bullshit made it sound like I was the only ex-cop who could possibly do justice to the job of animal control officer. I felt like I was a little kid getting picked last for the basketball team. Or, worse, that what he was offering to me was a handout—a pity play. I knew I wasn't fit for duty, at least not for any real police duty; even though my own physical injuries had begun to heal, my psychic injuries had festered. Maybe that's all I was good for, scraping up roadkill, getting cats out of trees. At least no one gets killed in a job like that; nobody expects you to be brave. I would have no emotional attachment to the animals I encountered. Even at six months, I wasn't at a distant-enough remove to believe that I could ever attach myself to another dog. The idea of partnering again with a canine was out of the question. *Is* out of the question, I still tell myself.

I know Lev didn't look at it that way—that he was tossing me a bone—at least I don't think he did. His point of view was that he had an opening and, clearly, I needed a job. I'd quit the force, tendering my resignation with relief. Maybe *relief* isn't the right word; more like *capitulation.* I'd given in to the overwhelming consequences of my loss. I was incapable of climbing out of the pit of despair that I had been blown into on that night in January.

"Cooper, with your experience, you'd be a real asset to me."

"I was part of a K-9 unit, not a dogcatcher."

"But you know dogs."

"I knew one dog." Argos. My German shepherd. No, the Boston PD's shepherd. My partner. For months, I'd been mourning his loss, and my inability to put what had happened into its proper compartment and get on with my life had made me vulnerable to losing control of everything else in my life.

The animal control job was a one-year contract. Temporary, a stopgap, Lev said, while I got better. Even so, I resisted the urge to hang up on the man who had once been a good friend, resenting both the suggestion that I might be interested in such a job and the barely disguised pity with which it was offered. "I know this is hard for you, Coop, but I really do need a good man in the position. The applicant pool around here is pretty shallow. The only other guy is a preppy grad student our first selectman is pushing on me. I thought of you because—"

I cut him off. I didn't want to hear his justifications. "You, of all people, know why I don't want to come back."

"It's history, man. Ancient history. There are so many new people around here, they don't even know who Bull is. "

"It's not just Bull, and you know it. I've spent two decades on the other side of the law from my brother. We Harrisons don't have a sterling reputation in this town."

"Harrison is pretty common name, and Jimmy's not around anyway. Hasn't been for years." As well I knew. My older brother was incarcerated in the prison at Walpole—in the eleventh year of his twelve-year sentence for drug trafficking.

Lev's words might, once again, have fallen on my—literally— deaf ear, but they came just when my wife, Gayle, had had enough. It was when Gayle broke it to me that she wanted me out of the house—she couldn't take what she called my "moods" anymore— that I finally listened to what my old basketball teammate had to say.

Gayle rested her fingers on the open mouth of the fifth of bourbon, which had become my drink of choice. "I'm going to the gym. Why don't you come with me?" She picked up the cap and screwed it back on.

I watched her slowly twist the cap, a casual motion. No recriminations, just a maternal "That's enough for you," acted out with a tightened bottle cap.

"No thanks. I'm fine. You go ahead."

It's a conversation we'd had over and over, and I could tell that she was growing impatient with me. No, *impatient* isn't the word. Worried, concerned. Maybe even bored. Tired of me and my inconsolable grief. She'd held my hand; she'd held my head when I'd gone too far with the bourbon. She'd held her tongue.

"Really, I'm just fine. Kind of tired. So you go." I had my eye on that bottle, wondering if she'd notice if another inch was missing when she got home from the gym. She disappeared into the bedroom, then reappeared, kitted out in flattering Spandex. "Hey, Gayle," I said.

The hostility in her eyes was liquid. There is a sheen to the human eye when anger and frustration sheath it in dammed tears.

"You look great." It was my clumsy attempt at a mollifying compliment, but she wasn't buying it.

"How would you know? When was the last time?" She didn't have to say anything more. Along with everything else I'd once held dear, our marital relations had suffered with my descent into the black hole of despair.

She knew I was lying. Gayle didn't look fine. She looked pinched and angry, and I knew it was my fault. But you can't stop being sad just because some shrink says that you should be "moving on."

Midnight and I was still awake, the ringing in my ear singing to me in the quiet of a lonely man's vigil. It sang of self-doubt, of regret. It sang of another night, deeply cold, stars so bright, they could make you believe in God.

I stood on the balcony, which was the real estate company's primary sales feature of the condo. Look, a view of the city, cheap at the price. Behind me was the closed sliding door that kept my wife from hearing the sound of the bottle repeatedly touching the rim of my glass. In the near distance, with my good ear, I could hear the barking of a dog. A throaty, "mean it," kind of bark. A warning. I was dwelling on my loss, maybe even wallowing in it. The good news for me was that I knew that's what I was doing. The bad news: It had become a comfortable place, but one that didn't really allow for anyone else. Gayle just didn't get my failure to get over Argos's loss.

I had Argos, my police dog, long before I knew Gayle. You don't get many dogs like Argos. Full-on police dog when tracking down felons, total puppy when playing in the backyard. His bark was deep, his bite crushing, but his love for me was unmistakable. Gayle had claimed to love Argos, as much as she could love something that was as devoted to me as he was. Her love was simply a normal affection for an animal, and why not? She didn't work with him, depend on him for professional success. He was the big dog taking up a lot of space in our condo. He wasn't her first love. He was mine.

It was a buddy of mine who got me interested in going for the K-9 unit. He'd been a dog handler in Afghanistan and couldn't say enough about the rewards of having a canine partner. I'm not going to say that meeting Argos for the first time was like love at first sight, more like a bromance. Unlike human partners, we didn't say good night at the end of a shift; we went home together. We spent holidays together. We played a lot of catch together. We had boundaries, like any good friends. He slept in his kennel at night. He didn't beg at the table. Argos never questioned my authority and I never questioned his dedication to the job.

When Gayle came into our lives, Argos accepted my sudden distraction with grace, placing her under his protection. Of course, he was not a pet. He was, for all intents and purposes, a tool. I was trained to use that tool. Affection and camaraderie were allowable, but not to the point of undermining the dog's purpose. Argos wasn't a therapy dog; he was a weapon. Tell that to the human heart. To me, he was the whole package.

"I'm done." That's what she said. She'd come back from the gym and I was exactly where she'd left me—slouched on the couch, still in the same sweats I'd started out in the day before, the bottle of bourbon down another four inches. "I can't take this drinking, this self-pity, this refusal to try." And then she said the killing words: "You're becoming just like your father."

So when Lev had called earlier that evening, instead of saying no, I'd offered to think about it. "I'm not promising, you understand, but maybe it wouldn't be a bad thing to get away for a while."

Lev shot the last arrow in his quiver—I could rent the old hunting camp on Bartlett's Pond. I knew what he was offering, even if he didn't. Solitude. Time and place to lick the wounds that had been inflicted on me.

"Come see me."

"Okay." I stood in the middle of the kitchen, my phone still in my hand. I placed it facedown on the granite countertop. I told myself that I hadn't said yes, but somehow it felt like I had made a decision. Gayle, holed up now in the bedroom, sleeping, or pretending to sleep, had made it abundantly clear that she didn't want me around anymore. She'd had enough.

So as dawn crept up over the horizon, I called Lev back and told him I'd take the job.

Part One

1

~❧~

My quarry is intelligent, experienced, elusive. I make a slow turn off the main road and head into a development, easing my government-issue vehicle over the numerous speed bumps designed to keep the rate of speed through the neighborhood down to fifteen miles per hour. I'm craning to see if my fugitive is skulking somewhere behind the cultivated shrubbery or hidden deep in the landscape architect–designed three-acre parcels of this, the most exclusive of all of Harmony Farms' neighborhoods. This isn't the first time I've had to collect this particular miscreant. He has a taste for the good life, a sense of entitlement that frequently brings him here to this covenant-restricted monument to suburban living.

I throw the vehicle into park, sit for a moment, collecting myself, running a hand over my military-short brush of hair. This is the most likely place. It is also where I need to be on foot. It's time to roll. I settle my cap on my head and gather up my equipment. I shut the driver's door very carefully so as not to alert my fugitive. Unlike me, my quarry has extraordinary hearing. The element of surprise is the only weapon at my disposal and the only one that gives me any advantage. The good news is, it's still early in the day, the better not to have interference in the proceedings. Once the neighborhood residents are up and about, my chances of capturing the escapee are pretty well shot. Nothing worse than a posse of vigilante home owners in pursuit of a trespasser.

Despite the similarities of tracking down an enemy or a felon or a missing person and tracking down this miserable runaway, there is no sense of danger, of imperative in this situation. Which, given my nightmares and panic attacks at the thought of returning to my former profession, is a good thing.

I shoulder the coil of rope and squat to examine a print in the dust, depending only on my eyes to tell me the whereabouts of my target. Back in the day, I would have depended less on my vision than upon my canine partner's acute sense of smell to determine the direction of our quarry, his acute hearing to detect the slightest sound. This entire hunt would have been a snap with Argos by my side. I could have been blind and deaf and it wouldn't have mattered. Now I'm just deaf.

It's a pretty morning. The rising sun breaks rosy above the lake that is this town's chief attraction—the view of which is the Upper Lake Estates at Harmony Farms' chief selling point. The bucolic name of Harmony Farms belies the discordant undertones that have developed in the three decades since urban flight brought an influx of newcomers to the village. It was once simply a farming community, carved out of New England soil, etched into hillsides with dry-stone walls, its pastures grappled from the stingy fists of old-growth timber, itself then committed to use as fence posts, firewood, and farmhouses. Lake Harmony is still its centerpiece, a ten-acre, pristine jewel in the crown, complemented by the half dozen spring-fed ponds that punctuate the terrain between gentle hills. Much of the shoreline is privately owned now, but the conservation people have carved out a nice public beach on the Lake Shore Drive side, the less pretty side, my side. It's where we swam when I was a kid, and where ice fishermen would slide their ice shacks out to the middle of the lake back in the day when it froze solid.

Old-timers like Deke Wilkins, whose family was one of the five original families given the charter for Harmony Farms back in the 1600s, have been pitted against the "new people," who arrived back in the glory days of the 1980s. People like the first selectman, Cynthia Mann, who leads the charge for quality-of-life improvements to the roads, the school, and the gentrification of Main Street. Or her husband, Donald Boykin, who sits on the land-use committee and likes to write big checks as "lead gifts" for a variety of big-ticket charities here and elsewhere. Theirs are the names you see on the top of donor lists, the ones who know how to throw a party.

But with influence come accommodations. A few of the niceties. In other words, bring all of the things we like best about city life to this hamlet where we fled to avoid the pitfalls of city life. And besides, twenty miles is too far to go to get a decent cup of coffee. Deke Wilkins likes the sludge that Elvin sells at the Country Market. He doesn't need any high-priced beverage too highfalutin to call itself small, medium, or large. *Grande.* He hoots when he says the word. At Elvin's, he can get a small coffee, and that's just fine with him. "Gimme a *petit*, will ya?"

I jog along a meticulously groomed driveway, following a scattering of prints pressed into the sprinkler-moist edge until I reach a gap in a determinedly trimmed hedge. On the other side, there's a depression in the grass that might be a print; a little farther into the property, I find another. I spot the best indicator that my quarry has passed this way, a small pile of manure. And there he is, happily grazing upon the expansive flower beds of Harmony Farms' wealthiest resident, Cutie-Pie, the miniature donkey, who has made a career out of escaping from his owners' inadequately fenced-in yard.

I pull a carrot out of my back pocket. Cutie-Pie eyes me with suspicion, gives me a wink, and goes back to eating the no doubt expensive and probably imported late-summer flowers. His little brushy tail twitches in derision. The thing with these miniature equines is that they don't think like real equines. They are independent thinkers. A horse will allow itself to be led. A miniature donkey will plant four feet and become an immovable object. A statue of a donkey. I swear that it's Eddie Murphy's voice coming out of Cutie-Pie. *Say what? Yours truly get in that truck? I don't think so. You're jokin', right?* Cutie-Pie is only the size of a large dog. Not even as tall as Argos was.

Right now, my goal is to get a lead line attached to this animal. I hold out the carrot. Cutie-Pie, without moving his legs, stretches his neck to its full length, reaching with his prehensile lips for the carrot. I keep it just out of reach, making the donkey choose: Flowers? Carrot? Cutie-Pie finally takes a step, then another. As soon as the donkey is within reach, I snag his halter, snapping the lead line to it. At least I've finally convinced the Bollens to keep the halter on at all times, even if I haven't convinced them to fix the freakin' fence. Nice couple, one tick away from doddery. They treat this out-of-control equine like a baby. Mrs. Bollen was my third-grade teacher, so it's pretty much impossible for me to threaten them with fines or confiscation. Besides, I really don't want a donkey at the limited facility my part-time assistant, Jenny Bright, refers to as the "Bowwow Inn." It's barely adequate for the canine inmates. I mean, it's better than it was when I arrived on the scene, but still pretty primitive.

Before I got here, there was no shelter, just the pound, which was nothing more than a wire run attached to the outside of the town barn. At least now the impounds have a proper kennel, proper care. Even if this isn't a job I want, I still have the integrity of purpose to make sure my animals are safe and rehomed. No animal on my watch will be put down unless critically injured or unequivocally dangerous, and I haven't encountered either of those circumstances to date, a third of the way into my twelve-month contract. I do that in memory of Argos. Argos, who could interpret what I was thinking even before I thought it. A pure white shepherd, his eyes deep brown, he was big for his breed, and maybe too pretty, but his magnificent nose was what made him the best of the best. Acute and never wrong. Not once. I shake off the thought. My shrink wants me to develop a mechanism to switch off those thoughts, develop what he calls "coping" mechanisms; adopt something that will bring me out of the past and back into the moment.

Half a bag of carrots later, I have the donkey crammed into the backseat of the town's white Suburban, a cast-off vehicle from the building inspector's department. Although I hope that Cutie-Pie doesn't let loose in the ten minutes it'll take to drive him home, I've set yesterday's *Boston Globe* under his back end. I've really got to lay the law down with the Bollens. Armand Percy isn't going to be too pleased to see his million-dollar gardens destroyed by a miniature donkey. Armand Percy isn't exactly a warm and fuzzy kind of guy. We assume he's some sort of venture capitalist who managed to survive the downturn. No one really knows what he does, just that he was one of the very first of the very wealthy to arrive in Harmony Farms thirty years ago.

What's certain is, Percy isn't likely to be the sort of fellow to overlook the destruction of his gardens. He's more likely to be the sort of fellow who will demand restitution. In all the years that Percy has lived in Harmony Farms, there isn't anyone who can claim to have seen him. Still, he keeps a cadre of housecleaners, yardmen, gardeners, and window washers employed year-round, most of whom come from the same side of the tracks as I did. Not the fancy side with the homes with a view of Lake Harmony and two bathrooms, but the rough side, where getting through high school was an accomplishment and home was often subsidized housing or one cheap rental after another, like the places we'd end up each time my mother left my father, dragging us boys with her.

Tina Bollen rushes up to meet me as I pull into the driveway. "I knew you'd find him!"

"Mrs. Bollen, this can't keep happening."

"I know." She says she knows, but I don't think she really gets it.

To her, and to her husband, Cutie-Pie is just a mischievous child. A bad little boy, which is exactly what she says as I extricate the donkey from the backseat.

"Oh, Cutie-Pie, what a bad little boy you are." She makes kissy noises and scratches his forehead, as if he's done something cute. This attitude puzzles me, given Mrs. Bollen's strict authority in the third-grade classroom. Oh, how times have changed.

"Some one of these days, a home owner is going to sue you if he finds Cutie-Pie munching on his flowers." I throw that out in the hope that the threat of litigation will bring her into reality. "That's if he doesn't keep a rifle." If litigation doesn't work, how about the threat of plain old violence?

But Mrs. Bollen just smiles. "I don't think so." There's a little of the old Mrs. Bollen in that remark, and something in her tone reminds me of the time she had me facing the blackboard, hands behind my back, all my pals outside at recess. Mrs. Bollen was sitting there at her desk, humming softly, as I anguished over being kept in, the sounds of school yard play in my ears. My friends were playing dodgeball, and every hollow bounce of the flaccid ball felt like a slap. I don't remember what it was I did wrong to merit so unfair a punishment. Unlike my older brother, Jimmy, I wasn't a bad kid, never intentionally fresh or into destructive mischief. I was probably caught chewing gum. Mrs. Bollen was a bug on gum chewing. To this day, I never put a stick of Doublemint in my mouth without feeling like I'm committing a misdemeanor. "Will you call someone to come build you a proper fence?"

Mrs. Bollen takes the donkey's lead line out of my hand. She doesn't look at me, just makes kissy sounds at Cutie-Pie. I look around, noting the flaking paint on the house and the poor condition of the roof.

"Look, if you can manage materials, I'll do it for you. I just can't keep chasing him down."

The Mrs. Bollen of my childhood was tall and imperious, her

steel gray hair disciplined into a crown of curls. This woman barely comes up to my shoulder, and her white hair is loosely gathered into a relaxed bun. She reaches up and pats my cheek, as if I'm still eight, not thirty-eight. I see a glint of that pity she once showed me, as if I haven't outgrown the need for it.

Mrs. Bollen was my teacher when my father was thrown in jail for drunk driving. Maybe she punished me that day because she wanted to keep me away from the other kids, the ones who knew what was going on. The ones who had heard from their parents that Bull Harrison had driven up Main Street in broad daylight, knocking down parking meters like toothpicks with his '68 Nova, until finally plowing through the plate-glass window of the Cumberland Farms. He climbed out of the truck, shook his head, bits of glass falling out of his beard, grabbed a half gallon of milk, and dug out his wallet. He looked at the shaken clerk. "Sorry about that." Three little words that became the town joke. No one was killed, thank God, and miraculously no one hurt, but Bull was—once again—the laughingstock of the village of Harmony Farms. Town drunk. Town joke. My father. *Sorry about that.*

Mr. Bollen has arrived on the scene, as bent over and plump as his wife is straight and thin. He gives Cutie-Pie a fond scratch on the neck. "That would be great, Cooper. If you'll buy the materials, we'll reimburse you. And for your time."

"No, no need for that. Maybe a plate of that lasagna Mrs. Bollen is so famous for." Somehow, I know that I'll be using my own account at the lumberyard for the fencing and that I may never have the chutzpah to hand Mr. Bollen the bill. But it'll be worth it to have that miserable little faux equine corralled permanently.

This is my life.

The dog waits patiently as the man who has kept him locked in the crate stands with two other men, a third man standing at a distance.

The dog can smell the sweet scent of fresh air all around him. The birds at this early hour have begun their chittering, and a new sun tinges the pond water pink.

The men are leaning against the big car, smoking cigars and passing a bottle from one to the next, pouring something into paper cups that smells sharp to the Labrador's clever nose. Unpleasant, as is the smoke drifting out of their mouths. The fourth man says something to the trio, and the man who seems to be in possession of the dog finally drops his cigar, stamps his foot on it, and snatches up the dog's leash. *"Come on, dog."* The dog tags along happily enough. The others follow. Like the man who holds his leash, they all cradle shotguns in their arms.

The walk is a pleasant one as they follow the fourth man, who moves quickly and quietly in the lead. They come to the pond, and a roofless structure, into which they go. Sunlight dapples the stamped-down riparian grasses under their feet. There's some talk, and then the three men all face the water. The fourth man walks away. The dog is uninterested in the absent man; it's enough to try to befriend the one in charge of him.

The dog doesn't know what they're waiting for, if indeed that's what's happening. He senses a general restlessness as the men, leaning through the open space above the low wall, shift on their booted feet and begin to mutter. Finally, a duck quacks, twice. The dog's ears perk up at the sound.

The explosion over his head launches the dog into a frenzy of panicked barking. Once, twice, three times the guns blast two feet over his head. It's only the grip the man has on the dog's leash that prevents him from running away. He's hauled back close to the man's legs, close to the discharged and stinking weapons, their heat and odor burning fear into the dog's mind.

He's given an order, but not with words he's ever heard before. It's a human-language mystery, what this man wants of him. He's pushed toward the water. *"Go, go, go. Get the goddamn, duck, you expen-*

sive goddamn piece of . . . " The dog is shaking, trembling, and the rage and frustration in the man brings the dog down to his belly; he rolls over, utterly submissive, quaking. The two other men stalk away, guns broken open, leaving the man and the dog alone on the edge of the pond.

The first kick hurts. The second kick breaks a rib. The blow with the stock of the shotgun cracks but does not shatter his skull. The dog scrambles to his feet, pulls against the leash, sets his feet against the constriction of the web collar, struggles, and finally slips free to bolt.

"Get back here, you mutt."

The man raises his shotgun, one barrel still loaded. Fires.

2

When I drop into Country Market to pick up a deli sandwich for lunch, Deke Wilkins is there, as he always is at this time of day, elbow resting on the meat case, that petit cup of coffee in his other hand. Jawing about who knows what with Elvin. The old man has been a constant in my life, and I can't think of a time when Deke wasn't in that exact spot, wearing those same overalls, his wiry gray hair sticking up like boar's bristles, and the nicotine of his pack-and-a-half habit staining the work-worn fingers of his right hand. Whenever my mother sent me into the market for a loaf of bread or a dollar's worth of bologna, there was Deke. On an ordinary day, he might have acknowledged me with a "Hey, kid." But when Bull was in trouble, as he often was, the old man sometimes stuck a packet of Twizzlers or pack of Doublemint into my pocket. When I'd mumble an embarrassed thanks, Deke might say, "Share with your brother. Come help me with my stone wall sometime. I could use a big boy like you."

Yeah, right. Share with Jimmy. More like, if Jimmy saw that I had a treat, my older brother would whack me in the back of the head and confiscate it.

Two little boys on a walk with their father. One boy is tall for his age, although compact, his jeans a little big, puddling over his worn Keds. The other boy still has that puppyish roundness to his face, a little boy's belly poking above the jeans he's already begun to outgrow. Like them, their father holds a fishing pole. In his rucksack is a plastic box of hooks and sinkers. The boys know what else is in his rucksack besides lunch and two bottles of Coke. Three cans of beer. Maybe a nip or two. Or three.

Their father has promised them he's going to teach them how to fish. The various NO FISHING *and* NO TRESPASSING *and* PRIVATE PROPERTY *signs that they've pushed past indicate that, once again, Dad is following his own devices. At six, the younger boy, Cooper, is old enough to read, and he has made a point of mentioning signs. Bull tells him to keep quiet. Mind himself. He knows what he's doing. "Trust me, boys."*

Eventually, they make their way to Lake Harmony, the eastern side of the lake, deep within the riparian territory of Upper Lake Estates. Home ownership there comes with waterfront access and the guarantee that no one else is allowed to fish at this particular spot. The exact spot where, for centuries, the best trout have congregated. Although there are only, at this time, three homes established in the development, all the amenities of curvilinear drives and new lush plantings, a boat ramp, and a brand-new pier are visual enticements for those urbanites considering relocating to the rustic—but sophisticated—Harmony Farms.

"Dad, I don't think we're supposed to be here." Cooper again. Fretting about signage.

"I fished here all my life. No newcomer is going to tell me otherwise." Bull snatches the pole out of Jimmy's hand and fumbles around in the rucksack to find the small tackle box.

Cooper hears the clinking of bottle against bottle as Bull finally locates what he's looking for—a chiming sound that he, at six, already associates with trouble. Sure enough, as soon as he's finished with the hooks, Bull sits down on the edge of the new pier and pulls out a nip and a can of beer. "Drop your lines, boys. Get me a fish."

Anyone looking at them might think that their trio looks like a family in a Rockwell painting. Two boys and a dad, poles twitching at their tips as false hope convinces them they've caught something. A bright orange life ring hanging from a peg is the brightest dash of color. Rockwell wouldn't have painted the ruddy flush darkening Bull's face as the hours pass and the nips go down. Sometimes Bull is a jolly drunk. Sometimes he's not. Cooper keeps his line in the water and his back to his father. He'd already figured out that it's best just to keep quiet.

They sit for hours, waiting for Bull to decide they've had enough, that the fish aren't biting, that occupying the private and forbidden pier hasn't brought them any luck. After the third or fourth nip, Bull lies back on the decking of the new pier and falls instantly to sleep, the sound of his snoring mimicking the sound of a distant motorboat. The sun has scorched the back of their necks and it becomes painful to look up. The creel beside them is empty, their sandwiches long since eaten, the Cokes gone, and there is nothing else for them to drink. Cooper nudges his brother and mouths, "I want to go home."

Jimmy reels in his line. Nods. Cooper reels in his. Bull's vigorous snores vibrate against the planking and they can feel it in the soles of their feet.

"Dad?" Louder. "Dad?" Jimmy steps a little closer to his father.

The snoring stops, but Bull's eyes remain closed. They wait for a moment. "Dad? Can we go now?"

Quick as a darting snake, Bull's hand grasps Jimmy's ankle and, with one smooth movement, he flips the boy off his feet. Jimmy's head nearly smacks the decking. "You catch any fish yet?"

Jimmy isn't crying; he's that stunned.

Cooper runs up to his father. "No. We tried. We tried." He's pushed aside, nearly falls off the pier. He catches himself, windmilling his arms to regain balance.

"Know what happens to boys who won't fish?" Laughing, Bull hauls Jimmy to his feet and tosses him off the pier, as if he's a too small fish. He's forgotten that Jimmy can't swim, that Jimmy is terrified of water.

Cooper screams and then runs, afraid that he, too, will end up drowning in the lake, the cold water taking him in and under, filling his lungs.

"Stand up, you pussy. That water isn't over your head." Bull is roaring with laughter. He pulls the orange life ring off the hanger. "You want I throw you this?"

Jimmy is thrashing, but finally he finds his feet. Bull drops the life ring, reaches down, and brings him up. Hands him his cap. "Time you learned to swim, boy."

Cooper is off the pier, standing on the shore, watching and ready to run for his life, but things seem to have simmered down. Bull unsnaps the useless hooks off their poles and shoves the plastic box back in his now-empty rucksack. He and Jimmy come off the pier, father and soaking-wet son. Bull strides past Cooper, confident that the boys are on his heels. Jimmy isn't crying anymore; he's wiped the tears and lake water off his face. As they fall in behind their father, Cooper reaches over and takes Jimmy's hand. Jimmy snatches his hand away from his little brother and runs to catch up with Bull.

What kept waking Cooper up at night after that wasn't nightmares about drowning, but the look in his brother's clear, cold gray eye. As if the Jimmy who had been his big brother had been utterly changed by his baptism in the lake and now was someone else entirely.

"Hey, Deke."

"Afternoon, Coop."

These days, Deke no longer buys me licorice or gum. These days, Bull Harrison is on the wagon and keeping his nose clean, and Jimmy is in Walpole, serving out his sentence for drug distribution. He was lucky that the value of the heroin found in the trunk of his car wasn't enough to get him sent away for longer. That he didn't plea-bargain himself down a couple of years only suggested to me that his contact is a very scary guy.

My way of dealing with my father is to avoid him. The first night that I was back in town, he spotted me in the market and enfolded me in one of his signature bear hugs. I extricated myself, maybe a little more roughly than necessary. He hadn't changed much since the last time I'd laid eyes on him. Still slovenly, still clueless.

"Hey, good to have you back, son. Put down those groceries and come have dinner with me." I hadn't told him I was coming back, but I wasn't surprised that he knew I had. Not at all. Not in this town.

"That's okay, Bull. I have a bunch of stuff to do. Another time." Another time in a pig's eye, I thought. I backed away as fast as I could, and the embarrassment that I'd left behind me so long ago worked its way up my face and I thought exactly like my younger self: Dear God, I hope no one saw me with him. My promise to myself in this reluctant return to Harmony Farms is that I have arrived as a stranger, not a native son.

"So, Cooper, I hear that Polly Schaeffer got another kitten." Deke settles his elbow back on the meat case. "Isn't she about over her limit?"

"Somewhat." The cop version of me keeps me from gossiping about my work, despite the juicy stories I could be telling. Polly, the local animal hoarder, being one such topic. Sweet, misguided, delusional, she's seeking something that her family, her onetime friends, her community simply can't provide. Maybe I should get Cynthia Mann to drum up interest in a mental-health clinic to serve the community, as she did with the new community yoga center. Never underestimate the power of a woman with money and time on her hands, coupled with a civic conscience that extends primarily to young upscale families. Maybe her hubby, Donald, can float the starter funding. No, on second thought, a mental-health clinic would disturb the equipoise between the fantasy Harmony Farms and the reality. These people came here to escape the touted evils of the city—poverty and drugs and abuse—and then they find themselves having to turn a blind eye to the rural poverty and spousal abuse and drug use, so that they can believe that they have bettered their lives.

"Can't her kids do something about her?" This from Elvin, who slaps a pair of neatly trimmed pork chops onto the scale.

"I'll go out. Talk to her again." I grab a bag of kitty litter and a flat of canned cat food.

Polly Schaeffer gave me the only other dog I had before my partnership with Argos. Back then, she was like any woman running a household. Back then, she had a husband, two kids, only two cats and one dog, a beagle bitch who'd wandered off in pursuit of a rabbit and come back *enceinte*. Polly, over some objections from my mother, and with Bull's grudging okay, gave me one of the puppies. Snoopy, I called him, even though he looked more pit bull than beagle. He was a good puppy, a perfect pal for a five-year-old boy living in the sticks.

I had to give up Snoopy when my mother left my father the first time, when I was six. Jimmy was eight. I begged her, if we couldn't have him, to let Bull keep the dog, but she said no. She said she didn't trust him with any living creature. Six weeks later, she moved us back into the ramshackle house on Poor Farm Road, but Snoopy didn't come back. I don't know what happened to him. Mom just said he had a new family, no one from around here. When I was a little kid, that sounded like he had a choice. When I was older, I envied him.

"You know what happened to that mutt?" Jimmy pushes Cooper's face into the mud at the edge of the lake. They've been fighting, squabbling over possession of a fishing pole. "They had him shot. That's what. Ha. You're stupid, thinking that poor old Snoopy is in some nice rich boy's home." Jimmy flips Cooper onto his back and shoves a handful of mud into his brother's mouth. "That pole's mine."

Polly took pity on me, let me walk Snoopy's mother, take her to the lake, play fetch with her. She never said anything bad about my mother's decision to get rid of my dog; she just kept her opinion to herself and was nice to me. Some years ago, after her husband died and her kids moved away, Polly Schaeffer began rounding up stray cats. What started as a noble gesture soon elevated to an obsession. But no matter how many times I've been out to talk Polly out of collecting more animals, I still think of her kindness and it makes my job all the harder to do.

I heft the bag of litter and flat of cat food out of my truck. I've swapped the town vehicle for my personal pickup truck because I'm here as an old friend. I never come in guns blazing with Polly. It's a matter of tact and finesse to get her to even open the door anymore. Over the years, as her hoarding has grown more pronounced, Polly has stopped letting her cats outside at all, fearful that someone will steal them, so I'm greeted with the eye-watering stink of too many cats in one tiny house. Cats are on the couch, the windowsill, and the television set, which blares with some talk show. Others weave themselves through and around my legs as I come in; a calico hisses and threatens me with polydactyl paws.

"Shut the door!" Polly stomps toward me, a kitten clutched to her pillowy breast. "You'll let them out."

"It's all right, Polly. No one escaped."

"How do you know? Now I have to count them again."

"And how many do you think you have?"

Polly throws me a coy look. "If I say, you're going to get mad."

"Why would I get mad?"

"I know you're not here just to say hi."

"That the new kitten?"

"Maybe."

"Not from one of your litters?" The one thing I've been able to do about Polly since I took the job is get all of her cats neutered. It's taken half my medical budget, but at least my pal Max Philbine, DVM, gives me a multiple cat discount. So, if she's adding to her collection through theft, at least the pride isn't increasing by uncontrolled breeding.

"Maybe not."

"You can't." I stop myself. "You should leave some kittens for other people."

"No one takes care of them like I do."

I have to push into the house to set my peace offerings down on the kitchen table, which is, predictably, layered with cats, cat hair, bowls of rancid milk, and something that may or may not be cat vomit. I have worked the mean streets of a major city, but this pretty much turns my stomach. When Lev Parker talked about my taking on the dog officer role in Harmony Farms, he left out the part about Polly Schaeffer's proclivities. I've chalked up a number of successes in this job—for example, rehoming seven stray dogs and an equal number of cats—but Polly stands out as my key failure to do my job. In my book, that failure has far more weight than the successes.

"Where'd you get the kitten, Polly?" I try to sound casual, simply interested.

"Found her."

"Okay, fair enough. Where did you find her?"

"I didn't steal her, if that's what you're suggesting."

I imagine putting Polly in an interrogation room and getting Lev to play bad cop so that I can be good cop, but here I've got to play both sides. "No. You didn't steal her, but is it remotely possible that she wasn't lost?" I don't allow myself to finger air quotes around the word *lost*, although I want to.

"She wasn't in a house."

"So, this kitten, which, if you ask me, looks half-grown, was just out wandering around?"

"Yes."

"And, if I call my office, Jenny Bright isn't going to tell me that someone has reported a lost kitten. Let's see, what is it? Gray and white, yellow eyes. Answers to the name of . . . "

"They let it out."

"Who, Polly?"

"I don't know. How should I know?"

A good policeman doesn't show frustration or impatience. But I'm not a cop anymore. "I'm calling Jenny."

"Okay. I found her wandering around in a yard near the old Callahan place."

"Near or *on* the Callahan property?" Despite how they speak of it, the place is no longer the Callahan family's landmark eighteenth-century homestead, but a completely remodeled version of the antique farmhouse with all the amenities, including pool house and five-bay garage.

"On." Polly is defeated, but only momentarily. "They're summer people. Probably left her behind when they went back home. People do that, you know."

"Yes. Occasionally, some summer person thinks that his or her impulsive vacation adoptee will survive on the charity of others. If no one answers the door, I'll entertain that notion." I hold out my hands. "Let me take her home, Polly."

"If no one's home, you'll bring her back, won't you?"

And this is where a lie is as good as a promise. If no one is home, or no one claims this kitty, my assistant will be tasked with finding her a new home. One, preferably, where there aren't already a dozen or more felines taking up space. So I lie. "Of course I will. You'll have first refusal."

I box the kitten and snug the crate behind my seat. As soon as the truck engine starts, the kitten sets up a pitiable yowling, as if she's being torn from the bosom of her family. I take care not to look up to see Polly's expression. I know that she knows that I've lied to her.

As I drive away from Polly's, I give Jenny Bright a call, and, sure enough, there has been a report of a missing gray cat. Not just a cat, but a rather expensive pedigreed Himalayan. Now, I know nothing about cats, and less about cat breeds, but it's pretty certain that this fluff ball is the missing feline. It seems easier simply to take the critter home than to have the family come get her. At the old Callahan property, I follow the new cobblestone driveway to the back of the house. No sign of life except for the faint scent of a Bounce dryer sheet wafting in the air. A woman in a gray uniform answers my knock. "Miss Mousy, where have you been?" She has an accent; I'm guessing Bulgarian. "I thought a dog got her. The missus would kill me if she knew she'd gotten out."

"So, you don't let her out normally?"

"No. Never. I think the pool man did it. I let him use the bathroom. Never again."

"Okay. Good to hear." It's good to think that Polly actually had found the kitten and not stolen it. It makes me feel a little better, knowing that at least she's not stealing other people's pets, that she hasn't gotten that bad. Yet.

I swing by the package store on my way home. I've given up the bourbon because I'm too often called to work in the middle of the night. But I haven't forsworn beer, and I open the cold case for a six-pack of Sam Adams. That and a couple of slices of yesterday's pizza are all I need. I head home, hoping that tonight I can enjoy a full night's sleep, uninterrupted by calls from the communications center reporting raccoons in trash cans or skunks holding dog walkers hostage. A night in my isolated cabin with just the radio tuned to NPR, loud.

Home is a former hunting camp on Bartlett's Pond, a bare-bones cabin with just enough insulation to call it winterized and just close enough to the main road to have electricity. My morning wake-up call is the sun easing itself up over the rim of the pond and the raucous sound of birds on the pond and in the woods. Lately, it's the honking of migratory geese and the sharp *come-to-tea* of the towhee that penetrates through the ringing in my ear. The red-winged blackbirds and their rusty-spring calls are gone. Chickadees chitter and complain and demand I fill the bird feeders *right now*. The rustic peace is shattered now and then by the early morning blast of shotguns obliterating some game bird—a sound that has the power to make my hands shake.

In the evening, as the light from the setting sun filters through the single window on the western side of the cabin, I can't tell if the silence is mine or if the birds have settled in. If I lived closer to town, I might go to the Lakeside Tavern every night instead of once in a while. I might find myself keeping upright on a bar stool, drowning my silence in a bath of noise from the old-fashioned jukebox and the cacophony that places like the tavern encourage. Instead, I turn on the radio and sit with my good ear closest to the sound of other voices talking about things that have nothing to do with me—things like war and famine and the state of health care.

Eventually, I will make myself go to bed, where I'll close my eyes and hope that I might enjoy a dreamless sleep.

Dusk comes so early these days. It's barely six-thirty, but I have my headlights on as I turn off the main road leading out of Harmony Farms. A few miles later, my headlights pick out the reflector nailed into a single fence post that marks the turnoff for my camp, a two-track driveway that meanders a half mile into the woods. A song I really hate comes on the radio and I reach for the off button. When I bring my eyes back to the narrow, rutted lane, something moves in the periphery of my vision. A shape, a suggestion. I'm tired enough to think that whatever it was moved like a ghost—dog-shaped.

It isn't so much the explosion as the exquisite silence preceding it that haunts Cooper's dreams. That awful silence like the air has been sucked into a vacuum. No air in his lungs. No way to scream. No way to stop the inevitable.

3

B arton "Bull" Harrison is a lumbering shaggy dog of a man. Built for strength, not speed. In a small town of increasing affluence, where the de rigueur Saturday uniform is Gap or Diesel, he stands out with his shock of gray-streaked hair and shaggy Fu Manchu mustache, sagging Wrangler blue jeans, and a flannel shirt no matter what the weather. He's most often seen pedaling his three-speed Raleigh on his way to his job at the lumberyard, where he ties two-by-fours or decorative lattice onto the roof racks of Land Rovers and Escalades or hefts six-by-six beams into the backs of carpenters' work vehicles. He's well liked at the lumberyard. Good for a laugh. Drinks Mountain Dew out of a can all day long. They say about him that he wouldn't hurt a fly. Some remember him from his bad old days, but most just know him as the affable guy at the lumberyard. One or two of the women who come in to shop for decorative molding or new drawer pulls remember him when he was a handsome young man. *Oh that Bull Harrison, you wouldn't believe it now, but he attracted the girls like flies. Shame about how he's turned out. Drugs, you know. Booze. Vietnam. Those kids. His wife.*

He's pretty happy about having his younger son back in town. It's been years since Cooper left town, getting away as fast as he could. Bull isn't ignorant about the whys and wherefores of Cooper's flight. It's pretty hard to grow up in a little town that witnesses your every movement. Because he, too, grew up in Harmony Farms, Bull remembers that sense of never having any privacy. Anytime he'd do something, well, let's be honest, stupid, the story would meet him at his own front door. Small-town fame is what it was. He was famous for trying, on a cow-tipping dare, to tip a bull over—hence his nickname—or for being the kid who could never resist a dumb challenge like driving his father's ancient and beloved '52 Ford truck across the ice of Lake Harmony from the boat landing to the opposite shore. Only he never quite got there. Pop was sure pissed off about that. Even today, when he tells the story, as he is given to do with the first sign of ice, Bull gets to laughing about the look on his father's face. He never mentions the whipping his old man gave him.

Ah, but Cooper is a different kettle of fish. Bull doesn't remember giving that kid a whipping very often; he kept his nose clean and hid in his room whenever Bull had to mete out punishment to his much more lively older brother. The things Cooper was famous for were, when you think of it, pretty good things—like good grades, like being a good basketball and hockey player.

It was hard on Cooper when Mona died. You would have thought that Jimmy would have been sorrier, but Cooper never quite got over it. Bull had tried, he really had, to be a good father, but back then he just couldn't keep clean. When you think about it, he couldn't keep clean when Mona was around; it's why she kept leaving. Then he'd straighten out, show her he was reliable, and she'd come back. Mona had very little faith in him but was eternally hopeful.

"Yeah, Coop fled the coop,"—that is what Bull likes to say whenever anyone asks him about his prodigal son. Took up a profession on the other side of the law from his brother, that's for damn sure. Jimmy, well, he's also a different kettle of fish, more like a barracuda. And from what Bull hears, that son, too, is on his way home.

Lenny Haynes stands in front of the bins of screws and nails.

"Getcha anything, Len?" Bull rocks back on his heels, takes a slug of his Mountain Dew.

"No. I got it." He grabs a paper bag from the stack and starts to fill it with roofing nails.

"Got a project going?"

"Maybe."

Bull doesn't take offense. This is the kind of conversation he and Lenny have been having all their lives. Lenny and his brother Bob live up in the hinterlands of Harmony Farms. About as prickly a pair as two porcupines in heat, as Bull likes to say. The kind of folks who protect their privacy with a barricade of NO TRESPASSING signs and hold the Second Amendment as sacred, convinced that every visitor is a potential invader, a threat to their sovereignty. Only the UPS man is welcome on their property. They are of the self-sufficient pioneer stock who make one trip to town a month. But Bull has known them forever and doesn't take their politics or their rudeness to heart.

"Got a sale on hammers. Buy one, get another for half price."

"What would I want with two hammers? Can't break 'em. Don't go bad. That's just bull crap and you know it."

Bull laughs. This is Len's humor. "I dunno. Maybe get that brother of yours to bang a few nails with you."

Len doesn't say anything, just drops the bag of nails onto the scale, waits while Bull writes him a slip.

There's a rangy yellow-colored dog in the back of Len's Ford truck. A short chain keeps it from jumping out of the bed. Bull walks over to give it a pat, but the dog snarls with an impressive show of teeth. Bull jumps back. Figure a Haynes to have a vicious dog.

"Watch it, Bull." Len makes no apology for his dog's behavior; in fact, Bull thinks that there's maybe a slight smile of pleasure in Len's face, a satisfaction. At his master's approach, the dog goes to his belly, his ears flattened back. His tail beats feebly against the metal of the truck bed. The dog looks anything but vicious; he looks defeated, and Bull kind of feels sorry for him.

4

⤳

Another day in paradise and I'm slowly driving up Main Street, looking for a loose dog that's been spotted by some concerned do-gooder. I'm of the persuasion that most wandering dogs make their way back home eventually. If I find it and it doesn't have a tag, then I've got to go through the hassle of locating its owner and, until I do, keeping it fed, and right now I don't have space in my shelter to house it, what with all three kennels occupied. Jenny Bright is exceptionally good at finding lost owners and has displayed an extraordinary capacity for knowing individual dogs as they come in. But she's off today. Getting another tattoo, no doubt. Or shacking up with her no-count boyfriend. Or reapplying the boot polish black to her chopped hair. For a girl named Bright, she's plenty dark, a small-town version of Goth.

I'm grouchy. It was a bad night last night. Even though the communications center left me alone, I was more restless than usual and unable to fall sleep. Some nights are like that. With no one else in my house, I'm free to get up and pace around, let my thoughts stream undammed and undeterred by the presence of another human being. That was the biggest reason for taking this cabin. I disturb no one with my pacing, my sighs, not even a neighbor who might be drinking a midnight glass of water and staring out his back window, idly wondering why his neighbor is up and every light in the house on. It's part of what drove Gayle out of her mind. She wanted me to take the damned Ambien, quit the bourbon. Well, she doesn't have to suffer my neuroses anymore.

Seeing the apparition that flowed past in my peripheral vision last night wasn't the first time that I've seen something like that. Easily explained away—fox, coyote, swamp gas, rising mist—but I'd rather wallow in the rather adolescent desire for the supernatural; think that, benignly, I'm being haunted by the ghost of my dog. There have been times when I was running and I had the unmistakable sense of being accompanied. I've seen his ghost in the blaze of rising sun on the pond—in the shape of a shadow. Heard his breath in the rustle of cattails as I pass by. I've heard him bark with such clarity that it wakes me from my sleep, and that's when I get up and pace and think.

I keep telling myself that if I *think* about it long enough, hard enough, I'll figure out how to accept Argos's violent death. Everyone kept telling me to *forget* about it, saying that was the only cure. It isn't just coping with the grief, although that's the part I understand. It's the fear, the liquefying fear that it will happen again. Every sudden noise sends jolts of anxiety through me. I couldn't bear to go to the Fourth of July fireworks. I jump out of my skin when the mechanic drops his wrench on the cement. Thunder makes me hold my hands over my half-deaf ears. With the start of duck-hunting season, every morning is torture, the erratic shotgun blasts ruining my place of refuge. The sound puts my teeth on edge and I have to leave long before I'm due at work, then stand at the door of the Country Market, waiting for Elvin to open at six, or burn expensive gas driving around Lake Harmony. I'm gun-shy. Worse, considering it wasn't a bullet that has caused this spiral, but, rather, my failure to use my weapon.

I am afraid to go back out there. There is a darkness, a hole, where my self-confidence used to be.

I spot my father as I turn the corner onto Maple Street. The old man is pedaling slowly, keeping neatly to the side of the road, so it will be impossible not to pass him. My Suburban wears the town seal on its side and he'll know it's me, maybe wonder why I'm passing without stopping.

It's the last game of the regular season and Cooper Harrison is on the bench, swiping a towel over his face and head, sucking in the fuggy, overheated air of the gymnasium. He's just hit a three-pointer. Lev is on the court now. In the way of best friends, he knows that Lev's hoping to best his three points and bring the exceptionally close game to a successful conclusion. There's a minute left on the clock. It's close, 81–83, but Cooper's pretty certain that the points that he and Lev have scored will hand the Harmony Farms Patriots a win and a spot in the play-offs. It's up to defense now.

Above the frenzied sound of screaming fans and bellowing coaches, the relentless chanting of cheerleaders, and the squeaking of basketball sneakers on polished hardwood, there is the awful sound of one man falling off the bleachers. Not a slip, a misstep, a thump, but a complete drunken tumble. The crowd's attention shifts from the game to the man. He gets up, shakes off helping hands, and purposefully strides right across the basketball court as if he's walking across the street, right through the ten boys scrambling for last points. Bull is so inebriated that he's forgotten where he is. The other team, grateful for the momentary distraction, scores before the ref can halt the game. The buzzer sounds, rude and final. The Harmony Farms Patriots have lost a heartbreaker.

"Your father has shit for brains, Harrison." Not quite playfully, Lev shoves Cooper aside as they head for the locker room.

I slow down, keeping well behind my father, who's pumping the Raleigh slowly up the rise. And then there he is, the runaway dog. I pull the Suburban over, wait a couple of beats until I'm sure Bull is out of sight, then get out to retrieve the dog.

Lucky for me the dog, Ralph, is a repeat offender and I know where to take him. Ralph's owner works over at the small medical center as a receptionist. She's a single mom, transplanted to Harmony Farms and then abandoned by her husband, who had the bad grace to die of a massive heart attack. She's a little dumpling of a woman, and her dog is the least of her problems. I haven't got the heart to fine her. She reminds me too much of my mother. Not the dumpling part, but the struggle to manage two boys with limited resources. She reminds me of the mother who moved her boys from one shithouse rental to another and then back to Bull's house when he showed signs of remorse and recovery. Brenda Connors works for the same practice my mother once worked for, which isn't odd, given that Harmony Farms has only one medical practice. It's bigger than it was when my mother worked there, but it's still in the same place.

I haul Ralph out of the Suburban and into Brenda's house. As is the case with most homes in Harmony Farms, the back door is unlocked, which is obviously how Ralph got out. I run a fresh bowl of water for the dog, then write a note. *Brenda, Ralph got out again. I think that the trouble is either your back door latch or your kids. Please get your latch fixed and remind your boys that someday Ralph may not come home. C. Harrison, ACO.* I tear the sheet from my notepad and stick it on her fridge with a magnet shaped like Cape Cod.

Scattered around the small, very messy kitchen is the detritus of active boys: remote controls and PlayStation handsets, mismatched athletic shoes, a sock. Ralph flops down on his bed, which is jammed into a corner, sighs, and closes his eyes, as if his wandering adventure was exhausting. Some dogs just love to wander; others never leave home. Maybe Ralph was just looking for his boys.

The very first assignment Argos and I were given right out of training was a search and rescue mission to find an autistic child. This was a city hunt, not a wilderness one, and exceedingly challenging. We went up and down city blocks, into alleyways, scaring druggies shooting up, but keeping to the mission. The frantic mother was pleading with me to find her child. What I remember most about that day is the moment that Argos hit the boy's scent—the way his tail wagged, the joy for him in completing the game. The dog was so clear in his surety that we'd found our man that it was as if there were a conversation between us. Argos said, *he's in there.* I replied, "Good boy."

The mother knelt in front of Argos. Her inexpressible joy over her son's return was almost painful to watch, and it was more painful to have to stand tall and pretend it was all in a day's work, to maintain the facade of dignified policeman. Argos didn't feel any such restrictions on his dignity. He licked the boy's face, making him laugh, and let the mom hug him, his tail beating from side to side with the pleasure of it.

I always looked on that as the moment when I fell in love with my dog. I'd loved him from the get-go, sure. Who wouldn't have? But the heroic accomplishment of finding that child, which this animal did with joy, transformed the mere affection of a man for his working dog to something I can only call passion—a pride-stoked passion. Maybe that's how normal parents feel about their children— that no matter what, there will always be love.

When I was a kid, the police were fairly regular visitors to our house on Poor Farm Road. Part of this was due to the number of times

Bull was brought home half in the bag rather than being dumped in the drunk tank, thanks to the kindness of one or the other of the town's two officers who had gone to school with him, one of them Lev Parker's father. Other times, especially as we got older, it had more to do with Jimmy being suspected of something—vandalism, theft. I would stand in the corner of the kitchen, unobserved, quiet, just in awe of the blue uniform, the duty belts with their serious hardware, how the officers exuded an authority like no one else I knew. It was the way that they were so in control, so confident, that put the idea of becoming a policeman in my head. I would grow up to be just like them.

5

I start my day, as I almost always do, with a five-kilometer run around the perimeter of Bartlett's Pond. Against the advice of my audiologist, I plug my earbuds into my ears, jack up the volume on my iPhone, and absorb the beats. It's cooler these mornings when I start off, but by the time I've made my first lap, I'm sweating and I yank my venerable Police Academy T-shirt off and drop it behind me, to be retrieved on my cool-down lap. The relentless music camouflages the ringing in my left ear and fills my head with enough noise that I can run without thinking. So I don't plan my day. I don't actually have to, as my days are pretty routine. I don't intentionally think about Argos. It's more the lack of a presence which brings that presence to mind. Does that make sense? Probably not, but that's the danger of the solitary life. You get away with random musings. Not all that long ago, Argos would have been attached to my side, and I deeply miss the sense of the dog beside me. Of course, if Argos were still alive, I wouldn't be running around this particular pond. Our favorite run was along the Charles River, on the Cambridge side. The tall military-looking man and the stunning white German shepherd garnered a lot of admiring looks. Argos ran with his nose at my knees, his elegant gliding stride matching his partner's pace beat for beat. He'd be panting a little, but not out of breath. It was more like encouragement. *Ha ha ha. Keep moving man, keep moving.*

At the end of however many kilometers I wanted to do, we looked for our reward, jogging over the Longfellow Bridge and up Charles Street to our favorite café. The owner had good cause to be happy to see me and Argos; we were the K-9 unit who had run down the man who had robbed him at gunpoint one foul November night. Despite the washed-down sidewalk, Argos had pinpointed the man's hiding place within minutes. I always left the equivalent of my "on the house" snack in tips. Argos graciously took the proffered gluten-free cookie, paying for it in his high five–raised paw before crunching the peanut butter–flavored treat.

It's a particularly pretty early fall day, trees a couple of cold nights away from blasting color, the tall grasses and bushes doing their own seasonal change of costume. The sky's a cloudless blue. As I trace the border around the pond, a turtle plops into the water. There are deer tracks in the soft mud at the edge of the pond. Soon enough, the pastoral quiet around here will be threatened by the groups of hunters that find Bartlett's Pond a fine place to bag pheasant, deer, and rabbit. Duck hunters have already been around, and the migratory water fowl that move out deeper into the pond as I pass by might end up duck soup soon enough.

I increase my pace with the change of tune in my carefully selected running music, going from a slow four beats to a rapid six-eight. Warm-up done, I sprint now. The soft burn of full-bore running reminds me that I haven't entirely erased the months of inactivity after what we all call "the incident," for lack of a better word. Other words have been auditioned—for instance, *event, trauma, horror, cri-*

sis, depression. And there's the always popular *self-pity,* the one that Gayle likes best. Or at least that's the one she chose as her default word to describe my rendering our marital life null and void.

I claim I can't think and hear music at the same time, but obviously, that's not quite true.

Another lap and I've hit the two-mile mark. I've calculated that five laps around the fairly large kettle-hole pond is about five kilometers. On bad days, I'll run it twice. I want to believe that actual running helps and isn't just running away. On good days . . . well, there aren't that many of those. Today, however, I have time for only one 5K.

My cool-down lap is the sixth and I slow to a moderate walk, letting the oxygen work its way back into my starved lungs, hunting for my discarded shirt. When I finally find it, some dog has planted one big muddy paw print on the front of my white Academy T-shirt. And no, I don't immediately think this is a message from beyond from Argos. I'm not quite that delusional. However, I haven't seen any dogs on my run.

We have three dogs in residence today. I picked up two of them together, a pair of nice-looking beagles. They've got tags, and we're just waiting for their owner to show up. Like many beagles, once these picked up the scent, they got too far away from their owner and didn't have the sense to turn around. The third is a solemn-looking mutt I brought in yesterday afternoon, probably a pit bull or some kind of AmStaff mix. Who knows where she came from. Maybe somebody failed in an attempt at a second chance for her in a country setting. Like the beagles, this girl is healthy and friendly. Jenny has her posted on social-media sites and has been running down leads. I can never figure out why people don't automatically call the shelter when their dogs go missing, instead of making us do the heavy lifting and spend taxpayers' money on classified ads.

Jenny and I go through the door that leads to the small indoor kennel area. All three kennels are empty, the inmates clearly in the outside runs, taking the air. The outside door sticks a little and I have to give it a shove with my shoulder. Two dogs behind wire enclosures look up at me with quintessentially beagle expressions of silly expectation. *A walk! Food!*

"Did someone collect the pit bull?" I ask.

"No." Jenny looks back indoors, as if the pit bull could be playing some sort of game of hide-and-seek with us.

It has been three-quarters of a year since I was a real cop, but the certainty that a crime has been committed is a liquid sense that flows through my brain, and I can feel myself tense with the muscle memory of being a cop. The runs don't have outside doors; the only access is through the shelter. The main door of the shelter is locked at night. The kennels are on cement slabs so that no dog can dig its way out. I gently back Jenny away from the area around the outside kennels. I'm looking for footprints, anything that will set me on the right course for solving this puzzle. The wire walls are over six feet high. There's no way a dog could jump that fence, nor a sixty-something overweight woman who prefers caftans climb up it. Polly Schaeffer is the first suspect to come to mind, although I well know from long law-enforcement experience that you can't always assume the obvious suspect is, in fact, the actual perpetrator. However, there is the theory of Occam's razor, that the most obvious answer is usually the correct one. Polly Schaeffer certainly fills the "obvious" bill with her recent proclivity for rescuing animals not in need of rescue. And unless I'm way off the mark, there's a size-six depression in the soft dirt, one that looks like it might have been made by a Ked, not by one of Jenny's honking Doc Martens.

"Looks like an inside job." Jenny can barely keep the smile off her lips.

"What do you mean?"

"Just joking. I mean, who else besides me is inside?"

"Right. And you had nothing to do with this?"

Jenny delivers me a cutting look. "As if."

"You were off yesterday."

"Yeah. And you were on."

"Right."

She stops smiling. "Coop, the back door wasn't bolted this morning. Just now. Neither of us had to unlock it."

I could swear that I locked the front door. I did; I distinctly recall locking it with the key that catches a little as you insert it. But did I bolt the back door? That I can't quite remember.

Mistakes come out of complacency, out of carelessness. Or out of distraction. I have little patience for mistakes like this. But I can only blame myself for failing to lock up properly last night. I remember now. The phone rang as I was getting ready to leave, someone with a complaint about a dog rooting in the garbage. A skinny yellow dog, a stray the person didn't recognize. There has been a rash of raided trash barrels in the past few weeks, and two other good citizens have called with similar sightings. In each case, as with this most recent sighting, the skinny yellow dog has been described as limping badly but fast enough on three legs to bolt as soon as he's discovered.

I can tell myself all day that a missing pit bull isn't a life-or-death situation, but this kind of mistake suggests that maybe I'm better off as an animal control officer in my former home town than being responsible for other people's lives.

I send Jenny out on a call about a missing bunny. I'm just not in the mood to be a comfort to someone who's idea of a pet is a caged rabbit. The beagles' owner has finally returned my call and is on his way in to collect his runaways. As if inflicting punishment on myself, I clean the empty run, vaguely hoping that it will give up the mystery of who took the missing pit bull. I've got to go to the town hall anyway, so I'll stop in and check with the town clerk to see if anyone has recently registered a bully type. Maybe the owner made an off-hours call and figured he could just liberate his dog and skip the ticket. But just in case, I'll casually drop by Polly's to see if she's acquired a dog. Although her preferred collectible is feline, she's fond enough of dogs, and a little loony, so my hunch that she made the heist is not exactly far-out.

I'm outside when a Range Rover pulls into the visitors' parking space. A stout man climbs out, two leashes in his hand and a disgruntled look on his face. "Got my dogs?"

"I believe that I do. Let's see and then do a little paperwork."

"How much?"

I name the fine, times two because of the double trouble.

The expression of annoyance on the man's face quickly dissolves into relief at the sight of his less than contrite hounds. "*Bad boys, bad boys,*" he says, but he hugs them and lets them lick his face in a rapture of reunion. I was wrong: He's not a hunter, but a middle-aged dog lover.

"Beagles are tricky. Best to have them on long lines when you're out walking."

"I will." The man offers his hand to me. "Thanks."

The gratitude coming from this guy makes me smile. Sometimes it feels good to be recognized for doing your job. Not exactly like the commendations Argos and I earned for bravery, but nice all the same. Mostly, with this job, the public regards me with something between disdain and annoyance. Despite the fact I'm working under the umbrella of the police department, the public really doesn't look at me as a cop. Barely an authority.

The beagle man shakes my hand vigorously. "I'd just die if anything ever happened to these guys."

Which pretty much sums up why I will never have another dog. Not a pet. Not a partner.

No sooner has the beagle man left than Doc Philbine pulls up.

"I was passing by, thought I'd stop in."

"I can give you a cup of coffee, maybe find a doughnut to go with it."

Max Philbine has the movie star good looks of a man more suited to a life in a power suit, not rubber boots and, during bovine breeding season, a plastic glove with a sleeve up to his armpit. But he's the son of a veterinarian who was the son of a veterinarian and he doesn't recall ever wanting to be anything else. Unlike his father and grandfather, though, Max can't make a living by being paid in eggs and pie, and the high cost of medical equipment and the sheer magnitude of laboratory tests and procedures never imagined by his forebears has Max wondering out loud to me if that teaching position at Tufts isn't worth considering.

"What, throw over all this glory for a three-day-a-week teaching load and a sports jacket?" I hand Max the sugar.

"And benefits and maybe a car that doesn't have to double as a portable office."

"Haven't classes started already?"

"The job would start in January."

The coffee in my mug is bitter, dregs left over from the first pot Jenny put on at seven-thirty, so I toss it into the sink. "Not to influence your decision, but you do know that you'd be leaving this town without veterinary care. You're all right with that?"

"I'd sell the practice. Actually, I'm pretty close to selling the practice anyway. Looking for a starry-eyed recent vet school grad hoping to become the next James Herriot."

I give him a blank look.

"*All Creatures Great and Small*? Books? Television series?" He shakes his head. "Never mind."

"You've made up your mind." I know that I sound like I'm interrogating a miscreant and so I busy myself with making a new pot of coffee. We really should invest in one of those single-cup dispenser things. Too much wasted coffee. The line item for office supplies, where I hide the coffee, is going over budget.

"What about you?"

Such an open question. Max knows my contract goes only to June 30. He thinks, like everyone else, that once my hearing improves, I'll be ready to go back to active police duty. He thinks that it's just a matter of decibels. He has no idea about the overpowering anxiety that squeezes my guts at the thought of taking on another K-9 partner. I can't lose another dog. And policing without one is out of the question. "We'll see."

"I'm heading out. You want to grab a bite at the tavern Friday?" Max rinses his mug, setting it into the little sink.

"Sure." It's become something of a regular thing for us, this Friday-night burger at Harmony Farms's local pub. It's my one concession to social activity. Otherwise, it's just me in my splendid isolation.

Max heads off on his rounds, which makes me think about starting on the annual farm visits as soon as Jenny comes back from her rabbit hunt. As my official title is Officer of Animal Control and Inspector of Animals, part of my job is to visit the local farms, count the livestock, and make sure that nothing inhumane is going on. I'll start with Second Hope Farm, the equine rescue on the other side of the pond from my cabin. But first, I'll pay Polly a visit.

"Nobody understands these dogs." Polly Schaeffer keeps one hand on the boxy head of the "rescued" pit bull. "They do terrible things to them." The pit bull is sporting a rhinestone collar and pink leash. She looks like a hooker. I think *that's* a pretty terrible thing to do to a dog.

"Polly, she's somebody's pet. Not a scar on her. She's friendly. She needs to go back to her people." I casually reach for the leash, but Polly jerks it away.

"She can stay here till you find her people."

"That's not possible." Once again, I feel like I'm in hostage negotiations. This time, I've arrived without litter or food, nothing to negotiate with. I've got nothing but the law on my side, and I'm tired and annoyed and pretty ready to use it against my old friend. "Polly, give me the leash."

Polly heaves a great sigh. "What if no one claims her? I know what you do to the unclaimed dogs."

"Polly, when I took this job, it was with the caveat that we find homes for the homeless. Or we place them with breed-specific rescues. I'll find her owner, or get her a new one. I promise."

"Or she comes back to me." Polly keeps the hand holding the leash behind her so that if I'm going to get to it, I'm almost going to have to knock her over. It's a far better thing simply to lie to her once again. "Fine. She comes back to you."

Polly gives me a girlish smile, coy and teasing. But then offers me the end of the leash. I replace Polly's blinged-out leash and collar with a nylon slip-knot leash.

"Just tell me one thing. How did you even know she was in there, and what made you think the door would be unlocked"

"You said one thing; that's two. It's pretty simple. Jenny posted her on Facebook, and I didn't know the door was unlocked. That was just dumb luck."

"My mistake."

"Oh, by the way, I saw your brother the other day, at the market."

"Jimmy?" I ask this as if there's another brother in my life. Jimmy. A white kid named for Jimi Hendrix. Born during my parents' brief hippie phase, which I figure was less about peace, love and rock 'n' roll than it was about drugs. I wrap the leash around my hand and give the pit bull a little tug to get her to follow me to the Suburban.

"This was definitely Jimmy. He greeted me like I was a long-lost relative. Kissed me on both cheeks, very Continental. I can't think that he learned that in the big house." Polly touches her plump cheek with the back of her hand, as if still feeling the smarmy lips of my ex-con brother. But she's smiling like a girl. Jimmy always did have that kind of dark attraction for women. That whole James Dean bad-boy look. What do they call it in the insurance business? "An attractive nuisance." The fun never stops here in Harmony Farms.

Lev Parker won't be pleased to know that Jimmy Harrison is back in town. Even if he's cleaned up his act and is now a model citizen, his history certainly means that Lev will keep his eye on him. When we were little kids, maybe seven, eight, Lev and I both looked at Jimmy as if he were some kind of god. Two years older, always on the cutting edge of adventure, he tormented the life out of us. He'd set us up for practical jokes, and just being victimized by his antics made us feel sophisticated and included. We thought it was cool and that it meant he liked us. Deluded little kids. By the time Lev and I were in fifth grade, and Jimmy was in junior high, the practical jokes and antics had evolved to serious mischief and an attraction for the illicit. My mother, Mona, couldn't cope with the seemingly endless round of trouble this kid was in, and Bull didn't care what Jimmy did as long as he didn't steal the beer money. Vandalism became petty theft, which became prescription-drug theft, which became hard-core drug dealing.

When my teachers saw my name on the class list, the automatic response was to look at me and tense their mouths. *Oh, here's another Harrison boy. Here comes trouble.* I spent a lot of time and effort trying to prove them wrong.

I might give Lev a call, just to let him know that Jimmy is back; but, on reflection, I figure that the chief of police has probably already heard that bit of news. Lev is a good cop, a good small-town cop. Looking at the well-tended gardens and high-end homes, the clean main street with its planters filled with seasonal flowers, and the cheerful banners suspended from the new Beaux-Arts–style lamp-posts proclaiming HARMONY FARMS WELCOMES YOU!, most people would assume that the worst crime in the area would be bad fashion sense. The darker secret is that the best customers for the drugs that men like Jimmy provide are the people who sit on the beautification committee and live in those megamansions that have taken over the old pastures and orchards of bygone days. Maybe they're not interested in heroin, but they have a hunger for prescription pills—oxycodone and Percocet—habits formed by the pain of living an active life, the wages of a good golf game or a face-lift, the upset of an occasional car crash. Or their kids party with the enhancements of whatever pills are available. It will be very hard for a man who has no moral compass to stay clean in a place that provides such an easy market.

As I don't have the heart to do it, instead of crating the pit bull and putting her in the back of the truck, I invite her onto the back seat of the Suburban. She immediately leaps over the seat to sit next to me like a date. I pet her, something I rarely do with these dogs temporarily in my custody.

When Gayle realized that I meant it, that I was going to take the job in Harmony Farms, be the dog officer in my old community, the first thing she said to me was that I wasn't going to be able to do the job because under my stiff exterior beat the heart of a pushover. She didn't mean it kindly. "You're too animal-soft. You'll never be able to keep an emotional distance." Which, on the face of it, was an odd thing to say for a woman who was making me move out of our home because she claimed I was emotionally distant from her. What she didn't seem to understand was that all of my "softness" for animals had been focused on my own dog. I am perfectly capable, even determined, not to engage with any of the animals in my care. I treat them well; I just don't get to know them. Sort of how I treated prisoners when I had occasion to transport them. Like I treat Bull and, now, how I'll treat my brother. Distant. No deliberate engagement.

No. I'm sure that Lev already knows that Jimmy's here. I can relax and add my brother to the list of people I'm trying to avoid. Contact with Jimmy is a lot like that old racist folktale about Uncle

Remus and the Tar-Baby. Getting anywhere near Jimmy is a bad idea, especially for someone who has worked for so long in the law-enforcement profession. There is nothing I liked more than bringing down dealers. Buyers were one thing, but these dealer guys were predators, benefiting from the weaknesses of others. Jimmy had skimmed along the edge of using, but he found a career in distributing.

My cell phone sounds off with the office ringtone, a series of barks. Jenny's idea. I push the Bluetooth button. "Coop."

"Did you find the pit bull?"

"Yeah. Polly had her."

"Good, cuz I've got her frantic owner on the phone."

"I'm on the road. Give me the address and I'll drop her off."

Second Hope Farm, Bates Road, third mailbox on the right."

Ah, the very place I intended to begin my farm calls. I love the old "kill two birds with one stone" theory of efficiency. I signal for a quick left turn and pat the pit bull on the head.

6

⤞⥳

Jimmy's being home is a mixed blessing for Bull Harrison. Jimmy has a driver's license and a used—or what he calls a "pre-owned"—Honda that he babies, so sometimes Bull can sweet-talk Jimmy into giving him a lift to work on those days when he can't bring himself to mount his old Raleigh, like on rainy days and those days when every abuse he's ever heaped on himself reminds Bull of his age. However, with Jimmy, everything comes at a price. Bull remembers back to the days when he and the boys were batching it, as Bull called it, trying to make living without Mona sound better than it was. Father and sons in the house on Poor Farm Road. With no feminine influence, standards slipped. They ate dinner in front of the TV and their housekeeping was pretty rudimentary. No one shouted at the boys about homework or bedtime. Clean laundry was optional and sheets were replaced with more convenient sleeping bags. The boys did their own thing, and he did his. Bull liked calling the three Harrisons "free spirits." It felt as close to being roommates as could be. In that spirit, Bull stepped further back from parental duties than he already had done with Jimmy, giving the boy carte blanche to run wild. Routinely, Bull ignored summonses to the school to discuss Jimmy's failing grades or misbehavior. He might say, "Hey, try keepin' your nose clean for a while" as he dropped a slice of pepperoni pizza in front of Jimmy, but mostly he just shrugged off the reports of bullying or fights. He overlooked the accusations of stealing wallets out of teachers' purses. Nobody had proof. Boys will be boys.

The truth was that Bull was a little afraid of Jimmy, of the way his cold gray eyes would harden like stone in his face whenever Bull tried a little authority with him.

The price he's paying now for the convenience of an occasional lift into town is Jimmy's taking over of the house. As much as he doesn't take care of it to any effective degree, Bull still likes his home, which he's owned since his parents passed it on to him. It's the house he's always lived in, except for the years he was in the army; the house he brought Mona home to and where he and she conceived the kids, in the same bedroom he'd always slept in and is still sleeping in. And now this old place feels invaded by the very kid, grown man now, who was one of those babies. Doors that never had locks are locked. He needs a freakin' key to get into his own house, and how hard it is to remember to take it with him? Jimmy gets mad when he has to cut his phone calls short to go let his old man in. "Wear it around your neck, for God's sake."

Bull touches his neck to make sure that the gimp lanyard one of the boys made in some day camp is there, the house key dangling from it. Jimmy is off somewhere and didn't want to wait around to give him a lift to work this morning. Jimmy goes for days at a time, driving off in the black Honda to parts unknown. Bull never, ever asks where he's been. He knows better. You don't ask Jimmy questions.

So he's got one son who is living back in the old homestead and the other one, who won't stop and give his old man the time of day.

Deke Wilkins has given Cooper a pair of Rhode Island Reds as a birthday present. He'd had the sense to ask Mona if that was okay, and she'd shrugged, figured that fresh eggs might be a good thing to have. Sometimes gifts just boomerang on you. First thing, Bull has to build a coop for them. "Coop's coop," he calls it. Six-by-six pen, five feet of chicken wire. Deke was clear on his instructions: "Stretch chicken wire over the top; keep the hawks out." Except that Bull runs out of chicken wire. "I'll pick some up." A promise forgotten almost as soon as spoken.

Cooper's stricken little face when he goes to feed his chickens and finds nothing but feathers and a foot. He doesn't cry, Bull will give him that. He gathers the feathers, putting them in a paper bag, like he was gathering the eggs that the two hens had produced only once or twice, careful, respectful. Bull watches as his younger son wanders off the property, heading toward Deke's place on foot. He should go get him, promise him another pair of birds, a better coop, but he doesn't.

7

~~~

I drive into the yard of Second Hope Farm and see right away that this isn't some dilettante's version of a horse farm. No miles of white fences, no massive barn with an artsy weather vane and imported wood and ironwork stalls. Nope. This is very much a working farm, plain old electric fencing, a dull red barn crying out for a coat of fresh paint. Various equines are distributed among the small dirt paddocks. The only grassy pasture contains a skinny horse, standing with one hind leg cocked under him, dozing in the warm fall sunshine.

A woman comes out of the barn at a run. "You have Betty? Oh my God, I was so upset." Even before I can climb out of the truck, she wrenches open the passenger door and the dog called Betty jumps out into her arms and nearly knocks her over. "I was freaked-out when I got home and found out that my house sitter had let her out. I couldn't believe that she didn't call and let me know right away that Betty had disappeared. I won't use her again, I can promise you that. The whole idea of a sitter is to take care of the animals. I'll just never go away again. Poor, poor Betty."

"We had her overnight, Ms. . . . ?" I need to get back on the official track here.

"Everett, Natalie Everett." She sticks out her hand as if we are standing at a cocktail party. Her grip is no nonsense and I can feel in the toughness of her skin the hard work that she's putting into the place.

"Cooper Harrison." I give her hand a firm shake.

"Well, thank you for bringing her home. Do I owe any fines or boarding fees?"

"We'll bill you."

"You have my address." She sounds a little like she is expecting me to say, "Aw shucks, ma'am, you don't owe the town anything for taking your dog off the streets."

One of the horses stamps, whinnies to a more distant pal, drops his nose into his hay.

I haven't forgotten that this is a two-part visit. "You weren't in operation last year, were you?"

"No. Last year was the dreaming year; this year is the action year." When she says this, Natalie takes a deep breath and waves a hand at the aggregate of animals and fencing, the shelters, and the hills that cradle the whole. "I chucked it all and bought a farm. Pretty insane, huh?"

"I guess that would depend on what it was you chucked." I think, Job? Boyfriend?

"Wall Street, Ann Taylor suits and three-inch heels."

Okay, a chucked career.

"Now it's Carhartts and muck boots."

"And this is a rescue, right? Not a boarding facility."

"Rescue and rehab. I give a few lessons on my two steady Eddies to supplement the income. Let me introduce you to the gang." Natalie smiles at me, the lovely sunshiny smile of someone pleased as Punch to be doing what she's doing.

"I just need to know how many equines and what other livestock you might have here. As long as I'm here, I'll do my annual farm inspection." I reach back into the truck and pull out my clipboard.

The sunshiny smile fades, quickly replaced by the face she must have most worn as a bond trader. All business. "Five horses, two ponies, one dog, and three guinea hens. And a useless cat."

"Cats aren't livestock." I write on the multipart form, then look up. "I need to inspect for water source, safe fences."

"Believe me, they've got water. And I'm doing the best I can with fences."

"Can I please inspect?"

Natalie hasn't given me back the leash I had on Betty, and she walks off, dog at her side, expecting me to follow. I'm wearing my cop face, I know. Straight man. It's my default expression. There is no need for such formality on a call like this, but I can't help myself, even in the face of a pretty woman whose only attachments seem to be to animals. Once a cop, always a cop. Sometimes I forget that I'm not an officer of the law, but a dog officer. A different man would chat her up, ask her questions intended to ease her mind, let her know that he's not an adversary, but—potentially—an advocate. Instead, I march alongside her in silence. For a small woman, she's got a quick pace. I check off a box on my form. "How many acres do you have?"

Natalie answers, and I can tell she doesn't know if this is a trick question or not.

"And you have seven equines?"

"Yes." She doesn't blink. Natalie knows exactly how many animals she can have on a property this size, but I see that she's expecting me to make her squirm.

"Zoning allows you to have up to ten."

"That may be, but prudence keeps me at seven. Once that off-the-track Thoroughbred puts on some weight and gets over his injury, he'll be adopted out. And, yes, I have all the licensing to do that legally." She points to the farthest paddock. "Shall we?"

"Hey, I don't need to see each and every bucket. Obviously, you're doing a fine job here."

"I guess I should say thank you." She's got the kind of blue eyes that echo the sky as it is today, bright blue, set deep.

"But I will need to see your instructor's license."

"Right." I follow her into the barn, where she has a corkboard with her license prominently displayed. "There it is, Officer."

We're standing in the aisle of the small barn. There's a bay horse in residence, her head leaning over the door to her stall. She reaches toward me, putting her warm, soft nose against my cheek, and I can feel her breath on my skin. "Hey there." I pat her neck.

"That's Moxie. She's my beginner horse."

"A beginner horse?"

"Sorry. A horse that teaches beginning riders."

I scrawl my signature on the bottom of the multipart form and tear away the pink sheet, handing it to her. "Looks fine. See you next year."

"I'm sure I'll see you before then. We do live in a small town." Her sunshiny smile has come back, although it's little more restrained. "Hey, thanks for bringing Betty back. She's a rescue, too, and hasn't quite figured out that she's safe."

"No problem." Stupid remark. I try again. "I mean, it's my job." Worse.

"And you're doing a fine job, too."

I point in the direction of the pond. "Do you ride around Bartlett's Pond?"

"Yeah. Why?"

"I've seen hoofprints."

"We hack the old schoolies. Keeps them fit." Natalie opens the door to Moxie's stall, slips a halter over the horse's head, and brings her out. "Do you ride?"

For the first time since arriving at Second Hope Farm, I give up a smile. "No, ma'am."

"Didn't think so."

"I run. Around the pond. Maybe I'll see you there sometime."

"Maybe." Natalie clips a line to either side of the horse's halter. She hands me a carrot, instructing me to break it into smaller pieces, then walks away to gather a saddle and bridle.

Her dog, Betty, is nosing along the length of the short aisle. Who knows what she's looking for.

"Betty doesn't go with you, does she?" Gingerly, I feed Moxie a piece of the carrot, amazed at how gently she takes it off my palm.

"No, she's not made for keeping up with horses. Why? Is there a law against that?"

"No. Well, technically a leash law, but I'm never going to enforce it on dogs away from town. It's just that some dog left paw prints on my shirt when I dropped it on my run."

She is obviously trying to treat this complaint as serious. "No, sir. Not my dog."

"Okay, then." I let Moxie have the rest of the carrot as Natalie tacks her up.

Natalie leads the mare outside, snaps her fingers to get the dog's attention. Two grays are engaging in a little horseplay, running and kicking up their heels, pretending to fight. A teenage girl I hadn't realized was there suddenly appears, takes the reins out of Natalie's hand, and leads the mare into the riding ring. I guess there's nothing left to say. Even before I climb into the Suburban, Natalie walks into the ring, into her chosen new life.

As I pull out of Natalie's barnyard, I'm thinking about how I should try to lighten up a little with these farm calls, take the authoritarian bit down a notch. Sometimes, when I got home from a long day of work, Gayle would have to remind me to drop the stiff, still, deliberately macho authoritarian demeanor of my job. "Take the dog out for a walk and pretend that he's just a pet." It's funny, but everyone hereabouts assumes that I, as a dog officer, would have a dog. When I tell them no, I don't, I get this look, like there's some-

thing wrong with me. Especially the fosterers. They just can't figure me out. Why wouldn't I have a dog? Might humanize me. I just
won't, that's why.

It's a beautiful evening and I take advantage of it by lighting a fire
in the fire pit, setting my wobbly camp chair in front of it, a beer in
one hand and only the sound of late-season crickets suggesting that
winter is coming. My thoughts circulate, undistracted by radio or
phone or anything beyond the stunning purity of the sky overhead
and the whispered, to me, sound of wind in the grasses and the occasional rustle of a creature making its way through the dead leaves
that blanket the ground around this one-man camp. Exhausted, I
doze off in the chair like an old man in front of the television, the
animation of the yellow flames of my campfire, colored now with
the umber and green of improperly dried wood, mesmerizing me
into a lulled state that might be sleep, or might be deep meditation.
In my dream state, there appears on the other side of the snapping
fire—something. A wraithlike form, indistinct behind the curtain
of flame. White. Like Argos. Vaguely dog-shaped, immobile. Watching me. A ghost of a dog. Argos. Standing in the flames. He looks at
me with wolfish eyes, his long tongue lolling, laughing. I reach to
take him out of the flames.

The fire pops like a gunshot, startling me awake, and the ghost
vanishes. I am left with a hard-beating heart, knocking so loudly in
my chest that I almost can't breathe. The adrenaline of panic forces
me out of my wobbly chair to pace around the dying fire, manic with
fear. It's what I can't conquer, no matter how many sessions with a
psychiatrist, no matter how many times I push the memories back.
I am afraid.

8

⚬

It's been a hard day. I went out to Deke's to inspect his farm and ended up spending three hours splitting and stacking two cords of wood for him. He's got to be in his eighties, and the idea of him still stacking wood is just wrong, so I volunteered and, for once, the old man didn't demur and send me packing. Which, in and of itself, is a little sad. When I was a kid, I hung around Deke's farm a lot. He had everything a boy could want—a pony, two or more cows, a small flock of sheep, chickens and ducks, and occasionally a pig; a fishing hole and acres of pasture and woods that were just perfect for a kid who enjoyed solitary wandering and secret fort building. He'd give me chores in exchange for a buck or two. Just like today, I'd stack firewood, or pull shingles off his chicken house. As when he used to give me Twizzlers or Doublemint, he'd be most generous on those occasions when I'd fled to his place to escape what was going on in my own, giving me the consolation of physical labor and a five-dollar bill.

His current dog followed me from woodpile to woodshed, her amber eyes fixed on keeping me in line. As long as I've known him,

Deke has kept a series of Border collies to work with the sheep. This one looked to be middle aged, and it struck me that this might be the last dog of his life. Which made me wonder what will happen to his place when he goes. I've never heard him speak of a relative, and he's pretty much outlived his friends. No doubt some rapacious developer will descend on it, unless Deke has made some arrangement. I could ask him, I suppose. But I won't.

His chief complaint today was that something had been bothering his chickens a day or so ago. Deke's old-school, keeps a shotgun at his back door. He may be in his eighties, but his hearing is damn good. The other night, he heard the squawking and leapt out of his bed to grab the gun. His hearing may be good, but his eyes aren't as reliable as they once were, so he missed the critter skulking around the pen. Because his first thought was that it was a coyote, he kept his old dog in. But the creature that ran away didn't run like a coyote. He said, "Think it might be a dog." Which is a bad thing. Chicken-killing dogs are trouble in a place like ours, where it's become fashionable to have free-range chickens. "Whatever it was, Coop, it was limping, dragging a hind leg."

"You should have called me."

"Hardly an emergency, and the shotgun scared it off. Haven't been troubled by it since."

It might not have qualified as a reason to get the ACO out of bed, but with the series of garbage can–tossing incidents and now this, it's pretty clear to me that I've got a problem dog on my hands.

Bad enough that I was knackered from the unaccustomed labor, but even before I could get back to the shelter, I got a call about the Bollens' freakin' donkey, gone again. This time, the little wretch gave me a good crack in the knee as I shoved him into the SUV. I swear, I'm building them a proper paddock, whether they like it or not.

The last straw was when I pulled up beside my cabin and saw

my single trash barrel rolled all the way to the pond. I was more pissed than curious. Already done in by the wood chopping, I had to retrieve the soggy paper towels and scoop up the mélange of garbage deemed inedible by whatever had tossed the barrel and gotten the bungee cord off it. It was too dark to see what kind of prints might be there, and I really didn't have the time or the interest in playing Tracker John. Because all of the other dog-in-the-garbage calls have been closer to town, I only considered for a moment that this might have been the same dog. More likely it was a raccoon. I don't think a dog could get the shock cord off. You need hands for that.

Max Philbine is already at the Lakeside Tavern when I get there, freshly showered and out of my work clothes and into clean jeans and a dark blue polo shirt. Max hands me a menu. "Hard day?"

"You could say that." I open the menu, although I know exactly what I want. We come often enough that I've got the limited menu memorized, and it's just for show that I even bother to open it. "Crazy day, and then I got home and found my trash barrel in the pond. That's twenty feet. I guess either some very determined raccoon gave it his best shot or we've got a bear in the neighborhood."

We both order beers and the house specialty—bacon cheeseburgers with sweet potato fries—making no excuses about the cholesterol therein, and toast each other with our first pints. We knock around sports and the current foibles of Congress before our burgers arrive, then sit in agreeable silence as we devour them. The server arrives with our second beers, at which point Max and I are ready to explore topics closer to home: his wooing by the university, my firm belief that he'll miss his practice if he gives in.

I don't know why I'm so upset by Max's temptation to leave Harmony Farms behind. After all, I'm not planning on staying here, so why should anyone else? This is a place easily left behind. At least it was for me. Max is as generationally rooted here as I am, except that his family has always been highly respected. Max doesn't have the stigma of a family's bad reputation hanging over his head, coloring everyone's opinion.

Maybe it's just that he's pretty much the only friend I have in town. The guys I hung out with in my youth are mostly living in faraway places, their parents still here, looking forward to the holiday visits from sons and grandchildren. One of the guys I knew was killed in Afghanistan. Another married his boyfriend last year but didn't invite any of us to his wedding. In adulthood, my friends have been my colleagues on the job. And now I'm no longer part of that culture, and that's made an unavoidable difference in our relationship. I represent the second worst-case scenario: unrecoverable trauma. We've lost touch.

I see her before Max does. Sitting at the antique oaken bar is Natalie Everett, a wineglass in her hand, out of her Levi's and now wearing jeans with a little bejeweled swoop on the back pockets. Her dark brown hair is loose and she keeps tucking it behind her ear as she laughs at whatever it is her companion is saying. Laugh, tuck, laugh. I find the unconscious motion unbelievably endearing. And am shocked at the thought. I don't even know her.

Natalie spins herself off the bar stool and, as she heads toward the rest rooms, passes our way.

"Hi, Natalie." Max calls out to her, waving as she passes. She seems not to notice me there at the same small table, and then does.

"Hi, Doc. Officer Harrison." She smiles at us and keeps moving.

"Nice view." Max raises his glass to his lips.

"I guess."

"Dead from the waist down, man?"

"What are you, twelve?"

"Sometimes. When it suits me." Max is a veteran of the marriage wars, and that's one of the reasons that he and I have become pals.

I say that it's because misery loves company, but Max says it's safety in numbers.

"Yes, she's attractive. But I don't think I'm her type."

"What type would that be?"

"A horse."

"That's no horse sitting next to her at the bar." We lean so that we can see the companion Natalie has just rejoined.

"Not from around heah."

"You're right. Not a rube."

"City boy for sure. Got Wall Street smeared all over him." I'm done with my pint and signal to our server for another round. To hell with my self-imposed two-beer limit. It's Friday, I've worked my tail off, and I'm a little weary of self-discipline. Despite what Gayle said, I'm not my father. I can handle myself.

Natalie and her companion are long gone by the time we're ready to split the check and head out. The temperature has risen since early evening, an early-fall warm front moving through, making Max conjecture if the latest tropical storm forecast to miss our area might not be moving in our direction after all. I can only repeat what I heard on the weather forecast this afternoon, possible thunderstorms passing through, followed by a cold front. It never fails to amaze me how much we New Englanders love to talk weather. It's like our comfort zone. What do people in temperate areas talk about during those last minutes of a late-night date or the awkward moments of waiting in a line at the post office with a stranger whose face is familiar but whose name you don't know?

We stand outside the tavern, staring at a blank canvas of sky. A bat fritters over our heads and we both duck, then laugh. A drop of rain. The first rumble of thunder and we say good night, running for our trucks.

My body aches, as if I've been lifting weights, and I regret that third beer a little. I'm not drunk, but it's a little hard to stay focused on the road. I'm really glad to see the reflector announcing the safe and solitary track to my cabin. It would not do at all to get stopped by one of Lev's real cops for a suspected DUI. I can just hear it, the "Like father, like son" condemnation. The storm is nearing and I'm gripping my steering wheel with each flash and boom.

A close flash of lightning. There it is again, a white wraith, a ghost of a creature, illuminated for a nanosecond. I can't explain why this *apparition*, for lack of a better word, makes my heart beat faster or why I call out: "Argos!" I shake off the feeling. Laugh out loud at myself. But I hurry down the dirt road, just in case there is a big white dog waiting for me at the cabin.

9

⁓

I wake with a jolt, sitting up, throwing off the sheet, and landing on my feet. It takes me a moment to collect myself, to remind myself that I'm in the old hunting cabin, that I'm fine, and that it's nothing but a lousy thunderstorm that has revved my imagination into nightmare. The lightning illuminates my room for an instant, my clothes on hooks, the single bed, the cheap nightstand with my books piled on it. Another flash so bright and I can pick out the colors of the braided rug under my feet. Like a little kid, I cover my ears to block out the thunder that follows. It percusses against my bare chest. This storm is sitting right on top of me. I sit up, cup my eyes in the heels of my hands to stop the flow of nightmare-induced tears. It just doesn't get any better. I have had this nightmare before. Some of my bad dreams have everything to do with inchoate fear. Objects and sounds represent terror—a solid wall, a tumbling rock, a cawing crow. My dream self sees the imagery and knows that it's the embodiment of danger.

Tonight, the thunder has evoked a more exact reenactment of

the explosion that has unraveled my life. Once again, I am the helpless witness in Argos's death.

In that split second after waking, I feel the relief of knowing it
was just a dream, and in the next moment, I know that the real nightmare won't go away. The loss is still there. The fear. In the daylight, I'll be able to shrug off this nightmare. Make it disappear. I
rub my face, a gesture that has become habitual. As I feel the night's
growth of beard beneath my fingers, I realize that the electricity is
out, ergo the pump, and so I head outdoors to pee. It's raining too
hard to venture off the porch, so I act like a little boy and aim my
stream into the downpour. Finished, I breathe in the sodden air, admire the distant light show as the storm moves away, a bolt or two
thrown in retreat, halfhearted. One Mississippi, two Mississippi,
three Mississippi. It takes six counts before the thunder reaches me.
As the storm slides off, heading for the city, where it will die, the
rain slows, lessens, and is done. In the sudden quiet, I hear something scrabble against the wet surface of the small porch, the unmistakable sound of claws against wood. I really wish that I'd brought
a flashlight outside. What kind of wild beastie is taking advantage
of the protection of the porch? Not under the porch, but on it. I turn
my head so that my good ear is able to follow the animal's movement across the rough boards of the porch, hoping to interpret by
sound what kind of trespasser I have. I don't think it can be a skunk,
but, nonetheless, I stay very, very still. A raccoon is a strong possibility, especially with the trash can incident yesterday, and that's a
little scary, as it's also possible that such a bold creature could be
rabid. Two towns over, they've had a case of rabies in a raccoon.
Puts everyone on edge.

I'm getting cold, standing outside in my underwear. The storm
has heralded the forecasted cold front and the air has gone from
muggy to chill. I shiver and whisper, "Hey, critter, move on. I want
to go back to bed." A flash of lightning and I see it. A dog. At least

I think it's a dog. A dog-shaped thing is huddled against the stack of firewood. As the animal is revealed in the brief flare of distant lightning, I can see that, whatever it is, it's wholly consumed by terror. Finally convinced that it really is a dog, I step closer, squat, snap my fingers. Ten seconds and the thunder finally reaches our ears and the dog bolts. I'm not sure if he's running from me or from the sound. The thing is, he is definitely on three legs.

"Hey, fella!" I know that shouting after a frightened dog is a recipe for failure, but I do it anyway. "Here, boy!"

I think that this must be my phantom, and I have to confess, I'm a little disappointed at the reasonable explanation.

I'm shivering and the cold forces my retreat into my chilled cabin. I pull an extra blanket off the shelf, find a pair of sweatpants to pull on. The temperature drop is quite astounding. It's as if fall has arrived at the flip of a switch. I climb back into bed, but sleep is elusive after that excitement, and it's just as the first birds announce the new freshly washed day that I finally fall into a deep sleep.

The power is still out, which kind of proves that I didn't dream the weirdness of last night's stormy encounter with the terrified dog. There are paw prints in the mud around the base of the porch, a skid mark where the dog must have slipped as he leapt off in his panic to get away from me. The storm has stripped some foliage from the trees, most of which are only beginning to color up. The thinned-out canopy lets in so much more light and makes the whole camp look more cheerful. I heat up some old coffee on the gas stove and sit on the porch to admire my new cleared view to the pond. A flat-bottomed boat drifts toward the middle of the large pond—duck hunters out before dawn, their Labrador in the prow like an ebony figurehead. Argos had a couple of Labs in his graduating class, great dogs for drug sniffing. They lacked the gravitas of the more serious-looking Belgian Malinois or the other German shepherds who came up in that class, but there was a lot to like about them. Half the pet dogs in this town are Lab or Lab crosses. Want to give away a dog, tell them it's part Lab. Jenny Bright isn't above doing that if we have a particularly unattractive inmate in need of a home. "Oh, yeah, he's part Lab for sure." Jenny's Goth looks are diametrically opposed to her persuasive appeal over the phone.

I'll set up the big Havahart trap I have at the shelter, bait it with a bowl of meat scraps, and I should have this phantom garbage-raiding, chicken-scaring dog caught within a day or two. That will be the easy part. The hard part will be to figure out what rabbit hunter went home without his dog, or what idiot thought dropping off an unwanted dog in the country would ensure its finding a nice new home. And then getting Jenny Bright to make sure that it actually does get a good home.

The lumberyard is Saturday busy and it takes a lap before I can find a parking place close enough to the fencing materials that I don't have to get a cart. I'm here to fulfill my promise to the Bollens to build them a fence that even Cutie-Pie can't breach. I'm here on a Saturday, on my own time, because, as far as I know, Bull doesn't work on Saturdays. A million times a week I pass by Crane and Sons Lumber, and on any one of those passes I could have pulled the town's SUV into the lot and gotten what I need to do the job. Fortunately, my own vehicle is more than sufficient to hold the posts and rolls of thick narrow-gauge wire I'm going to use. Gayle got the Jetta; I've got the Ford F-150 crew-cab four-by-four pickup with the United States Police Canine Association decal on the back window.

Crane's Lumber is like my own backyard; I know exactly where to find what I'm looking for, as I've been coming to Crane's all my life. Even when I lived in Boston, when I had occasion to need a lumberyard, this was the one I came to. The business is over a hundred years old, and there are no longer any Cranes, sons or otherwise, by that name still alive, but the sense of its still being a mom-and-pop operation persists.

I pull a crumpled piece of paper out of my pocket to check my estimated measurements against the size of the rolls and the height of the posts. I'll need a posthole digger, and I can rent one here. There is little that Crane's doesn't offer the DIYer or helpful neighbor or former student doing an old teacher a favor. One of the better things Cynthia Mann and her exurban cronies have done is to prevent the encroachment of big-box stores within the borders of Harmony Farms. On the outside, yes. Over the edge into the less pretty, less prosperous, less desirable areas, sure. Plenty of Harmony Farms residents take their business over the line, but I'm not usually one of them. I just don't patronize Crane's on weekdays, when Bull might be there. Any encounter with my father inevitably makes me feel bad. Bad because I can't look at the guy without cringing, what with his outdated Fu Manchu mustache, crumpled-paper-bag face, sick bloodhound eyes, pale and always looking a little wet, his shock of defiant gray hair, and his mostly toothless grin, every time he sees me, his younger son. Bull is a wreck of a man, and I would feel sorry for him, except my father did it to himself. Every helping hand, Bull managed to slap away.

As a city policeman, I saw plenty of human train wrecks—the druggies and the prostitutes, the lost souls who found themselves in trouble with the law out of stupidity or bad judgment, or poverty or mental illness, not necessarily anything as straightforward as malfeasance. Some were even quite likable, almost sublimely ignorant of what was wrong with taking a few bucks for a blow job or selling an ounce of weed to a college student. Each one, in some way, reminded me of Bull. And as was the case with a lot of those jerks, everyone likes Bull Harrison.

"Hey, son. Whatcha buyin'?"

Bull. I'm guessing that he's working overtime. 'Tis the season when home owners and caretakers get started on those projects that have been waiting for the cooler weather.

"Bull, how are you?" I have long since stopped calling my father by anything other than the nickname he earned long before I was a glint in his eye.

"Sittin' up, takin' nourishment. You're lookin' good."

"I'm all right. Can't complain." My God, this could be a bit of bad dialogue in a bad sitcom set in Rubesville USA. "I need fencing for the Bollens' donkey." In other words, this is business, not a social call.

"Right over here." Even though I really don't need an escort, Bull tags along beside me, chatting away about nothing. Ignoring him, I slide a metal fence post out of the pile. "I want to build a twenty-by-thirty pen. What heights have you got for wire fencing? I need something at least four feet high."

"With that mule, I'd go five feet."

He's right. I choose a taller post.

Pulling the stub of a pencil out from behind his ear, Bull does a couple of calculations on a scrap of paper, figures out how many posts and how much fencing, and hands me the results. "Take that in and pay for it. I'll throw the stuff in your truck."

I pay, then carefully fold the cash register receipt and put it in my wallet. I'm still not sure I'll hand it to Mr. Bollen, but this is a pretty expensive good deed if I don't. I head outside to where my father has neatly stacked the poles and rolls of fencing in the back of the truck. If this was the other yard guy, I might hand him a five and tell him to go get a cup of coffee and a doughnut on me, but it's not, and the best I can do it clap Bull on his meaty shoulder and say thanks.

"Don't be a stranger, Coop." Bull runs fingers down the length of his tobacco-stained Fu Manchu mustache, then spits.

Bull's tired phrase reminds me and I say, "Hey, I hear Jimmy's back."

Bull repeats the grooming and spitting. "Yeah. Got sprung a week or so ago."

"Where is he living?" I know I sound more investigatory than curious.

"With me."

"Watch out for him. Don't get involved. . . ." This is not good news.

"I know. Don't worry about us. He's clean. I'm clean."

"This isn't about *clean*. It's about keeping out of jail."

"Been there, done that. Don't intend to do it again. Neither does Jimmy. He's reformed."

I have enough self-control to refrain from saying "Yeah, I've heard that before." I don't say anything else to the old man; there's no point in it. I'll just get frustrated. I have no doubt that Jimmy is holing up till his next opportunity to make a buck outside of the law. He's a recidivist, not capable of true reformation, real change. Just thinking about him makes me mad.

I walked out of our house the day after high school graduation. Bull was somewhere, probably at a bar, and Jimmy was sitting on the couch in his boxers, smoking a joint. He took a hit, holding on to it like a little kid holding his breath. His hazed-over eyes studied me until he let the stream out. "Where you goin'?"

"Away." Far, far away from being the *other* Harrison boy, the boy people thought I must be, given my family history. No one ever again would know about my wreck of a father, or my having a brother like Jimmy.

"Where?"

"To the rest of my life." The sudden notion of freedom swept through me, making me laugh out loud with the joy of it.

That was twenty years ago, and, kind of like Jimmy, I have proven to be a recidivist, returning to the place I once fled and to the people I thought I was done with.

I slam the truck door and drive away from my father. I don't mean to, but I glance in the rearview mirror. Bull is there, waving good-bye to me.

Mrs. Bollen has sent me home with a rectangular Pyrex dish of her signature lasagna and instructions on how to heat it up. There's enough here to feed a family of four, and that's great, except I'm not certain if my electricity is back on, and I'd hate to lose this national treasure because there's no way to keep the leftovers cold.

Natalie Everett is in the Country Market when I stop in to pick up the makings of a salad and get some scrap meat from Elvin for the Havahart trap. I'm behind her in line and can't help but notice that three bags of carrots and a Lean Cuisine box are the sum total of the contents of her basket. What I also can't help noticing is that she really doesn't need to be eating Lean Cuisine.

It isn't my style, and I wouldn't have said anything, but Natalie happens to glance back and catches me looking at her groceries, so I make a weak joke and say. "You can tell a lot about a woman by the items on her grocery list."

"Officer Harrison, hello. Yes, I spend more on carrots than on anything else in the market."

I point at the Lean Cuisine box. "That's hardly a fit dinner for a woman who does physical labor all day."

"Cheap, nourishing, and fast. Three qualities I require."

I think of the lasagna sitting on the seat in my truck. "Are you vegetarian?"

She smiles, as if she thinks that she should be, given her chosen vocation. "No. An unrepentant meat eater."

"I have incredible homemade lasagna in my possession and there's no way I can eat it all by myself. Would you like some?"

"Oh, I couldn't."

We dance around the idea in a conversational two-step as I insist and she demurs. After several more rounds of this, I insist one more time for emphasis and, as she pays for her groceries, I realize that I've inadvertently arranged a date with Natalie Everett. I give her directions and my phone number just in case she thinks better of this impromptu dinner.

"See you at six." She hefts her cloth grocery bag of carrots over her shoulder. "I think I can find it, but if not, keep your phone handy."

I throw my package of meat, the head of lettuce, the two small tomatoes, and the single cucumber back in my basket and back out of the line. I'm going to need more stuff. And I hope to God that the electricity is back on. Dinner by candlelight would be way too predatory.

Then I think, Hey, it's just shared lasagna, no big deal. From what I saw at the tavern last night, she's got a boyfriend—a thought that doesn't make me feel any less awkward. Grow up. This is just neighborly breaking bread together. A chance to show that I'm not really an asshole.

Cooper is almost surprised that Celia said yes, that she agreed to go to the prom with him. They've casually dated since midwinter, a movie, a ride to the lake. Made out a little bit. But the prom is a big deal. It's the kind of event where you have to invite your date over to meet your parents, have pictures taken. Celia's parents don't know that they're dating. She's never suggested that he have dinner at her house; she's never let him pick her up at home. Cooper is no fool; he knows that her parents will flip at the idea of their college-bound daughter mingling with a Harrison boy. The fact of his prowess on the basketball court or the ice is nullified by his family history.

He's nervous as he arrives at Celia's house on Sunset Lane, the rented tux making him feel ludicrous instead of suave. He nearly drops the plastic box with the corsage in it. The front door opens and Celia comes out in a rush. Her face looks flushed, and he realizes she's been crying.

Behind her come the parents. No one looks happy. Cooper recognizes family discord and moves to disarm it with an outthrust hand and a smile on his face.

"Mr. and Mrs. Laughton, so nice to meet you. Celia, you look beautiful." It's as if he's taken his lines from Leave It to Beaver, *but it works and the parents stand down. Mrs. Laughton has the pair of them pose against the open front door and takes one picture. Cooper doesn't think she gave them time enough to smile. It's going to look like a double mug shot.*

"Home by eleven." Mr. Laughton doesn't say this with a wink. Cooper will have Celia home by ten-thirty. A day later and she says she thinks that they should take a break. After all, she's leaving for college in eight weeks. Long-distance romances really don't work. Cooper doesn't even try to argue her out of it. He understands the power of parental disapproval.

Natalie and I sit in the harsh light of my two camping lanterns, one on the small kitchen table and the other on the counter. The lasagna, reheated in the gas oven, has been invaded and still half of it remains. I'll insist that she take it home, making the case that I'm not being polite but that I have no way of keeping it cold. In the old days, the camp had a propane generator, but that's long gone, the advent of reliable electricity making it pointless, unless you have a situation like this. I could have lighted candles, kept the glare of the battery-powered Coleman lanterns out of our eyes, but I thought better of it. I keep telling myself that this isn't a date, that she's only here for the meal. She's got a boyfriend. So I use the lanterns.

We've chatted about the weather, finally seasonal; the high cost of grain, climbing every time she buys a bag. She asks a polite question about my job, so I entertain her with the antics of the Bollens' mischievous miniature donkey. Conversation lags a little. It's only seven-thirty, and already dark, and to two people who have been up since dawn, it feels like the middle of the night. My restless night, and the effort of building a donkey-proof fence for the Bollens, and her own physically demanding job of stall mucking, hay bucking, and saddle time have worn us both out. Natalie apologizes for yawning, so I suggest a breath of fresh air. "It's not too cold; let's sit out on the porch."

I grab the bottle of pinot noir that Natalie, arriving a little late and wearing those dressy jeans, handed me upon arrival, then open the door for her as she shrugs on her jacket. It is so dark and so quiet here on this little piece of paradise. Even the crickets have quieted down. Natalie stands on the edge of the porch, leaning out to look at the stars now crowding the sky above the pond. "I get a pretty spectacular view of the night sky over my place, but not quite like this—too many neighbors living around me." She takes the refilled wineglass. "I suppose your neighbors are without electricity, too. Makes it look like it must have looked a hundred or so years ago."

"No neighbors to speak of, although I do get a glow in the sky from all the streetlights in Harmony Farms. Come over here." We step off the porch and move to the side of the small cabin. I stand behind her, directing her to look toward the northwest, where the sky is indeed more pale. "Clear nights, it's harder to see, but on overcast nights, the lights bounce right off the cloud cover and it looks like the end of days." Her hair smells nice. I lean in a little, then pull myself back. Not a date.

"Speaking of the end of days, I'd better call it a night. Early chores." She's still got her back to me, inches away from my chest. She finishes off her wine.

"Me, too." I take a backward step. "Hey, you've got to take the rest of the lasagna."

She turns around, shakes her head. "Only because you don't have electricity. You know, you should have picked up bags of ice at the market. That would have held you."

"I did, but my cooler is only big enough to hold milk, beer, and dog meat."

"I didn't see a dog. Of course you'd have dog. Where is he?"

"I don't." *Not anymore.* "The meat is for a feral dog that I have to trap."

"Trap?" The way Natalie says the word, I might be some fur trapper about to commit an atrocity.

"Havahart. No harm will come to him. That's assuming he gets to the meat before the rest of the critters out there find it. Trap's too big to prevent a skunk or raccoon from getting there first, snatching the bait, and scurrying away."

"Feral, huh? Should I be worried?"

"No. I think it's just a dumped dog. He'll come in from the cold with a little encouragement."

We go back into the cabin to wrap up the remainder of the lasagna. Suddenly, the electricity flares on and the refrigerator rumbles to life. "Take it anyway." I put the Pyrex pan in her hands. "Just drop the pan off at the shelter and I'll return it to Mrs. Bollen."

"It's just me; I can't eat all this."

"Freeze it, then. You'll have it when your boyfriend comes."

"Boyfriend?"

"Fiancé, then? The fellow you were with at the tavern last night."

"My brother?"

"Even the best detective in the world couldn't have deduced that by observation."

"We look alike."

"Can't say I saw the resemblance. So, next time your brother comes, you've got something to feed him."

"Okay, I'm not going to keep playing pass the lasagna with you. I'll take it, but then you've got a meal owed." She takes the pan out of my hands with a little jerk.

"Thanks for coming. And for the wine."

"Thank you for asking. Neighborly, right?"

Why do I feel wrong-footed? "I'll walk you out to your car, fend off the skunks." I grab my flashlight, the big serious one that I use when trying to locate kittens or bunnies or snakes stuck in odd, dark places. Given that I now know that she's single, there is a whole new matzo ball hanging out there. Should I kiss her good night? A cheek kiss? Both cheeks? Something Continental? Boy, am I out of practice.

"See you. Thanks again." She's in her car, keys in hand, lasagna pan on the seat beside her, but her door is still open. "Hey, good luck with that dog."

Screw it. I lean in and give Natalie a gentle kiss on the cheek. Nothing overtly meaningful, just a friendly, neighborly peck on the cheek.

The way she smiles at me, I know that I may have blown the evening but that I've gotten that just right.

It was getting harder to get around. At first, the wound had been exquisitely painful, but after days of licking at it and lying in the soothing mud at the edge of the pond, the dog had managed to adapt to the constant ache of the pellets embedded in his hip. He was more hungry than hurting after a week. Instinct and experience kept him away from humans, but not from human habitation. As his mobility briefly improved, his ability to focus on finding food also improved. A visual learner by nature, he observed the raccoons, which tolerated his presence, neither threatened by him nor very interested. But he was interested in their habits, their routes into the neighborhoods that grew out of the woods and fields. He watched as their clever paws lifted trash-can lids and they hoisted themselves inside. The mouth-watering scent of offal and rotted vegetables encouraged him to limp closer. A flash of wisdom and he chased off the raccoons, taking the contents of the trash barrel for himself.

Other creatures, crows and skunks, led him to compost heaps. He attempted to chase a skunk away from its feast only once. Ignoring the pain in his hip, the dog fled, stopping every few yards to try to roll the stinging, stinking spray out of his eyes and off his skin.

It was the clever coyote who led him to the chickens. He followed her at a distance, upwind, so that she wouldn't know he was there.

They'd met only through scent marking, hers distinctive from the older, potent male who owned this territory, but the dog knew her the moment her rangy gray form slipped out from between the dense trees and glided silently down the hill toward the house and barn. He stayed behind, keeping to the trees, aware that there was a dog somewhere on the property. He watched as the coyote bitch circled the quiet pen, poking a paw here or there to see if there was an opening. Suddenly, she raised her head and looked right at him. There was no challenge in the look. The dog licked his lips, yawned. Nervous, tempted.

He took her invitation and in an awkward three-legged trot came down the hill, his clumsy noise alerting the sleeping hens. At the first squawk, the coyote was gone. The back door of the house slammed open and the yard lights burst on. Fighting the weakness in his leg, the dog bolted for higher ground, the double shotgun blast reminding him of the treachery—the danger—of humans.

As the weeks have passed, it's grown harder and harder to travel any distance away from his makeshift den. Not only has his hip wound festered but every bone in his body screams with a feverish ache that makes even sitting painful. He's been living mostly on crickets and what frogs he can catch, and the cold penetrates his now-fleshless body.

His dinner of crickets has not satisfied him by any means. He's spent all day limping along, sniffing every likely hiding place for some edible and catchable creature, with limited success. Grass and water are all that he can depend on. It's too much now to venture as far as the houses that have trash barrels. He's tucked into his den, exhausted. His acute ears hear the man who approaches at a run. The scent of fresh meat is somehow attached to him. The dog gets up and moves gingerly through the tall grass to where he can observe.

He watches as the man sets up the crate in the middle of the path that he runs along every day. He pulls the meat-scented package out of his pocket and opens it up. The overpowering scent of raw meat fills the air, bringing saliva to the dog's mouth. He swallows, yawns. Keeps his eyes on the man as he places chunks of the meat inside the crate, the bright cone of battery-powered illumination casting the man into shadow but the meat into the spotlight.

Now satisfied with the arrangement of the meat and the openness of the crate door, the man gets to his feet. He stands over the crate, walks around it, examining the ground with the sweep of his light. The dog is fixated on the scent of the meat within the crate but is unwilling to reveal himself. He waits, patient as a statue, for the man to go away. Finally, he does, striding quickly along, following the beam of his flashlight. The dog hunkers down in the tall grass, unaware that if the man's flashlight should sweep his way, his wide open eyes would give him away.

The man is gone, and the dog hears the cabin door shut, the sound of windows being cranked back in. He hears the man's human sounds without paying them any attention. His eyes and nose are on the meat. And he understands the price to be paid for getting it. He remembers the crate he was placed in by humans. He remembers how the door was shut and latched and how he was lifted into the back of a truck. He remembers only pain and torment after that.

The meat has attracted others. A red fox tiptoes out of the cattails, his brush outstretched and proud. The fox is startled off by the sudden advent of a larger predator. The adolescent female coyote sniffs the air but doesn't come close to the meat-baited box. The dog understands. There is too much human scent lingering around it. Of the three members of the Canidae family, only he has had true contact with these two-legged creatures. But she makes no move to leave, and the dog sees that this tantalizing offering is subject to loss. He may be afraid to retrieve it, but he doesn't want anyone else to have it. Even as emaciated as he is, he's still bigger than this adolescent coyote. He emerges from his cover and walks toward her. He growls. She lowers her head, waggles it, then bolts.

Alone now with the crate and the untouched meat, the dog lies down in the path, his nose pressed up against the mesh of the cage. He breathes in the odor of the fat, the bones, and the stringy red flesh. He sticks his tongue in, stretching it as far as he can against the obstruction of the wire mesh, and is rewarded by a taste. He struggles to his feet and circles the crate, standing for a long time in the obvious entrance. Some deeper caution prevents him from entering. The meat is a full body length away from the opening, too far to commit to trying to get at it. He settles down beside it once again, protecting from others that which he cannot, will not, get for himself.

Then another, stronger scent of coyote comes to him. This isn't the young female. This is the coyote who has left the scent marks defining his territory, his range. The dog has been aware of living within that range, and the inherent danger of it. And now this big male will demand that meat. The dog struggles to his feet. Once upright, he lowers his head, pulls his lips into a snarl, vocalizes his possession.

The male coyote, bigger than the dog, heavier and healthy, stiff-legs toward him, his hackles up, his yellow eyes fixed and hostile.

10

E ven before the lazy sun fully lights up the pond, I'm up and dressed and tying on my venerable L.L. Bean boots. I'll run later, if I run at all. Right now, I want to get out and see if the dog is in the trap. I've got a catch pole and a second Baggie of food and every expectation that a dog, no matter how feral it's become, won't have been able to resist the smorgasbord of meat products I baited the trap with last night. I'm less certain about what I may have captured—whether it will be a domestic dog or something I'll have to call the Wildlife Service to come deal with.

I check my messages as I walk out the door. Nothing this early from the communications center. Good. A voice-mail message from Max, wondering if I want to come over for the game. Better. And a text from Natalie saying she enjoyed herself last night and asking if I'd like to take a riding lesson sometime. Best. I text a quick yes to Max, saying I'll bring the beer, and, before I can overthink my re-sponse, text a yes to Natalie.

There is something that appeals to me about the idea of having an activity in place of an awkward reciprocal dinner. I do much better when I'm doing things, rather than just making conversation. Gayle and I spent the first few months of our courtship hiking and biking and river rafting. It was a long time before I realized that conversation with her was no longer contrived, but natural. And it was even longer before I realized that we both saw silence as a welcome thing. And then my silence went from a comfortable manifestation of our relationship to being withdrawn and guarded and maybe even hostile. No wonder she found a new guy.

Knock it off. Enough with the thoughts of that which is no longer in my control—*id* freakin' *est*, my marriage.

The October morning is lemon-colored, and I tilt the bill of my hat as I head due east toward the location of the trap, catch pole over my shoulder like a kid going fishing. I swing left along the path, and when the trap is only a few yards away, I start talking, alerting the animal, should he be incarcerated, of my approach, and my non-threatening intentions. "Hey, boy. Good fella. Did you enjoy your meal?" I whistle, a dog-calling "Come to me" whistle like the one I used for long-gone Snoopy and the one I used to call Argos back from his dog park free time. A towhee mocks me with its own sharp two-note upbeat whistle. *Tow Hee!*

The trap is in shadow, but I can see right away that not only is it empty but it's overturned; the trap's door is sprung and the bait is gone. I wish I was enough of a tracker, a hunter, to thoroughly assess the clues. There are definitely paw prints, but of a size to be the dog's? Maybe. Maybe not. It's also possible that there are two sets of prints. There's definitely fur. I pick up a silvery tuft. I need forensics out here. There's something very dark brown spattered on the pounded-down grass beside the trap. Another hunk of fur, this one with a little skin attached. More pale yellow than silver.

Max hands me a bowl of popcorn and a beer.

I set the bowl down on the coffee table and flop onto Max's ancient leather couch. I've been telling him about my failed attempt at capturing the feral dog. "He's not the first fugitive I've had to pursue using a couple of different methods." I take a swallow of beer. "I may have to track him and see if I can get him with a tranquilizer gun."

"If that's what you want to do, let me know and I'll give you the right dosage."

I don't mention that my tracking skills are nonexistent. Despite a couple of years in the Boy Scouts, I never earned a merit badge for tracking. Even when Bull offered to take me hunting, teach me how to find rabbits, I declined. Not out of any squeamishness, but because I didn't want to be anywhere near Bull and a gun. Later, professionally, my tracking was all done via canine nose.

We settle to watch the Patriots beat up on the opposition, and the conversation is essentially nothing more weighty than cheers, second-guessing referee calls, and epithets. By halftime, the Patriots are well ahead and Rocco's, the one pizza place in town that delivers, has brought us dinner.

"Maybe you shouldn't try trapping him. Maybe something a little less aggressive would work better with a dog like that."

"What do you mean?"

"He needs to be brought back into the fold, so to speak. The human fold. If he is a runaway, or a lost dog who's figured out how to survive without humans, he needs to be reminded that people are okay."

"How do I do that?"

"Don't try to trap him."

"I should just invite him into the house?"

"Something like that. Be around. Get him used to you."

The game is back on and that's it for conversation.

Jenny Bright isn't at the shelter when I get to work on Monday morning. I know that she'll pull in any minute now, and, because it's Monday, she'll be carrying a bag of what she calls her "go-to-work-on-Monday incentive." Harmony Farms, so far, has avoided any chain doughnut shops, and what those shops offer cannot be classed in the same genus as what she brings from Darlene's Bakery. Homemade, still warm, not quite perfectly ovoid, tantalizing doughnuts in a waxed white bag, wafting out of which is the scent I believe heaven might smell like.

My job is to get the coffee started. That set, I do something I should have done far earlier—pull out my logbook and review all the lost, missing, misplaced dogs over the past few weeks. Dogs wander, dogs get lost, but usually they find a human and turn themselves in. It's also possible that whoever lost this dog never thought to alert the dog officer. Some folks in this town are still unaware that they even have a dog officer. Still, my finely honed animal control officer instincts tell me that this is an abandonment case. His avoidance of humans is suggestive of human-caused trauma. Something I understand.

There's nothing logged that remotely resembles a missing mid-size yellow dog with a limp. I look at the reports of garbage tossing, plus Deke's chicken harassing, add in my own sightings, and there develops a territory of sorts where this stray dog is hanging out. My cabin's in the dead center.

I slap the book shut. Jenny has arrived and the sweet scent of freshly made doughnuts preceding her makes all else unimportant.

"Is that coffee ready?" she asks.

I get us both mugs from the chipped collection as Jenny divvies up the contents of the bakery bag. The first time Jenny brought doughnuts to the office, she made some remark about cops and doughnuts. Nothing particularly witty. I gave her a deadpan lecture on profiling and how making assumptions most often leads to personal offense. She blanched even whiter than she normally is under her Goth makeup and fell all over herself apologizing before I laughed and made a cop and doughnut joke myself. Jenny is the daughter of the golden couple of my first year in high school. Mark Bright and Olivia something. The homecoming king and queen, the couple all the other couples wanted to be. I know the story, but I'd never say anything to Jenny, who is the daughter of their teenage passion. College scholarships lost, the golden aura tarnished. Mark is in his father's business, plumbing, and Olivia works as a bookkeeper somewhere. Good people. Raised a quirky, if nice, kid. Their only child.

"I take it you didn't catch that dog, the one you took the big Havahart for?" Against her Goth-blackened lips, the white sugar of her powdered doughnut makes an interesting contrast until she licks it off.

"I'll get him. I was just checking to see if we had any reports on a lost dog in that vicinity, but the only unaccounted-for missing dog is that Lhasa apso that went missing a year ago."

"Coyote, my guess." Jenny breaks off another piece of doughnut and dips it into her black coffee.

"Probably."

Jenny pops the last of her doughnut into her mouth. "Poor family. It's tough not knowing."

"They're telling themselves that some well-meaning but misguided Samaritan picked it up and took it home. Home being a penthouse overlooking the Charles in Boston."

"You have to tell yourself whatever you must to gain acceptance of the unanswerable."

"Wisdom from a chick with seventeen piercings and a tattoo of Cookie Monster on her bicep."

"Yes, my son." Jenny crumples the paper bag and tosses it, then heads to the rest room.

I brush the crumbs from my glazed doughnut into my palm and then, with an eye to the closed rest room door, lick them off. Jenny's offhand pseudophilosophic remark floats in the air. Maybe she's right, and I wonder what I'm telling myself to get through my own unanswerable questions.

I pull into the uphill driveway of the Haynes brothers homestead, ignoring the array of NO TRESPASSING signs nailed to the stockade fence, as well as various other signs, all variations on the same theme: *Stay out.* BEWARE OF DOG. NEVER MIND DOG, BEWARE OF OWNER, PROTECTED BY MAGNUM. Sweet boys, Len and Bob. I'm here because I've gotten a call from an anonymous whistle-blower reporting animal cruelty. Anonymous because no one wants to be on the wrong side of the Haynes boys, but I'm pretty sure it's the electric company's meter reader.

Behind the stockade fence, the Haynes property makes Bull's shabby Poor Farm Road house look pristine. Blue tarp on the roof, random piles of salvaged wood, roofing shingles, rocks. A rusted-out John Deere sits cattywumpus against the side of a tilted outhouse. It's not deer season, but there's a carcass hanging from an oak tree, gutted and bled out. At least I think it's a deer. The Haynes are meat-on-the-table hunters, not sportsmen. Some speckled hens scrape at the dirt. So far, no one has called out to warn me off the property. But my instincts tell me that I'm being observed. The big Suburban with the town seal is announcement enough of who I am, and probably why I'm here. I climb out of the SUV, stand tall and bold as I take a quick survey of the yard. And there they are, three mongrels attached to short chains, which are fixed to a bare wheel rim from some kind of big vehicle. They fan out like spokes on a wheel and their chains are so short, they can't reach one another. No water. No food. No shelter. Feces everywhere.

They are on their feet, big dogs, hounds, by the look of them. They growl and then, at the approach of the two men, grovel.

"You got a warrant?"

"Hey, Bob. Len." I want to keep this on an even keel, but I know my job. "I don't need one. But you've got to provide shelter for these dogs. Basic needs."

"They're fine."

"No, they're not. And you want to keep them, you provide shelter, food, and water."

"You and what army going to take them away from us?" This is Len, the elder.

"You don't want to know." I hate bullies, especially the ones that have no original material.

"Get back in your town vehicle and get off the property."

"Neither one of you wants real trouble, so just move the dogs into that crappy shed, or lose 'em."

Len takes a step closer to me. "I said get off my property."

Although my voice is steady, there is a terrible roiling in my blood right now. I can hear the pulse in my ears, overriding the tinnitus. I don't want to lose my temper, my professionalism. I fall back on my training. "Please step away, sir." *Sir*, the default method of address for the irrational. Respect but no fear.

The dogs are back on their feet now, ears pinned, tongues popping against lips, nervous, anxious dogs. I decide that I should take a closer look. I shoulder myself past the barricade of Len and Bob. "Hey, pups. Good boys." I don't try to touch them; I'm only looking for signs of starvation or injury. They bark at me, but the look on their faces is pure fear aggression. They look well-enough fed. No obvious signs of injury. I notice a fourth chain, a collar still attached to the clip. I face the Haynes brothers. "I'll be back in a few days. See that they're sheltered properly."

I climb back into the SUV, back out slowly, implying that they haven't chased me away.

It's a beautiful, cool early October night and I'm camping out. I've got my sleeping bag and my camping lantern, a book, and a pot of stew simmering on my camp stove. I've chosen a spot where the feral dog can't miss my presence in the woods. There was enough daylight when I got home from work for me to scope out where the dog might most likely be living. It's not unlike hunting, or chasing felons. It just takes thinking and observation, measurements, and luck. I've chosen a flat, more or less comfortable site just inside the woods, a few feet from the path, twenty-five yards from the driveway. This is where I'll eat and sleep until the dog grows used to my nightly presence. If Muhammad won't come to the mountain ... . Fill in the rest for yourself.

I scoop some lukewarm stew out of the pot for myself, then ladle a second helping into a dog dish. This I set out ten feet from where I sit with my back against a scrub oak. I whistle twice and then settle in for what I know may be a very long wait. It could take days, maybe even weeks. I'm not sure I have the stamina—or interest—to do this for long, but, for now, it's a beautiful fall night and it isn't the worst place I've ever slept.

Two little boys, too young really to be out at night on their own. Lugging He-Man sleeping bags never meant for outdoor use. They set up camp on the imported sand of the small public beach at the edge of the lake, ignorant of the fact that the nylon bags will soak up the moisture from the ground, leaving them both soggy and shivering in the morning. Cooper thinks it's worth it, this discomfort, to have the benign attention of his older brother. He spends most of the night shivering and trying not to think about how badly he needs to pee, but he's afraid to climb out of the bag, afraid that some creature of the night might get him. The night birds and the bullfrogs sound so ominous when you're lying awake and cold and desperate to pee.

"I've got to go take a piss," Jimmy says.

Cooper didn't know his brother was also awake. "Me, too."

They crawl out of their damp sleeping bags to stand side by side as they urinate against a tilted tree. A screech owl cries out across the lake, making Cooper shiver.

"It's just a bird, stupid."
"I know." But it's good to have confirmation.

I wake from a surprisingly dreamless night. The sky is just beginning to turn gray and it is light enough that I know I won't be going back to sleep. Far from being cold or sore from a night on the ground, I feel, for the first time in a very long time, refreshed. Instead of awaking to my collection of stressful thoughts, I think immediately of my canine quarry. I struggle out of my sleeping bag to check the dog dish. Untouched. Disappointed but not surprised, I leave it, break camp, and head home for a shower. I'm a patient man. I can do this every night if I have to. Maybe there is even something pleasurable in the quest. It's been a long time since I've had a challenge that engages both my intellect and my competitive nature.

11

〜

I think this one will fit you." Natalie pulls a riding helmet off a shelf, hands it to me. "Buckle the strap. Make sure the harness is tight."

She's giving me that promised riding lesson today and I'm feeling like a new recruit trying not to piss off a drill sergeant. I take the helmet, put it on, buckle the chin strap as directed. She's told me to wear the most worn jeans I own and sturdy boots with a heel. If I like riding, I can invest in the right gear later.

Nat's already kitted out in riding pants, paddock boots, and half chaps. In a graceful, practiced motion, she gathers her hair into a knot and puts her black-and-brown riding helmet over it. If I survive the lesson, she'll take me out for a quick trail ride, so two horses are tacked up. I'll be on the bay mare that kissed my cheek the other day, and she'll be on the big chestnut, a rescued "off-the-track" Thoroughbred she's rehabbing for a new career in dressage. This, it seems, is her specialty, buying broken-down racehorses and retooling them.

I always admire people who know what they're doing, whether it's hammering shingles, directing traffic, or tracking felons. Natalie exudes the confidence of someone who is completely at home in her job. I can't imagine that she was ever a bond trader. I can't picture her in a suit, with high heels, a briefcase. She couldn't look any more attractive than she does right now, leading her horse out of the barn, every contour of her very well defined posterior perfect in mouse gray breeches. I pull myself back into the moment. Right now I'm with an attractive woman and about to climb aboard a horse for the first time since Deke let me swing a leg over his elderly pony when I was a kid.

It's one of those mid-October days that sparkle and make you squint against the angle of the sun as it grazes the tops of trees dressed in flaming red and orange leaves. The faded red of the barn somehow compliments the foliage, and the pasture grass has greened up again after a long, hot summer. The rustic charm of Natalie's Second Hope Farm is picture-perfect.

"Use the mounting block." Natalie holds the mare as I mount. "Have you ever ridden before?"

I mention the pony rides.

"Okay." And, with that, Natalie takes my left leg and positions my foot in the stirrup, telling me to do the same with the other leg, hands me the reins and shows me how to hold them properly, steps down from the mounting block, and walks to the middle of the ring. "Squeeze with your legs."

The mare moves toward the middle of the ring with a shuffling walk, her ears twitching from side to side. She ends up standing next to Natalie.

"Around the ring, not in the middle. Look where you want to go."

I look, squeeze, and the mare, reluctantly, shuffles off to the perimeter of the riding ring.

"Squeeze harder; make her move."

I do, and suddenly I'm riding. A walk, to be sure, but I have the horse moving forward and, with Natalie's order to "shorten" my reins, I have the feel of her between my hands and legs. I feel pretty good, pretty accomplished for a first-timer. This isn't so hard. We change direction, make some circles. I'm feeling pretty good.

"Want to try a trot?"

Half an hour later, I understand very well the location of what Natalie calls my "seat bones." I'm pretty sure that I will recognize them every time I sit down for the next week. My lesson is declared over; she's up on her chestnut, and even a first-timer like me can see the world of difference between my riding skills and hers. On his long dancer's legs, the horse appears to be floating above the ground as she trots him around the ring. I think of the hours of practice Argos and I put in, drills designed to make action into reaction. Hours of practice takedowns, searches, refinements to our skills. What Natalie and the chestnut are doing is more like a ballet lesson. I am seated on my mare in the middle of the ring, watching Natalie's face as she concentrates on moving her horse in gliding lateral moves. I know that kind of concentration, the kind that blanks out the rest of the world. When Argos and I were on patrol, the only thing on my mind was the task at hand. Not hunger or thirst, or weariness, for either of us. A goal was set, to find a missing person. Or to take down and hold a criminal until backup arrived. Nothing could distract us from that goal.

"Get 'em, boy."

Argos is a streak of white motion, accompanied by the throaty music of his trademark growl. More than a growl, a roar, a fearsome vocalization guaranteed to frighten the most aggressive criminals.

"Get him off me! Get him off me!" The perpetrator rolls on the ground beneath the big dog's savage advance.

"Argos, all done." Cooper has his handcuffs out, and the perp is almost glad to have him snap them on. He hauls the guy to his feet. "You have the right . . ."

Argos fairly dances beside the pair, cop and collar, his amber eyes fixed on the man in Cooper's grip, silently reminding the captive that he, Argos, is still on the job and he'd better not try anything.

This collar is the twenty-first for Cooper and Argos and it gets the attention of the papers, and the local news station does a little story on it, on Argos, which makes Cooper feel like a proud parent.

Natalie's goal is a little more obscure, but I think it involves perfection in movement. I stroke the silky neck of the mare, Moxie, and feel her relax under me, dropping her head, her thick black tail casually swishing behind me. She blows air gently through her nostrils, the horsey equivalent of sighing. A peaceful, contented sound.

"Got enough energy left in you? Want to go out for a hack?" Natalie is walking her horse, his neck stretched out fully, his ears drooping with relaxation.

"I do." I may never walk again, but I've got enough energy for a trail ride. As instructed, I "gather" my reins, which gets Moxie's attention and she perks up.

We leave the paddocks behind, moving slowly toward the hillside bordering Natalie's pastures, on the other side of which is Bartlett's Pond. My mare takes the lead without my express say-so, but Natalie just says that's who she is. The big chestnut docilely follows along, putting his trust in the smaller mare to save him from scary things. Or to be eaten first. Warm from my riding-lesson exertions, I've left my jacket behind, and the cool October air feels good. The movement of horse hooves through the dry fallen leaves is a cheerful sound, like crunching bran flakes. Once in a while, I hear Natalie's voice behind me, but I can't catch what she's saying over the rustling of the leaves. I haven't mentioned my hearing loss, although she must have wondered about me, as I wasn't quick to respond to her instructions as I tracked to the left in the ring. She had to repeat herself enough that she must have thought me a student with very poor retention; after all, I'd done so well going clockwise.

Very quickly we are at the pond and begin to circumnavigate my running path side by side, which makes conversation a lot easier.

There's a gathering of Canada geese on the bank, muttering to themselves as the horses pass by. They glide out into the water, complaining of the intrusion.

"Did you ever catch that dog you were after?"

"No. He's savvy enough about traps to keep out of them. I've been trying to get him to know me by dropping some meat as I run, leaving my dirty shirt where he can smell it, that sort of thing."

"Tame him?"

"I guess you could say that, although I don't think he was born feral. But clearly something happened to him, and I'm afraid that if I don't get him pretty soon, before the real cold settles in, I'm just going to find a corpse one day. No dog deserves that kind of end."

"I know. That's how I feel about the horses I rescue. You wouldn't believe the conditions some animals are kept in. By well-meaning idiots mostly, people who have no idea what it takes to keep a horse healthy. They get one for their kids, keep it in a backyard in a six-by-six pen. Or find out they can't afford to feed it and let it loose. Or race it at age two with damaged ligaments masked by drugs." Natalie is getting wound up.

"But we can't save them all."

"But you're going to save this one. I just know it."

We veer off the trail around the pond, following a narrower path.

"Max told me you were a cop before you were an animal control officer."

"That's right. K-9 unit."

"That must have been pretty exciting work." Subtext: So how come you're a lowly ACO in a Podunk town.

"It had its moments." I'm not going to be sucked into a conversation I haven't had with anyone. "Bond trading must have had some heart-stopping moments, too."

"There were days, sure. But I didn't quit because it was too exciting."

"I assume you quit to follow a dream."

"Second Hope?"

"Isn't it? Your dream, I mean."

"It's more than a name, Second Hope. More than a dream. It saved my life." She doesn't look at me when she says this, and I know that she, too, has a story she'd rather not get into. She strokes her horse's neck. We pause at the edge of a small field that I recognize as Deke's back pasture. "Want to try a canter?"

It's just like in the cowboy movies; the wind in my face, my eyes watering, and the sense that I'm either going to fly or fall hard keeps me smiling. I'm just beginning to relax into the rocking horse rhythm of this mare when Natalie brings her horse down to a trot and my mare suddenly follows suit, almost unseating me with the abrupt change of rhythm.

"How was that?" Natalie has dropped her reins, her horse completely ready to head home without guidance.

"Amazing." I give my mare a pat on her neck and a little scratch. "Where do I get the right gear?"

It has been a very long time since a woman looked at me with approval, and I bask in the radiance of Natalie's smile. She's got dimples I haven't noticed before. I've always liked dimples.

We make our way back to Second Hope at a walk, side by side.

12

Roger Schaeffer is a pudgy, balding, colorless man dressed in the überbland colors of beige and taupe. In the harsh fluorescent overhead lights of the animal control office, his skin is as mushroom-colored as his pants and his eyelashes are so pale that his watery blue eyes appear bald. He is the polar opposite of his florid, caftan-wearing, overblown mother, Polly. And it's his mother he's come to see me about. About her animals.

"I guess you could say that we're staging an intervention. We'll get her out of the house; you collect the animals and get them out of there."

"And where am I supposed to take them?" I point to the three-dog kennel and the short stack of cat cages, two of which are occupied by cats, and the third contains a black-and-white rabbit. "I don't have the room."

"She can't go on like this. I'm afraid that the Health Department is going to come in."

"Look, Roger." I sit forward in my office chair, put on my

authority face. "I'm keeping tabs on her and she's got a lot of cats, yes, but she's not breaking any laws."

"She's a crazy cat lady." To my surprise, Roger is on the verge of tears. "How would you like it if everyone made fun of your mother?"

Don't you remember what folks said about my family? I think. My mother may not have been made fun of, but she sure was an object of pity. *What does Mona see in him? Why does she keep going back to that drunk?* Funny what a kid overhears. Some adults think that a child who appears to be focused on his Legos isn't aware of their conversation—teachers, baby-sitters, neighbors—that a little kid doesn't understand that his mother is gossip fodder; that he isn't listening.

"No one is making fun of her." I get it now, Roger's distress. It's no laughing matter to have a parent who is out of control, or a danger to society, or an embarrassment to you as you grow up and you have to distance yourself from their foibles. "Have you ever gotten her help? I mean, you know, a psychiatric evaluation? If there was a diagnosis, maybe something could be done."

"We've tried, my sister and I. At first, we thought, Great, she's got an interest, and something to keep her company because neither one of us lives here. That was for the first three cats. Now I can't take my kids to see their grandmother."

"She's a good soul, Roger." I could mention the puppy that she gave me, but I am squeamish about reminding Roger, who has about fifteen years on me, about that grubby little poor-side-of-town kid who would show up at his house to play with his dog. I want Roger to know that his mother has friends. "Folks like her. She's active at church." But I don't tell him that no one will go to her house to visit. I also don't tell Polly's son that sometimes I have to remove her "rescued" animals and return them to their rightful owners

Roger knuckles away a tear, sniffs. "We'd just appreciate anything you can do. Maybe even just take a couple of the cats? Even that would help."

I slide my rolling chair to my office door. "Hey, Jenny, can you come in?"

Jenny Bright has a file folder with the names of local residents who have been willing to foster some of the inmates of the Bowwow Inn. She works with a variety of rescue organizations to place the unclaimed dogs that occasionally languish in the kennel here. If a dog fits a breed type, Jenny has the capacity to sweet-talk even the most reluctant of program directors to take a chance on the animal.

I ask if she can come up with a few animal lovers willing to foster a cat or two.

"I don't know, Coop. There aren't a lot of feline fosterers around. Not quite as glam as dog fostering." She squeezes one of her multiple ear studs in more securely, the movement showing to advantage the red-and-green lizard tattoo crawling along her forearm.

"Work your magic."

"I'll see what I can do, but no promises."

Roger is staring after Jenny as she walks out of my office, his round face a pale mask of doubt.

"Don't worry. She's very good at what she does."

I walk Roger Schaeffer out of the building and to his, unsurprisingly, beige car. "Give me a call in a couple of days, and I'll let you know if we've got places for some of the cats." I'm not about to empty Polly's house out. I can't do that to her. But, as Roger says, she's a crazy cat lady and I need to do something.

As he drives away, it occurs to me that he has no idea that I'm one of *those* Harrisons. What a pleasant thought. Maybe Lev was right when he said no one would remember me.

It's been almost a week, but I'm still feeling my first horseback ride in my thighs. It's kind of a good pain, a reminder of an enjoyable experience and something that is beginning to feel like a new friendship. Tonight, Friday, I'm taking her out properly, to the Lakeside Tavern. The tavern is perfect because it's so local, so unassuming, we can be perfectly relaxed and not look like a couple out on the shakedown cruise of a first date. Besides, it isn't a first date, not technically. We've already broken bread together—which reminds me that I still have Mrs. Bollen's lasagna dish in my truck—and shared an outdoor experience. So, to be accurate, this is the third date, practically routine. Still, I'll go home and shower before driving to her place to pick her up. Maybe take her one of those ten-dollar bouquets from the Country Market.

Max Philbine is the only one who knows that I'm testing the dating waters with Natalie, and that's only because Friday is usually the night he and I hit the tavern ourselves. I felt a little like a playground fink, breaking a date with a pal to go out with a girl. Max laughed and forgave me. "Hey, she's a great girl. Go have fun. I've got other friends, you know."

"Max?"

"What?"

"Why haven't you asked her out?"

"I did." Max waits a beat. "Kidding."

"Seriously, why not?"

"Coop, old man, I've been down the marriage path twice and have foresworn ever becoming entangled in that again."

"I'm not talking engagement here, but a date, you know, two people of the opposite sex talking over a plate of linguini."

I certainly have no ulterior motive, no desire at all to go down that path Max referred to, not at all. It's just a date. Besides, Natalie's made it fairly clear that she's glad of a date but not looking for a lifestyle change any more than I am. Phrases clutter her conversation—"I'm so busy," "I'm so focused on my work, I can't think of anything else"—in a pretty obvious deflection of unwanted intentions. I'm not courting, or seducing, and I think that suits us both.

I'm only buying her a meal to say thank you for introducing me to a new sport. That's all. Really. It's what friends do.

Before I can turn my attention to the pleasures of my upcoming evening, I have to go check on the Haynes's dogs. It's must be the Puritan in me, do the hard thing first so that you can enjoy the fun thing later. I keep my fingers crossed that not only will the brothers be away from the property, which would make my inspection a lot more pleasant, but that they have heeded my warnings. I'm one for two when I pull into the yard. No dogs in sight. This is encouraging, but then I don't hear them, either, and I think that I would. Len comes out of the house. I get out of the truck. We meet like the sheriff and the gunslinger, halfway. "Len, where are the dogs?"

He doesn't say anything; neither does he meet my eyes. He blows his nose into a red bandanna, stuffs it into his overall pocket. "When you were here last time, I didn't know you were Bull's boy. Thought you were a newcomer."

Bull's boy. "Right. Cooper Harrison."

By virtue of knowing my family, of my being determined a native, as it were, I am suddenly okay in Len's book.

"I'll show you." Len leads me around the tilted shed to a flat shaded area where he's erected a proper kennel, not luxury living by any means, but each dog now has its own doghouse and run. There are still only three dogs, but he's built a fourth kennel.

"You didn't happen to lose a dog recently, did you? I've got a stray I'm tracking."

"Nope. Had one die."

"How?" I have to ask.

"Bone got stuck in his throat." Len turns away from me. Our conversation is ended.

As it turns out, I don't have time to run by the market and buy flowers for Natalie. The truth is, I kind of chickened out. Flowers just seem too suggestive of intentions she isn't interested in. I may not have had time to buy flowers, but I have built in time to take a two-lap run around the pond and drop some stew beef as I go, feeding the dog and making inroads against his distrust of me. When I get back tonight, I will fill the bowl with meat, add a couple of dog bis-cuits, and set it, as I always do, ten feet from my sleeping bag. Far enough away that the dog knows he can't be grabbed, close enough that he will identify me with the food. This morning, I was over-joyed to see that, for the first time, the food was gone. Of course, without having actually seen the animal that took it, I can only hope that it was my target dog, not some sneaky woodland creature un-afraid of humans. One of these nights, I should really try to stay awake, watching for the glitter of animal eyes in the dying flames.

It's already dark by the time I pull into the yard at Second Hope Farm. The barn lights are on, the doors wide open, and the effect is warm and welcoming. Natalie's dog comes out to greet me, as if wondering where I have been all her life. I squat to pat her, stand up, to see Natalie coming toward me, the lights of the barn illumi-nating her way.

The water is the only thing that feels good against his wounds. It was only the looseness of the skin around his neck that saved the dog from the fangs of the male coyote, suffering punctures but not a broken neck. His forelegs bear the gashes inflicted by the bigger canine. The punctures and the gashes are filled with pus and the stink has attracted flies, which torment the dog.

Every day, he awaits the sound of the man running along the path. Only then, after the man passes, does he rouse himself from the shelter of the reeds and pick up what the man has carelessly left behind. Chunks of meat. Because it's daylight, and the man scent lingers, there is no competition for it. The dog swallows the cubes whole.

The dog closes his eyes, almost as desirous of sleep as he is of food and water. Even for a young dog, not even a yearling, this constant discomfort is wearing, and he could be an old dog just at the end of his life for the amount of will left in him.

13

The meeting had been a good one. Someone had brought seasonally decorated doughnuts, and the coffee was a little less acidic than usual. Maybe whoever brought the orange-and-black sprinkled goodies had plumped for Dunkin' Donuts coffee. Couple of new guys, shy first-timers mumbling through the introductions. Bull didn't usually speak at these things; he was happy to sit in the back and listen to others relate how many days it'd been since their last drink or what extraordinary efforts they were making toward sobriety. Or why they were starting over again at day one. He'd had a lot of day ones. The novelty of sobriety would wear off and things would happen. Right now, he was clinging to day 753. But, hey, who was really counting?

Jimmy's got stuff locked away. But Bull knows where it is. For the first few days that Jimmy was at the house, he'd done what a lot of guys do when they get out—gone on a drunk. It was as if he didn't know that Bull was on the wagon, that he'd gone over two years without a drink or a hit. But Jimmy was a man coming off the desert, so he brought a boxful of liquor into the house, setting it on the banged-up kitchen table. "Oh, yeah, right. You're off the sauce, right, old man?"

"Seven hundred and thirty-six and counting." Bull was proud to tell his boy this. The last time he'd seen Jimmy, Bull'd been sober, too, but only since dawn, which was when Deke picked him up to drive him to Walpole for a visit with his elder son. It was a long ride and a longer day, being without the anesthesia of alcohol. Made the visiting room all the more depressing.

"You keep a calendar?" Jimmy asked.

"I have to."

"Well, I hope you don't mind, but I'm indulging. I counted days, too, and by my calculations, I'm at day four thousand and something." Jimmy opened a cabinet and pulled out an old jelly glass with the cartoon images of Fred Flintstone and Barney Rubble decorating it. Jimmy filled the glass to the top of Fred's head with the whiskey and raised it to Bull. "What should I toast?"

"Freedom?" Bull takes a Coke out of the refrigerator, pops the top. The sizzle of carbonation tickles his mouth. "Good health?"

Jimmy studies Fred's face on the glass. "To old friends and new endeavors." He throws back a deep swallow, winces, bangs the tabletop with an open hand. "Good stuff."

Jimmy keeps the booze in his room, the same room that he slept in all those years ago when the whole family was living on Poor Farm Road. Back in the day when Mona was here and things were better. Not good, but better. She was so beautiful. At least until the lines began to develop and deepen around her eyes and in her cheeks, and eventually there was a hardness to her eyes that wasn't there back in their early years. Even then, defeated by the life she'd gotten, Mona was beautiful in Bull's eyes.

A singularly golden spring evening, two kids about to fall in love. Bull in his leather jacket, Mona, a fragile-looking seventeen, in a miniskirt. The sweetness of that first kiss, the feel of her breast under his hand. There is an urgency, more than just desire; in a month, maybe two, Bull knows that he'll be drafted. He's been dealt a lousy number, and he's not college material. That's okay. It means that he and Mona can get married all the sooner. It's all he wants, to give her his name and have her back home waiting for him. She's smitten by his hasty proposal. There is a certain romance to the idea of being a war bride. Like her own mother had been. No one tells Mona "Marry in haste, repent at leisure." She's known Bull all her life but has loved him only since that first kiss, the smoky taste of passion.

He looks so handsome in his uniform; she looks so beautiful in her wedding dress. Two kids, stars in their eyes. They have no idea that Bull will never be the same man as he is in this moment. All of the optimism and happy expectations of building a better life will have been replaced by inertia. A new conviction: What's the use?

"How you doing, Bull?" One of the newer guys had clapped a hand on Bull's shoulder. He was new to the group, but not to Bull's acquaintance. He was one of the Highway Department guys Bull used to work with back in the day. He was a kid back then, fresh out of high school and delighted to be on the crew, a family sinecure. Now he'd risen to department head, just like his dad and his grandfather before him.

"Hey, Tom. Good enough. You bring these?" Bull stuffed a doughnut into his mouth, tongued the sprinkles off his lips.

"Yeah. My turn."

"Rite of passage. There are enough of us, you won't have to do it too often."

"Hear that Jimmy's back."

"That's right." In another man, a red flag might have snapped to attention, but Bull wasn't suspicious. Tommy was here, in a meeting. He couldn't have been looking for trouble. He'd just told thirty sweaty men how he'd been sober so many days and clinging to his

Higher Power. Then again, Jimmy never dealt in alcohol. Bull knew all too well the rationalizations an addict can conjure. But, as far as he knew, Tommy was a run-of-the-mill, too many G&Ts after work kind of alcoholic, there at the meeting because Lev Parker had nailed his ass doing fifty in a twenty-mile-an-hour zone and had given him the choice of AA or thirty days. "He's doing okay," Bull said, referring to Jimmy.

"He got a job yet?"

"No." At least not one he clocks in for, Bull thought. As part of Jimmy's probation he had to at least appear to be making an effort to job-hunt.

"Tell him come to me if he's interested."

Near as Bull could figure, his boy had no marketable skills. He had no CDL license or experience on a factory floor. He'd never had so much as an after-school job. Unless they'd taught him some trade in Walpole, Jimmy's résumé only boasted selling illegal drugs. "Jimmy's not the pick and shovel type, if you get my meaning."

"Naw, nothing like that. No heavy lifting." Tommy laughed, reached for a glazed doughnut. "I could use someone in the office to do scheduling, that sort of thing. Detail stuff."

"Okay. I'll mention it." Bull didn't think that Jimmy would be interested, but he hated to discourage people. Besides, it was nice of Tommy to make this offer. He was a stand-up guy. Not too many employers around there were going to want an ex-con on the payroll. "Thanks."

Tommy clapped Bull on the shoulder again, the gesture both empathetic and patronizing.

14

The bar is three-deep when we arrive at the Lakeside Tavern. There's a twenty-five minute wait for a table, so we join the throng at the bar and order a drink. For a relative newcomer, Natalie seems to know half the people here and she air-kisses and nods to faces that I don't recognize or have a name to put to. I know the bartender, Guy, simply because Guy has been behind the oak bar since I used to come in here to pull my father out. I see a couple of folks whose dogs I've nabbed, the woman who runs the natural-foods store, where I occasionally shop.

In an unusual show of rubbing shoulders with the proletariat, the town's power couple, Cynthia Mann and her husband, Donald Boykin, are here. I know Cynthia a little, Donald not at all, and yet they wave to me in a friendly manner. I almost walk over, then realize that they're gesturing to the person behind me.

Max is at the corner table next to the fireplace, which is glowing now with the first fire of the season. He's got a guy with him, no one I've ever seen before, and I wonder if this is someone from Tufts here to further seduce our town's only veterinarian.

The Irish music trio is warming up, and the whole scene seems so cozy, so cinematic. The jolly neighborhood tavern, gathering place. Maybe I should have suggested getting out of town, going someplace more sophisticated, a place where we might have had to wear something other than jeans. A place where we would have to pay attention to each other, without the comfort of the familiar, the buffer of other acquaintances keeping us safe.

"Marla's flagging us."

Of course Natalie would know the hostess.

"She's a student. Decent rider. She rides the mare you rode."

Marla seats us at the table opposite Max's, flanking the other side of the fireplace. Natalie greets Max with a peck on the cheek. Max does introductions. His tablemate is not from the university, but another vet. I get it: Max is vetting—no pun intended—a potential replacement for himself.

That bit of civility done, Natalie chooses the chair at our round table that puts her back to them. Behind her, Max nods to me, then lifts his glass in a little mocking salute. Natalie's eyes are on me, or I might have good-naturedly flipped Max the bird.

On the ride over, we covered the easy topics of my sore ass and her crazy, busy day. As we have already dealt with the obvious elements in our current lives—her farm, my job—now, we both know, it is the time in our acquaintance to begin to burrow underneath the known surface. We've touched upon the observable, and if we are to become friends, we need to pry a little into each other's lives.

Fortunately, our server arrives just in time.

The special sounds good enough for Natalie, and I fall back on my usual cheeseburger. We order a shared appetizer and new beers. The Irish trio are in full volley and it's impossible for me to hear anything that Natalie is saying over the relentless fiddle and tabor. I keep leaning in, finally shifting my seat over so that my good ear is near her. "I can't hear." I point to my left ear. "It's damaged, and this doesn't help."

Natalie leans in close, so close, I feel her breath on my cheek. I slide an arm around her to keep her there, to hear her.

"How? How was it damaged?"

"Bomb." I take a sip of beer, think about it for a second, then add, "It's when my K-9 partner was killed."

And, as simply as that, I have finally neutralized what happened. Not diminished or defined, or with any less grief, but honed down into a sentence that informs, without killing me by saying it out loud.

The tabor player's mallet beats out a frantic pulse and the fiddle screeches with the same six bars in manic repetition until, at last, the reel comes to a merciful end and I hear Natalie's response clearly. "I'm so sorry." She touches the back of my hand, one finger gently pressing on my knuckles. "Is that why you're here?"

Slowly, I take my arm from around her shoulders, smile up at the server bearing our appetizer of baked Brie and warm bread. A lock of Natalie's dark hair has tangled itself around the button of my shirt cuff and I'm a little stuck. I untangle myself without pulling a strand out.

"Is it?"

"Yes." I stab the Brie with the knife and the warm cheese oozes out over the white plate through the split. I have said enough. I'm not going to reveal to this relative stranger the core disease of my heart, the depth of my grief, the chasm of my fear.

Natalie takes the bread and cheese I hold out to her, rolls her eyes heavenward at the taste. I can see her watching me, waiting for more from me. And then comes the glimmer of understanding. "Okay. Another time."

"Fair enough. Now I'll ask you one, and you can duck it. Why Harmony Farms?"

"You mean, with no connection, no family, no reason to choose this rural location rather than one closer to my origins?"

"Yes. Exactly."

"For exactly those reasons."

"You needed to get out of Dodge?"

She laughs, the first full-throated laugh I've heard from her. "Yes. Something like that."

"As a former law-enforcement officer, I have to advise you that anything you say can only make me curiouser."

"Like Louis Carroll's Cheshire cat?"

"I thought it was Alice who first used the term."

"With you, Mr. Harrison, I suspect that things do get curiouser and curiouser."

The Brie is gone, the white plate nearly licked clean, and our server has appeared with our main courses. Natalie orders a glass of white wine to go with her swordfish and I switch to root beer. "Designated driver."

"How nice for me."

The trio has started up again, this time with a set of sweet ballads. It's easier to talk, but we don't. The silence is comfortable and the food good. Max and his potential replacement have left—Max slapping me on the shoulder in a good-old-boy manner on the way out—and the crowd has been winnowed down to the point that their table remains empty after having been cleared by the busser.

Even a nondate like this needs a second half. Dinner is the first part; a movie or a concert or a couple of strings at the bowling alley, if Harmony Farms had a bowling alley, would make up the remainder of an evening between people not ready for a third act. I am so out of the dating scene that I haven't given any thought to what we might do as a postprandial activity.

As if there had been no pause, Natalie says, "I came to Harmony Farms because the property was for sale and I could afford it. The reason I could afford it was because I was awarded a fairly large sum in a lawsuit. Ugly, but that's the truth. It's when I knew that I had to do something different from what I'd been doing. This was a God-given opportunity."

"I'm going to assume you won't tell me what kind of lawsuit."

Natalie touches the bowl of her glass, stroking away the moisture glistening there. "Wrongful death."

"I'm sorry." There are so many varieties of wrongful death—parent, child, spouse. Medical malpractice, car accident. Shooting. The dead child on the street, caught in the cross fire.

Like me, she's not quite willing to give up her story. I stifle the urge to interrogate her, suppress my curiosity. Whatever her story is, I'll let her keep it to herself until she's ready to tell me. It's a comfortable thought, this idea that there will be other times.

Natalie excuses herself for a moment, leaving me to decide if we should stay for a last drink or take off now, find somewhere else to go for a nightcap. I'm sober, and I can certainly indulge in a glass of wine at that new wine bar on Main Street, the place that took over the space once occupied by Marie's Yarn Shop. Then again, maybe we aren't dressed appropriately for something called a wine bar.

When she gets back from the ladies' room, Natalie decides for us. "I have about an hour left on my internal clock before I crash and burn. Would you like to get out of here and finish up with pie and coffee at my place?"

Yes, please.

Timing in life is everything. A minute less in the ladies' room, a server quicker to bring the check, one less minute in the Lakeside Tavern and I could have avoided my father and brother. It might even have been possible if only they hadn't made a beeline for the empty table for two vacated by Max and his friend. There they are, Bull grinning at me and Jimmy looking at Natalie with his cold gray eyes.

"Hey, Cooper, how they hangin'?" Bull wraps a meaty hand

around my neck, shakes me like a cat with a mouse in her mouth. "You treating this girl all right? He treatin' you right, ma'am? You tell me he's not and I'll kick his teeth in."

"Oh, he's a perfect gentleman." Natalie steps back, her booted foot stepping on mine, her head against my shoulder.

I am blocked against the table by my family. There is no escape. Natalie's body against mine is like a shield, and I think of captors and hostages. I notice that the pint glass in Bull's hand is clear, a wedge of lemon floating against the ice.

"So, we don't get an introduction?" Jimmy has changed since the last time I saw him. He's put on jail weight; he looks more like Bull, less like me. He looks like what he is, a middle-aged ex-con. Unlike his still-on-the-wagon father, Jimmy holds a glass of dark beer; a thin creamy head tilts slightly as he maneuvers closer to Natalie.

I can feel the skin of my face tighten with anger. I will not lose control of myself. I will not let them get the better of me. "Natalie, this is Bull, and Jimmy." Do I deliberately leave out the common factor of our last name? Maybe, but Bull chimes right in.

"Bull Harrison, pleased to meet you." Bull smiles at Natalie with what amounts to a toothless smile, yet, like a baby's, somehow charming.

Jimmy snatches her hand, gives it a little shake. "Natalie, you want to have fun, you call me. My brother's never been much fun."

"You bet." Natalie extricates her hand from his grip, shoulders her handbag and, with the coolness I've seen her use in the paddock when walking between fractious sixteen-hand horses, pushes through the wall that Bull and Jimmy create.

I feel a deep need to apologize for my family, but I don't really have cause. After all, except for being who *I* know they are, for being crude, they hadn't committed any egregious crimes. Besides, the less said about Bull and Jimmy the better.

So instead of opening up a can of worms with my apology, I

open the passenger door for her and ask, "What kind of pie are you offering?"

"I only know how to make one kind, apple. Hope that's all right."

"My favorite."

The yard light comes on as we pull into the parking spaces by the barn. Moisture shows in the cone of light. The air has grown colder, more in line with the time of year than previously, and for the first time I'm not looking forward to sleeping outside. My sleeping bag is rated for twenty degrees, and it's well above that, but, still, the idea of a warm bed after a pleasant evening is a sweet one. And no, I wasn't thinking of hers. Not exactly.

I follow Natalie as she does her late-night barn check. The barn smells of warm animals and hay, shavings and manure. The horses chuckle, used to having their naps interrupted, expecting treats. Natalie hands me some carrots and I find Moxie and feed her snapped-off pieces. I love the touch of her muzzle against the palm of my hand.

We're done in the barn and head to the house, where the pit bull, Betty, greets us as returning heroes. Of course, Natalie has brought some leftover swordfish back, so, in fact, she is a hero. I'm comfortable at the kitchen table. Natalie's got one of those single-cup coffeemakers and a carousel with varieties of coffee in small containers. "I've got to fall asleep outside in the cold, so you'd better give me decaf." I hope that doesn't sound like a bad play for an overnight stay with her.

"Still trying to lure your dog in?"

"Yeah. He's not cooperating. Max said if I showed kindness that he'd be enticed into capture. So far, not so much."

The pie is good, the coffee hot, and the evening's energy is spent. I don't hesitate this time to kiss her good night and am rewarded with a second kiss. "Hey, take the rest of this fish; maybe your ghost dog would like a change from meat." She hands me the ecofriendly cardboard box. "Betty can share."

The wind has picked up by the time I get out to the campsite. I'm too tired to get fancy, so I open the cardboard container for the dog, whistle twice so that if he's around, he'll know I'm there, and climb into my goose-down bag. The ground feels particularly hard tonight. With the colder air, the sky has dried out and the stars are amplified against a jet black sky. No moon. No fire. Just the light from my lantern before I shut it off. I stare up at the sky and wait for sleep. There is Sirius, the dog star, faithful companion of Orion. Mythical dogs. My dog, Argos, was named for the faithful hound of Odysseus, who recognized his master first upon his return. Legendary dogs.

Argos wouldn't recognize me now.

The dog waits for the man to come back. It has become a habit by now, this expectation that the human will join him for the night. The food that he drops, the sound of another animal's breathing, vocalizations, movement—these have become something the dog has accepted. But the night grows colder and darker and there is no sign of the man. He waits, sniffing the air, hearing his own vocalizations, an interrogatory rumble in the back of his throat: *Where are you?* It could easily become a whimper.

The dog hears in the distance the sound of the truck that he identifies with the man. The headlights glance through the trees and vanish. With his acute hearing, the dog follows the man's path from truck to porch to house. He merges with the thick brush, waits until the man appears bearing the sweet scent of cooked food. The dog, shivering, licks his dewlaps, pants with widened mouth, trying to gather in more of the sublime odor.

He hears it, the whistle, the man's voice. The words *come* and *boy*. He can't yet bring himself to be seen by the man, so he stays where he is until his fellow night creature climbs into his nest, and only then does the dog venture close enough. At first sniff, the man is the same, his scent as it always is, an amalgam of sweat and laundry soap, and the debris of skin cells that offer so much detail to a dog. But, tonight, there is an overlay, a sexual tinge to his odor, a loosening of pheromones and anxiety that brings a new texture to the information the dog has been garnering about this man. The man makes soft noises in his sleep, utterly confident that, as a human, no harm can come to him out here in the dark woods.

The yellow dog limps over to the open box, carelessly left on the ground by this very careless man. Inside, there is a new treat, the sweet, salty scent announcing something he's never had before. He wolfs it down, his eyes at all times on the form of the sleeping man. The fish and vegetables are gone, but their odor clings to the textured interior of the cardboard box. Eyes still on the man, the dog deftly picks up the box; the flavorful, ecofriendly cardboard box will help to fill his belly.

The dog comes closer to the man. Still hungry, always, but tonight his curiosity has brought him as close to this person as he has ever dared before. Confident that this human is completely unaware and won't suddenly leap up in a startled reflex, the dog stretches his neck out, the better to breathe in the scent wafting up from the only exposed part of him, the top of his head. He is almost leisurely as he sniffs, loosening his dewlaps to gather in the scent molecules that drift out of the warm-scented sleeping bag. The idea of warmth is beginning to grow in importance, along with finding food. With none of the fat that his breed normally carries, this dog feels the cold in his scant flesh. He lacks the layers that will let him survive the coming winter. Even this early in the waning season, he feels the cold seep into his bones as he burrows into his place beneath the fallen tree. Even if he can manage to find enough to eat to keep alive, instinctively the dog knows that it will still be hard to survive once winter sets in.

The man rolls over, dragging the sleeping bag over his head. The dog backs up, a movement that pains his hip. The hip wound has opened up again, and he's spent hours licking the place, tasting the rot within. The dog positions himself behind the form of the sleeping man. He should retreat to his nest, to his safe place, to the hollowed-out protection against the rising wind. He listens carefully to the exhalations of the man, watches his restless motion inside the cocoon of the bag, which makes it wriggle, as if a butterfly is about to emerge.

The flavorful box is gone and the dog rests his chin on his paws, his eyes on the man. Simply being there, in the presence of a sleeping human, gives the dog an oddly contented feeling. As long as the man remains asleep, the dog is going to enjoy this temporary companionship.

15

I awaken in that last moment before dawn, when the suggestion that night is over is confirmed by the first note of the first bird, close enough and loud enough that even I can hear it. My neck is stiff and it feels like I've been sleeping on rocks. The wind has died down, but the cold front that was pushing it has arrived and I can see my breath in the predawn gray. Okay, I've had enough. This is the last night for me on the ground in this Ahabesque quest. I lie there, gathering up the courage to emerge from my warm chrysalis into the cold day. In my good ear, I hear a sound, so faint that it might be a leaf scraping stubbornly against a branch, a leaf that is particularly rhythmic. I know that sound, a hind foot motoring against ribs in an ecstasy of scratching. Unbelievably, my quarry is right behind me. I don't dare move, but I need to see for myself what my good ear is telling me.

I am so excited at the prospect of finally seeing my elusive ghost dog that I can hear my heart's systole in both ears. Slowly, millimeter by millimeter, I roll my head toward the noise. In some foolish notion that I can convince the dog that I'm still innocently asleep, still harmless, I keep my eyes closed.

Argos always knew when I was awake, never falling for a pretend sleep, or a desperate attempt to regain sleep, but nosing me under the arm as soon as my eyes had flickered open, as if he was waiting just patiently enough to hear the sound of my blink before bounding into action.

Maybe that was the time when I loved that dog the most: his pesky insistence that I get out of bed, start his day, go for a walk, go to work, take advantage of being together, partners, pals. Argos, bearing little resemblance to the all-serious working K-9 that he would become the moment I opened the door to the cruiser, would prance and play-bow and carry on like any dog who loved his human unconditionally.

Once we'd moved into the condo, I'd broken a lot of the rules, no longer making Argos sleep in his kennel, blaming it on the condo board for prohibiting an outdoor kennel. But the truth is that I'd stopped treating him like a weapon that needed locking up. I'd started treating him like a member of the family. A pet.

The scratching has stopped, so I'm certain the dog has bolted. I open my eyes and I'm not wrong. With nothing to lose now, I softly say, "Hey, boy. Come on, fella. I'm not going to hurt you. You're all right. Come on over." I keep my voice gentle, nonthreatening. I whistle, the same two-note whistle I use when I run and drop the food along the path. For the first time since I started this quest, I feel encouraged. The dog, it would seem, has made contact.

I crawl out into the cold. My jeans and jacket are stowed in the bottom of the bag and I dump them out, dressing quickly. I roll up the sleeping bag, think about maybe one more night, one more try, now that I'm coming so close to making headway with the dog. But the idea of another night on the hard ground reminds me that I'm closer to forty than twenty.

Back at the cabin, I light the first fire of the season in the wood-stove, hoping that the flue will draw and the chimney is clean enough that I won't start a chimney fire. As part of my incredibly cheap rent, I have all of the responsibilities of a caretaker, and some of the expenses of an owner. Like gas for the stove, and electricity, a woodstove is a utility. I've been stockpiling wood all summer, but my kindling pile is a bit small. Along with making a note to call the chimney-cleaning people, I jot down a reminder to stop by the lumberyard and pick up some broken shingles and a bucket of two-by-four trim ends. I can do that on my way to the tack shop Natalie told me about, where I'll buy my own helmet and half chaps. It's Jenny's weekend to tend the inmates, so I indulge in a long hot shower, give myself a fresh buzz cut, and settle down with yesterday's newspaper.

My cell phone barks twice and my quiet, well-planned Saturday is out the window.

There's been a dog-versus-car incident out on Route 114. The spot is closer to my cabin than to the shelter, so I don't bother to stop and swap my personal vehicle for the town's SUV. When I arrive, there's a cruiser with all lights flashing and a Subaru Forester tipped nose-down in the gully. I set my flashers and climb out of my truck with a black trash bag in my hand. The rumble of a Jerr-Dan tow truck announces its arrival to haul the unfortunate Forester out of the hole. I walk over to the visibly shaken driver, who is standing with one of Lev's officers. I don't yet see the body, but in my heart of hearts, I just know that this is the dog I've been pursuing.

"Ma'am. Officer Taylor. Where's the . . . " I hesitate to use the word that I should, *carcass*. In my previous life, I would have said "the victim."

"He ran off. But I hit him, I know I did. He was just standing in the middle of the road as I came around the curve. It was horrible.

I tried to miss, but . . . " Her voice trails off. She's confirmed my worst fear and I have to look away. It sucks. It would have been better to have had a clean kill. Now an already-compromised dog is more damaged, and this ups the ante on the game of luring him in. "Which direction?"

She points across the road. I start tracking, following nothing more than her pointing finger, because there are no prints on the pavement, no blood, which I allow is a little encouraging.

I trained myself to not be sensitive. Sensitivity in my line of work—my real line of work—is useless and boneheaded. That notwithstanding, I remember the pressure of those times when something or someone got under my skin and close to my heart. The lost child found—or not. The child caught in the cross fire. The stranger tying a necktie tourniquet around the leg of a homeless man hit by a car. I wouldn't be human if those kinds of things didn't affect me; but I wouldn't have been a good cop, a successful policeman, if I had let it show. Only some nights, after dinner was done and Gayle and I were doing the dishes, I might have mentioned the child or the stranger, and been content that my wife understood that I needed to tell these stories not out of hubris or self-importance, but so I could sort out the emotions that had gathered in my chest. Gayle might have said nothing at all, simply lain the palm of her hand against my cheek. Even Argos, who had been with me when I was searching for the missing child, or chasing the shooter who had killed the bystander in the street, or watching me taking over for the stranger with the necktie tourniquet, couldn't quite relieve my unwanted emotions as effectively as the touch of my wife's hand.

Now it's more than I can bear, the idea of coping with things of this nature. There is no sense to the cruelty that put this dog into this situation. The idea of one abused dog's life ending under the wheels of a car eats at me and I no longer have the comfort of my old dispassion. Nonetheless, in front of my fellow officer and this lady, I must put on a mask of occupational indifference. But inside, I wonder, can

I ever protect myself again with the armor of true bravery, of stoicism? My professional reserve has become jellied.

If a dog's endangerment affects me this way, how can I ever return to a profession where I encounter human suffering on a regular basis? This is why I can never have another dog, K-9 partner or otherwise. I can never put myself in this vulnerable position ever again.

I keep walking, swiping away tall grass and sweetbriar until my hands are dotted with spots of blood. I call for him. Ludicrous, I know, a nameless dog that has never but that once—this morning—come close to me is hardly likely to respond. He'll be in shock. Dragging himself off to his death.

I've been stupid, listening to Max's Buddhist idea of seducing a dog. I should have been out hunting him like I might a deer, a felon. Getting a dose of tranquilizer into him three weeks ago instead of believing that this Zen approach would somehow work. I'm a marksman. Shooting him outright rather than prolonging his suffering would have been the kinder thing. But I'm not that brave.

Cooper holds his weapon in both hands as he has been taught, as he has practiced for years. Safety off. Finger on the trigger. He has only to squeeze the round off and put an end to this. But he doesn't. He hesitates. In all the years he's been a cop, Cooper has never fired a weapon at a human target before. Has never had to. Argos has always sufficed. But this time, it's different.

There is no sign of the wounded dog. I've circled back to my truck. The Forester, the cruiser, and the tow truck are all gone. Only a streak of tire marks on the state road suggests that anything untoward has happened here. And then I see it, hidden in plain sight. There's a rocky apron around a storm drain at the foot of the sloping verge. The car strike sent the dog into the rocks and its coat color has camouflaged it. I unfold my black plastic bag and carefully retrieve the body of a speckled spaniel I'm pretty sure belongs to Cynthia Mann.

She's waiting for me as I pull around the circular drive fronting her Georgian-style home. I've called, so she knows why I'm here. For all her lofty position and relevance to the life of the village, Cynthia is still a grief-stricken pet owner, and I feel for her. I know what it's like to lose a beloved animal to violence.

I take up my burden and present the bagged body of her beloved pet to Cynthia with the same heartfelt words of condolence I all too often had to use in my former life when speaking to parents of lost children, to the grandmother of a murdered drug dealer who had raised him, to the wives of men lost in the line of duty. I tell Cynthia, "I am so sorry for your loss." The adverb is my own, and off-script: *So* sorry.

Donald Boykin brings his Land Rover to a halt behind the Suburban, rushes over to his wife, who is still cradling the black-shrouded body of their dog. "Honey, how did this happen?" He looks at me with a look of puzzled contempt. As if I'm the one who hit the dog that shouldn't have been loose in the first place. "Who did this?"

That's the question I was pretty certain he'd want an answer to. Donald Boykin doesn't strike me as a man who thinks unanswered questions are acceptable.

"I'm not at liberty to say." I actually don't know and I'm leaving any repercussions regarding that poor woman to the discretion of the local police. "Purely an accident; your dog ran out in front of the car No way to avoid it."

Boykin wraps an arm around his wife, who is obviously suppressing tears while I'm still there. "I want the name. I want it now."

"Why don't you contact Chief Parker." I'm not getting any vibe of grief from this man, only anger that something of his has been devalued. Maybe I'm being unfair, but that's what I think.

"What's your name?"

I know this tack. The "I'll put you in your place" tack beloved of the powerful, of those who seldom don't get their way.

"Harrison." I don't touch my forelock, shuffle my feet. I pull my shoulders back. "Once again, my condolences."

"Officer Harrison." Cynthia adjusts the inert bundle in her arms. "Thank you. It's been a bad year for dogs for us."

As the first heavy drops of rain begin to fall, I sit at the drop-leaf kitchen table, the radio on but not much company, the newspaper spread out in front of me, although I'm not reading it. The wood-stove pops as the heat builds up; a slightly damp log sizzles. The rain spits against the skylight with a cold sound, and I am glad that I'm inside, a proper bed waiting for me, for the moment when I think that I might be able to fall asleep.

I'm glad I'm inside, but I can't help but think of the feral dog. I'm a little ashamed by the relief I felt in discovering that the victim of the car strike wasn't the yellow dog. But maybe it would have been better. This dog, this ghost of a dog, cannot survive a night like this, when the rain beats down and the temperature drops. I get up and pace around the living area of the cabin, straightening a faded photograph on the wall depicting long-ago hunters with their old-fashioned rifles against their shoulders and their game bags full, dogs sitting patiently at their sides.

"Cooper, there's plenty of time to make that decision. You get better, then come talk to me." Lieutenant Carter hands Cooper back the resignation letter he's carefully written, printed out on smooth ecru stationery.

The gathering has been as close to a funeral as possible without disrespecting the memory of fallen humans. Cooper's brothers in arms, his fellow K-9 officers and their dogs, have shown the fallen K-9 Argos every honor due his name.

Glasses have been raised and toasts made. Moments of silence. Inclusion in news-
paper reports and Facebook postings and Web-site memorials. Hero. Brave.

It's almost impossible for Cooper to look at the other dogs, the way they keep
to their handlers' sides, the way they look at their human partners, the way it's
assumed that he's going to partner with another K-9 just as soon as his hearing is
better, when his back heals. He keeps his mouth tightly clamped, gritting his teeth.

Lieutenant Carter is correct. It is too soon to make a career-altering decision,
life-altering. But that doesn't stop Cooper. There's no way he can ever endure
this kind of pain again. It's like a sickness, a cancer growing in his psyche.

The rain is coming from the southwest, smacking against the windows on the unprotected side of the cabin. I flip on the porch light.
The rain drips in attenuated lines from the overhang like a beaded
curtain, but the porch itself is bone-dry. I empty the large wicker
basket filled with split logs. I stack the logs and then get my sleeping
bag. Out on the porch, I set the basket against the wall of the cabin,
slide the sleeping bag out of its nylon carry bag, unfurl it, and layer
it carefully inside the concavity of the basket. I go back in and bring
out a bowl of dog meat and a water bowl. Something will find this
and eat it; something might even poke a hole in the sleeping bag and
take out the lovely goose down for its own nest. But maybe, just
maybe, the dog will accept this humble offer of shelter for the night.
As I always do when dropping the meat as I run, or leaving the bowl
filled with dog food, I whistle, two notes, sharp and consistent. Then
call, "Come on, boy. Come on get your dinner." I whistle again. I
can hear nothing except the sound of the rain beating down on the
porch roof.

16

The ambulance blows past Bull as he pedals his bike to work, rocking him in the backwash. Seems like there's an ambulance roaring down the main street or Route 114 every fifteen minutes lately. Just another symptom of an expanding population in a small town. Jimmy keeps talking about it, how all these rich people living here in those big houses just means more money being spent on infrastructure. You'd think he paid the property taxes. Funny the stuff he takes issue with. Still, he's good for a meal now and then, like the other night at the tavern. Funny, too, seeing Cooper there with that little horse lady who comes into Crane's for stuff. Weird having both boys back in town after so many years. Bull knows that he should feel lucky; lots of parents never see their kids. Polly Schaeffer is always moaning about the fact her kids won't visit her. But when you think of it, the Harrisons don't really enjoy a warm and fuzzy Hallmark card kind of relationship. Any family gathering is a contest with those boys.

Jimmy was in a good mood that night, flashing a wad of cash, telling Bull to order anything he wanted off the menu. Just seeing that much cash fanned out in Jimmy's well-manicured hand put Bull off of mentioning Tommy's offer of a desk job for Jimmy. Clearly, Jimmy wasn't in need of an eighteen-dollar-an-hour handout.

Jimmy flirted aggressively with their waitress, a cute kid Bull remembers used to work in the Cumberland Farms store. Way too young for the likes of Jimmy, but that didn't stop Jimmy from hitting on her. Bull admits that it was a little uncomfortable when Jimmy wouldn't stop flirting. When his hand grabbed hers as she reached for the check holder, stuffed as it was with more than the cost of the meal and a huge tip, it made Bull feel more than a little awkward. "Come on, Jimmy, let the girl do her job." The look Jimmy gave him could have frozen water, but Bull laughed, wanting the girl to understand that Jimmy was only kidding. That Bull was in her corner, that Jimmy really meant no harm. That Jimmy would never do her harm.

Guy, the bartender, had his eye on them. Bull waved, a careless, "Everything's fine" kind of wave, and then put his hand on Jimmy's arm. A silent caution: Don't make an issue of this. You don't want trouble.

"Next time, sweetheart." Jimmy shoved his chair back, nearly toppling it against the people behind them. "I'll see you around."

The waitress had the cojones to snark back at him as she marched back to the kitchen, "Not if I see you first."

"I won't overtip her again."

"Come on, Jimmy. She's too young for you."

"Can't fault a man for wanting to get laid."

There was an ugliness to Jimmy's turn of phrase. That girl was only a couple of years away from being jailbait.

As they worked their way around the collection of tables to the exit, Guy kept his eye on them, and the look on his meaty face was clear: They would not be welcomed back. Which kind of sucks, as Bull really enjoys the Lakeside. It's the one place he was welcomed back into once he was firmly established in the program. The other bars still won't let him in, even if his drink these days is only seltzer and lemon.

But that's Jimmy for you. Tough guy, full of himself. Doesn't give a rat's ass about what other people think. Never did, even as a kid. Bull can't think of one person Jimmy ever deferred to. Not a teacher, a parent, or even a cop. He would stand there, that flinty look in his eye, just daring whoever it was to carry out their threatened punishment. Wouldn't even plea-bargain for a reduced sentence. Took the whole stretch—less a few months for good behavior, what a joke—keeping his mouth shut and his loyalties solid. Now he's reaping the benefit of that sacrifice. "It's only time," he'd said. "Just time."

Jimmy is still young enough to believe that he has unlimited time.

17

～

Waking up on this rainy Sunday, I think first of the dog, surely dead by now, my impulsive gesture of last night a pretty foolish one. I'm so convinced that this quest is over that I don't even take a peek out the window to see if he has actually taken me up on my offer of a warm bed. The one thing I've never done is allow myself foolish hope. Not now. Not ever. Not even when I regained consciousness after the blast; I knew even before I opened my eyes that Argos was dead. So there is no subterfuge in my clumping around the cabin, adding wood to the fire and getting the coffeemaker going.

The coffee is ready, the fire cheerfully crackling in the Jøtul; my bed, in military fashion, is made up tight. Unlike what I do on a workday, I'm letting myself enjoy a first cup of coffee while still in my pajama bottoms and T-shirt. Maybe I'll get really lax and skip shaving. Except for Elvin at the market, where I'll pick up a paper and possibly one of those lemon squares that sit temptingly in a clear case above the paper rack, it's unlikely that there will be anyone today who will see my unshaven face. The Patriots are on this afternoon, and I don't know if I'll listen to the game on the radio or if Max will invite me over to watch the game at his house. The truth is, I'd really rather stay put and listen to the game by myself. I'm not in the mood for company.

Thinking that I've got another chance to have a quiet day at home, I duck outside to the porch to bring in more split quarters to dry by the fire.

Because I have no expectation that the dog took advantage of my hospitality, I am completely shocked to see him curled up in the basket. Shocked and then alarmed as the dog, doesn't even raise his head. It's only the slow rise and fall of the animal's emaciated rib cage that tells me he is still alive. As if I've cornered a wanted man, I take my time assessing the situation. The first thing that I see is the festering wound on the dog's hip. I can see it, and can smell the putrefaction oozing out of it. Gunshot, I'm pretty sure. It bears the hallmarks of an old unhealed wound. What looks like dark fur is actually filth scored into the yellow. What toenails I get a glimpse of are broken off, shattered into frayed remnants. But mostly what I see are ribs, and a spine with each and every vertebrae detailed beneath the loose skin. With no muscle, the skin looks like it belongs to a larger dog. There is nothing to this animal but skin and bones and patchy, filthy fur.

The animal is so still that at first I think the dog has come up onto my porch and died. But with each slight rise and fall of his rib cage, I understand that, in his weakened condition, the comfort of the goose-down sleeping bag has lured the dog into a deep sleep. Every instinct that has helped this dog survive in the wild has been subverted by the simple warmth of a sleeping bag.

I don't move. I deliberately soften my muscles, relax my breathing, as if I'm meditating or practicing that yoga my first shrink recommended I do to try to alleviate my "tension," as he called it. The ringing in my left ear increases, as if my blood is gushing into it with every pumping heartbeat. What I hear is my uncertainty, the chiming of indecision. I simply don't know what to do with this turn of events. I need my catch pole, or another handful of meat to keep the dog's attention when he comes awake and realizes he's compromised his freedom. And then it hits me: Maybe the dog has volunteered his freedom. Maybe that's why he's so sound asleep. I've seen this in captured fugitives, this sudden exhaustion, as if capture has broken the strain of trying to stay free. They take to the narrow mattress of the holding cell and sleep the sleep of the dead.

The water bowl is empty, the dog dish licked clean, so at least I'm confident that dog is hydrated and his hunger assuaged for the moment. In a very literal sense, I'm getting cold feet. I stepped out here barefoot and this wet October Sunday morning feels more like a November day. The rain has finally let up and the sun is breaking without warmth through the sooty cloud bank malingering over Bartlett's Pond. A duck calls to a mate, twice, and I think that it's a man-made duck call, that there must be hunters out on the pond this morning. It always strikes me as funny: If I'm not fooled, why are the ducks? I turn my good ear toward the pond, and when I turn back, the dog is sitting up, looking at me.

"Hey, fella," I whisper, trying to find the right pitch. "Hey, boy. Good boy. You want some breakfast? I've got some in the cabin. I won't hurt you. I'm here to help." As long as the dog doesn't move, I natter on like a nervous suitor, hoping that the sound of my voice is soothing, not frightening; cajoling and harmless. "Good boy. I can help you. You just gotta trust me." I take a step closer. This dog is so weak, I know that if I can just grab the loose skin around his neck, I'll be able to hang on to him.

The dog pushes himself more upright, cocks his head, listening to my voice, deciding. His eyes are runny; mucus whitens the lids. Fully engorged deer ticks cling to his ears, his cheeks, little pale brown dollops of disease. I wonder if the dog is so weakened that he actually *can't* stand up. I move about a foot closer. Now the dog does get to his feet, if only three of them. The right hind leg dangles, as if he's lost the use of it. I take another cautious step, putting myself close enough that if he will simply step out of the basket, I can maybe grab the skin around his neck. First one front leg, then the other, and the working hind leg hops over the edge of the shallow sleeping bag–filled nest. Close enough. I take a step backward. The first sign of a good negotiator is to know when to step back. Let the opposition relax a little. The dog lowers his head, sniffs the air, taking in my scent. I'm hoping he reads that I mean him no harm. I'm hoping that he associates me with the food I've left him, the nest I built for him. I whisper reassurances: "You're okay. You're okay."

I kneel on the decking, bringing my eyes down to the dog's eye level. He looks left and right, as if assessing an escape route. I make a kissy noise and the dog cocks his head again, interested. He's got wrinkles above his eyes, and I think that this wreck of a dog could actually be a Labrador. Slowly, very slowly, the dog takes a step closer, his eyes on mine, begging for kindness.

Just as the dog finally, cautiously, comes close enough that I should be able to put a hand on him, a shotgun blast rends the quiet, followed by a second blast and then another. He yelps as he scrambles to jump off the porch, landing in a three-legged heap. He yelps again as a second volley brings him to his feet, and in seconds the terrified dog is gone. For such a physically compromised animal, he moves incredibly fast in his panic. Although I leap, I have no chance of grabbing him. I end up on all fours, staring at the porch floor. "Shit." Freakin' hunters have chosen this delicate moment to fire. I jump to my feet and off the porch, stupidly chasing after the animal in bare feet, a clumsy predator after a terrified dog.

Two more shotgun blasts. This poor dog is probably in the next county by now. I pull up from my foolish pursuit. So much for the quiet Sunday. So much for getting the paper. Probably so much for the football game. I have no choice, I'm going after the dog, and this time I'm going to find him. But first I have to head into the shelter to pick up the tranquilizer gun. The options for bringing this dog in have been whittled down to one. I have to shoot a dog that is clearly terrified of guns.

It felt like the sound of the gunshot was inside his head, hollowing out his brain, echoing through his skull, and blinding him to anything but movement. Even the agony in his hip was obliterated by the sheer terror caused by that sound. And it came again, over and over. Volley after volley blasting away in astounding cacophony. The dog kept moving, dragging the useless leg, his aching forelegs pulling, his good hind leg pushing him over the ground, through the grass, and into the deeper woods and beyond. Running, he makes an anguished crying, a primal sound of expected death. The memory of his original terror at having a gun fired over his head keeps him moving even after the firing ceases; he can smell the sharp, mean scent of fired gunpowder and hot metal lingering in the air, drifting over the place where he's denned, tainting it.

He is past his den; he is traveling far away from the familiar pond side. He is distancing himself from the cabin and the man there who offered him food. As long as there is that sound reverberating in the air, there is no place safe for him.

It had felt so good, that soft, warm, comforting circle of basket and bag. It hadn't felt like danger or capitulation to take advantage of it. For so long now, the running man had been a part of the dog's daily experience, it was becoming harder to stay away from him than it was to actively avoid him. The forgotten food, the quiet solace of sleeping within proximity. The memory of better things influenced his slow loss of caution. How wrong he had been.

The dog can run no farther. His lungs are burning and his whole body is trembling, all energy spent. Even the fear can't keep him on his feet, and he crumples to the ground, his sides heaving with oxygen starvation. His tongue lolls out of his wide-open mouth and he tastes the dirt.

A red-tailed hawk soars above the prone body of the dog, limning slow arabesques in the overcast sky. Behind it, bullying it, a pair of crows defend their territory. The hawk isn't particularly bothered by the crows, and it continues its slow wending. It screeks once, rises higher than the crows care about, and departs to hunt live game elsewhere. The crows then turn their attention to the dog. They land and pompously stride over to see if this inert form is already carrion, or if they must wait until more time has passed before they begin to peck away at the soft parts.

The dog lifts his lip and growls. The birds back off, consult with each other, and then elevate to a pair of low branches to patiently wait out the inevitable.

18

Max, can you set me up with the right dose of tranquilizer?"
I'm trying to keep the frantic out of my voice, but I'm sure
that Max got a hint of it. I don't panic, ever, but sometimes my voice
hits a decibel that suggests I'm in a hurry. "I don't want to kill him."

"I'm just on my way to Second Hope. Meet me there."

"What's going on?" I don't know a lot about horses, but I know
that they have a tendency toward fatal bellyaches. I immediately
think of my little quarter horse mare, Moxie, and have a moment
of concern before Max tells me what's happened.

"One of her horses stepped on a nail. Puncture wound."

At least it's not a life-threatening incident. "I'm on my way to grab
the dart gun. I'll see you there."

I'm out of the truck and into the shelter, unlocking the cabinet
that contains the dart gun. I also grab the catch pole. Jenny, there
to feed the inmates, hands me one of the donated blankets and a
couple of bath towels off the shelf. I don't know if I'll find the dog;
if I do, it's more than a safe bet that I'll be coming back with its life-
less body wrapped in the towels.

"You'll find him, Cooper. I know it." Jenny gives me a smile, but I see the doubt in her eyes. If I haven't been successful yet, what makes me think I'm going to be now?

I wish that I had a siren on the town's Suburban. I really miss those things at times like these when I'm in a hurry and every freakin' Grampa Goosie is out on the road and oblivious to my flashing red lights. I can't help it, I feel like there's a ticking time bomb about to go off and every second counts. Even heading out to Second Hope is going to cost me time in what I know is likely a losing race. That dog isn't going to survive the night. It's amazing that he even survived last night, and the weather forecast predicts that the temperature tonight is going to fall off to below freezing. But even if I get going in record time, I still have to find him. It might not be a needle in a haystack, but it's acres of conservation land. *If only I had a dog.* A tracking dog. Argos. But if I still had Argos, we'd both be working and it wouldn't be trying to find a feral dog, but feral humans. The circular nature of that logic is enough to make me laugh out loud in what Gayle used to call my "humorless laugh," the one I'd employ when I was in a bad mood, which became all too often after the last night of my career.

By the time I pull into the yard at Second Hope, Max is there in the barn aisle, tending the horse with the nail puncture. Nat's student Marla is holding the horse steady. Max is bent over the horse's left front hoof. In a neat motion and without setting the foot down, Max reaches into his vest pocket and pulls out a vial of tranquilizer.

"Thanks, Max."

"What are you going to do?" Natalie comes around the other side of the horse. As anxious as I am to get this party started, I take in her worried frown and the way she keeps one hand on the horse.

"Hopefully, find him alive. I had him this close." I demonstrate with thumb and forefinger a quarter of an inch apart. "Some asshole duck hunter fired his gun and that dog took off like his tail was on fire."

"Do you have any idea where he might be?"

I motion toward the wooded hillside between our places, dull now with the fading glory of late October. "He could be anywhere out there. He bolted in this direction, but I can't imagine that he made a straight line."

Max sets the wounded hoof into a bucket of water and Epsom salts, straightens up as if he's fighting a bad back. A lot of his work requires awkward bending. "Good job not pulling that nail out, Natalie. You do that and you end up introducing bacteria into the puncture. He'll just need a little soaking twice a day, and I'll leave antibiotics." Max gives the horse a pat on the neck.

Natalie fingers a carrot chunk into the horse's mouth. "Cooper, I've got an idea."

A precious half hour later, I'm mounted on Moxie and Natalie is leading her favorite gelding out of the barn. I'm torn between thinking that I'm wasting time when I should start looking for the dog closer to my place and grateful that there will be two of us on the hunt. I'm waiting on the patient mare for Natalie to adjust her girth, when Max closes the hatch of his Jeep and walks over. "As soon as you find that dog, you call me. I'll meet you at the office."

"I will. And, hey, thanks for making it sound like I'm not on a fool's errand."

"I didn't say that." Max gives the mare a pat on the neck. "Ride safe."

So here I am, mounted and riding beside Natalie along the trails wending through the conservation land surrounding Bartlett's Pond and along the fence lines of the last remaining working farms of Harmony Farms, including Deke Wilkins's place, an area deeply familiar to me from my youthful adventures when I would stay with

"Uncle" Deke. Although it has stopped raining, the air is chilly and I wish that I'd dressed in warmer clothes. We ride through an orchard of untended and gnarled apple trees, along the ridge with views that open up, revealing the pewter surface of distant Lake Harmony. Here and there, a curl of smoke rises in the still, damp air, marking the place where one of those big houses lurks, hidden in the landscape.

And all the time we ride through this scenic countryside, I am searching for the dog and seeing nothing but ground. We ride in silence. Even the sound of hoofbeats is muffled in the deep, wet leaf mold beneath us. We should be bushwhacking, pushing our horses through the briars and low-hanging pine boughs, because the dog is certainly not going to be handily waiting for us on the main trail. As we descend the ridge, we come to a fork in the trail. One way leads to Bartlett's Pond; the other will take us to the open field the conservation group has cleared to encourage certain kinds of birds to choose Harmony Farms as their seasonal home. It's a place popular with dog walkers, as their dogs can run free, and I often stop by just to see what's going on, who's out there with what dogs, and generally just to offer a friendly face. It's a good policy, in police work—and in animal control—to know your population by name.

Natalie pulls up her gelding. "What do you want to do?"

One way leads back to my place and to the area around the pond where the dog has apparently been living. But it also leads toward the place where the hunters were, where the firing of their guns had freaked the dog out and sent him running. The question is, How far could the dog have gotten before he had to stop? Was he scared out of his usual haunts and even now holing up in some new hideout? How easily my thoughts revert to the lexicon of my past: *holed up, hideout.*

"Let's head to the field. I doubt he could get that far, but we can eliminate it as a possibility pretty quickly."

Natalie gathers her reins and pushes her gelding forward. We follow at a safe distance. The field opens up in front of us as we emerge from the woods, four or five acres of grass and empty bluebird boxes surrounded by a perimeter of bramble and pine, juniper and scrub oak. The rain has kept the dog walkers away, which is good, I think. We ride a slow circuit around the edges, but I wonder if the dog, if he's there, will be visible against the grasses, which are nearly as yellow as he. "We should split up and ride through the field itself. If he's there, he's camouflaged."

I like how Natalie doesn't spend time revising my plan, even though she also doesn't say "Good idea." We ride to the center of the field and then set off in opposite directions, making loops so that more ground is covered visually than in a straight line. I am about halfway down my section of the field when I notice the crows.

I've only been on a horse twice now, but that doesn't stop me as I charge across that field like I'm some kind of cowboy running down a calf. It doesn't even occur to me that I might not be in control. All I know is that where there is a murder of crows, there's carrion, and I think it has to be the dog. I'm moving so fast that I barely hear Natalie bellowing out instructions, probably thinking that I'm being run away with.

The crows reluctantly move aside, but I don't know if it's the full-bore approach of the mare or my hollering that convinces them they need to get to safety. I pull back on the reins with an awkward elbows-flying grab. The mare drops into a teeth-jarring trot and I nearly bounce off of her, but by the grace of God, I don't. I stay on and manage to slow her to a walk before leaping off her back as I see the body of the dog nestled in the tall grass. If it hadn't been for the crows, even with my careful survey, I might not have seen him, he matches the yellow grass so perfectly.

Then Natalie is there, and she takes the reins from me as I squat next to the dog. His eyes are open, but do I see a flicker of life left in them, or just the dull reflection of the overcast sky? I reach out, wave my hand close to his face, and am relieved to see the blink impulse still there. "Hey, fella. We're going to get you some help. Just stick with me, okay?"

The fear is still in his eyes, but there is something else there, as well. I'm a human being, and I want to think that maybe, just maybe, there's some hope there, too. Do dogs hope? I don't know. If Argos could show enjoyment and anticipation, why can't this wreck of a dog feel hope?

Natalie is on her phone, calling for her student Marla to bring her truck to the field parking lot. I like her initiative. I hadn't considered how I was going to transport the dog if we were on horseback. I pull the bath towel out of the saddlebag attached behind my saddle. I place it on the ground and, together, Natalie and I lift the dog onto it. He's long, but he weighs nothing, and I can see the horror in Natalie's eyes.

"At least I didn't have to try to dart him. I expect that even a little tranquilizer would likely have killed him."

"Probably. You dodged that bullet."

"Ha."

"Sorry, bad choice of words." She gently folds the ends of the towel over the dog, packaging him like a burrito. Thin lines of red seep through the worn terry-cloth; his skin is sliced into ribbons from his mad dash through the vicious briars that grow in the underbrush. "You take my truck. Marla and I will take the horses home." I am absurdly grateful to her. There doesn't seem to be anything else to say as we wait for Marla, the horses happily grazing the meadow for the last green of the year.

When the truck shows up, I gather up the dog in my arms, trying not to think of how little he weighs, or how much this feels like it must when you carry a sleeping child. My other failing. I didn't fail at the idea of having kids; I failed at trying to make it happen. I tell myself that it's probably for the best. I don't think that I would make a good father. You have to have a model for that.

The dog moans with a surprisingly human sound as I bundle him into the truck. "Hang on, pal. You can do it."

As he promised, Max is waiting for me at his office. He's changed out of his farm-visit clothes and is wearing scrubs, as if he's betting that he's going to be doing surgery on this dog. I set the dog down on the examining table and step back as I would once the EMTs had arrived on the scene, respectfully letting the professional assess the situation. But I watch his face and know exactly what he's going to say. Max won't be telling me anything I don't already know.

Part Two

19

Bull Harrison is pedaling his beat-up old bike along Route 114. Despite its designation as a state highway, Route 114 is a quiet country road that attaches Harmony Farms village to the far-flung world like a frayed string on a yo-yo. No longer the main route from here to there, it serves as the quickest way to get to the main north-south highway and thence to the civilization of Starbucks, Pottery Barn, and Wal-Mart. The road follows the contours of the metes and bounds of long-gone farms, the farmers' names recalled now only in the signs that fingerpoint up narrow, unlined roads: roads called Barnaby, Fletcher, and Winkler. Others bear the names of their past purposes: Mill and Orchard, Quarry and Church. Bull pushes hard against the pedals to gain the top of the rise to the turn off to Poor Farm Road. His road.

Poor Farm Road has the distinction of having once housed the indigent of Harmony Farms, where they were put to work in the fields in exchange for a roof and meals. Farmers who had lost their farms due to bad yields or bad management or bad health might have ended up there. Others who made up its workforce might have been the

unemployables, or the men who were drinkers and had no homes
to go to.

The actual poor farm is featured prominently in the historical
society's pictorial display of old Harmony Farms, but no one still living remembers it in operation. The buildings are long gone, the fields
turned into Harmony Farms' cash crop, housing estates. Bull has
lived on Poor Farm Road all of his life. His is the eyesore that has
the real estate brokers take prospective clients onto Poor Farm Road
from the other end. That way, they can fall in love with the pristine
model homes on their three acres of meticulously kept lawns without ever seeing Bull's place, with its sagging porch and algae green
roof, the wheel-less Nova moldering out front and the row of trash
cans filled with empty Coke cans that line the driveway, Bull's savings account.

Bull is just the most recent Harrison to live in the house. He got
it from his parents, and they got it from his paternal grandparents
and so on, back to 1849, when the original Barton Harrison bought
it and a hundred acres of stony topsoil-deprived hillside. It has always been Bull's intention that his sons would follow him in home
ownership. For a man who seems not to be in control of his life, Bull
is surprisingly efficient. He had a will made out, years ago, even before he went on the wagon, and divided up the property between
his sons equitably. The fact that Cooper has no interest in the house
or, to be truthful, in him doesn't mean that he'll just give Jimmy the
whole enchilada, even if Jimmy seems intent on making the place
his own. Bull thought that he'd like the company, but Jimmy isn't
the same kid who used to be fun to be around, getting into mischief,
sure, but still willing to hang out with the old man, especially when
Bull was willing to provide a little liquid refreshment for Jimmy and
his underage buddies. Nowadays, he's moody, secretive. He yelled
at Bull just yesterday for opening up a cupboard. As if he had every
right to lock a cupboard in Bull's own house, Jimmy went out and
came back with a hasp and padlock, which he screwed to the cup-

board, then snapped the padlock shut and glared at Bull as he ostentatiously dropped the key into his shirt pocket. "You stay out of my business. Okay?"

"I don't care about your goddamn business."

"Keep it that way, and you'll be better off."

Bull thought that Jimmy's threats sounded like something out of a B movie—Cagney menacing some weak-chinned underling. He wasn't spying on Jimmy, hell no. All he had been looking for was a jacket that he'd been missing. He couldn't remember where he put it, and he was looking everywhere. And everywhere included that cupboard under the stairs. Even though he's been dry for a long time, there are times when his memory of doing things is completely shot— like sticking a winter coat in that cupboard, or arriving at the market with no idea why he's there. Or, worse, arriving at the market with no recollection of how he got there. Senior moments. That's what he calls them, even though the holes in his memory are a titch more unnerving than a momentary lapse. He can't recall going to his father's funeral. He knows that he must have, but his dad passed so close to Bull's return from Vietnam that the funeral, along with a lot of other things, just never stuck in his memory. Those first months stateside remain a long blur. It sometimes seems like he only woke up on the day that Jimmy was born.

Jimmy is out in the yard when Bull gets home. It's nice having a working car in the yard, and Jimmy's is pretty decent. If Jimmy is in a good mood, maybe he'll ask his son to drive him down to the Wal-Mart to stock up on paper goods and Coke. He's going through a lot of stuff, having a permanent houseguest now. Jimmy's been back for several weeks and hasn't even hinted at when he might find himself a place of his own. He can't enjoy being a grown man living with his dad, but the rent is cheap—that is, free. Guess you can't beat that when you are first getting back on your feet after incarceration.

Bull remembers the days after he'd been sprung from his little sojourn in the county jail. It was hard, really hard, to find work, especially with a permanently revoked driver's license and a long history of walking-off the job for no reason. Well, not exactly for no reason, but his chief reason for wandering away from a job site was to get a drink. The county jail's program of locking inmates away from the nearest source had gotten Bull on the right road for a while. But, within a few months of his release, he was at it again, helpless without the county's oversight and daily AA meetings. Instead of finding a meeting to help him stay out of trouble on the outside, Bull had exchanged the bottle for something a little more efficient. The best part was, except for his dealer, he hadn't had to efface himself to get his fix, like he did when he was in the liquor store every day, handing over crumpled dollar bills for a few nips and a six-pack. Then everyone who saw him go in or out of Ray's Bottle Shop knew that Bull Harrison was feeding his need.

In those days, Jimmy's easy access to drugs was a poorly kept secret. With his son's ready supply of relatively cheap stock, Bull realized that he could hold his head up as he walked past Ray's and pretend he was in recovery. Of course, that had ended when Jimmy's first business associate was busted. Jimmy himself disappeared for a while after that, and Bull was back at Ray's, keeping his eyes down as he pocketed the nips.

All water under the bridge now. Bull leans his bike against the porch, pulls a pack of Camels out of his shirt pocket, and joins Jimmy, who's standing beside his car. He offers his eldest a smoke, but Jimmy waves him off.

"I quit. You know that." He's got that impatient, the-old-man's-acting-senile-again tone to his voice.

"Good, just checking." In fact, he has forgotten that Jimmy arrived fresh from the state pen a reformed smoker. You can say this about Jimmy: He keeps himself pretty clean. No tobacco smoking. Back in the day, once he'd started selling drugs, Jimmy had stopped using, preferring to pocket the dough rather than enjoy the high.

No free samples, he says. Bull is no dope; he knows what Jimmy's keeping in that locked closet. Sometimes it makes him want some, just a taste, just a little reminder of what painlessness feels like. It's only knowing that it's so close at hand that reminds him of the need; he wouldn't think of it otherwise. He also knows that his son would kill him if he stole anything.

Bull doesn't want to get back on that merry-go-round. He likes his job at the lumberyard. He likes that now some people actually say hi to him when he pedals by. "Hi, Bull. How's it going, Bull?" Sometimes he even feels like a regular guy, someone who is an upstanding citizen of this town. No longer the town clown.

Jimmy is cleaning out his car, stuffing a plastic grocery bag with receipts, used tissues, paper coffee cups, and soda cans. He looks maybe too busy to ask for a lift to Wal-Mart. Maybe he should give Cooper a call, see if he's available sometime for a paper-towel run. Bull drags on his cigarette and blows the idea out of his mind with the exhale of smoke. Nah. Bad idea. Cooper's made it plenty clear that he's not looking to renew any family ties.

Bull drops the cigarette on the ground. "You wanna head over to Wally World?" He presses the heel of his boot onto the smoldering butt. "I'll buy you a Big Mac on the way."

Jimmy neatly ties the grocery bag's handles together. Grins at his old man. "You still think that's appealing? Like when we were kids?"

"It's cheap, tastes good."

"Funny, but the first few years I was in, all I wanted was a Big Mac. Don't ask me why, I never ate that many of them. Then once, for some reason, you brought me one. Remember? I couldn't eat it. It was cold and the grease was tasteless. After that, I don't know. Guess I lost the taste. Guess I grew out of them."

Bull doesn't like it when Jimmy reminds him of where he's been the past dozen years. That an entire decade of his life has passed mostly out of Bull's sight. "So does this mean you won't take me?"

"No. I can't. Sorry." Jimmy slam dunks his makeshift trash bag into the barrel.

The four of them pile out of the Nova, the boys running ahead, heedless of the cars in the drive-up line. Usually, they get their McDonald's to go, but tonight they're there to eat in, as if this Friday night is special. Happy Meals for two. Mona and Bull get Big Macs and share a box of fries. Milk shakes so thick, they give Bull brain freeze.

Who knows what starts the fight. They have reached a point in their marriage when anything and everything provides a trigger point for an argument. Maybe Bull got greedy with the fries; maybe Mona got snarky about something. Then Jimmy did something to Cooper. Probably took his Happy Meal prize. So Mona's mad, and Cooper's screaming at Jimmy to give it back. Jimmy's running around the restaurant, rolling the purloined plastic toy over the backs of seats and benches, even those occupied. Mona's yelling at him to stop.

Bull gets up, walks out. He's left the keys to the Nova on the table and has ten bucks left in his pocket from what he spent on dinner. It's not much, but enough. He's not thinking at all about how he's going to get back to Harmony Farms from here; he's only interested in the VFW-post bar he knows is on the next block.

20

I'm in the tiny lab-cum-drug closet of Max's office. I left the exam room and the dog to Max's ministrations, using the privacy to call Natalie and let her know that I am at Max's and that when I'm done here, I'll return her truck and pick up mine. Instead, she offered to meet me here, so I'm looking through the blind slats at the three parking spaces in front of Max's storefront practice. The cop in me is thinking that he really shouldn't have his drugs in a room so close to a plate-glass window when he comes into the room to deliver his pronouncement.

"Cooper, I think that a merciful euthanasia is the right thing to do."

"Euthanasia?" I don't know why I am shocked by Max's all-too-reasonable suggestion.

According to Max, the dog is near death; the infection has traveled deep and the wounds on his legs and neck are from another dog, or, worse, a coyote, which suggests rabies. Stupidly, I ask if he can do a test to find out, and Max tells me that the only test for rabies is postmortem.

Even if I had the budget to take care of him, it wouldn't be humane to put him through the trauma of surgery and what would likely be an unsuccessful recovery—in effect, prolonging the inevitable. Why would I do that? It makes no sense. So why am I so upset at this verdict? Nothing Max has said comes as a surprise. All I have to do is say 'Okay.' Not exactly the executioner, but certainly the judge and jury. But I can't say the word. I've worked too goddamn hard to bring this dog in. How many nights of sleeping out? How many attempts to lure him in? How much time have I spent thinking about this miserable beast?

It reminds me of something. Like the memory of a dream. The quest had a purpose, and maybe I've inflated its importance. But here he is at last, my quarry. A wounded and traumatized dog. I think what it reminds me of is that moment when a job is done, when it's time to stand down.

"Are you sure?" I feel a little foolish saying this. Of course Max is certain. He's too fine a vet to suggest euthanasia out of laziness. If he thought there was hope, he'd be in the OR right now. I sigh, let the decision settle in. It just seems wrong to reward this dog's fight to survive with death.

"Right. Look, I'll go in with you. He shouldn't be alone." I want this over with by the time Natalie arrives. I don't want her looking at me with the disapproving eyes of a professional rescuer.

Max reaches for the barbiturates and I leave him to it, going into the exam room, where the dog is as still as if he's already gone.

But he's not, and he raises his head as I come in. Looks me in the eye. Looks at me with Argos's eyes.

No two dogs are exactly alike, not even dogs of the same breed. Dark brown eyes reflecting from a white face aren't the same as these pained and equally dark brown eyes buried in the yellow mask of this dog. Argos's eyes were never troubled, never anything but alert and game. This yellow dog's eyes tell me that he is deeply afraid.

I hear Max come in, the squeak of his trainers against the worn linoleum of the exam room floor.

"Max, don't. Let's just try. Okay? Give him a couple of days."

"Cooper, you really want to put this stray dog through that?" He's holding two hypodermic syringes, both capped with plastic guards.

"I do." As I say it, Natalie comes into the exam room.

Max looks at me, then at Natalie. He shakes his head and sets the lethal injections down on the counter. "Your call."

"Yeah, I know. Probably the wrong one, but I think we should give him one more chance. He's hung on this long."

"I've never known you to be sentimental."

"It's not sentiment. At least I don't think it is." Natalie moves into the room to stand beside me. She reaches over and gently runs her hand over the dog's skull. The very tip of his tail flutters into the semblance of a wag. "It's common decency."

Max shrugs with an elegant capitulation that says he thinks I'm nuts but that he'll humor me. He shoos us out of the room, and for a brief, distrustful second I wonder if he'll do it anyway and claim the dog died on the table. The two hypodermics are on the counter, and Max sees me glance at them. "Put these in the med room, will you?" I'm embarrassed at my obvious skepticism. Max deserves better than that from me.

There is something, something in the way this dog has led me on a merry chase, something in the singular fact of his having survived against the odds clearly stacked against him. He's tougher than he looks. And right now he's looking at me with Argos's eyes, saying, *Give me a chance.*

It's only one o'clock, although it feels like I've put in a whole day. I'm exhausted and, frankly, sore from my morning on horseback. I don't want to sit in the waiting room, watching a clock hand move minute by painful minute, but I don't want to go home, either.

Then I feel Natalie's hand on my back. "Let's go. Max will call when he's done." Natalie has stepped up in a quintessentially female way to assess and act. It is so comforting, like having a mother say, "Time for bed," or "Eat your peas." We leave the office and I suggest that she doesn't have to spend who knows how long waiting for me.

"Look, I'm starving. Why don't we get lunch first? Besides, the Patriots versus Jets game is on at the tavern."

When we get to the tavern, we're able to squeeze in by the bar. We order sandwiches and root beer. I check to make sure that my cell phone is not only on with the loudest ring but also on vibrate; then I place it on the bar in front of me so that I have a visual. In a noisy football crowd, the chances of my hearing my phone decrease drastically. Natalie doesn't waste her breath mouthing platitudes like "He'll be fine," or "It's in God's hands." It's almost like having a buddy as she turns her attention to the screen with the closed captioning and devours her fries one after the other.

Second quarter, eighteen seconds left on the clock. I'm studying the time display on my phone, trying to calculate how long Max has been working on the dog. It seems to me that the longer he takes, the worse the news. He said that he wouldn't attempt a surgical fix to the hip wound until the dog was stabilized. I understood the words, if not the specificity of them. Fluids, antibiotics?

Natalie nudges me out of my thoughts. "I have to go. I've got to soak that hoof again." She's had the good grace to wait until halftime. Bless her heart. After a small scuffle, I pay the tab; then she drives back to Second Hope Farm and I go back to Max's, fully expecting the worse.

21

I t'd be a good idea if you made yourself scarce." Jimmy slathers a gob of mayonnaise on the sandwich he's making. "Just for an hour or two." He picks three slices of ham off the pound that Bull has brought home and lays them on the bread, adds cheese, a swath of mustard. "You got someplace you can go?"

Where's he going to go? Library's closed on Mondays. In the bad old days, this needing a place to hang out wouldn't have been a problem, and Bull smiles reflexively at the thought of a couple hours spent like any other joker, belly up to a bar, soaking up the suds, laughing with perfect strangers. He sighs, waits for his son to recall that his father has only a bicycle for transportation. Maybe he should take in a movie. That'd be fine. He hasn't been to a movie in years, but that would mean getting Jimmy to take him out of town to the mall. "It's raining, Jimmy. I'll just stay in my bedroom. You'll never know I'm here."

"No. I need a little privacy. Trust me, Bull. You don't want to be anywhere near this house a couple of times a week. That's all I'm saying. Make yourself scarce."

"Then make your arrangements for when I'm at work." Bull pulls a slice of the ham off the pound, folds it into his mouth.

"I serve at the pleasure of my clients."

"Yeah. Right. Clients."

"Shut up, old man." Jimmy isn't smiling, isn't kidding when he says this, and this is what's beginning to get on Bull's nerves—his son's disrespect. Worse than disrespect, downright meanness. There is something dead in Jimmy's eyes, like whatever he experienced in the state pen killed the last bit of the boy he'd once been, the boy quick to laugh. Quicker, sure, to bully, that laughter generally at the expense of someone weaker, vulnerable.

"Jimmy, you in trouble?"

Jimmy chews his sandwich, says nothing. Then he meets Bull's eyes. "What if I was? What could you do about it?" He shoves the rest of his sandwich into his mouth. "Just be out of here for an hour or two."

"It's raining, Jimmy. I don't want to get wet."

Jimmy doesn't respond, he's making himself another sandwich. Annoyed, Bull pretends he's just had a great idea: "I know. I'll call Cooper, see if he can pick me up. He hasn't been by since you got here."

"Not on your life. I don't want you to bring him here under any circumstances. Especially when I got company coming. Got it?" He seems to swell up as he takes a hostile step toward Bull. His chest expands and the belly that he grew in prison widens, draping over his belt. Cherries of color dot his pallid cheeks. The pale water gray of his eyes darkens perceptibly.

"Calm down. I was just trying to figure something out."

Jimmy shrinks back to size, steps away. "All right. All right, I'll drop you off someplace."

"And pick me up."

"Get your jacket." Jimmy walks away from the ham and cheese

on the counter, the open jars of mayonnaise and mustard, the loaf of bread.

They don't speak as Jimmy drives to the village. Bull can see the tension in his son's softened jaw, how the muscle in his cheek keeps working with his very private thoughts. He's hatless and there's more skin at his temples than he had before he went away. Bull is surprised to find himself the father of a middle-aged man. One not aging particularly well. Even though he's been out for weeks, Jimmy hasn't lost the tallowy look of a man who has spent years with less than an hour of sunshine a day. Sometimes that gray pallor never really goes away, as if the lighting of the prison has entered your pores.

Why does Jimmy treat him like a pain in the ass even as he has come back to the Poor Farm Road house of his own volition, holing up with his old man while trying to get his life back on track. He should be grateful for a free roof over his head, not ordering his father around like a servant, or, worse, like Bull's an annoying child. This business of being put out of his own house rankles; he can't deny it.

Beyond the irritation, there lies a subtext of worry. Jimmy is up to no good, not even giving it six months of good behavior before falling into recidivism. Bull knows that word all too well. *Recidivism.* A word so often applied to himself during the bad old days. A week, a month, a half year in the county jail and they'd pour good sense down his throat, warning him off becoming a recidivist. Like Jimmy, Bull couldn't make it stick the first few times; he reverted to type within hours of release. But that was just being a drunk, a drug addict. What Jimmy's into is certainly far worse. The temper. The secretiveness. The lock on his bedroom door.

Jimmy drops Bull off at the intersection of Route 114 and Main Street. It's pouring, and Bull pulls up the collar of his ancient army-surplus jacket, puts a soggy Camel between his lips. "Don't forget to come back and get me."

Jimmy pulls away even before Bull slams the Honda's door, and Bull wonders if he's been abandoned.

In Harmony Farms, all the stores close at six o'clock. The only place open on Main Street is Cumberland Farms, so Bull goes in, buys a pack of smokes, lingers at the magazine rack. Bull knows that the kid behind the counter has his froggy eyes on him. He buys a coffee, then spends a long time leaning against the counter, sipping it until it cools to tepid, tasteless. He throws it out. Bull uses the bathroom, then buys another coffee. The kid openly stares now, as if the tractor beam of his gaze will move Bull out of the store before he has to ask him to leave. The NO LOITERING sign is outside, not inside. Ha. Take that, Frog Eyes.

No one who comes into the Cumberland Farms greets him. He doesn't know anyone. It's like he's been dropped into a foreign land, a place that is unfriendly to strangers. He was born and raised here, so how can it be that no one is familiar? He's not so old that all his peers are dead. At least not the peers with whom he grew up. He has lots of dead peers, dead in a foreign land, a land unfriendly to the strangers sent to win their war. Ducky and Marvin, Whip and Del. Names now. Just names.

Knee-deep in a rice paddy, wearing blackface like some old-fashioned minstrels. Every flicker of movement brings a jolt to the gut, a griping like cramps, pure fear. An ugly cow stands in the middle of the paddy; the dull moonlight glints off her curved horns. A woman wearing the ubiquitous conical hat stands on the edge, staring at them; her hands are down, flattened palms against her skinny legs. She calls out, but none of the men—boys—speaks a word of the language. To them, it's gobbledygook. Gook. They don't know if she's warning them that the Vietcong are ahead, or if she's alerting the VC to their presence. Maybe she's just yelling at them to get out of her paddy. No one has any idea, and that makes her dangerous. Bull doesn't know who gives the order, or even if an order has been given—a critical distinction.

With one shot, the woman crumples to the ground, her hat rolling down the slope to the rice paddy, a loose wheel. When he walks past the body, Bull can see that by Vietnamese standards, she is an old woman. Maybe fifty. Her vacant eyes look right at him.

The platoon moves on, wading deeper into the paddy. The ugly cow lowers its head and makes a moaning, lowing sound. The conical hat floats in front of Bull. He picks it up, drains the water out of it. Breaking away from the line, he trudges through the underwater growth to place the hat over the woman's face.

Bull walks out of the Cumberland Farms, trying to walk away from the thoughts that burn at him. Nearly fifty freakin' years, and yet the suddenness with which the war memories rise up still has the power to bring on the shakes. If he can keep his memories at bay, he can keep the thirst, the cravings, at bay. It's as simple as that. Stop thinking.

The rain has leveled off to a cold drizzle that glitters in the streetlights. A car approaches, and Bull hopes that it's Jimmy, but it keeps moving, its high-tech sodium headlights like the eyes of some prowling animal, washing the street with sharp white light. Bull begins walking; he'll stick his thumb out and catch a ride with someone. Anyone.

22

I see him, caught in the headlights of the car in front of me. I'm on my way back to the cabin after work, and when I see the figure on the side of the road, I can't immediately tell if it's man or beast. In the dusk Bull's bulk is bear-shaped.

Lying on his good side, recumbent upon the flipped-down rear seat, in my custody and my care, is the yellow dog. Max confirmed what I suspected, that this is a Labrador retriever, although he's such a bag of bones, it's hard to imagine that he could ever weigh eighty pounds. Because Max doesn't have a twenty-four-hour presence in his office, the dog had to go home with me. So I've shoved painkillers and antibiotics down his throat and applied the veterinary version of Neosporin into his wounds. The ticks are gone, but Max didn't want to bathe him until he's recovered enough to take the soaking. So he stinks. And he's afraid. Really afraid. He shakes like he's got the d.t.'s when I approach him, no matter how softly I try, how Mother Teresa I try to make myself. I've had him in an empty kennel all day, but I can't leave him at the shelter, where he belongs, because he needs meds every six hours. I feel like a new parent, fussing over timing and warmth and food, coddling an infant. Except that every time I stood by the cage, even just to make sure he was still breathing, he struggled to withdraw deeper into it, like I was going to haul him out and beat him. Whoever had this dog has some dues to pay. In the drama of trying to save him, neither Max nor I thought about wanding him, see if he's chipped. He's got a recheck in a few days; I'll get it done then.

I realize that it's Bull standing by the side of the road in the drizzle, and I immediately think that he's been out drinking. He's going to get hit by a car. When he's drunk, he has no sense of self-preservation. I don't want to, but I pull over. "Get in the truck."

"Good to see you, too, son."

He climbs in, and I feel myself recoiling, anticipating the scent of alcohol fumes coming from him, but there are none, just the benign odor of coffee. I don't ask him why he's out in the rain on a Monday night. I don't really care. Bull is a world unto himself and there is very little about it I'm interested in. Actually, there's nothing about Bull's life that interests me. The solid wall of indifference is how I am maintaining this separation of my childhood self from my adult one. I have come back to Harmony Farms a different man from the one who left twenty years before. I have had the satisfaction of people asking me where I'm from, never connecting this Harrison with that one, who is, at this moment, looking over his shoulder at the recumbent dog. I always say I'm from Boston. I pull away from the side of the road a little fast. Gravel spits out from beneath the rear tires.

"Layin' rubber?" Bull chuckles, like I'm trying to entertain him.

"I assume I'm taking you home."

Bull doesn't answer, letting me take that as a yes. Then, ursine, he shakes his head. "No. I don't think so."

"You have someplace to be?"

"Not really. Where you going?"

"I'm taking you home. You need groceries or something?"

"I'm good. Just drop me at the Lakeside."

"I'm not going to do that."

"You think I drink anymore?" He pulls this magnificently offended face. "I'm strictly on fizzy water and lime these days. My television doesn't work. I want to watch the game."

"There's no game tonight."

"Okay, you caught me. *Dancing with the Stars.* I like watching the
ladies in those naked-looking costumes."

This is almost plausible. But, however diminished I am, I am still,
at heart, a cop. "Why don't you want to go home? What's Jimmy
up to?"

Bull doesn't answer, he's looking again at the dog on the rear seat.
"What's with this dog? Is he yours?"

"No. He's been injured and I'm taking care of him until I can
either find the owner or get him fostered out."

"Poor guy. He looks pretty bad off. Lab?"

"Yeah." I think about it for a second. "He look like one of the
Haynes's dogs to you?"

"Possible, though I think they keep hounds."

He's done it, distracted me from my question, so I repeat it.
"Where's Jimmy?"

"Home."

"And you don't want to be there with him?"

"Coop, I told you, I want to watch TV."

I wonder if the dog behind me is listening to this conversation. I
wonder if he understands the subtle tone of a born liar. Argos was
like a polygraph machine when it came to liars. It was like he could
smell dishonesty coming out of their pores. This dog just sighs, a
sound even I can hear in the silence of the cab. It's a deep, cleans-
ing sigh, and I worry for a moment that it is the sigh of death. That
he has, after all our efforts, breathed his last. At the next stop sign,
I turn around in my seat and flip on the overhead light. The dog's

head is still on the seat, but his much brighter eye is open, and he is looking at Bull.

I flip off the light and take my turn through the last village intersection. Three miles up the road and I'll take the right onto Poor Farm Road.

"Coop, Jimmy just needs a little time alone. Without his old man hanging around. You get what I mean." Bull gives me the old wink, wink, nudge, nudge, implying that my pasty-faced, overweight ex-con older brother is entertaining a woman.

I'm taking Bull home out of decency, but mostly I'm going to see if Jimmy is there, alone. I don't know why it should matter, why it's got my hackles up that he's sent Bull out in the rain and told him to keep away. There can only be one reason, and I don't think for a minute it's because he's got a girl in the house. I have no authority, no warrant. No reason to get involved. But I do.

"What's Jimmy up to, Bull? And don't tell me he isn't up to anything."

"The God's honest truth is that I don't know."

"He's making sure that you don't."

"Yes. It's better that way."

"Is he dealing? I mean, do you think that he might be? Take an educated guess."

"Cooper, if I did, and I don't, why would I tell you that? I'm *his* father, too. I wouldn't turn on you, and I won't turn on him."

"I'm not asking you to; I'm just putting it out there. Bull, you don't want to have the kind of trouble that comes with Jimmy."

"I only know that you're both my sons and I'm no snitch. Especially with no what you lawmen like to call *evidence*." He waits a beat, maybe two. "And you'd be some kind of asshole to turn your own brother in, specially without any proof. You go be a cop in Boston; don't try to be a cop here.

"In case you haven't noticed, I'm not a cop anymore." I mean this as a way to make him understand that I don't have any real intention—at the moment—of doing anything about Jimmy, but even to my sorry ears it sounds petulant.

The dog behind me sighs again. Bull turns around and speaks to him with a soft garble of baby talk. I can hear the thumping of his tail on the backseat, a little heartbeat of a sound in my good right ear.

"Why don't you drop me at the end of the road? Better for both of us."

Hey, what would I prove if Jimmy is at the house, that maybe he has company? That maybe Bull isn't, well, bulling me and Jimmy is just entertaining a woman? Can I just let this go for now? It's not raining anymore, and Bull can use the exercise. I pull over at the bottom of Poor Farm Road. A Lexus goes around us, high beams undimmed. Bull gets out, but before he closes the door, he reaches in to pet the dog, who is still lying on his side, as if the motion of the truck is soothing him. He doesn't growl, doesn't make any sound at all as my father gives him a gentle pat. "Take care of this guy. He looks like he could be a nice dog."

"I will." I am more puzzled than jealous; the dog still cringes in fear at the sight and touch of me, but for this wreck of a man who has blown every chance he ever had at a normal life, he thumps his tail.

23

Bull Harrison stands by the side of the road, his younger son's taillights moving away from him at a clip a little too fast for the road, as if he can't get far enough away from his father fast enough. Well, Cooper's always been like that, always had a bug up his ass. What are you going to do? Bull accepts the fact that he might have been a better father, but, hell, the boy isn't a kid anymore; he's a grown man. Get over it! Bull trudges along Poor Farm Road, nursing his indignation.

A little too close for comfort, a car zips by Bull, and a fine spray of runoff hits him at knee level. Bull waves a fist, but he moves to the other side of the dark country road to face oncoming cars. Now his pants are wet, and after that last cup of coffee, he needs to pee. Home is a quarter of a mile away, and he has no idea if Jimmy will welcome him back or not. Sometimes it just seems like life sucks. The ornate sign announcing Poor Farm Estates—does no one but Bull see the irony in that?—is one of those artfully carved hand-painted gated-community signs gracefully illuminated by uplights, situated on its own little island of grass, with twin entrances bifurcated to either side of it. Six-row cobblestone aprons demarcate the entrances to the development from the road. The fine drizzle sparkles in the soft beams like fairy dust. Bull steps beside the sign, unzips, and waters the well-trimmed burning bush shrubs that embrace the entrance. Now he can make it the rest of the way home.

The house is dark, no welcoming porch light turned on for his benefit, which may be due more to the fact that the light hasn't worked in donkey's years than any malintent on Jimmy's part. It's actually been kind of nice, coming home from work most evenings to a light in the parlor, the clutter of another person's belongings. Jimmy may not be easy, but it's kind of nice to have someone to watch TV with of an evening.

The kitchen is at the back of the house, and if Jimmy is home, he's probably in there. Bull checks for any other cars in the driveway, but there's only Jimmy's Honda and his own up-on-blocks '68 Nova. Now, there was a car. Bull had many a night in that automobile he'd love to relive. Runs out to the lake with Mona, who was at her hottest back in those days, a six-pack and a handle of Jack in the trunk. Wearing that aged leather jacket he eventually lost somewhere in the last quarter century. Bull runs his hand along the old car as he works his way in the dark around to the back door of the house. Sure enough, there's a light in the kitchen. Jimmy is framed by the curtainless window like he's a piece of art. A piece of work, more like. He's on his phone and gesturing, as if his caller can see him, punching the air with his forefinger. Bull recognizes the gesture as one of his own. The emphatic forefinger. You. Will. Do. What. I. Say. Yeah, half the time his kids would flip him the bird and do what they damn well pleased. Looking at the expression on Jimmy's face, though, Bull thinks that no one is going to disrespect this guy. It is a look of smoldering anger. Dangerous anger. Bull turns around and climbs into the front seat of the Nova. The bench seat is pushed way back, so he stretches his long legs into the well on the passenger side. He folds his arms across his chest against the chill night air. He'll give Jimmy a few minutes, then go in. It's his house, damn it. He won't be kept out of it. Bull feels the pull of gravity against his eyelids. He closes his eyes, just to rest them; another minute and he'll go in. He nods off.

Bull has no idea where he is when he is startled awake by the blast of high beams sweeping through the Nova's windows. Oh, right. Stuck out here in the car while Jimmy's on the phone. The high beams belong to a car Bull doesn't recognize, and instinct makes him hunker down lower in the front seat. He doesn't know how long he's been asleep—a few minutes or an hour—but it's no longer raining and the stars have finally broken through the three days of heavy clouds.

The car is a late-model bullet-shaped thing. Black, wire rims. Nice. The man who gets out of it pauses to get his bearings. Without a porch light, the yard is dark, and Bull sees doubt in the way the guy keeps one hand on the handle of his fancy car. Maybe not doubt. Wariness. He'll bolt if he thinks he's in the wrong place or that maybe something isn't kosher. But the front door opens, a box of light with Jimmy in the middle. The man trots into the house and the door closes with a thump.

Now he'll have to stay put until this visitor leaves. Bull is savvy enough to know that whatever Jimmy planned, did not happen at the appointed hour and that things are pretty tense. Jimmy wants to keep him in the dark about his "client" and Cooper wants him to blab about Jimmy's dealings. Jekyll and Hyde. No, these boys aren't two halves of any whole. More like those biblical brothers, Cain and Abel. Bull shivers as the cold front that has pushed away the clouds settles in. No, that doesn't sound right, either. Cooper and Jimmy are just a pair of dissimilar men. Same upbringing, different results. Well, he's no fool, and he's not about to let Jimmy think that he saw this car or that man, and he's not going to breathe a word to Cooper about his brother's nighttime visitor. Bull's just glad he had the sense to hole up in the Nova. And then he thinks, What an awful thing it is to be afraid of your own son.

Bull doesn't have time to nod off again before the visitor emerges from the house. Jimmy doesn't linger in the open door, shutting it even before the stranger has reached his fancy car. Even after the car leaves the yard, Bull stays in the Nova for a little while, giving Jimmy a grace period, giving himself enough time that there will be no question but that he hasn't witnessed any comings or goings. The trouble with deception is that you have to think of every contingency. What if Jimmy, business conducted, suddenly remembers he has to go fetch his father and then doesn't find him? It's been five, six minutes. Bull cracks open the rusted car door, pulls himself out. His pants are dry now.

"Shit, Bull. I'm sorry. Things went long and I forgot." Jimmy seems genuinely contrite. "I'd of remembered in a couple of minutes. You should have stayed put."

"S'okay. I hitched." Bull heads to the bathroom, noticing as he goes, that the padlocked understairs closet is open.

"Who picked you up?"

"No one you know." This is, kind of, the truth.

24

"Come on, boy, take it." It's been three weeks and the dog and I are still in the hostage/guard mind-set. Apparently, I'm the guard and he feels like he's a prisoner. I'm hopeful that we'll achieve some sort of Stockholm syndrome soon and that he'll begin to look to me for friendship and validation. I have yet to get his tail to wag even in the slightest. At least he's no longer pressing himself against the bars of his kennel to get as far away from me as he can. And at night, in the cabin, I've actually been able to walk past him in his basket to the bathroom without his scrambling behind the couch. Small steps. Natalie has been invaluable to me as I try to socialize this animal. "Rescues have such baggage," she says. I say, "This isn't a rescue"—and I finger air quotes around the word—"I may have rescued him from the wild, but I'm not a rescue operation." She always gives me this look, like she's hearing what I'm saying but not giving it much credence. I don't think she knows exactly how serious I am about keeping this enforced companionship with the dog all business.

Frankly, he should be kept in the shelter, but until the course of antibiotics is done, he's got to have me near. With all those ticks that had been clinging to him, in addition to the infection in his hip, he's also got Lyme disease and—drum roll, please—ehrlichiosis. Max says it's just dumb luck that he hasn't got the other tick-borne illnesses available to mammals, or heartworm. So a normal course of antibiotics for the infection was extended to sixty days. The fun part is, of course, to pill a dog who is terrified of me.

In order to not traumatize the dog further by shoving the capsule down his throat while I have him in a headlock, I've been opening up the cap of doxycycline and mixing it in with a potage of rice and hamburger. Soft foods, Max says. Easy on the tummy against the ravages of the doxy. Still he looks at me like he believes I'm poisoning him. I've never seen a dog eat with such an expression of fatalism. It's as if he's saying, *I know you're trying to kill me, but I'll eat it on the off chance you're not.* He makes me miss Argos in the strangest ways. Argos, who would take his dinner bowl in his teeth and present it to me if he thought he should have seconds. Argos, who would lick the bowl until there was no point in putting it in the dishwasher. We worked hard and we deserved good meals. Argos frequently inspired me to break the cardinal rules instilled in us in training. I fed him the ends of my sandwiches, the crusts from my morning toast. I even cooked us bacon and eggs. Hearty breakfasts to keep us strong.

I crouch down, place the plastic bowl next to the basket containing the yellow dog. "Hey, fella, you should eat this. I made it for you with special rice and special hamburger. The expensive stuff from the Country Market. Elvin is a highway robber when it comes to meat, but it's worth every penny. Eat up. Come on." I am cajoling and wonder if I sound like a daddy playing "One for the airplane, one for the baby." It's not hot, although I've poured the grease from the frying pan over it to give it even more flavor and more needed calories.

The dog gets to his feet, climbs over the edge of the basket like a deposed king mounting the guillotine. The good news is that he's bearing weight on the bad leg. Last week, Max finally chanced anesthesia and removed the pellets, confirming my belief that some asshole duck hunter shot his own dog—whether intentionally or accidentally is irrelevant to me—and then drove off without him. I asked Max to wand the dog, but the microchip reader came up blank, which means either the dog isn't chipped or that it's the type of chip that requires a different reader. Max will try to get one on loan.

I sit down on the floor beside him and he turns to look back at his safe place. "If you don't eat it, I will." He knows that threat is toothless. He sits. I push the bowl closer. He definitely looks better than he did, now that he's all cleaned up and his eyes are much brighter. He's gained some weight, but it's an uphill battle. Maybe he's anorexic. Can dogs be anorexic? I give up and get off the floor to see about my own breakfast. I push the bowl under his front legs. As soon as I turn my back, he goes at the food, inhaling it in three gulps. Now I get it. He won't take it if I'm looking, as if he expects me to snatch it away from him. I can see my shrink nodding with a grim expression and declaring, "Trust issues." Guess this dog and I are well matched. We both have issues.

My phone rings just as I set down my own plate of bacon and eggs. It's not the barking ringtone, so I know that it's not work-related. It takes me a minute to locate the phone, which has fallen between the nightstand and the bed. The number displayed isn't one I recognize and I'm tempted to let it go to voice mail, but it's a local number, so I don't. In the end, I'm glad that I didn't, as the caller is Polly Schaeffer. In some moment of weakness that I don't remember, I must have given her my personal number. Or maybe she spotted it on the board at the shelter during her little B and E attempt. Whichever the case, she's bawling like a baby and can hardly get the words out.

"Polly, settle down. Tell me what's the matter."

"They took them. They took them all."

"Who took what?" I'm asking only to get her to take a deep breath. I know goddamn well what she's talking about and I'm furious. I told Roger Schaeffer I'd deal with it. I have dealt with it. Jenny found nice permanent homes for a couple of the cats and Polly let them go more or less willingly. And she found four foster homes for up to six of Polly's collection. These things take time, as I told Roger, and to strip the old lady of all of her pets is simply cruel. If I thought for one blessed moment that any of Polly's cats was in any way suffering from an excess of companions, I would have had no compunction against taking them all. But, despite the rank odor of too many cats in too small a house, they are all clean, fat, neutered, and, according to Max, up-to-date on their vaccines. There's just no law against it as long as everyone is healthy.

"Roger took my babies. He said that the Health Department was going to arrest me."

"Jesus, Polly." I really don't know if he can do that, or even if the Health Department has the authority to arrest anybody. I think of them more as a fine-imposing department. I think Roger has played a mean trick on his mother. "Give me an hour; I'll stop by."

I thumb off the phone and go back to my breakfast, which is gone. The dog is back in his basket and the slow stroke of his pink tongue along his lips incriminates him. Not only is my cooked breakfast licked off my plate but the half pound of bacon left on the counter and the two raw eggs sitting in their cardboard cradle are gone, too. Shells and all. The only thing untouched on the table is my mug of coffee.

"What's the matter? You don't like my coffee?"

The dog just looks at me with those sad, innocent brown eyes.

"You're a thief, aren't you? Won't take what's offered. You prefer to steal it? Okay, if that's how it's going to be. So be it." At least I know now how to get food into him. Just turn my back or leave it on the table. Bingo. It's going to be hard to adopt out a dog who steals off a table, so that habit has got to be broken pretty quickly. But, I know, first I have to get him to relax around people. Nobody wants a cowardly dog, a dog that shrinks from every human touch, casts craven, pleading eyes at the friendliest of folks..

What am I thinking? I need Jenny to find this boy a foster home ASAP. As I have said to Jenny and Natalie and anyone else who thinks I should be rehabbing this mutt, I have neither the time nor the inclination to retrain a dog I have no intention of keeping.

I guess the silver lining to Polly's lament is now that Roger has removed all of his mother's cats, Jenny can focus on finding this boy a home. Not me. We've got forty-five more days of meds and then off he goes. I just have to be more diligent about where I put my food. It's like having a bear in the house.

The man is patrolling the room, clearly aware of the theft of the food, which is sitting rather heavily in the dog's belly right now, having followed the large amount of just slightly off-tasting meat and rice. He's not yelling, which is good. But he's not sitting still, and that means he's a threat.

Although this is a pleasant sort of captivity, it is still captivity. The interior scents are fully human—the sweetish odor of soaps, the fulsome odor of food hidden most of the time behind impenetrable doors. And there's the odor of the man himself, tainted perhaps by the soap smells, but still clearly identifiable, different from that of any other person this dog may ever encounter. He is attached to a leash when the man carries him outside to relieve himself. He is behind a closed door otherwise—in the basket, with the soft man-smelling sleeping bag, subjected to pills being shoved down his throat, but then rewarded with bowls of room-temperature meat, fresh water. Wary and worried, the dog keeps his eyes on the man until he retires to his own bed. The man's touch isn't unkind, but it lacks the meaning that would finally put this dog at ease. It is the touch of business, not affection. There's the awkward demand to open his mouth and have things forced down his gullet, always followed by a voiced "Good boy." It's confusing. Still, he can't trust that this man won't one day hurt him, and so every time the man brings him food, or takes him outside, or makes him swallow the pill, the dog cowers in his corner, shrinking himself down to as small a target as he can reasonably become. *Don't touch. Don't touch. Don't hurt me.*

During the day, they go to that place with the other captives. The cage is not quite as comfortable as this place, but his aches are beginning to lessen and the foam rubber pad is good to stretch out on. There is no fire to lie beside, but the place is warm enough. Certainly far warmer than the nest he had under the fallen tree. Even a dog knows when there have been improvements in his living situation. The only time the dog can truly relax is when he's got the two other dogs beside him in an adjoining kennel; only then can the dog drop his guard long enough to sleep, leaving the watching to his comrades.

The other two dogs are friendly enough, poking curious noses through the diamond-shaped spaces of the wire that separates him from them when they are outside. It is clear to him that this pair has a family bond. Littermates certainly. They carry their tails at exactly the same plane and they move as one unit, patrolling the limited space of their run, communicating effortlessly as they mark and remark the same four posts. The yellow dog envies them. He'd like to be a part of their pack, but the wire prevents him from testing their openness to a third party. Still, it's nice to have company. He can sense that their lives have been disrupted, that this isn't their normal place any more than it's his. They whine sometimes, a soft, plaintive sound that speaks to his own distress. Unlike him, however, whenever the man or the chatty woman comes in, they wriggle and yap and leap in the air like they expect kindness. They get excited about these humans, and not just for the food that is offered. It's like they are excited to see these captors. He is simply worried. The woman will snap leashes to their collars and take them outside, beyond the confines of the run, to sniff and mark and even chase balls. There is something about that little sphere that keeps his attention. A vague notion of how it tastes, a desire for it.

The yellow dog stands in his isolation, watching, panting with anxiety, pacing from side to side until the aching in his hip starts up and he crumples to the ground, a low and involuntary whine coming out of him.

"Easy, fella. No ball playing for you till you get better. Doctor's orders."

The dog has no idea what the man is saying. One ear turns back toward the man, listening, analyzing, parsing out of human language the man's intent. He's recognized a few words from his early life: *boy, fella,* and the one the woman uses often—*sweetie.* Some words are becoming familiar from hearing them over and over: *easy easy it's okay okay okay.* Then the man barks loud human words and any fleeting sense of safety flies away.

He simply doesn't understand what the man wants of him.

25

Polly is sitting in a lawn chair in her front yard. Her voluminous caftan is mottled shades of pink and lime, a curious but unidentifiable pattern smeared across her body. Her reddened eyes clash with the pink. Her beehive hairdo is tilted slightly to one side. As I climb out of my truck, she pushes herself out of the chair and stomps over to me, apprehending me before I set a foot on her property. One finger points at me. "How could you?"

"Simmer down, Polly, I didn't—"

"You colluded."

She's got me on that one. "I talked with Roger, sure. But I told him we wouldn't—"

"Give them back."

"Polly, I don't have them."

Her mouth begins to quiver, a word I'd heard but never before actually seen happen. As the realization dawns on her that her cats are long gone, she begins to make disjointed utterances, and I worry that she's having some kind of seizure or stroke. Then she pulls herself back from the brink. "Why, Cooper? Why did he take all of them?"

Somewhere in my training, there must be a protocol for this. But if there is, I don't recall it. I reach out and pat her shoulder, a pat that becomes a full body hug as she throws herself against me. Her weeping is dampening the front of my uniform.

"I want to press charges."

"For what?"

"Catnapping."

I literally bite my tongue against an inappropriate chuckle. "Let's call it feline theft."

"Purr-loined." I can feel her laughter against my chest. A laughter that evaporates pretty quickly. Roger is a shit.

"Make me a cup of tea, will you, Polly?"

The yellow dog is sitting in the backseat. His head is framed by the window; he is looking at us with a curious expression of concern. As he's regained his body mass, the wrinkles around his face have become expressive instead of simply too loose skin.

"That the dog you rescued from the woods?"

"Yeah. He look at all familiar to you?" I ask everyone I meet this question.

"Maybe. Lots of yellow Labs in Harmony Farms.

"What about the Haynes?" Polly is one of those rare people whom the Haynes brothers seem to like. She's hired them for years to do her odd jobs.

"I don't think they go in for purebreds, but maybe. If somebody gave it to them, say. Why don't you go ask them?"

Oh, I will.

The dog in the back of my truck is not just a mystery; he's a crime. Or, rather, a crime victim. If he were a human being, the cops would be all over this, trying to find the perpetrator and bring him to justice. To me, it's obvious that someone abused this animal, certainly left him for dead, even may have actively tried to kill him, and here I am, treating him like a regular old lost dog, albeit one who needs more care than most, and, as with the rest of the unclaimed freight languishing in my kennel, I think that my main job is to find a new home for him. I've missed the big picture. Just because the victim is a dog, there is still a bad guy out there needing punishment. This line of thinking gets my juices flowing. I'll deal with this. I'll figure it out, and breathe a little life into my job.

With no tag and apparently no chip—Max hasn't picked up the other reader from his colleague, too busy with his plans, I guess—I'm going to have to figure out another way to find this dog's owner. Jenny's done the social-media posts and we've looked at registrations to see if any yellow Labs about this guy's age have been licensed in the past year. I have a list that is a starting point, but my gut tells me that anyone who would do something like this isn't going to have been inclined to register his dog. And that surely smacks of Haynes.

It gives me a nostalgic feeling to think that, as a dog officer, I am still, in some small way, an enforcer of the law. It's all I ever wanted to be. From earliest childhood, I wanted to be a cop. Every consecutive Halloween until high school, when I hung out with a group that inclined toward dressing like thugs, I dressed up as a policeman. Squirreled away in some shoe box that I've carried around since forever is a snapshot of me in my miniature uniform, plastic badge pinned on my chest, hat positioned perfectly on my crew-cut head. Unsmiling, like a true officer of the law. All business. Thinking about investigating this crime reminds me of all those make-believe games I played as a kid. The sweetness of pretend because you were always successful. Fearless and successful. Bad guys didn't try to blow you up in those days. You never failed to pull the trigger.

"What do you say, fella? Want me to bring your assailant to justice?"

The dog, typically, says nothing. Not even a whimper. Not even the comforting sound of his tail thumping on the car seat.

Well past Halloween, a little boy dressed in a well-loved policeman's costume comes into the kitchen, the scent of peach pie imbuing the room with a sweet warmth. The ancient wood and kerosene range is fired up, and his mother is lifting pies out of the deep and mysterious cavern of the oven. The man they have always called Uncle Deke is at the kitchen table, a cup of coffee already in front of him, his fingertips splayed against the mug.

"You ever need anything, you or the boys, you come to me." The old farmer reaches out and takes Cooper's mother's right hand, shaking it so that she meets his eye. "Hear me?" Cooper is a little scared by the force of Uncle Deke's quietly spoken words, the fact that he's grasping Mona's hand. He can't fathom what their old friend means. If they needed milk? A ride someplace? Cooper needs new shoes, and he wonders if Uncle Deke is offering to buy him new ones. He's done things like that before, arriving with groceries and saying that he over-bought, that he'd take it as a favor if Mona would take some of the extra cans and jars, these gifts coinciding most times with Bull's absence. When Cooper's mother would cry in her bedroom when she thought the boys were outside.

"You don't have to put up with this. His parents may have been my dearest friends, but I don't mind saying . . . "

"I can take care of myself, Deke Wilkins. But I appreciate your kindness." Cooper's mother sets a piece of too-hot peach pie in front of Deke and the filling slides out from under the crust, coloring the white plate. "I'm not going to be here, me and the boys, when he gets out."

"I've got room, Mona. It's a big house for one old man."

"No. But thank you. It wouldn't be right to put you in that position, you being like Bull's own family."

At that moment, Jimmy comes through the back door, bringing in with him the cold late-afternoon air; a finger of breeze chills the back of Cooper's neck a moment before Jimmy knocks the toy policeman's cap off his head.

"Yeah, Deke. It's Cooper. Thought I might come by this afternoon." I know that I'm shouting into my phone, but the old farmer has grown increasingly deaf. "You need anything? I haven't seen you around much."

"No. I'm fine."

I hope that this is true. Deke's of the old-school Yankee mentality. Wouldn't ask for a Band-Aid if he was bleeding to death.

"See you soon." I sign off and decide to ignore Deke's assertion that he doesn't need anything. I'll take over a few supplies. Maybe get him a peach pie. It'll help assuage the flicker of guilt that I have regarding my real reason for paying this call. I need to make sure that Deke's aim wasn't better than what he admits to and that he didn't, in fact, hit the dog that he chased away from his chickens.

Jenny is back in with a pair of setters that I've taken custody of recently. Sad case. Their elderly owner dropped dead and the dogs were left alone until some neighbor realized he hadn't see the old man for days. They'd stood guard over him, loyal to the end.

Working with a setter rescue, she's lined up a potential foster home for them. I am amazed at Jenny's network and how she seems to have the confidence of every breed-specific rescue group within a three-hundred-mile radius. This potential foster couple are an hour away and Jenny has volunteered to check them out for the rescue group. I have to note that she's volunteering her time, but it's during regular work hours, and as she's worked hard to find the right situation for these orphaned dogs, I've signed off on this junket as being part of the job.

I go into the kennel room to fish the yellow dog out of his cage.

Just once I wish he'd not look at me as if I'm the Grim Reaper, shrinking against the wall, tail tucked. I have to confess that I'm getting a little impatient. If you could have two thoroughly opposite dogs, it would be my magnificent and brave Argos and this, well, yellow, dog. One inspiring, the other despairing.

Argos never lacked for courage. It was as if he were a structure built around a solid core of bravery. I'll tell you what: There were moments in our career when I was the one who was afraid. You might say, yeah, sure, he didn't know that there was an AK-47 behind one of those hollow-core doors, or that he didn't have the intellect to be worried. You'd be wrong. But his courage under fire, or his determination to track down his man, would often fire up my own rectal fortitude and persistence. I never wanted to let that dog down. I knew that, like a human partner, maybe even more than a human partner, he had my back. A human partner can disappoint; a canine cannot. A human partner can make the wrong call. A human partner can fail.

I finally manage to get my patient out of his cage and into my truck. Because of his wound and his stubborn reluctance, I have to lift him onto the backseat, and his reaction is always like I'm about to throw him over a bridge. Ensconced on the rear seat, he heaves a great sigh and settles down. At least he's not the kind of truck dog that hangs his head out the window and barks at everything. I'll give him that. It's actually almost easy to forget that he's back there.

In exchange for the junket on company time, Jenny's agreed to do the night check for me. I'm driving away, thinking that I'm a free man, my evening is my own, and that I intend to pull one of those "Hey, I have a thought" pseudoimpulsive calls on Natalie. I'm hungry, she's hungry, and it's two-for-one night at the Lakeside. What'd you say? Not a date. Definitely not a date. I continue to be of the opinion that Natalie would prefer that to a standard date. Just sayin'. She's an interesting mix of hot and cold. Totally wonderful and then doesn't return texts. I'm not looking for anything big and scary, but a little encouragement might be nice.

A fresh, still warm peach pie is beside me as I arrive at Deke's. His place has that early-November look about it, russet leaves on the ground from the line of ancient oaks that border his drystone wall, the big pasture a mix of wheat-colored tall grass and short emerald green last-of-the-year growth. His pair of milk cows are recumbent, idly chewing their cuds, contemplating whatever it is that cows think about. Deke's chickens are behind bars 24/7 ever since the advent of coyotes in the area, and I kid him about no longer being able to sell his birds as free-range ones.

It is a quintessentially pastoral scene, up to and including the wisp of smoke that is rising from the foursquare center chimney of Deke's eighteenth-century house. Except for the 2011 Nissan truck in his driveway, it could be a scene from two hundred years ago. It makes you think about why folks like Deke and Elvin, and maybe even me, get frustrated with the influx of newcomers bent on taking the bucolic nature of Harmony Farms and making it suit their needs. Deke's been making a subsistence living on this land all his life, and his family before him, back to the first influx of newcomers, who, admittedly, pushed the original inhabitants into a war. I guess that's just the way of the world. No one much likes the imposition of change.

Deke comes out of his barn, followed by his old dog, adding to the sense that I've driven back in time, this time only as far back as the mid-1950s. Trucker cap, heavy green duck-cloth coat, jeans so faded and stained that only a trace of their original blue shows, knee-high black rubber boots. Scowl. It's like I've come home. "Hey, Deke."

"Hey yourself. That a pie?"

"Peach."

"I won't say you shouldn't have. Come in. I'll fix some coffee."

I fall in behind him, and I can't help but notice the rocking side-to-side gait that suggests the old man's hips or knees or back are slowing him down. Once again, it occurs to me that, with no kids and no help, he's going to be forced into a hard decision sooner rather than later. My grandparents would be in their late eighties if cancer hadn't gotten my grandmother and heart disease my granddad. Deke and my grandparents were in eighth grade together, which was as much education as they were offered in Harmony Farms in those days, so I know that he's very definitely in his eighties, maybe even in his nineties, so I guess you could say that he's not doing so bad. Still bucking hay bales and shoveling manure. Riding his tractor into the fields and planting corn. I kind of hope that he simply drops dead in his barn or out in his pasture before he's faced with having to sell up because he physically can't cope with the farm anymore. Too bad there's no one to leave this chunk of paradise to, a thought that really saddens me.

Deke may be an octogenarian farmer, but he's got a fancy single-cup coffeemaker and plants a cup of high test in front of me within a minute of my coming into the house. He makes his, sits down, and says: "What's on your mind, son?"

"Just paying a call." I fork a hunk of pie into my mouth.

"Right. And the queen of England is on my social calendar for bridge."

"I just wanted to see how you're doing out here."

"Same as always. Sitting up and taking nourishment."

"Haven't seen you at Elvin's."

"I been there." He takes a bite of pie, admits, "Maybe sticking a little closer to home. Most of the old crowd are gone. Dead or gone to assisted-living hellholes. Even Elvin's gone to Florida."

"Since when?"

"You're not a very observant officer of the law. He's been gone since last month."

"Hey, I'm just the dogcatcher here. And, speaking of dogs, come out with me and take a look at the one I've got in the back of my truck." Nice segue, Cooper.

Like a good guest, I take my plate to the sink, swallow the last of my coffee, and wait for Deke to shrug back into his ancient jacket. He gives his sleeping collie the command to stay. I'm not sure she is even aware of our leaving.

We stand in front of the open truck door, staring at the dog, who has pushed himself upright. In his eyes is the seemingly permanent look of worry at the approach of two men, one of whom has been attending to his every need for weeks. The dog's brown eyes won't meet ours; he turns his head sideways, as if to pretend we aren't there.

"Any chance you've seen this dog before?"

"Nope. Never. Ones like him, but not this one."

"Might have been a lot bigger; he's been feral for a while, down to skin and bones when I captured him."

"Nope. Can't say I've ever seen him."

"Okay. "

"Why are you asking me?"

"What about that dog you saw poking around the chicken coop. You fired at him, didn't you?"

"I told you before, I didn't hit him. And that dog, well, I still don't know if it was a dog. Too dark to see and he moved too fast."

"Okay. Just had to ask."

Deke nods his head, then juts his whiskery chin in the direction of the dog. "Looks like a nice dog, though. Skinny, but nice."

"He's better than he was." Who am I kidding? The dog has tried very hard to become one with the backseat, shrinking himself as best he can against the opposite back door.

I close the door and follow the old man back into the house, where the sleeping dog rouses herself enough to wag her tail. Given that Deke's place was a sanctuary of sorts for me when I was a kid, I haven't spent near enough time here since I came back. I'm hungry for another piece of pie and I think that Deke is hungry for the company. Or maybe that's me.

At any rate, I've given myself the rest of the day off and he's grateful for an extra hand with the cows.

It's a two-edged sword, having someone know you for your entire life. On the one hand, there are no mysteries. It's all just hanging out there. On the other, there's no shield against probing personal questions.

"How come you're still here, Coop?"

"Don't feel like going home." I dump the bucket of feed into the trough in front of his dry cows. They're old girls, living out their natural lives in this small paradise of Deke Wilkins's farm.

"That's not what I mean, and you know it. I mean, why aren't you back to work, your real work?"

"I still have ringing in my ears."

"They don't have any desk jobs on that force?"

"I don't want a desk job."

"So, when the ringing stops, you'll go back?"

He means go back to the K-9 unit. Deke was enthusiastically supportive of my decision to join that unit after several years as a patrolman. He told me it was a natural fit. He even came to our graduation, beaming like a real grandfather as Argos and I received our commission.

I don't answer, as if, due to this oft-cited tinnitus, I can't hear his question.

"You were a good cop, Cooper. It was your dream, wasn't it? Why'd you give it up so easy?"

"It wasn't easy."

"You fell off your horse. Get back on."

"No sir." He's not the first to use that shopworn adage. I didn't fall off a horse; I was blown apart.

Deke pats his knee and his collie moseys over. I don't want to be angry with Deke, but he's got me pretty riled. So I say something that's really none of my business, but I want to let him know that we all have things we give up.

"You weren't always a bachelor, were you?"

"Never married. That's a bachelor."

"But you were engaged. I remember hearing about it. My mother was talking to someone about it."

"Then you know what happened." ·

"She died, didn't she?"

"Don't. It's not the same, and don't you dishonor her by comparing Isabel's death with that of a dog."

Argos wasn't just any dog. "I'm just saying that sometimes the pain of loss becomes fear. The fear of loss."

But Deke's gone, his old Border collie trailing along behind him.

I should go in, apologize, but I don't. I climb into my truck and drive away.

26

S ince Jimmy is apparently uninterested in getting his own place, it seems to Bull like it might be kind of nice to have some Christmas decorations up at the old place. It's been donkey's years since he did so much as hang a wreath on the door, much less drag some unfortunate balsam out of the woods and prop it up against the living room wall. It's been just him here, alone on Poor Farm Road, the scratching of the mice in the walls keeping him from being entirely by himself as he watches marathons of *It's A Wonderful Life* or *A Christmas Story*.

Even when Jimmy and Coop were still kids, they didn't do much in the way of celebrating the holidays. Bull would give Jimmy a few bucks in an envelope. The kid might buy him a pack of smokes; well, maybe not *buy* exactly, but would hand him a crisp pack on Christmas morning. And Cooper, jeez, that kid. He was the kind of kid who wanted to believe in Santa and, all evidence to the contrary, never quite got over the hope that some Christmas morning, that spindly tree in the living room might have that new bike under it. And that line of thinking gets Bull to chuckling. He did manage to get a bike under the tree one year, one that he "found" in the open garage of one of those new houses down the street. Nice BMX. Sweet ride. Jeez, the look on Cooper's face when the cops took it back.

Crane's sells trees and wreaths. Maybe he can get a good discount on a little one. Dress it up with popcorn and spray-painted pinecones. Bull has a vague memory of construction paper chains by the yard, projects both boys did when they were real little. Before things got really bad, before his demons stole the life he had hoped to live back in the day when he and Mona were courting and the draft was the only threat to their happiness.

Aw, Mona. My beautiful Mona. She dazzled the eye. She dazzled his eyes. Tall and slender, a body made for the low-slung bell-bottoms and flower-power shirts. Blond hair as perfectly straight and long as a model's. It swished every time she turned her head, and Bull teased her into turning her head just so he could hear the sound. Her hair smelled of lemons; she smelled of Jean Naté. She had those clear gray eyes that her sons would inherit. Bull had admired Mona from afar all his life, from kindergarten, where she was the popular girl, the one that all little kids gravitated around for games. In middle school, where she was the first girl most of the boys had a crush on, and where she was the fashion arbiter for the rest of the girls in their class. To high school, where, miraculously, she noticed him and pulled him to his feet at the homecoming dance. Not that Bull hadn't enjoyed a certain amount of popularity himself. Big, strong, athletic, and funny, he had never lacked for friends or girlfriends. The girls told him he was handsome, and, well, maybe he was. Thick hair the color of oak, fashioned into an earnest rendition of Elvis's pompadour, the strong square-cut jaw that would be his legacy to his sons. Together, he and Mona cut a swath through the high school.

Bull misses that Mona, the one who looked at him with happy eyes. Not the one who she became, sad and defeated.

"*You can't keep doing this.*" *Mona stands in the doorway of the house on Poor Farm Road. He can see Jimmy behind her; Cooper is hitched to her hip. She looks like that Depression-era picture, the woman who looks old but probably isn't, sitting in front of her tumbledown house, kids with hungry faces around her, worry working ugliness on her face. He'd quit his job again. Plenty of good reasons, but he knows that Mona will say the biggest reason is the drink. Which isn't true, not this time. She's wrong. Nonetheless, he knows it is possible that she will finally make good on her threat to leave him if he loses another job. But, technically, he hasn't lost the job; he gave it up—before he got fired. Bull might be working his way through every low-level job in town, but he has his dignity, so it doesn't matter to him that the job, sanitation worker, had come with the first health benefits he had ever brought home as part of a job. First time his wife could take the kids to the doctor for any minor sniffle and be proud to hand over that insurance card like anyone else. Well, shit, he'll find another job with benefits. That was the benefit, pun intended, of quitting before getting fired. His terms. All the way home Bull had thought about what he was going to tell Mona, what spin he was going to put on the tale of high dudgeon and dignified resignation.*

"*Just tell me that they gave you a reference.*" *Mona shifts Cooper to her other hip.*

"*Hey, we'll be all right. The Highway Department has an opening.*"

"*Not for a quitter. For someone who maybe applies for it, for a department transfer maybe. I just don't understand you, Bull. I just can't keep doing this.*"

"*It was their fault.*" *Bull wants to launch into his grievances, shift out of the role of screwup to that of aggrieved victim, but Mona won't hear it. She shuts the door of his own house in his face. He doesn't carry a key, so he's left banging on his own front door, pleading with his wife to let him in. It's cold out. It's going to rain. He doesn't deserve this. He's the man of the house. In moments, the door opens and Mona, dragging a black trash bag behind her, shoving the two boys ahead of her, walks out of his house without a word.*

"*Where you going, Mona?*"

She doesn't answer, just shoves the bag into the backseat of the Nova and hurries the boys along with a frantic gesture, as if she's afraid Bull will chase them. Cooper is crying, upset at a situation he cannot begin to understand. But Jimmy, who's maybe four years old, stares at Bull with those hard crystal eyes. Without a word, Mona slams the door and guns the Nova out of the yard. Jimmy is kneeling on the backseat, looking at his father through the rear window. As Mona pauses long enough to let a passing car go by before she peels out of their driveway, Bull can see his elder son, his childish fist raised in an eloquent gesture of disdain, a single middle finger extended.

It wasn't so many years ago when he and Mona had made that kid in the back of that car. Back when he was first home from Vietnam, back when the only thing in the world Bull wanted was a good night's sleep and to be held in the arms of this beautiful woman.

Funny how just thinking about Christmas trees can bring the early days to mind. There's a lot Bull has forgotten, or maybe stored away in some unreachable corner of his mind. Or forgotten because he was so blind drunk that he never stored the memories like a normal person. She came back that time, and he thought that she always would, once she got over her mad; once she discovered that even a bad husband was better than no husband. Not crawling back, though. It was never like that. She'd just show up, the kids a month or two older, she a little calmer, standing in his kitchen like she'd never left. He'd go back to meetings and she'd let him sleep with her. They even tried having another kid, like that would fix what was wrong, but it never happened. But it was good, those times when Mona came back, to sleep beside the one person he couldn't live without. To have someone there to wake him from his nightmares and not ask him to talk about them.

Bull sets his Raleigh against the back of the lumber shed and pulls on his deerskin gloves. He goes over to where the Christmas trees are displayed, studies them for a moment, and then picks out a skinny six-footer, gives it a little shake, watches the needles rain down. It'll do. He walks the tree back to his bike without wondering how he's going to get a six-foot tree home by bicycle.

Jimmy is at the house when Bull finally gets home. It was a long, awkward walk from work to home with a bicycle and a Christmas tree, and any number of times Bull thought about abandoning one or the other along the road. He called Jimmy about every quarter mile to see if his son was around and could come get the tree. Jimmy never answered the phone, and Bull figured that he must have forgotten to charge it, or had it off. Neither excuse held water, but Bull always prefers to give folks the benefit of the doubt. Jimmy is pretty much attached to that phone, like he was to his security blanket back in the day. Bull remembers throwing the filthy thing into the fireplace to burn it. The kid threw a fit, screaming and crying and carrying on. Well, now he's got a new toy, and no one would dare separate him from it. "It's my office," he told Bull. "My workplace."

"Hey, you got that thing off?" Bull drags the tree in by the stump, sprinkling pine needles behind him. "I been calling you."

Jimmy holds the phone up, waggles it. It's a different phone. Bull can see the difference between the fancy phone Jimmy usually uses and this one. And even Bull knows what Jimmy has in his hand is what they call on TV "a burner." Disposable. Untraceable.

Bull sets the tree, sticky with pine pitch, against the wall. It's going to take Lestoil to get the pine tar off his hands, and he has no idea if he has any. In the meantime, he has to remember not to touch anything, lest it stick to him.

After supper Bull goes up to the attic to try to find some ornaments for the tree.

"What are you doing?" Jimmy's sudden appearance startles Bull from his attic search. All he can see is Jimmy's head; the rest of him is on the rickety foldout attic steps.

"Looking for the ornaments." He's been through the two upstairs rooms, rummaging through boxes and trunks that have been up there since he himself was a kid, finding nothing remotely ornament-like.

Jimmy laughs like the Grinch. "Right. And I'll just get the mulled cider going. Ornaments. Anything we ever had as kids is long gone. Used to keep them in the shed out back and, don't you remember, one year you decided that we'd been so bad, you'd just use 'em for target practice?"

Bull doesn't remember doing that. He does remember Jimmy being so angry one day that the kid went into the shed and smashed everything in it with his baseball bat. He doesn't even bother wondering why Jimmy has a completely different memory. As a kid, even a little kid, Jimmy liked to break things, and sometimes after smashing a pal's radio-controlled car or Cooper's rabbit cage—who knows what happened to the two rabbits—Jimmy would have no idea he'd done it. He wasn't faking it; the kid really did black out some of these violent acts. Not all of them, though. He'd own up to one or two a year, like the time he took a baseball bat to the principal's headlights. He'd owned up to that one because it made him a hero in his pals' eyes, but mostly he'd deny any wrongdoing. He'd look at Bull with those clear gray eyes and say, "No sir, I have no idea what happened." He was a cute kid, almost pretty, and it was painful to believe he was capable of such anger. Of course, after Mona died, he stopped being pretty. And his behavior went from delinquent to criminal.

"Guess I'll have to go to the Dollar Store and see what I can get," Bull says.

"You do that. Why not buy a big inflatable Santa while you're at it." Jimmy's laughter is infectious, and Bull laughs, too, but it doesn't feel jolly.

It was a busy night last night, two customers tapping on the front door. Furtivelike. Tap, uh, tap. On his way to the front door, Jimmy told Bull to go to his room, like he was the kid and Jimmy was the dad. "Stay there," he said. "Don't come out and turn up your TV loud. This is private."

"Bullshit." That's what Bull said, and left his room to amble down the hallway to the bathroom, right past the kitchen. Jimmy had said he was on Weight Watchers. That's why he'd gotten the scale. Right. And Bull was born yesterday. Skinny guy arrived first, dressed in nice clothes, shiny shoes, with only a thin ridge of mud on them from the front yard. Second guy wasn't a guy. Bull didn't need to go to the bathroom when she arrived, but she was so nervous that her voice carried, a high-pitched, nervous voice trying to sound not nervous, but experienced. Jimmy's quick, "We don't need any conversation" silenced her. Jimmy always said he was having a client stop by. Jimmy, Bull knew, was back in business.

It would be easy to blame Mona for the way Jimmy turned out. What kid might not be forgiven for going bad when his mother upped and died on him when he was at such a vulnerable age; what was he, thirteen? But the fact is, Jimmy was always a difficult child. From birth, if you want to believe it. Defiantly refusing to sleep, using his baby toys as weapons, smacking his parents with rattles and teething rings, yanking the cat's tail not like some normal kid, but really wanting to pull that tail out by the roots. Biting anyone and anything that got in his way.

"So, you want me to take you to get some decorations? I could use a run to the mall."

"That would be great. Yeah." Bull grins at the unexpected offer. You just never know with Jimmy. That's what makes him dangerous.

27

Any luck with that list of dog licenses?" Natalie hands me two flakes of hay. "Toss those to Silky."

I get a kick out of how Natalie seems to think I know the names of all these horses. I don't, but I have noticed that every stall has a dry-erase board with names and instructions, so I find the right one and toss in the hay. It's lovely to be in the animal-fueled warmth of the barn. They're all sporting blankets, plaids and solid blues or reds. Dignified black for the handsome gelding Natalie rides. The mare I ride—Moxie—is dressed in girlie pink. Frankly, if she was my horse, I'd get her one of those plaid blankets. It's such a silly thought that I have to smile at myself. I've never thought about dressing animals. Weird. Except for his bulletproof vest, Argos was au naturel at all times.

"Not much." Actually, none at all. I've called everyone on the list who had a male yellow Labrador registered in the last year, and although I've had a lot of pleasant conversations, no one has a missing animal. At least no one has admitted to it. "Next step is that I'll start with a couple of assumptions and then move on. Assumption number one: This is a hunting dog and his owner was hunting; ergo, there should be a permit. With a little digging, I might come up with a few names to look at."

"That sounds a little like a needle in a haystack to me."

"Perhaps. A lot of police work falls under that category. It's not all guns blazing and heroic rescues. Assumption number two is that there is a microchip between those shoulders and assumption number one can be vacated."

Natalie hands me another pile of hay. "I'm not going to ask why you're numbering your assumptions in such a strange order. But I will ask why Max hasn't already checked to see if the dog has a chip."

"When the dog was first brought in, we were too concerned with fixing him to remember to do it. And then, when we did, we found out that Max's reader pings only on a certain kind of chip. He borrowed one from another practice, and that one was broken. Now he's so wrapped up in getting ready for his new job, he's hardly around. He's basically closed the practice until the new vet arrives."

"It makes me so nervous not having a vet close by. I just hope that the new vet is good with horses. Not every veterinarian deals with large animals."

"I can't imagine that Max would ever hand his practice over to someone who handles only small animals. Half his practice is equine and bovine." I take the armful of hay and drop it into Moxie's stall.

I'm here to pick Natalie up for dinner. The weather has been better and I've had a few more riding lessons, a couple more casual dinners at the tavern. I feel like we're slowly sculpting the definition of our relationship. Sometimes she's my instructor; sometimes she's my friend.

We've gotten a little exotic and are heading an hour down the highway to Boston to a North End restaurant, so we're wearing actual dress-up clothes. This time, we both agree it's a real date. She's in black silk pants and I'm in my chinos, and now we're littered with hay. I pluck a stem out of her hair; she brushes chaff off the sleeve of my blue jacket—a possessive gesture.

I've cleaned up my truck for the occasion so that we don't have to worry about dog hair on our nice clothes. The yellow dog is in my cabin, with a bowl of water and a warm bed, and he's been medicated for the night. I'm sure that he'll be fine alone for the very first time. Shoot, he'll probably finally relax. I'll be home, if this date goes south, by ten. If it turns into a good night, I'll be home around midnight, and I'm sure he can hang on till then. At the very least, he's definitely housebroken. A tiny little bell rings in my head and I think that might be my tinnitus: *Put him in the shelter. No,* I say to the little voice in my head, *he'll be fine.*

The best way to get from Natalie's farm to the main highway is by taking Poor Farm Road. I won't point out the family homestead, but I do slow as we go by; this is where the road narrows, and for some reason deer like to play roadside roulette at this point in the route. In the house, the overhead living room light is on and there is a bulky form in the window. It takes me a second to realize it's a tree. An undecorated, unlit Christmas tree. In the yard is a car I assume is Jimmy's. Behind it is a black Lexus, angled in such a way you know that the driver isn't planning on staying but for a minute. I can't help it: I slow even more, as if I expect that the backup lights are going to go on at that moment. It's just a lucky guess, but they do, and I let the Lexus back out of the driveway, as if I'm a good neighbor. Then I think about following it. Natalie seems unaware of my little game. She's still chatting about her success with some arcane movement with her gelding. Renvers? I am surprised, however, when the Lexus makes the next right-hand turn into Poor Farm Estates. Hmm.

Bull's isn't the kind of place anyone would choose to stop by to get directions, and in this day and age of GPS and navigational devices, there's no chance that anyone would mistake the muddy driveway of 179 Poor Farm Road as the entrance to Poor Farm Estates. Too late for trick or treat, and too dark for Jehovah's Witnesses. In my overactive but police-trained imagination, it's way more likely that it's one of Jimmy's buyers or suppliers come to call. Someone who lives nearby.

I must have hmm'd out loud, because Natalie says, "What?"

"Nothing." Nothing at all. I really should stop this nonsense.

Villa Rosa is one of those Italian restaurants that is unprepossessing on the outside, a basic storefront with philodendron plants filling the window, but when you're inside it's like being in a neighbor's dining room, if one's neighborhood was in northern Italy. I've been going there since I was introduced to the Villa Rosa by a classmate in the Police Academy whose parents were friends with the owners. Villa Rosa is small enough to be intimate, which is a good thing, unless you happen to be seated very close to someone you'd rather not be near. The hostess leads us to our reserved table for two right beside my ex-wife and her boyfriend.

My first and probably best instinct is to back up, tell Natalie that I've changed my mind, that we should eat French, not Italian, but the moment comes upon us too quickly and the space is too tight for a graceful exit.

She is seated facing us; her gentleman friend has his back to me. "Cooper. Hello." The moment she says my name, Rudy gets to his feet. He's about my height, but not in good shape. I could take him if I had to. He's one of those pale types, thinning sandy hair, blue eyes, no definition to his jaw, a little saggy but not bad-looking. We've met before—at our divorce hearing, Gayle's and mine. Rudy was being "supportive."

There is that drawing-room-drama moment of how to introduce everyone. What are we to one another? Gayle and me. Natalie and me. Rudy and me.

Natalie takes over by offering Gayle a hand. "Natalie Everett." She's ingeniously vague about who she is in my life.

"Gayle." A two-beat pause. "O'Neal." That's not going to clarify things. "This is Rudy Verdick." I notice she doesn't give Rudy a playing position. These women are two very good chess players.

"I'm a little surprised to see you here," I say. I'm looking around to get the hostess's attention. There's no way I'm spending my first actual date with Natalie almost knee-to-knee with my ex-wife.

"I don't know why you should be. Unless you've forgotten that it's my favorite place."

I bite back some smart remark about who got custody of this place and every other restaurant we both liked.

Natalie pulls out her own chair, sits down side by side with Gayle. I'm pretty sure she's figured out who Gayle is. She immediately flashes Rudy a big smile, both of them costars in this marital play.

"Hey, Nat, let's go someplace else." I'm not sitting down next to Rudy on a bet.

"No need. We're done here." Gayle stands up, swivels her way out from behind the round table with just enough motion in the swivel to remind me of what I've left behind. Maybe *forfeited* is a better word.

Rudy hasn't said a word. He offers a tepid handshake, goes off in pursuit of their coats.

Gayle lingers. "So, tell me, Cooper, are you enjoying your job as a dogcatcher?"

"I prefer the term *animal control officer*."

"Of course you do."

Rudy returns with her coat, holds it open like a proper gentleman. Gayle slips her arms into the sleeves. "Natalie, so nice to meet you."

"It's been very nice meeting you." Natalie wears the delighted look of a woman about to interrogate a man.

I sit down as soon as they vacate the space. "I am so sorry."

"What did you ever do to her?" Natalie takes up her menu.

"I failed her as a husband."

"Oh. I had no idea that's who . . . " By the way that she flushes,

I don't entirely believe that Natalie hadn't figured out who Gayle is. I know that Natalie wants more. I'd certainly want more of the story if I were her.

"Good evening, folks. May I interest you in a glass of wine?" Our server has arrived, setting the house specialty of warm crusty bread and olive oil to dip it in on the table.

I am very grateful for the performance-art quality of our server, a handsome young man who might be a son of the owner or an Emerson student working his way through college. He distracts what is an awkward silence with his rendition of the specials, rolling the Italian off his tongue as if tasting the food himself. Playing for a little more time to recover from my shock at seeing Gayle, I ask him to repeat them with more detail.

When he leaves, I hand Natalie the basket of bread. "He should be wearing a pencil-thin mustache."

"And a pinkie ring."

I laugh harder than the weak joke deserves, but I am relieved to have hurdled the moment.

Natalie dips her piece of bread in the dish of oil, swirling it in a pretty gesture that spreads the darker balsamic into the oil. "Cooper, I won't pry into the whys and wherefores of your divorce, trust me. It's not that I'm not curious; of course I am. It's that I really hate being asked probing personal questions, so I won't ask any." She takes a strong bite of her bread. "However, I wouldn't mind hearing your public version."

"Irreconcilable differences. I stopped being the man she married. I have been, since Argos, I've been . . . " This is not easy. I've never used the word before out loud other than in a clinical setting. "I've suffered from depression. It kind of runs in the family." I'm not sure that's true, but, having endured the black dog, I think that it's likely that my mother also did. "But I'm better now. I think."

"Argos. Nice name for a dog."

This from Natalie makes me smile. "From Odysseus."

"You were supposed to get over it."

"Yes."

"I get that." She keeps her eyes down. "We're really allowed to grieve for only a little while nowadays. We don't go from black to lavender like the Victorians. We're expected to compartmentalize, not to offend or disturb others with our unbearable grief."

I reach across the table and take her hand, squeeze it gently, release it. "I won't ask you anything, either. But I am a good listener."

Our plates arrive and I pour us a second glass of the outstanding red.

It's not late when we head back to Harmony Farms. We've had a good meal, walked around and admired the city's holiday lights, held hands. I think that we've had a good time; at least I did after I settled down from having run into Gayle.

Natalie is such a hard read. The silent moment had given way to the set piece of two people enjoying a fine meal, and it wasn't until we were in that satisfied stasis of postprandial and precheck when she finally told me her story. I listened, knowing that, with Natalie, commentary and bluster and a sympathetic show wasn't necessary to prove my interest. She didn't want outrage on her behalf; she only wanted me to know what had pushed her from Wall Street to Harmony Farms.

"I was married." She immediately paused, and I wondered if that was all she was going to say, the past tense enough of a clue that I could make my own conjectures, the most obvious a bad divorce. A beat or two and she went on. "He was killed."

"How?" I gently prompted her, afraid that she wouldn't push herself to give me the story. I figured she'd back out. She was a little like that lazy ex-school horse rehab project of hers, if she didn't give him a little encouragement with her crop, he wouldn't move. Natalie, too, needed a little encouragement.

"Shot to death. By a frightened home owner." She gestured toward her glass and I poured more of the very good red wine into it. "He made the mistake of being black in a white neighborhood. A flat tire and a forgotten cell phone and little option but to knock on a door in broad daylight and hope that he'd be met with human kindness. Instead, he was met with panic and fear and prejudice and a legally owned handgun."

"I am so sorry." I'd heard this story, or stories like it, all too often. "A case of stand your ground?"

"No. Fortunately, this wasn't Florida. I mean, if there can be a fortunate side to it. My husband was dressed in a business suit and not a hoodie, a pair of expensive shoes and a rep tie from his prep school, and was clearly no threat. The shooter was a known hothead; he'd been arrested twice before for threatening neighborhood children. Between the criminal trial and the civil suit that followed, he'll never threaten anyone ever again.

"But the point here is that when I went back to work that first day after my allowable bereavement leave was over, it was business as usual. Forget your personal drama and jump right back into the important drama of buying and selling money, making money. Put your loss behind you, Nat, and let's read some prospectuses. I went into the ladies' room and threw up, then wrote a resignation letter out by hand. I didn't take anything but my photo of Marcus. I walked out."

I hesitated a moment before I reached across the table to take her hand for the second time that evening. I wasn't sure if she'd let me, or if she'd pull it away in a show of whatever the female equivalent of machismo is. She let me take it, squeeze it gently, even though she works too hard for her hand to be soft and fragile, as it must have been back when she was on Wall Street. "How did you get from walking out to owning Second Hope?"

I was rewarded with a genuine smile. "It's more a case of how I ended up on Wall Street when a place like Second Hope had been a dream of mine since I was a little girl in braids riding a fat pony."

She fingered the rim of her glass and I split the remainder of the bottle between us.

On the way home, I again take the shortcut through Poor Farm Road and again I slow as we pass by Bull's house. It's before eleven on a weekend so yet another strange car in the driveway shouldn't be suggestive of anything going on. Except my father has no friends and my brother is hardly likely to be entertaining. No porch light, no lights on at all in the front of the house. No lights on that Christmas tree.

Natalie invites me in. For us it's late, but neither one of us remarks on the time. She lets Betty out and I give the yellow dog a brief thought, quickly deciding that he can hang on another few minutes. I hope so at least. She offers me another glass of wine, but I decline. She offers a cappuccino instead and that sounds good. We are standing in her small kitchen, where traces of her previous life show up in the expensive-looking cappuccino maker. She hands me the tiny cup and we move into the living room, sitting side by side in the embrace of her ultrasoft microfiber-covered sofa, a fabric, she says, that is her second favorite, after polar fleece, being both dog hair– and horsehair-resistant.

My cappuccino is gone in a sip. I set my cup down on the glass and wood coffee table and she does the same. I take her cheek in my palm and she presses her hand against the back of my hand. She feels warm, her cheek and her palm. I lean in to kiss her and her mouth is warm, too, and tastes wonderful.

It's the first time he's been left alone since the man brought him inside. The novelty of it is quite invigorating. Now that the pain is mostly gone from his hip and his other more internal aches and pains are all gone, the dog moves quite ably through the small cabin, sniffing luxuriously at the man's objects—the bed, the clothes dropped on the floor, the shoes. The shoes. He picks up one shoe and mouths it like a puppy does a soft toy. The mouthing is comforting and quickly becomes chewing. The relief of using his jaws is intoxicating, equally entertainment and relaxing.

Midway through the shoe, the dog feels hungry; the chewing has gotten his juices flowing. He drops the shoe and heads into the kitchen area of the cabin, laps water from his bowl and licks the empty dinner dish. He'd been fed, but he doesn't remember when. In his mind, nothing is certain; one meal may have happened, but another may not. Still, the scent of food fills this room, his good nose telling him that behind those doors lies paradise. The man may never come back. Or he may come back and not put food in the bowl. Or he may be replaced by another man. Life's uncertain. Get those cupboard doors open. He scratches at the under-the-counter cupboards, leaving long claw marks. He throws himself against them, and the force of his body blow bounces the door to one of the cupboards open. Ha, ha, ha. Therein lies the bag of kibble that the man has begun to mix into his moist food. He takes the top of the bag in his teeth and pulls. It falls open with a satisfactory thump, scattering the kibble from one end of the room to the other. The yellow dog begins to vacuum up the spill.

Enough with the kibble. There are far more interesting things to investigate. The dog lifts himself up on his hind legs and taps the hanging cupboards with a paw. Like the body blow he dealt the lower cabinets, the force of his big paw bounces the weak magnet keeping the door shut and it pops open. He's got the door open, but he can't reach inside the cupboard for the few items that aren't in cans and unassailable, things like cookies and a box of cereal, another of crackers. The dog stands on the floor on all fours, contemplating the largesse just out of reach. With a grunt and a surge of desire overcoming waning disability, he jumps onto the counter, knocking off a can of coffee and a bowl of sugar. Utensils drying on a dish towel scatter into the sink and onto the floor in a twangy cascade of sound.

A few hours later, back in his basket bed, sated and working now on the other shoe, as happy as he's been in a year, the dog hears the man's truck coming down the track. It doesn't occur to him that he's done anything wrong. He's a survivor, and that's what he's ensured for himself while alone here in this place, his survival.

"Oh my God." The man stands in the open door, his hand still on the light switch. "What have you done?"

The dog shrinks deeper into the protection of his basket. He can sense the change in scent even as the man walks gingerly through the debris field of his cabin. He came in smelling of food and contentment, and a certain kind of animal satisfaction, but that olfactory story has quickly changed to the sharp scent the dog most associates with escalating human anger. He makes himself smaller, hoping that the man won't take out his anger on him. He doesn't know why the man might go from content to angry in a split second, but he's not going to provide a target. He's had that experience before and he's not about to make the mistake of nosing up to an angry man.

"Guess I shouldn't have left you alone."

And then the man makes a sound that the dog hasn't heard come out of him before.

The man laughs.

28

My first thought was that my solitary cabin had been tossed. The scene looked exactly like a botched burglary or a hate crime. Funny how professional experience overrides common sense. Claw marks on the cabinet doors and paper trash strewn all over pointed a pretty convincing finger at my houseguest. I was so tired, so content, I just left the mess and went to bed. It isn't till I get up this morning that I notice my only pair of running shoes have been destroyed. I find one in the bedroom, the other peeking out from under the dog's heavy head, like he's trying to hide the evidence from me. They have been systematically chewed into pulp; the only thing that makes them recognizable as footwear are the soles. I've put a lot of miles on those Nikes and they had a lot of miles left in them. A new pair isn't exactly a budgeted line item in my personal finances for this month.

At least he had the good grace to look ashamed when I came in last night and took in the magnitude of my mistake in assuming that he wouldn't take advantage of being left alone to wreak such havoc on my possessions, ignoring that little voice telling me to put him in the shelter. I guess I didn't think that this dog had it in him. I'd never had a dog that willfully destroyed property before. Then again, except for the brief time Polly let me have Snoopy, I'd only ever had Argos. And my belongings were sacrosanct to him. Another good reason to stay dog-free.

The sugar is gritty and sticky on the wooden cabin floor and there isn't enough ground coffee left in the can to make a cup. I'm not a good candidate for caffeine withdrawal. The kibble is all gone, and if it hadn't been impossible for the dog to get the refrigerator door open, he wouldn't have any breakfast, either. I warm up the rest of the hamburger and rice mix, dump in the contents of his last two capsules of medication, and smile. He's finally done with the meds. I can take him back to the shelter and get him out of my house. Monday. Jenny's on this weekend and I have no interest in going to the shelter even to rid my tossed cabin of the tosser.

"Okay, no running today. But we're going to have to go find coffee." I don't know why I'm telling the yellow dog this; it's not something I've been doing, talking to him, but he is listening to me from a distance, those soulful, guilty eyes not meeting mine. Submission, I know. A dog who meets your eye is challenging you, or trusts you. I suppose submission is a good thing, but I'd love it if, just once, he'd look at me without looking like he expects me to beat him. Jimmy used to smack me because he said he didn't like the look on my face. All I wanted was for him not to hit me.

I clip a leash to the new flat collar the dog is sporting, an impulse buy when I was in the hardware store, and we go out to the truck. I'm still lifting him into the backseat, but now I wonder if I haven't just inadvertently trained him to expect to be lifted. Next time, I'll invite him to jump up. Surely he knows how to do that. After all, he most likely got out here in a truck, a thought that renews my determination to find out who this dog belongs to. As Natalie says, sifting through the Massachusetts Division of Fish and Game's computer records to find someone who might theoretically fit my mental description of the asshole who might have shot his own dog, and assuming my lone contact in that department is willing to give me access, is pretty much a long shot. Like winning that lottery my father insisted would change our lives. There was a time when he substituted the lottery for drinking. I'm not sure we were any better off; the money was still spent. So, I'll leave a message for Max to see if he's finally gotten a working microchip reader. Another gamble, another chance at the lottery.

I lift the yellow dog into the backseat of my truck and race off in pursuit of caffeine. And, having found coffee and lemon squares at the Country Market, I buy two and drive over to Natalie's.

Despite the cold, Natalie is out in her ring, schooling the off-the-track Thoroughbred she calls Lew. He looks like a fire-breathing dragon as jets of frozen breath plume out of his nostrils as she asks him to collect. I can see her breath, too, as she talks to him in both spoken language and the language of seat and hands. Her dog, Betty, greets me, and after a minute's internal debate, I decide to let the yellow dog out to have a little fellowship with his own species. His tail beats from side to side, and I'm surprised at the thrill I get out of seeing it wag. They perform the customary canine greeting, taking turns putting nose to anus, checking out whatever it is dogs check out. Salutations done, Betty gets playful, and the yellow dog goes into a play bow. Against my better judgment, I decide to let him off the leash. I figure either I have half a chance that he'll run off again, which is sort of seeing things glass half-empty, or I'll be pleasantly surprised if he doesn't. I have a moment's trepidation before getting it—Betty will keep him close. And, sure enough, he happily follows Betty as she heads into the relative warmth of the barn.

"I'll be done in a minute; I just want to repeat that movement. He's coming along so well once I get past his stubborn streak." Natalie puts the horse into a canter and I lean on the top rail of the fence. I'm not at all sure what's she's asking for, but all at once she smiles and transitions to a trot, then a walk. She drops the reins, Lew drops his head, and they make a slow circuit, slow enough that I hand her the rapidly cooling paper cup of coffee and she sips it as she cools out a horse in twenty-degree weather. By the time Natalie decides that the horse can stop moving, my feet are numb from standing in one place. She pulls up and dangles her own feet. "The hardest part is getting off once my toes are dead. The rest of me is plenty warm enough."

"I'll catch you." So I do, in a fairly awkward and silly attempt to prevent her from having to hit the ground with frozen feet. I have her in my arms and that feels pretty good, and she lets me kiss her. Then she pulls away to grab the soft, fuzzy blanket hanging over the fence and drape it over the horse, commencing to walk him around and around the ring. We walk together, and I'm holding the hand that isn't holding the horse's reins.

We head into the barn and I greet Moxie, who dangles her head over her stall door. She nuzzles my palm, hoping for treats. Lucky for her, I know where Natalie keeps the mints. I feed her a few, and my hands are warmed by the soft feathers of her breath. The tack room is heated, and I retreat into it to get my own frozen feet thawed while Nat pots around untacking and blanketing the horse. In the time that I've been hanging around Second Hope Farm, it seems to me that horses are mostly about dressing and undressing. Finally, Natalie joins me and we sit enjoying the warmth of the tack room, eating our lemon squares. The room is decorated by the saddles on their wall racks and the collection of bridles dangling from hooks. An umbrella stand shaped like a Chinese vase holds an assortment of crops and whips. The room smells like leather dressing, not a scent I can describe, but one that I associate with things well cared for.

The temperature has dropped further and the early-morning blue has paled to a cottony white. As we head back to the house, I can taste snow in the air. Maybe the weather guy has it right this time; they're predicting the season's first real snowfall tonight.

I realize that I don't see either dog, and Natalie tells me that while

I was thawing out in the tack room, she's put Betty and the yellow dog in the house. "He was a little skeptical about it, but he was cold enough that he finally agreed to go in with her."

"Wait till I tell you what he did." I make the story a lot funnier than it was, make myself out a lot more forgiving than I am. "I hope that Betty is a good-enough chaperone that he hasn't tackled your pantry."

The two dogs meet us at the back door, tails wagging. I take a quick survey of the kitchen, but the only thing out of order is the sloppy-dog ring of water surrounding the water bowl. "Looks like you're safe."

"You really should have known better than to leave a dog with issues alone in the house."

"I know that now and I sure won't make that mistake again. Trouble is, it's going to make his a hard adoption. People don't want destructive dogs. Dogs with *issues*."

"So you are going to adopt him out?" She leans a little on the word *are*. Like she's been entertaining some storybook notion of my keeping the animal.

"Of course."

"Oh."

"Why?"

"I just thought that, well, because of how hard you fought to rescue him, and then keep him alive, that you'd want him."

"No." That sounds so abrupt. I don't really have the words to express why I can't bring myself to ever have another dog. So I fall on the simplest explanation. "I've had my dog."

"So, what does that mean? There's some rule that says you can't have another?"

"I don't want another."

"That I understand. Sort of. But, really, you've devoted such good care to this guy, how can you not be attached?"

"Just doin' my job, ma'am. Doin' my job."

She doesn't smile.

I change the subject posthaste. "I think it's going to snow. What would you say if I suggested we hang out, watch it snow?"

"It's not snowing yet and, as much as I'd love to hang out, I've got things to do."

"How about tonight? I could bring over some of my famous chili."

"I didn't know you were famous for chili."

"Oh, there's lots you don't know about me."

"I'll bet." She's smiling at me, and then she stops smiling, as if she's been caught doing something wrong. She turns away from me, puts one hand up like a traffic cop. "Cooper, this is good, but I need to slow down a little."

"I thought that men are supposed to say that." I want it to sound funny, but it sounds petulant.

"You, too. I mean, we both need to take this a little slower."

Slower? In my view, we've been taking this—whatever it is—pretty damn slow already. "Hey, Nat, it's not rebound; it's been too long, for me, for it to be anything but really liking you. Wanting to be around you."

"Cooper. It isn't rebound for me. It's grief."

I'm put in my place. "Right. I'm sorry. I've been hasty." I get it. Despite what we talked about last night, I know that unless she gives herself permission to get on with her life, her love life, she's never going to be happy again. Or maybe I'm just not the guy to do it.

"Coop, I'm sorry."

"It's okay." To prove it, I hug her and am saddened by her sigh, not of relief, but of something deep within her. It's time for me to go.

It takes a few minutes to get the leash on the yellow dog. As usual, he shrinks away from me, which is embarrassing in front of a woman who rescues animals. I assure Natalie that despite the dog's implication, I really don't eat dogs. This dog is falsely accusing me with his tucked tail. I make a joke of it and am rewarded with her laughter. Finally, just to heap more embarrassment on me, she puts her hand out and the dog goes to her. She hands me the leash. "You really must stop beating him."

"Righto. I'll try to remember that."

"Seriously, you've got to at least make an effort to befriend him. It's clearly not enough to feed and medicate and keep him safe. He's got to learn to trust you. Do you think that mare you ride was always such a love? No way. She came to me so head-shy and nervous that she was a danger to ride. It took me months to earn her trust, and now, here you are, a rank amateur, completely confident on her back."

"I'll do my best." I zip my jacket, pull open the back door. The dog balks at the doorway. Fighting the urge to yank his leash, I say gently, "Come on, fella, time to go. Say bye-bye."

"You know, training exercises are a nice way to bond."

"I'll keep that in mind."

Training exercises. A few rounds of "Sit, stay, heel" are kindergarten compared to the kinds of things Argos and I did together. I don't think she'd toss that out so casually if Natalie really had a clear understanding of the kind of work I did before. She knows the basics—that I was a cop, that I was a dog handler. But she can have no concept of the complexity of partnership I enjoyed with Argos. He wasn't a pet, or even, to use the more politically correct term, my companion; he was my partner, my backup, my wingman. And, yeah, my companion. It's not something that I can talk about. Not now. Maybe not ever. Argos was my one and only. And then I think: Kind of like Natalie and her murdered husband.

The yellow dog traipses behind me, as if using every inch of the six-foot leash to keep his distance. He's not pulling back, or resisting, just keeping distance between us. I open the back door, point. "Up."

He gives me a hangdog look. His root beer–colored eyes, clear now and brighter, are cast down and, despite the frigid temp, he pants, yawns. I speak enough dog to recognize that he's having one of his panicky moments. "Okay. No new tricks today." I heft him into the backseat. I turn around to make a joke of it with Natalie, but her door is closed.

When their mother died, Bull's reaction was to go on the bender of all benders. That was hardly a surprise; he went on benders at the drop of a hat—when the Sox lost the pennant or when things simply got a little tougher than usual, like coping with a rainy day. This time, a single day after the funeral, he gets tossed into the drunk tank, and Jimmy and Cooper pretend that they have an uncle living with them so that they don't get shipped to foster care. They're lucky; in a way, they do have an uncle. Deke Wilkins parks his seldom-used Oldsmobile Cutlass in the front yard of 179 Poor Farm Road to make it look like someone is living with the two boys. Jimmy point-blank refuses Deke's offer of staying with him at his place. They are thirteen and eleven, and Jimmy says that they will be fine alone. That they want to be alone. The boys will wait out Bull's episode, living off food dropped off by neighbors like Polly Schaeffer and the third-grade teacher, Mrs. Bollen. They have food, a roof over their heads. The one thing that no one offers, though, is an explanation of how to live with the loss. Cooper cries for a couple of days, until Jimmy smacks him and tells him to grow up. Cooper never sees Jimmy cry about their mother's death. Even the sudden death of his mother fails to penetrate the hardened heart of that boy. He fends off all attempts at consolation with sharp elbows and by disappearing for hours. As a result, everyone leaves Cooper alone, too.

I do understand Natalie's need to pull back. Grief, after all, is a mercurial element, shape-shifting and breaking off to bury itself in different regions of the heart. Sometimes you just want to go back to normal, stop being the kid everyone feels sorry for. And sometimes you need to crawl into the bedroom closet and cry.

29

They're never going to get here in time. We are completely alone. The big white dog is following me at heel like a shadow. We have tracked down the perp. He is our quarry. Where the fuck is backup? It's dark now, and on this dead-end street, there are no streetlights, so the stars embedded in the night sky are visible, glittering in the cold air. It's so cold, but so beautiful. A night when you might believe in God if you weren't standing outside a crack house, pretty certain that there is someone pointing a weapon in your direction, and your backup wasn't taking forever to arrive. Argos growls. His sharp ears have heard the sound of the back door opening. Our shooter is going to make a break for it.

I swallow the taste of bile. I have no idea what the population is inside that house. The perp could have dashed in for protection, or he's got a posse sitting there, guns drawn. There could be women and children in there, potential hostages, or nothing but rats.

I speak into my radio, keeping my voice low and in control, but I can't hear my own words. They are garbled, as if my tongue is stuck to the roof of my mouth. What I want to say is, "We have the shooter." But what comes out of my own mouth is gibberish. I can't form the words. There is nothing, not even static, to suggest that I am connected. The darkness feels like someone has put a blindfold *over my eyes. I reach out to touch my dog but can't find him. The darkness is liquid; the silence is a weight. But I know that he's there; he's still with me. Finally, the brush of a cold nose touches my hand.*

Something's keeping my reinforcements from getting here. It's just me and my dog. And that's enough. I won't wait; I won't take a chance that this mad man gets away. Argos is backup enough. "Let's go."

In my blindness, deafness, I stumble up stairs and am in a large empty room brightly lighted, bringing sight back to me. It looks like a gymnasium. Mats hang from the walls and ropes dangle from the ceiling. There is a trampoline in one corner and a small child bounces and flips, bounces and flips.

The large form of a man materializes, bulky, misshapen. His face is obscured, blurry, inhuman. I feel a building terror. Argos barks twice. I try to tell him to stay, but again, nothing comes out of my mouth. Without the order to stand down, Argos flies away from me, intent on his man.

With a slow, graceful gesture, the bulky man, bear-shaped and faceless, pulls the detonator.

I wake up screaming, screaming and screaming until I feel a warm, wet nose pressed against my cheek. I clutch the dog around his neck, press my face into his fur, breathe in his wonderful animal smell, and weep with relief. It was all a dream. It was just a terrible dream.

And then, fully awake, I realize that the yellow dog is the dog in my arms, not Argos.

It was the sound that brought the yellow dog into the man's room. Whimpers and moans, meaningless words in his tongue language that weren't meaningless to the dog in their timbre. The man was making the sounds that the dog heard himself make. Usually when the man made noises, the dog sought out his bed, his safe place, and stayed there, head down, tail tucked. But this night, when it was almost no longer night, but graying toward a new morning, there was something in the man's cries that reached into the dog's own experience, and he rose from his basket and stood in the doorway, breathing in the scent of the man's dreams, pungent, sour with distress.

When the man called out in his sleep, his arms reaching out to grasp something that wasn't there, the word he used, the *name* he called—Argos—meant nothing to the dog, except that he knew that it was a name in the way that the man said it, with deep fear, with deeper love. It was like he was being called, although that wasn't his name. Was the man calling him? He'd talked before, but never asked him to *come*. It was a word he knew.

His almost-healed hip creaked a little as the yellow dog tentatively took a step toward the recumbent man. One step, then another. If the man had awakened, looked at him with wide-awake eyes, the dog would have bolted. He aligned himself against the side of the narrow bed, sniffed at the man's sweaty neck, took a careful taste with the tip of his tongue. The man said the name again—Argos— this time with a reverence, a softness in his voice that the dog had never heard him use before. The dog knew that the man wasn't calling him by that word, that name, but it didn't matter. There was enough kindness in that tone that the yellow dog's self-protective fear eased even when the man, in his sleep, flung an arm over his back. The touch was not gentle, his arm in sleep heavy, but the face buried against the yellow dog's neck was warm and wet and harmless. The dog sighed and let himself be hugged, and he found a great comfort in that creature-to-creature touch.

Even when the man woke, the dog remained as he was, pressed into the man's arms, not struggling.

"Come on by the house. I got something for you."

I'm gassing up my truck as Bull comes out of the Cumberland Farms. It's Christmas Eve, a day that pretty much feels like any other day of the week to me. Not a creature is stirring. The setters are nes-tled into their new home and for once we don't have any stray cats in residence, so I've given Jenny the afternoon off. I've been mostly just hanging around the shelter, catching up on paperwork, basically dogging it. Too many cups of coffee and a little too much time doing playful Internet searches on random topics like the weather in Ta-hiti and what a one-way ticket would cost. Too much is the answer.

"You got plans for the holiday?" Bull is persistent; I'll give him that.

"Yeah, I do." I don't, but my nonexistent plans don't involve a family gathering at the Harrison homestead.

"That's good. But come by when you can anyway."

"I will." I hang up the hose and plug in the gas cap. I don't see Bull's bike and I wonder if he's on foot. I will say this: He's looking better, and by better I mean a little thinner and a little less unkempt. His clothes are clean and he's clean-shaven around his mustache. Guess he's still keeping sober. He's trying. And I know that I will probably drop by the house, if only for a minute, and that I should go get some little thing to give him for Christmas.

"That's good. That's good. So, see you later?" He's grinning that big baby grin of his.

I go into the store to get some milk and bread, and when I come out, he's leaning into the backseat, petting the dog.

"You got a name for this dog?"

"Nope. His new owners will get to name him."

The truth is, I'm still a little shaken up from finding the dog in my arms this morning and by how much that gesture of comfort has touched me. I have no explanation for what happened, only that it did. I guess you could call it "creature comfort." I almost tell Bull about it, but I don't. I remember those times, when I was a kid, hear-ing him crying out in his sleep, wild, anguished sounds that fright-ened me. Mona would wake him up. I'd hear their voices through the wall as she kept telling him it was just a dream, just a dream.

I don't want to talk about nightmares; that might just lead to talking about fears. I've had that nightmare before, or ones similar to it—subconscious reenactments of painful memory decorated by random images.

The dog is sitting up, for once not shrinking back against the opposite door. Bull strokes his bony head with his big spatula of a hand. "That's good; he'll be a good dog for someone."

He will. Bull's right about that. With the right family, people understanding of his shyness and shoe-chewing quirks, he'll enjoy a long, happy life. Jenny's in discussions with two potential Labrador rescue outfits. I should let go of the idea of bringing his assailant to justice and just get the poor animal into the adoption pipeline. I would, but that seems so, I don't know . . . unfinished.

Max called me a little while ago to say that he's got another microchip reader and that if I've got a minute, I should drop by, see if the dog is chipped. I'm really hoping that he is. I've struck out with tracking down a hunting license. My one contact at Mass Fish and Game practically laughed me off the phone at my suggestion that their computers could locate, out of all the license holders, one random hunter who might have been in Harmony Farms over the last year. Who did I think they were, CSI Boston? If the microchip doesn't pan out, after the holidays I'll check with the Conservation Commission, which hands out written permission to carefully selected hunters who want to hunt on some of their properties. The odds with that are only a little more in my favor. I could be cold-calling fifty hunters to ask if they'd lost a dog. This is one reason I was never interested in moving up to detective—too many phone calls.

Max isn't alone when we get there. He's got his replacement with him. I am prepared to be nice, but I want her to understand that she's got some big shoes to fill. It's not all kittens and puppies around here. I think of Natalie's remark about not all vets working with large animals. Horses. Max makes the introductions. She's Amanda Davios, DVM. He rattles off her credentials as she takes the dog's leash out of my hands and drags him into the exam room. For some reason, I think of the Cloris Leachman character in *Young Franken-stein*. What was it? Frau Blücher? I expect to hear horses neigh. Like minions, we follow.

"He's looking pretty good. Eyes are much brighter. We'll weigh him before you leave, but he definitely looks less ribby to me. Keep up what you're doing, Coop." Max hands Dr. Davios the new reader.

As she waves it over the dog's shoulders, I feel an excited thumping in my chest. It's like it's tomorrow, Christmas morning, and all I want is to know who shot and dumped this dog.

"Bingo." Dr. Davios is actually pretty when she smiles. "I've got a number."

All I have to do now is call the microchip company and see who's registered to it.

God bless us every one.

The village of Harmony Farms looks pretty, dressed as it is in holiday finery. The planters that in summer are filled with pansies each contain a small Christmas tree, little red-and-gold bows providing daytime interest and, at night, glittering on the verge of tawdry, with tiny white lights. We have learned how to celebrate a secular Christmas, no crèches on the lawn of the town hall, but loads of trees and swags of greens and HAPPY HOLIDAYs! posted everywhere. Even Max's storefront window boasts a massive wreath, eight tiny reindeer climbing diagonally across the center.

I couldn't get a parking space in front of the office, so the yellow dog and I have to walk a half block to reach my truck. He's anxious, panting in the cold December air, but there's no avoiding this short walk down a sidewalk crowded with last-minute shoppers. He's not a tugger; he's more a lag behinder. "Come on, dog. Pick up the pace a little. I've got things to do." Top of the list, call the dog-finder company. He suddenly goes belly-down, literally trying to crawl away from oncoming foot traffic. I haul him to his feet.

I'm embarrassed to be seen by Donald Boykin, embarrassed to look like a dog officer without patience, and am relieved when he walks into the next store he comes to. Lucky Cynthia. Her husband has just gone into Harmony Farms' version of Victoria's Secret: Mandy's House of Lingerie. Funny, Cynthia doesn't look like a garter belt kind of girl. I've heard it said that Mandy's caters to a, shall I say, *Fifty Shades* kind of client.

Finally, the yellow dog agrees with me that moving toward the truck is the better idea, and he pulls me along with a new strength. I have to wait for Bob Haynes to climb into the passenger side of his truck before I can open my door and lift the dog in. He nods to me. For a Haynes, that's tantamount to a conversation. I nod back. Once in the backseat, the dog squeezes himself into the right-side foot well.

The dog tethered in the bed of the Haynes's truck growls at me as they pull out of their parking space.

The scent had come to him, barely filtered by the tangle of humans crowding him, the one other scent he recognizes from among the myriad human scents. A scent that sends his sensitive nerves into a frenzy. The scent of pain. Of violence. Panic closes in on him; he drops and crawls away from it, instinctively making himself less of a target. And the man holding the leash continues to insist on heading toward the scent, not away from it. But then, there, safety: the open truck door.

I want to make this call on a landline. The ringing in my left ear is definitely letting up, but it's still better to use a landline than jack up the volume on my cell phone. I head back to the office, leaving the dog in the truck, where he's comfortably curled up on the seat, and fish the paper with the number on it out of my wallet. As I dial the microchip registry, I'm thinking that I will have to put on my best officer of the law voice. The voice on the other end of the phone is male. The man identifies himself as Dan and I identify myself as Officer Harrison, Harmony Farms. He takes the number, says he'll make the call and give the owner my contact information. I start to insist that I be the one to make the call to the owner, but Dan is adamant, saying that's not the way it's done. I could pull the officer of the law card, but I figure, What's the point? Unless I don't hear from the owner; then I can get assertive with Dan the microchip man. I wouldn't want some guy on the other end of my headset bullying me out of doing my job correctly.

I hang up and sit by the phone like an idiot or a teenage girl waiting for a boy to call. Just as I shove my rolling chair away from my desk, the phone rings. I'm startled to my feet. It's Dan from the registry and he lets me know that I don't have the final answer to the conundrum of the yellow dog. The number is for a kennel, Barkwell Kennels, Labradors and Golden Retrievers. He doesn't want to linger on this problem anymore than I do; it's Christmas Eve, after all, so he gives me the information and wishes me well. I call the number and, like Dan, get an answering machine wishing me Merry Christmas and Happy New Year from Bob and Donna Stinson. According to their message, the Stinsons are enjoying a rare vacation in Hawaii. My policeman reaction is to think, You idiots! Never leave a message like that unless you plan to invite mayhem.

My dog officer reaction is, frankly, a little bitter. Now I'm going to have to stick it out until they get back. I really wanted to get this solved now. It's been weeks. Almost three months if you count the time I spent trying to lure the dog in. It's the holidays, the shelter is finally empty, and Jenny's off, so I can't simply leave the mutt in the shelter like I would a normal impound unless I want to be driving back and forth three times on Christmas Day. Then again, that would be a good excuse to duck going to Bull's.

When I climb back in the truck, the yellow dog sits up and gives himself a healthy shake from nose to tail. He puts his head over the back of my seat, breathes in my good ear. I reach back and give his head a pat. He doesn't immediately shrink away, a first for us. "You want to spend Christmas with me?"

He shakes his head again, ears flapping. I take that as a yes.

It's late, and I really should do that bit of last-minute shopping, find a present for Bull, and, what the hell, one for Jimmy. Go to the Stop & Shop and pick up something to take tomorrow for lunch, because I'm pretty certain that Bull won't have thought about a Christmas meal. One of those preroasted chickens would be good. "What do you say, fella? Let's go shopping?" I'm talking to the dog again.

The yellow dog apparently doesn't disagree, so I head out of town.

30

Y ou did what?" Jimmy shoots out of his chair like a Roman candle on the Fourth of July. "Tell me you didn't invite Cooper over here."

"Hey, I did. So what? It's freakin' Christmas and he's my son, too." Bull grips the can of Coke so hard, he can feel it dent.

"What did I tell you? How we can never have Cooper over here. He's a nosy cop."

"He's not. He's the dog officer."

"Bull. Get real. Once a cop, always a cop. Okay. Damage done. What time is he coming?"

"Don't know exactly. Kind of open-ended."

"Christ." Jimmy sits back down, takes out the most recent of his cheap cell phones, and starts thumbing through contacts. "Get out of here for a little while. I got to make a couple personal calls."

"You've got business on freakin' Christmas? What are you, a doctor or something?"

Jimmy grins at his father. "Something like that. Now, get out of here."

Bull lingers, defiant.

Jimmy gives him the stink eye and presses the burner phone to his ear. "Hey, yeah, it's me. Change of plans."

Bull tosses the empty Coke can into the sink. The clatter of hollow can against stainless steel follows him as he walks out of the kitchen.

"Personal calls"—that's what Jimmy calls them. Calls to one or two of the guys he's been dealing with since his last trip to juvenile hall. Used to call them classmates, like he'd been to prep school instead of incarcerated. Type attracts type. The last time Jimmy was sent to juvie was for breaking and entering and theft of more than five hundred dollars' worth of electronics. Just like with the first time he went, everyone—counselors, teachers, lawyers—hoped that yet another turn in reform school would finally straighten him out. Feel-good programs hadn't. Counseling hadn't. It hadn't been his first B and E. But it was his first time charged with assault, which was the main reason the judge decided that Jimmy Harrison wasn't going to get anything out of a few months of doing community service. Lucky for Jimmy, he was under seventeen, barely, and didn't get sent up to an adult facility, where, with his pretty-boy looks, he might have been made some guy's girlfriend. On the other hand, he met these two characters in juvie. What he didn't already know about trouble, they were happy to teach him. Guys with such ordinary names, Mike and Dave. Sound more like furniture salesmen than hard-core drug dealers. Come on down to Mike and Dave's Furniture Emporium and drug shop. Bull remembers them coming to the house, holing up in Jimmy's room, smoking dope, laughing. They didn't look like teenagers then, and he supposes that they haven't changed much.

What got lost in all that business was the reason Jimmy broke into the Slaters' house and beat the crap out of the Slaters' kid. The kid had bought an ounce from Jimmy and didn't pay him. And the guy that Jimmy owed for the weed wasn't happy about that and gave Jimmy his orders. So in effect, the Slaters' kid brought it on himself. He didn't do any time for having bought the weed; that part got swept under the rug, and Bull has never been able to forgive the little shit for the injustice. Now that kid is a partner in the town's oldest law firm. Funny, huh? Funnier still, Jimmy never ratted on the dealer, even though he could have avoided jail time by turning him in. Even at seventeen, that kid had cojones.

Bull really doesn't want to know what Jimmy is up to, but it's hard not to imagine that whatever credit he earned by not succumbing to a plea bargain this last go round has earned him a higher rung on the ladder in his field. Jimmy likely made some pretty good contacts at Walpole, and, along with his old friends Mike and Dave, he's clearly been elevated into the big time. Maybe not cartel level, but definitely involved in something bigger than selling nickel bags to kids on the street. It just sucks that he's decided to use the homestead for his base of operations. Makes day-to-day living with him a challenge. And Cooper, there's no figuring him out. Bull's got enemies who treat him more cordially.

"Come on, Bull. You've had enough." Cooper is skinny, too skinny even for a high school junior. Like no one ever feeds him, which isn't true. He's a ravenous eater; it just doesn't show. *"Now."* Cooper slides a hand under his father's elbow, knowing that he'll have a hard time finding his balance once he vacates the bar stool. Bull's a sailor finding his land legs.

"I'm fine. You go home, boy."

"They want you out of here, Bull." The bartender nods in agreement. Fink. Rat fink. Isn't his money as good as anyone else's around here? *"I'm not making no trouble. Why can't I stay till last call?"*

"It was last call half an hour ago, Bull." The bartender takes the glass locked in Bull's fist, tugs it free.

"You should be in bed, Coop. You got school tomorrow."

"Yeah. I do." Cooper reaches to take Bull's other arm; like assisting an in-

valid, or teaching a toddler how to walk, he guides his father to his feet. "I have the AP English test in the morning."

Bull isn't sure what an AP test is, except that it's something Cooper is doing that separates him from his dropout brother. And probably something he should be getting a full night's rest to do.

Bull sleeps all the way home. Roused to get out of the car, he stumbles through the doorway, finds his bed, and flops facedown.

Cooper fills a glass with water, lays out four aspirin on Bull's nightstand, then falls into his own bed but does not go back to sleep.

Bull shuts his bedroom door and turns on his television. There's a Christmas special on. He'll wrap the presents he got for the boys and watch it. Pretend like he's got normal kids.

31

It's Christmas morning, although I don't remember that until I turn on the radio and get a blast of prepackaged seasonal music on our local radio station. It's six o'clock in the morning and they're playing the whole of Handel's *Messiah*. I can live with that. I peek at the outside thermometer and decide that, even with the new running shoes that I got yesterday at a last-minute shopper's extreme discount, I'll give myself the day off from running. "That okay with you, pal?"

The yellow dog is sitting in the exact middle of the ancient braided rug that serves less as decor and more as a dirt catcher. His tail twitches from side to side, and he bobs his head. I can't tell if he's agreeing with me or trying to talk me into running around the pond at eighteen degrees Fahrenheit.

I'm not that much of a masochist. "Give me a break. It's Christmas, or have you forgotten?"

The dog steps into his basket, shakes, turns three times counterclockwise, and tucks himself in.

I have to admit that I'm a little surprised at myself, talking like

this with this dog. Now, with Argos, conversation was a given. We
had a great back-and-forth. I'd ask hypothetical questions like "Think
we should tell Gayle we want pizza for dinner?" Argos would tell me
with wise eyes that Gayle would not be pleased with pizza; that it
was my night to cook and cook I should, not bail out on my responsibilities. He was tough on me.

I'm still in my T-shirt and pajama bottoms, the woodstove cranked
up to sultry, a messy pile of breakfast dishes on the counter—except
for the egg-smeared plate that I've put on the floor for the dog to
prewash for me. I've got the latest Carl Hiaasen and I'm deep into
the fantasy life of a disgraced but lovable detective when my cell
phone goes off. It's not the bark ringtone, so I don't flinch. It's
Natalie.

We haven't been in touch much. At all. I've been "giving her
space." "Hey, Nat. Merry Christmas."

"Same to you. Having a good one?"

"Actually, very peaceful." I look at the yellow dog, tucked in his
basket like a cashew. "Just me and the dog."

"Still no owner?

I give her a brief synopsis of my thwarted investigation.

"I think he's growing on you."

"Like a wart. What are you up to?" It crosses my mind that maybe
I can duck going to Bull's and spend the rest of the day in her company. No implications, just a little time spent together. I've got that
chicken in the fridge.

"Stuffing a turkey. My in-laws are coming for dinner. It's the first
time they've seen the place."

"You nervous?"

"Kind of. I mean, if Marcus, if it hadn't happened . . . "

"Hey, they'll be impressed with the place. They'll be happy to
see you happy."

"Thanks, I hope so."

"Who wouldn't be?"

"Coop, I wish I could invite you, but I . . . "

"Nat, don't. Besides, I'm expected at my father's."

"That's good. It's a good day to be with family."

Right. Family. Always a good thing.

"I'm glad you called, Nat. Merry Christmas."

"I'm glad I called, too."

I sit for a long time, my phone still in my hand. The radio station has switched to secular Christmas songs, bouncy and all holly jolly. The fire in the woodstove has burned down and I feel a cold draft against my neck. I need to add some wood, get dressed, take the dog out. But I just sit here. Smiling.

As much as I understand Natalie's cold feet, her putting the brakes on what could be a developing relationship, or nothing, I've missed her. I like her company.

I've put off going to Bull's as long as I can. In the old days, I would have taken him a bottle of Jack and a carton of cigarettes. Now I'm just aiding his nicotine habit with a carton of Camels that I picked up at a gas station convenience store where I never shop. I've added a pair of thick work gloves and a knit cap to replace the one he wears, which stinks. I mean literally stinks—of unwashed hair and cigarettes. For Jimmy, the perfect gift that says, *I'm just being polite*, a box of Russell Stover candies. The wrapping paper cost more than the chocolates. I've got the cooked chicken as my edible contribution to the family reunion. I put the chicken and the candy into one carry bag, grab the gift bag with the hat and gloves, pull on my Carhartt jacket, and hunt around for my own hat and gloves. I'm the only person living here, and yet there are times when I swear gremlins have moved my stuff. It's really just an example of how far I've come from the structure that ruled my life, where my bed was made tight and my possessions were put where they belonged. My scalp was visible beneath a buzz cut and I never went a day without shaving. I run a hand over the three days' stubble on my face right now and tell myself that, at last, I've become fashionable.

Now all I have to do is figure out what to do about the dog. I suppose that I can lock him in the bedroom, as long as I'm careful to put all my footwear out of reach. I don't dare leave him alone in this rental cabin otherwise. But when I call him to follow me into the tiny bedroom, he balks, as if he's being asked to take a perp walk. He retreats to his basket and turns his back to me.

"Hey, come on. You can sleep on the bed." I try to make it sound like I'm offering him a Caribbean vacation; instead, I sound like a huckster selling swampland to retirees. "It's great, soft and warm. You'll be fine. Besides, I won't be long."

Nothing except a great sigh.

Short of dragging the dog by his collar into the bedroom, an act that would surely set him back to whimpering in the corner, I'm out of ideas. I gather the bag with the presents and the chicken in its plastic sarcophagus and call to him. "Okay. But you're going to have to stay in the truck. Come on." I open the cabin door and walk outside, pause on the porch. The yellow dog emerges from his basket, stretches fore and aft, and walks out of the cabin as if he's expected this all along. His tail isn't wagging, but it's not tucked, either. For once, he jumps into the backseat under his own power.

The afternoon is nearly over as I head toward Poor Farm Road, taking the longer Lake Shore Drive route as much for the scenery as for procrastination. The sky is that dull shade of gray that defines a winter sky in our minds when we think of winter. The dark days of winter. Gloomy and threatening.

I might take a run by Deke's on my way home from Bull's. I feel bad about how things went the last time I saw him. As annoyed as I was by his bluntness, he didn't deserve my bringing up what is still a painful subject for him. Besides, the old bachelor doesn't have anyone to "drop by" on a Christmas day. I could leave the chicken in the truck and take it to him instead. Maybe even the candy. Jimmy doesn't need any candy. He needs a diet.

The Nova up on blocks on the front lawn is crowned with the three inches of snow we had earlier in the week. It has been in that spot now for a quarter of a century, a monument of sorts. Jimmy's car is cleaned off and backed neatly into the turnout. There are tire tracks of varying widths in the gritty snow, like various vehicles have pulled in and backed out. They pulled up close enough to the front door that it couldn't have been drivers who missed the turn to the estates and used the driveway to turn around. It doesn't mean anything, but I'm enough of a cop still to stop and look at those tread marks, determine that they are from two different vehicles, and that neither one was Jimmy's Honda. I file that thought away for future reference. It makes me feel, briefly, like a cop.

I pull the bag with the stuff off the front seat, think about my idea of going by Deke's, and take the cold chicken out, putting it on the seat. Then I look and see the dog sitting there, ears alert to my actions. I can't leave the dog and the chicken in the same vehicle. Nor can I leave the candy instead. Chocolate is toxic to dogs. "This should be interesting." I open the rear door and invite the dog to go with me into Bull's.

It is every bit as depressing as I thought it would be. The place even still has the same sour odor of unclean beds, dirty wet towels, and overfilled garbage pails as I remember from my childhood. I never brought friends home, afraid and embarrassed at what they might think of me if they saw the inside of my house. As a kid, I was painfully aware that the "bachelor pad" of my father and older brother was actually a grotesque pit. But, as a kid, I also never did anything about it. Instead, I spent as much time out of my house as I could reasonably carry off. I hung out with friends, or made my way to Deke's place to help him feed his cows; sometimes I got only as far as Polly's. I put a lot of miles on my bike. As I walk through that storm door-free front door and take a whiff of the interior fug, I am cast back into my youth.

"When Mom gets home, she's gonna be pretty mad. We should at least get the dishes done. I can do the laundry; she showed me how." Cooper stands with his small fists planted on his skinny hips, facing his father. He has to look up to see the man's eyes, which are obscured by shaggy hair flopping down into them. His father sways slightly, as if there's a breeze in the kitchen.

"Waste of time. Throw the suckers out. I'll buy more. Better yet, we'll eat on paper plates from now on. No dishes to wash." Bull chortles, a gurgling sound in the back of his throat, like he needs to hawk and spit. "We'll live like bachelors. All pizza and football. That's how we Harrison men will live from now on."

"Bull, we can't do that. When Mom gets home, she's going to be disgusted with us." Cooper feels an urge to shove his father, to see if he can knock him over, to see if he's full of hot air.

Bull pulls out a chair and sits down, so that he and Cooper are now eye-to-eye. He shoves the hair out of his eyes and Cooper sees something in them that frightens him. They're rimmed in red, the whites crazed with blood vessels. He's seen his father's bloodshot eyes many times before, but this time there's a scrim over them, and it seems like his father's pale gray eyes are underwater. As if they're floating beneath the surface. Drowning. "You know she's not coming back, don't you?"

"Bull, she always does. She will this time, too." Cooper knows that his mother didn't run away this time, didn't leave them deliberately, but had an accident. That's what Bull said, that she had an accident and the Nova hit a tree. But, it wasn't a bad accident; there's just a crimp in the hood, and the cracked windshield. He can see that for himself; the car's back in the yard. It doesn't look that bad. Fixable. But Mom's in the hospital; that's where they took her three days ago. They won't let the boys in. They're too young, Bull says. Too young to be visitors.

"I'll wash if you'll dry." Cooper thinks that he's making a deal. If they can get the house cleaned up, Mom will come home. She's holding out on them cause she knows they've trashed the house in her absence.

Cooper runs the hot water, stacks the pots with dried-on tomato soup or canned chili, the plates with greasy slicks, and the forks with hardened food stuck between the tines. He squeezes in too much liquid soap, splashes hot, soapy water onto the floor. Bull stands beside him, grubby dish towel in his hands. Cooper bangs the pots and runs the water hard so that he can't hear his father's sobs.

Bull is kneeling beside the needle-challenged Christmas tree, trying to find the socket to plug it in. I'm a little afraid that the whole thing will go up like a torch if he manages to get the lights on, but it doesn't, and it is, surprisingly, kind of pretty. He hoists himself back to his feet, claps his hands together like he's accomplished hard labor. "Want some Christmas cheer?" He ambles into the kitchen. "Got hot cider. Not much kick, but it tastes good."

I take the paper cup with the mulled cider. He's been a little heavy-handed with the nutmeg, but it's not bad. The yellow dog has followed Bull into the kitchen, has been following Bull around since we got here. It amazes me, because he never follows me around. But I suspect that Bull has been feeding the dog crap from the array he's put out on the table—peanuts, a bowl of chips, salsa, a plate of pepperoni disks, hacked-off cheddar cheese, and crackers. "So, where's Jimmy?" I make a cracker sandwich out of the pepperoni and cheese. I've been in the house for six minutes and no sign of my brother.

"Jimmy? Oh, he's seeing a pal, but he'll be back in a minute."

"His car's here." Jimmy isn't exactly the type to take a walk.

"Guy picked him up."

"What guy? Who does he hang out with?" Hang out, like a teenager.

"How should I know?

"He dealin' again?" I hear myself slipping into the sloppy language of my youth.

Bull fixes his gimlet eye on me. "It's Christmas, for Christ's sake. Give it a rest, won't you?"

"All right." I catch him slipping the dog a slice of pepperoni. The dog takes it from Bull's hand as gently as a lapdog would. As concerned as this once-starved creature is about food, he does have good manners. He's going to make some family a real nice dog. I wonder when the Barkwell Kennels people will be back from their vacation. Wonder what they've done with their dogs while they're away. Wonder if maybe someone is taking care of things and might have access to records. I feed the dog a slice myself and go back into the living room. My plan to do a drop-in has been derailed, since Bull tells me he's got a frozen lasagna heating up. I guess I can't really bail on him if he's done that. Besides, I don't want to miss a chance to see my big brother.

The house is one of those uncharming antique places that are hard to heat. The living spaces are chopped up into small square rooms of practical purpose: kitchen, bedrooms, sitting room. The room that might have started out as a birthing room—the house is that old— is a bedroom, mine when I lived here. There is a second floor filled with the remnants of our forefathers which is closed off by a door at the top of the stairs to keep the heat from being lost upstairs. As Bull goes in to check on the lasagna, I take a little walk around the house. The first thing I notice is the padlock on Jimmy's bedroom door. There's also a padlock on the cupboard beneath the stairs to the unused second floor. When I was growing up here, there wasn't even a Schlage lock on the front door. My cop radar is pinging.

The wash of headlights through the front window alerts me to Jimmy's return. I am standing at the foot of the stairs, my elbow casually resting on the age-blackened newel post. The yellow dog has wandered into the room, his ears lifted and his nose pointed toward the front door. As my big brother pushes open the heavy door, the headlights are in my eyes, so I can't see the vehicle behind him, but I do notice that they're that sodium-style, a curving pattern of small bright lights, suggesting the eyes of a predator. Suggesting an expensive car like the one that backed out of here the other night and turned into Poor Farm Estates. Jimmy is bathed in that harsh bluish light. The dog growls.

"Hey, Coop, how the hell are you?" Jimmy slams the front door and grabs me in a headlock, throws a mock punch at my face.

Again, the yellow dog growls, a throaty warning. He's got his eyes on Jimmy, the first dominant gesture I've ever seen him make. His ears are flattened against the side of his lowered head and he growls a third time. His whole body is stiff, his tail straight out behind him.

"What the . . . " Jimmy releases me and for a sick moment I think he's going to kick him.

"Don't touch him." I push between them. I'm not under any illusion that the dog is protecting me. As soon as I speak, the dog moves behind me, trembling visibly, head lowered, tail tucked as if embarrassed at his own temerity, waiting for punishment. He begins panting, emitting a barely audible wheeze.

Jimmy scares him. Jimmy scares me a little. I'm not afraid of him, but I am afraid of the man he's become. Yeah, you might say that it was inevitable, but it still shocks me to see just how hardened he is. It isn't just the prison time, or his choice of career. I've known plenty of parolees and career criminals who had more than a flicker of humanity left in them. With Jimmy, it's an evolution that began a long time ago. There is a deadness in his eyes. He is capable of kicking this dog, and enjoying it. "Back off, Jimmy."

"Put him outside. I don't want no dog wandering around in here."

"He's not a sniffer dog, so I guess you don't have anything to worry about."

"What's that supposed to mean?"

"Means whatever you want it to." I put my hand on the dog and feel him trembling. He shrinks away from my hand and I know that I've lost ground with him.

Bull comes in. "Knock it off. Both of you. It's freakin' Christmas." He's got a dish towel over his shoulder, a can of Coke in one hand. "Come on, dog. I got something for you."

The yellow dog slips out from behind me and follows Bull into the kitchen.

"Why all the locks, Jimmy? What are you hiding?"

My brother stares at me for a deathless moment. "Keepin' Bull out of my booze. That's all. Nothing for *you* to worry about."

32

The lasagna is a little cold in the center, but Bull sets it on the table and they each hack off a block, eating without speaking. As soon as Cooper finishes his, he gets up and clears his place like a good boy. He snaps his fingers at the dog, who is pressed against the back door, as if hoping someone will let him escape. "Thanks for dinner. I've got to be going."

"Wait, Coop. I got presents." Bull shoves his plate to the middle of the table, tries not to notice the look on Cooper's face, like he's afraid this Christmas family reunion will never end.

In the sitting room, Bull hands Cooper a wrapped box, embellished with two stick-on bows, one red, one green, and gives another box to Jimmy, who sets it beside his chair. Cooper gives Bull an unwrapped carton of Camels and a gift bag with snowflakes all over it, then hands Jimmy a wrapped box. He isn't going to think about the fact that Jimmy hasn't bothered with presents. Jimmy's a busy guy. He doesn't have to buy presents for his father anymore. He's too old for that sort of nonsense. He's sitting there in that chair, both feet planted flat on the floor, fidgeting with a hangnail, preoccupied.

When Cooper was a little kid, it was tradition for him to open his presents first because he was the youngest. This time, he tells Bull to open his first. He's pleased with the gifts from his second son, says that they're real thoughtful. He puts on the hat and models the gloves. "Thanks, Coop, they're perfect."

Jimmy shakes his box of chocolates and says. "So much for Weight Watchers." Bull wonders if Jimmy is saying this for effect because he thinks that Cooper has noticed the food scale sitting out on the cluttered counter and suspects what that scale might really be for. Bull's never seen Jimmy weigh any food.

"I think that you can allow yourself one a day. That won't push the scale over." Cooper glances in the direction of the kitchen, where the scale is.

"Open yours." Bull has cracked open the cigarette carton. "Go on." He pulls out a fresh pack, taps it against his knee.

Cooper pokes a finger under the tape and pulls away the wrapping. Bull remembers when it was almost as exiting for him on Christmas morning as it was for the boys. That exquisite moment just before they opened the boxes, when you hoped that you'd been a good Santa. That nanosecond before you saw the disappointment that the Nintendo was used or the sneakers weren't Air Jordans, but a Kmart knockoff.

Cooper opens the box and looks up. "Hey, thanks, Bull. That's nice." He holds up the tie. It's a paisley design, greens and blues and yellows.

"I figured you could use it; you know, a man can always use a tie."

"It's great. I'm sure I'll have an opportunity to wear it." Cooper carefully returns the tie to the box, folds the tissue back over it.

"Like maybe New Year's Eve, like if you go to a nightclub or something." Bull is scrambling to figure out how to justify this gift, but Cooper eases him.

"Exactly what I was thinking."

"Jimmy, open yours."

Bull has picked out a tie with tiny fleurs-de-lis in yellow against a blue background for Jimmy.

"Oh good. A tie." Jimmy dangles the tie in the air, then drapes it over his neck. "Perfect for meetings with my parole officer."

Bull makes himself laugh; he's learning to treat a lot of what Jimmy says as if he's playing him. Kidding around. As if the son who has come to live with him—uninvited—is just joking around. That half of what he says or demands is him being deadpan funny. Not abuse.

"You guys can swap 'em if you want." Bull hadn't labeled either box, just handed them to his sons randomly. Like everything else in his life, random always seems to work best. Planning and thinking ahead are for other people. One day at a time—that's all he can cope with.

Cooper makes his good-byes, calls the dog, and is gone. Jimmy is in the kitchen, microwaving a second helping of the oily lasagna, the tie still draped around his neck. Bull taps a Camel out of the new pack, pats his pockets for his little green Bic lighter. He lights up and Jimmy swings around. "Outside with that. I don't want any more of your secondhand smoke"

"My house."

"You can kill yourself with those things, but not me."

"Nothing worse than a reformed smoker." Bull jets a stream of smoke in Jimmy's direction. "Holier than thou."

"Want me to crack out the Jack Daniel's? I got some in my room. Finish yourself off properly."

"I'm touched by your concern." Cigarette between his fingers, Bull points at Jimmy. "You got the end of that tie in your plate."

After the warmth of the house, the air outside is cold but nice. Bull stands there, looking at the stars, smoking one cigarette and then another. He can't seem to get it off his mind; just behind a locked door is his former best friend, Jack Daniel's. Glancing through the kitchen window, Bull sees Jimmy, the bottle in his hand. This is Christmas; surely there'd be no harm in a finger or two. A little celebration. Leave it to Jimmy to poke him with the pointy end of the stick of temptation.

He sucks down another lungful of smoke, exhales into the night sky. He's gone this long without it. He can keep going.

Bull goes over to the Nova, brushes the last of the snow off the roof with the side of his hand.

33

I t's not that late when I leave Bull's, so I head over to Deke's. The old man is happy enough to get the chicken, calling me "real thoughtful," but I think that he would have been happier with the candy. He doesn't say anything about our argument, and neither do I. We're New England men; we don't have to say "water under the bridge" to know that it is forgotten.

What is weird, though, is the dog. We're inside the house for a few minutes when the dog starts up again with his fearful trembling, eyes glazed, tongue hanging out, panting in the decidedly under-heated house. At first, I think he's having a seizure, but then I figure it out. This was exactly how he reacted to Jimmy. He'd already let Deke pat him on the head, so I know it isn't fear of this male human that is causing his panic. I glimpse Deke's shotgun by the back door. It's an old one, his father's gun. Now his gun. Right there.

"Can I look at your gun?"

Deke gives me a puzzled look; this gun has been in this house since I was a kid. He picks it up and hands it to me, at which moment the dog literally cries out—a yowl so plaintive that I feel cruel for instigating it. Deke's sleeping collie lifts her head from her paws and gets to her feet, shakes, and goes over to where the yellow dog has pressed himself against the back door. She gives him a nuzzle, as if to say, *You're okay.* He visibly relaxes.

"I think maybe he's gun-shy." Deke kindly takes the gun away from me, putting it in a closet, out of sight of the dog.

The power of a dog's olfactory sensors is astounding. It isn't out of the ordinary for a dog to know the scent of a firearm, especially one that's been fired. Argos could ferret out a handgun on a perp even before we frisked him. But having a dog react with a fear association is pretty odd. Unless you knew that he'd been shot. Dogs aren't necessarily tuned in to cause and effect, but this pup clearly understands the relationship between the scent of a gun and the hurt of a gunshot wound. And now I have a hunch why, far from his usual stranger/danger cower, the dog overreacted toward my brother with fear aggression. Carrying a concealed weapon is a big no-no when you're a parolee, and so I have something else to add to my growing list of suspicions about my dear brother. I have no doubt in my mind that Jimmy was carrying somewhere on his person.

There are two sides to the equation of drug dealing: the dealer and the buyer. If Jimmy is back in business, then who are his buyers? The third player is the supplier, the one who provides the merchandise in quantity to the dealer. My question about Jimmy isn't whether he's back in the business, but at what level. Is he supplying small-time dealers, or is he selling the stuff himself to stupid college kids who want to ace physics exams with the help of speed, or bored housewives nostalgic for their hippie youth and looking for an ounce of weed? And, who's bankrolling him? He certainly didn't come out of prison with a savings account.

I have to stop doing this, thinking like a cop. I'm not a cop. Not anymore. As far as I know, there's no law against keeping a food scale on a kitchen counter. There's no law against locks on doors. I don't have enough hard evidence to get a search warrant, even if I had the authority to ask for one. Even if it walks like a duck and quacks like a duck, you still need to be an officer of the law to convince a judge to issue a search warrant. But I do have Lev Parker. Maybe tomorrow I'll drop into Lev's office and put a bug in his ear. Lev is a good cop and I bet that Jimmy is already on his radar, but I can add a little inside information—the locked doors, the possible concealed weapon—and maybe get Jimmy on Lev's to-do list. How's that for brotherly love?

"Jimmy stop it. Stop it." The smaller of the two Harrison boys is crying, bloodied, on the ground and his older brother won't stop pummeling him. Cooper has no idea why his brother is beating him up after accusing him of a theft he didn't commit. No one touched his precious stash of pot. Cooper didn't even know Jimmy had it. But Jimmy has lashed out and accused Cooper because he's the only one who's ever followed Jimmy into the shed. But that was months ago, and he didn't see anything more than Jimmy firing up a cigarette. A cigarette. Nothing that Cooper would ever be interested in. He hates them, how they make his house stink, how they make his father's breath foul.*

"You stole it. Either give it back or give me the money." Jimmy punctuates each word with an open-handed slap against the side of his brother's face. At thirteen, he outweighs his brother by twenty pounds.

Cooper is pinned, crushed by his brother's weight and fury. "I didn't take anything. I didn't."

Suddenly, a massive hand has Jimmy by the collar, lifting him up and off of his brother. Cooper gets to his knees, gasping, crying like a baby.

"What the hell are you doing to your brother?" Bull shakes Jimmy. "You trying to kill him?"

"He stole from me."

"So what? That's what brothers do. I stole from mine, and I may have smacked him, but I sure didn't beat the crap out of him. Cooper, go to the house."

Cooper is rooted to the spot, still crying.

"What do you think he stole, Jimmy?"

Jimmy is dead silent. He's nearly as tall as Bull, and he straightens him-self so that the distance between their eyes is only a matter of inches. "Maybe it wasn't Coop. Maybe it was you."

With singular clarity, Cooper understands that this time Jimmy has it right.

Bull starts to laugh. "I'm saving your ass, boy. You're too young for that stuff."

"I don't use it, Bull."

"I see. Cooper, I told you to go back in the house."

Cooper stays, fascinated.

"How much you pay for it?"

"Less than I'll earn selling it."

"I want a cut."

"No."

"Ain't negotiable."

Jimmy has lost entirely the aspect of boyhood as he jabs a finger into his father's chest. "Mom sure would love to know you're using again. What was it she said the last time? Oh, yeah, that she'd leave your sorry ass forever if she found out you were back on drugs."

"She never meant pot. Besides, you tell her, and she'll flush it. You'll get nothing."

Jimmy contemplates this. "All right. No more than five percent."

"Ten."

"And you tell Cooper to keep his mouth shut."

"You hear that, Coop? This is our secret. Now go get washed."

In the house, Mona finds Cooper in the bathroom, bloody washcloth in his hands. She wants to know what happened. "Nothing. Me and Jimmy got into a fight."

"About what?"

"Nothing."

"Sure doesn't look like nothing to me." Mona takes the washcloth, rinses it, and gently cleans Cooper's face.

He won't tell her. He knows that if she ever leaves Bull again, she'll leave them all behind. Jimmy is too much for her, and Cooper knows it. He hears her crying when she thinks that no one's at home, frustrated by yet another call from the school, or a complaining neighbor. The "Bad Seed," that's what she calls her elder child. "Damien." "Rosemary's Baby." She has lots of names for her elder son, who, for reasons she cannot fathom, has taken all of the worst of both of them and become something wholly frightening.

If it wasn't for Jimmy, maybe they'd be a happy family. His father could stop drinking for real without the stress of a juvenile delinquent in the house. His mother could relax, not keep waiting for the next bad thing to happen.

I've struck out with the dog today. Two fear-inducing incidents in one day has proved too much for him. We leave Deke's and I practically have to drag him into the truck. Like a wrong-headed horse on the end of a lead line, he bucks and kicks and almost wriggles out of his collar. I lift him into the truck and slam the door. I'm exhausted. This day, which started out so peacefully, has gone south. I should drop him off at the shelter, give us both a night away from each other, but the shelter is out of my way and I just want to go home.

And so I drive back to my isolated cabin, one unhappy dog in the backseat, my stomach rebelling against the glob of undercooked lasagna sitting in it, and all sense of the Christmas spirit dissolved away.

34

B ull asked Jimmy to give him a ride to work, it had been raining all night and more rain was predicted. Jimmy wouldn't
leave the house to give his father a ride to work because he said he
had "friends" coming over and he didn't know when they'd show
up. As if real friends wouldn't sit and wait for him. Such crap. As
he was pedaling his Raleigh bicycle down the shoulder of Route 114,
an approaching car hit a massive puddle and the spray hit Bull
with full force, soaking his jacket and pants. Having dicked around
waiting for Jimmy to offer him a ride, Bull was already late to work,
no time to turn around and get dry clothes on. So he spent the day
in the lumberyard, wet and cold. Try though he might, he couldn't
talk the boss into finding him an inside job today, and he had spent
the last eight hours in varying degrees of wet and cold, culminating
in the long bike ride home along poorly drained roads, once again
being hit with the backwash of cars passing him. He knew he should
quit that friggin' job. He'd quit better jobs for less reason.

Now he's home, and even if he's changed into ratty sweats, he's
still shivering with the kind of deep internal cold that can be heated

up only by one thing. Bull knows that Jimmy has a bottle of Jack in his room. He brings it out now and again when he's in a mood, teasing his old man with it. "Want some? Oh, right. You're a teetotaler now. Bottoms up." He always was a little prick. Even as a kid. He used to tease Cooper unmercifully, giving him a Matchbox car that the kid coveted and then taking it away. Later, as they got older, he stole Coop's homework and burned it up or threw it into the toilet. Kid stuff. Wasn't happy till he got Cooper crying.

That lock wouldn't really keep him out. A Phillips-head screwdriver would fix the problem, and then he could put it back, with Jimmy none the wiser. Just a swallow. Just enough to get the old internal combustion going. A finger. Two at most. Bull stands at the kitchen junk drawer, his hand on the pull. Sure, there's got to be a screwdriver in there. Everything finds its way into this drawer. One of Mona's pet peeves. "Can't you ever put your tools back where they belong and not in my kitchen drawer?" she'd say. She had a lot of pet peeves, like putting dirty clothes in the hamper, not on the bedroom floor; never driving the boys when he'd been drinking, which was a hard one, because he was always drinking in those days.

He tries hard not to think about it, what happened. Just accept it. That's what they say. Accept what you can, change what you can, and know the difference. Bull's a little tired of having to hold up everything he does or thinks against a saying. He yanks open the drawer and, sure enough, underneath the crazy salad of string and bottle openers, broken crayons, dry Sharpie markers, spatulas, and paper clips, there is a screwdriver. A nice Stanley. Probably the one Jimmy used to install those locks in the first place.

The Nova is facing the road. He's been meaning to get the brake fluid into it for a couple of weeks now. When you step on the brakes, the pedal goes almost to the floor. He's pretty sure it's just low on fluid. Nothing more serious. No big deal, not really. He'll pick up some brake fluid at the gas station next time he gets gas. But he forgets. Mona's car is fine except for that low tire. Cars. Jeez, always something to worry about. No big deal, either. She's plenty capable of putting air in her own tire.

The school has called and Mona has flown out of here like her tail is on fire, equally angry that she's going to be late for work again and angry that her elder son has committed yet another schoolboy crime. She's left Bull in the kitchen, his head in his hands, completely incapable of handling this latest incident with his son. "Don't come," she'd said. "It's worse when you come." Not mere bullying this time, but the principal has accused Jimmy of nearly drowning a fourth grader. Not just shaking him down for his lunch money but then sticking his head in a toilet. Bull sits at the kitchen table, protesting: "If they had a separate junior high in this town, he wouldn't be picking on little kids for their lunch money." Mona tells Bull that he's missing the point. He always misses the point. Something has to be done about Jimmy, before he kills someone. Can you imagine a mother saying that about her kid? Bull gets to his feet, fighting to get his balance. It's ten-thirty in the morning and he's well into his daily drunk. He's unemployed again, and Mona's job as a medical receptionist is the only thing keeping her head up as she hands food stamps over to the cashier in the grocery store. "He'll be fine," he says. As he always says when the subject of Jimmy's increasingly antisocial behavior is the only topic Mona is chewing on.

Then she asks the one question he's been hoping she won't. "How do you suppose Jimmy came by that new PlayStation? The one he thinks I don't know he has? Stolen? Or paid for? How, Bull? Fourth grader's lunch money? I don't think so. And I think you do know. This has got to stop, Bull. I can't take it anymore."

Mona didn't slam the door when she left the house to meet with the principal. She'd gently shut the front door, the click of the latch echoing in the suddenly silent house. The sound of finality. Bull leaned one sweaty palm against the windowpane to watch her drive away, thinking that she shouldn't have taken the Nova.

Six months after Mona's death, Jimmy did his first turn in juvie, not quite fourteen years old.

The sizzle of sleet smacking against the kitchen window snaps Bull out of his reverie. He has the screwdriver in his hand and he's staring at it as if it's a mystery how it came to be there.

35

It's Friday night and I don't have a date. Max isn't coming home from his week at Tufts until tomorrow and Natalie is picking up a new rehab project.

Rather than spend yet another night with only the company of a dog who keeps himself to himself, I head out to the Lakeside Tavern, dog safely in the backseat. I can't afford to lose any more running shoes. It really is time to incarcerate my canine roommate, but I don't. I've got Jenny on the case, building up a nice Facebook presence for him, and she tells me that, given his pathological shyness, the more home time he can get, the better it will be. I suggest she offer him accommodations, but she demurs. Can't. Boyfriend is allergic. Yeah, right.

The calendar has tripped over into a new year, and the Barkwell people are still away. I've filled their answering machine, so I don't even get the recorded beep anymore. They have a fairly amateurish Web site, loads of pictures of cute puppies interacting with cute toddlers, but it's very static, no e-mail-contact button. I'm just a hair short of driving up there to wait it out on their front step.

The yellow dog settles himself down on the foam dog bed I've placed on my backseat. I bought it because I'm sick of dog hair all over my truck. He does seem to like it, and I know that it keeps him warm. I've tossed an old blanket over him just so that I won't be accused of leaving a dog out in the cold. Food, water, shelter—the basic tenets of good pet keeping. Not that I'm keeping him.

The Lakeside is bustling, so I head to the bar and squeeze myself in to stand between two guys perched on tall stools; nod to my left, nod to my right. The bartender knows me well enough that he brings over an IPA without my having to order it. I don't know if that's scary or an endearing example of life in a small town. I'm thirsty, so I go with the latter. The best part about standing at the bar is the fact that with your back to the room, you might not see people you don't want to see. You don't watch the door; you don't have to greet every person who walks by your table. In effect, it's perfect privacy. My left-hand neighbor isn't chatty; his eyes are fixed on the closed-captioned evening news. The guy to my right has a girl on his other side and he's playing one of those little wooden pegboard games with her, taking every chance he can to touch some part of her body. Sweet. Sort of. Or creepy. I don't know. I can't see her face, so I don't know if she's lapping up the attention or ready to slug him. I stand ready if she should choose to protest his attentions. These are the thoughts that are bouncing around in my mind when I hear a familiar voice and a meaty hand claps me on the back hard enough that I knock my beer over.

Bull, fully shit-faced. My father, fallen gloriously off the wagon.

I shovel Bull into the front seat of the truck. The yellow dog gets up and pokes his nose over the seat back, sniffs Bull's cheek, and then retreats to his bed. Bull stinks so badly of booze that even the dog has turned up his nose. I have no idea how he got himself to the Lakeside. I don't see his bike, and the bartender was pretty quick to say he hadn't served him. I have one idea—other than that he was hitchhiking and some sap picked him up—and that's Jimmy.

"Bull, what the hell happened?"

"Nothin'." He's got that belligerent tone I associate with his mid-drunk state. Early, you can hardly tell he's been drinking. Late, and he's soppy and your best friend. Somewhere between the extremes, Bull's latent anger begins to show.

I look over at him. In the quick dash of light from a streetlamp, I can see that he looks like he's been smacked around.

"Did you fall?"

He doesn't answer right away. Then: "Yeah. I fell."

"Off your bike."

"I guess."

"Did Jimmy hit you?"

Bull closes his eyes and they sink beneath the swollen flesh of his cheeks.

"Is he at the house?"

"I don't know. I guess." There is something else in his tone now. He's afraid I'm going to take him back there, to his own house. He's squeezing his hands together, fingers intertwined into a prayerful fist. For some reason, I notice that he's still wearing his wedding ring, a thin gold band that has embedded itself into his finger.

"What happened? What did Jimmy do?" I can't keep the anger out of my voice, the simmering rage that I have toward this brother of mine who is at the heart of all the bad things that ever happened to my family.

"Shut up, Cooper. Just please shut up."

Behind me, the dog whines.

I have no choice but to take Bull home with me. I half-carry, half-drag him out of the truck, forgetting for the moment that the dog is loose, free to walk off and back into the woods. But he doesn't. He follows us in and watches from the safety of his basket as I drop Bull onto my couch in an inelegant maneuver that nearly takes me off my feet. He outweighs me significantly and I certainly don't have the upper-body strength I used to when part of my daily routine was weight lifting in the precinct gym. Bull is either instantly asleep or unconscious. He's breathing, so I leave him there. Funny, but all I want right now is a beer. The one I didn't get, courtesy of my father's drunken greeting. I'm not sure I even paid for it. Great, let's add drink and dash to the list of sins of the Harrisons of Harmony Farms.

I grab a cold one out of my fridge, go out on the porch, and sit in one of the two plastic chairs my landlord has thoughtfully provided, slowly drinking my beer. By the time it's gone and I'm chilled to the bone, I've calmed down, made a plan. Bull can stay tonight, and tomorrow I'll get him to see that he needs to get Jimmy out. Now. Better yet, I'll try to talk him into pressing charges against Jimmy for assault. Parental abuse, for God's sake. Even as I consider that lovely thought, I know that there is no way I could ever get Bull to turn on Jimmy. He never has, and he never will. Jimmy is like his blind spot. I remember it so well, Bull defending Jimmy over and over. No matter what the infraction, it was always someone else's fault.

I push the door open and am blown away to see the yellow dog nestled in beside Bull on the couch, stretched out full length beside the snoring man, his head cradled in the crook of Bull's arm. He rolls his brown eyes toward me, and the very tip of his tail thumps against the cushion, as if to say, *It's okay. This is where I'm supposed to be. He'll be fine.*

Bull is standing in my kitchen, a quart of milk up to his nose to see if it's gone off. He's made a pot of coffee and the table is set for breakfast. He looks at me, smiles his patented big baby grin, and says good morning. I've been awake most of the night, fretting over him, and here he is, none the worse for wear except for the bruise on his left cheek and the dull shiner above it. I look around for the dog.

"He's been out."

"Okay. You walked him?"

"No. He went out; then he came back in."

Guess I shouldn't worry any more about his taking off. That's progress of a sort. I take the mug of coffee Bull hands me, sit at the table. He's fussing over scrambled eggs and I'm cast back into a time when he was the chief cook and bottle washer of the family. We didn't eat at McDonald's, at least not every night. Bull may have been half in the bag, but he always put a home-cooked meal on the table. I don't think I ever gave it a thought. Hot dogs and hamburgers, spaghetti, meat loaf—basic stuff. And something he called "slumgullion"—hamburger and stewed tomatoes with elbow macaroni. I get a craving for it as I sit at my own table, a grown man.

"Bull, are you going to tell me what happened?"

"When?"

"I don't know. Let's start with last night and work backward. What happened?"

"I went where I shouldn't have." Bull pulls the other chair out and sits heavily, props his elbows on the table and cradles his coffee mug. "End of story."

"And Jimmy caught you."

He nods.

"And smacked you around."

"I fell."

The eggs are starting to smoke a little and I jump up to rescue them. The dog has come into the room, takes a lap at his water. Bull pats his knee and the dog joins him on that side of the table. I look at the back of my father's head and am filled with despair. A first cousin to the kind of despair I felt in those first dark days after I lost Argos.

"Why, Bull? Why now? You've been sober for years."

"No, son. I've been sober for about eight hours."

"Will you start again, staying sober?"

"I can't say."

"Will you at least try?"

"You can't ask that, Coop."

"Maybe not, but I can ask what pushed you off the wagon this time." I spoon eggs onto his plate, onto mine. Grab the already-cold toast out of the toaster.

Bull gets up to get the ketchup out of the refrigerator, shakes a puddle of the stuff onto his plate, and tucks into his breakfast. He sips his coffee, looks at me, then sets his plate on the floor for the dog. "I can't tell you why I went off. I don't rightly know. Sometimes the trigger isn't obvious. I was cold, tired. Didn't think to call my sponsor. Was thinking about things I haven't thought about for a while."

"What kind of things?"

"Just things." Bull doesn't look at me, a classic avoidance technique used by liars. I didn't do a lot of questioning in interview rooms; my job—our job—was to catch them, not interrogate them. But on more than one occasion, I did question a felon, maybe even threatened him with the dog if I didn't like the answers he was giving me. Except for Jimmy, who can look you in the eye and tell you the most outrageous lie, most liars can't look you in the eye. They don't even know they're doing it, looking away. It's instinct.

I snatch up Bull's plate from the floor, drop it in the sink. I school myself to remain patient, like Natalie working with a stubborn horse. Never show anger. I think that it's important to know why Bull drank, because my own instincts suggest that Jimmy is behind it. So I don't face Bull when I ask the same question in a different way. A leading question. "So, why were you so cold?"

Bull has the dog's head in his hands and he's playing with his muzzle. The dog's tail swings back and forth in a languid sweep. His eyes are closed.

"Got wet going to work; boss kept me out in the yard all day. I was freezin' when I got home."

"Couldn't you have grabbed a ride with Jimmy?"

Silence.

I run the hot water, squeeze in too much liquid. "He's too busy?"

"Yeah. Something like that." Bull runs his hands down the length of the dog, scratches at the base of his tail.

"What else does he have in his room, Bull? You notice anything?"

"I was fixed on that bottle. There it was, sitting there in the middle of his bureau like it had my name on it."

"I think that it probably did." I wouldn't put it past Jimmy to entrap Bull this way. Just for fun. And if that was the case, then why did he get violent with Bull? Why did he smack him? Dump him at the Lakeside? He'd do that only if he was angry, and he'd most likely been angry because Bull did more than swipe that bottle. "When did he hit you?"

"Who said he did?"

"That shiner."

Bull touches his eye. "I told you, Coop, I fell."

"Can't you at least be honest with me? Jimmy hit you and it wasn't just for taking that bottle." I'm fast losing any advantage I have; losing my temper. "Bull. He needs to get out of your house. I can help you. You don't have to let him stay there."

Bull gives me a baleful look, slowly shakes his head. "But then I'd be alone."

36

Polly Schaeffer sits in front of me, her usual caftan abandoned in deference to the polar vortex we're enduring this winter. She's in a full-length faux-fur coat, equally faux Russian soldier-style hat. The warmth from the office has steamed up her glasses and she pulls them off, looking at me with myopic intensity. Ever since Roger spirited away her cat collection, Polly has been a ghost of her former self. She's lost her sparkle, her smile. I really think that what her son did was pretty reprehensible, even if understandable on one level. But he could have left her one or two. I'm hoping that I can cheer her up.

Jenny has tendered her notice. Just before we left work on Friday, she came up to me, handed me an actual resignation letter, and then burst into tears.

Like a good boss, I read the letter, folded it, and put it back in the envelope. She's got another job. She's taking what she does here and going to a big nonprofit shelter in New York State. "That's great, Jen, really great. They're lucky to get you." I'm not the world's most demonstrative man, and I knew that I was perilously close to overstepping the boss/employee boundary, but, what the hell, I got up from my desk and gave her a big hug. She pulled herself together and we had one of those clumsy laughs that people whose connection is about to be severed enjoy.

She's the one who suggested Polly as a replacement. "She's got a lot of love in her just wasting away. She knows her way around a kennel."

"She'll want to take them all home."

"She'll need boundaries, sure. But you're good at boundaries."

"Polly, would you be interested in a job?" I ask her now.

Polly has enough self-respect to act like she's weighing the pros and cons of the offer that I've made her. "I'm a little *mature* for a lot of heavy lifting."

"No heavy lifting."

"I won't watch you put them down."

"I don't put them down. Part of your job is to find them homes."

"What hours? I have my shows that I like."

The finance committee is going to be very pleased with me. I give her several hours less than what Jenny worked, and offer her a step-one salary, which is a tick above minimum wage. The town is going to be saving a little money. Go me.

Which makes me think about my own future. My audiologist has given me the good news about my hearing. The tinnitus is nearly gone, and although I'll never hear well out of my left ear, I made the thirty decibel or better benchmark. The rest of me is back in form. The running and the wood chopping, the lifting of cages and canines has brought me back into shape. In other words, for the first time in a year, I'm fit for duty. At least physically.

I've left the yellow dog with Bull at my cabin. I offered to drive him to work, but apparently Monday is his day off. Neither was he in a hurry to go back to his own house. I kept my mouth shut. He spent the weekend with me, and it didn't suck. Sober, he's a pretty good cribbage player. We walked the perimeter of Bartlett's Pond, the dog with us. For the first time, I dared to let the dog off the leash and was gratified to have him chug along with us, sniffing and peeing, crushing the new ice beginning to form at the water's edge as he waded in, lapping at the cold pond water.

"I was glad when you didn't go into the service." Bull said this apropos of nothing. "Glad you didn't follow in the old man's footsteps."

I could hardly tell him that there was no way I'd ever consider following in his footsteps, but civility kept my mouth shut. So I just asked why he was thinking of that.

"I don't know. I guess because sometimes I think that what happened to you was a little bit like what happened to me. Over there."

"Vietnam?"

"Yeah."

"How so?"

"Sudden death. It haunts you. Nothing clean about it. You wonder why you survived and other guys didn't."

I was speechless.

"I heard you last night." Bull patted his leg and the yellow dog left the edge of the pond.

"Heard me what?"

"You know. Dreaming."

"Yeah. I was." I snatched a stick up from the ground, flung it into the pond. "Does it ever get better?"

"For some, I guess. Not so much for me."

I wanted to ask him if he thought I'd ever recover. But I was afraid of the answer.

Jimmy called to ask if I knew where Bull was, as if he didn't have anything to do with his absence. I played it straight, as if he actually didn't. "He's a little banged up. I told him he could stay here."

"Good. Keep him."

"Hey, Jimmy?"

"Yeah?"

"What are you selling?"

Jimmy didn't even bother to tell me to go fuck myself, just hung up.

I took Bull's house key with me when I left the cabin this morning. I slipped it out of his jacket pocket and kind of forgot to mention it to him. I think I'll just stop by the house and get him some clean clothes. He could use some clean clothes.

An emergency call keeps me from going home at lunchtime. Bull doesn't have his cell phone, so there's no way I can call and tell him I won't be back when I said I would. What the heck, he's probably forgotten that I said I'd be home at noontime. I feel kind of bad about that. The call takes me out to the highway, where a dog has been sighted wandering along the breakdown lane. I'm dreading what I might find, but the gods are with me and I slip in behind him as he trots south. He's a fairly sizable mutt, what I would call a collie-shepherd cross, but for all I know, he may be some kind of designer dog. He's all business, ignoring the backwash of semis and cars merging onto the highway. I set my flashers and get out, catch pole in one hand, liver treats in the other. "Hey, bud." I guess my experience of trying to catch the yellow dog has jaded me, so I am completely surprised when he turns around and walks right up to me, takes the treats, lets me slip a noose over his furry neck and walk him to the truck. That's how it's supposed to be done. Even better, he's got a tag.

Two hours later, I'm still at the office, waiting for Mugsy's owner to show up, and I'm starving. Jenny offers to go get me something, but I decline. I'll deal with Mugsy and then I'll call it an early day. I fill up on yet another cup of coffee. Mugsy's owner isn't going to get the easygoing Cooper Harrison.

By five o'clock, Mugsy's gone home with his grateful family, adorable little kids hanging off his neck and the dad sheepish with relief. I don't even fine them. They're too damn cute to be angry with.

The temperature has dropped considerably from this morning, which started off in the twenties. I hope that Bull hasn't set my cabin on fire stoking the woodstove. Speaking of Bull, I think that maybe now's a good time to take a run past his place on my way home. Any luck at all and Jimmy will be elsewhere and I can, well, I can fetch my poor old dad some clean duds. A legitimate errand even if Jimmy is there. I put my hand in my jacket pocket to make sure that the house key on its plastic fob is handy.

As I pull out of the parking lot, my phone rings. I can't see the display, so I'm flying blind when I push the Bluetooth on. It's Natalie.

"Cooper, how are you?"

"Fine. You?" I recalculate my route to include the scenic drive along the lake, give myself more time. "Did you get that rehab horse?"

"I did. He's a wreck. Worst case of rain rot I've ever seen, and his feet are so overgrown that he can barely walk. I'm sitting here waiting for my farrier and I was just thinking that I hadn't talked with you for a while." There is something in her voice: a weariness I've never heard before.

"Natalie, is everything okay?"

"Sure. "It's just . . . "

"What, Natalie?"

"You ever just want to quit?"

"Yeah. Every day." I'm halfway around the lake. "But I didn't set out to be an ACO, so that's sort of understandable. What's going on with you?"

"I spent my morning breaking ice on the tanks and then trying to get an electrician here to figure out why the heaters keep blowing the circuit breaker. That's the kind of thing that sometimes gets me to wondering why I'm doing this. Is it worth it? To save, what, four animals? There were three others at this place, just as bad as this one, and because I haven't got the room, I can't save them."

"I know. Sometimes it just sucks." I get brave. "Want me to come by?"

"I wish you would. How about you bring dinner? Something easy."

I think that's about the best offer I've had in a long time.

As I had hoped, Jimmy's car is gone. I pull in, boldly parking the truck in front of the house. If Jimmy comes home, he'll have no doubt that I'm there and he'll be a trifle concerned at what I may have discovered. Maybe it will be enough to give him a little hint that his operation, whatever it might be, would be better served elsewhere. I walk around to the back door, past the up-on-blocks Nova.

Inside, I quickly grab a plastic bag and fill it with Bull's stuff just in case; if Jimmy does show up, I'll have my prop handy. While in the kitchen, I yank open the fridge and help myself to some leftover pizza. Then I get to work.

This would be so much easier if I had Argos. I have to stop thinking like that, I know. But it's true. Although, technically, he was a tracker, a dog trained as a sniffer would be able to pinpoint the location of Jimmy's stash without my having to resort to screwdrivers and guesswork. My guess is that Jimmy has a bunch of red herrings in this house. That is, these padlocks aren't all securing his merchandise. He's probably got one, maybe two hiding places. I mean, who would be so obvious as to put up padlocks like big red arrows saying: Something's hidden in here! I think that he's been playing with Bull's head. However, I know, I just know, that he's got something stashed in this house, and that's why it would be great to have a drug-sniffing dog with me. Save a heck of a lot of time.

I have to go with the obvious first, Jimmy's room. The hasp and padlock are on the floor; no doubt Jimmy found Bull in flagrante delicto. So the door's wide open, and I boldly enter Jimmy's room, experiencing a subtle flashback to when we were kids and he'd pound me for so much as appearing at his door. It really hasn't changed much. No Arrowsmith posters on the walls anymore, but it still wears the same faded brown-and-white-patterned wallpaper, which is at least three generations old. It still smells like unwashed boy. I don't bother with poking around in the bureau drawers. If he's got something in here, it's beneath the floorboards or in the wall. These antique houses are good for loose floorboards, and Prohibition encouraged the art of hidden cubbies. I step, rock, feeling for a subtle give in the floor, then move the bed, do the same. I slide the bureau away from the wall, knock, listening with my better ear for any hollowness. Jimmy's been hiding drugs in the house since he was a kid; I just have to think like him. Think where he might feel secure leaving his stock. It has to be someplace both secure and handy. Giving up on his room, I decide to check out the closet under the stairs. I pick up the screwdriver from where Bull left it on the floor.

There's no light in the cupboard, and I left my flashlight out in the truck. I can't imagine that there's a working flashlight in this house, but I scurry around to the logical places one might be kept. I locate one, but I'm not surprised to find the batteries dead. I'm running out of time. It's getting dark and I have no idea when Jimmy will come back. Pushing aside coats and boots, I feel around as best I can in that small closet before I screw the hasp back in place.

I've got the plastic bag with Bull's change of clothes and a toothbrush. I take one more circuit of the downstairs, hoping for that aha moment. Nothing. I grab another slice of cold pizza. And then I remember something.

As with a certain subset of rural home owners, ours was a family that never threw anything out. Not string or paper bags, not buttons or Christmas boxes. A Yankee heritage writ large on the back porch, where a doorless refrigerator and a baby carriage still reside long after they reached the limit of their usefulness. In the kitchen, too heavy to move out to the porch, is the aged cast-iron range that my maternal ancestors used, and what was at one time the only source of heat for the house. Tucked up beside it, its successor, a seventies-era white Westinghouse electric stove. The old range has devolved into a kind of handy countertop, piled with pots and pans, a cookbook, magazines, empty salt and pepper shakers. Once, when the electricity went out, I remember Bull firing it up again. There was just enough kerosene left in the glass jug that fed into the burners to get it going so we could have a hot meal. That was okay, but the house was freezing, so Bull then loaded the firebox up with scraps of two-by-fours. Within minutes, the kitchen was filled with smoke. The long-unused chimney was backed up with bird nests and the detritus of years of leaf fall. We survived that, but it was clear, that we should never use that range again, not for cooking and certainly not for heat.

Which makes it the perfect hiding place.

There are two things that a drug dealer generally carries: the drugs and the cash. I open the left-hand oven door, then the right. No drugs. Then I lift the burner plates off the top, reach in. Nothing. Then I smile, tapping the sheet-metal pipe that leads from the back of the range to the chimney. I should hear a hollow ping. I don't. It's more like the sound you get when you knock on a solid wall. Carefully, I pull the stovepipe out of the wall, put my hand in, and touch a brick, and another. Not clay bricks, but bricks of pure heroin. I've been around drug busts enough to know that what my dear brother has stashed away in our childhood home is a freakin' mother lode of heroin. I pull one package out. The trade has its own standards; in my hand is a package of neat little white powder–filled baggies, like the kind jewelers use, banded together and then wrapped into neat bundles. It's hard to say how many bricks are tucked into the stovepipe, but it doesn't really matter. I've seen the evidence with my own eyes. It could be ten bricks or fifty. Thousands or hundreds of thousands of dollars in street value. Plenty to send my brother back to jail for a very long time.

After slipping one tiny Baggie out from one bundle and putting it into the inside pocket of my jacket, I carefully tuck the package back into the stovepipe, then reattach the pipe to the hole in the wall. Then I open the cast-iron door to the old firebox. And there's the cash. Like the heroin, all sorted into neat packages of various denominations, none less than fifty. And there are a lot of them. Makes one wonder why Jimmy is driving a banged-up old Honda. He's got enough here to buy himself a Lexus. I close the door, throw the heavy latch back into place. Or maybe his handler has the Lexus. Again I have to wonder where Jimmy is in the food chain.

I don't have time to ponder this existential question, as the front door opens and Jimmy comes in.

"What are you doing here?" He tosses his keys onto the kitchen table, goes to the fridge, grabs a bottle of water. He's good; I have to give him that. Not once do his eyes go to the old range. He gives off virtually no "tell."

"Just collecting some stuff for Bull." I hold up the plastic grocery bag, take a bite of the old pizza. All perfectly natural.

"You going to keep him? Probably a good idea."

"Just one more night. And it's his house, Jimmy, not yours."

"Will be." He laughs, slugs back half the bottle of water. "Your turn to watch him. He really needs a keeper."

"Maybe so, but you're in his house."

"A couple more nights? Okay?"

"Why?"

Jimmy doesn't answer me. He sits and finishes the water, then shoots the empty bottle into the overflowing trash.

"You should recycle."

"Hardly the worst of my sins."

Jimmy is only a couple of years old than I am, but right now he looks like a middle-aged man, or a man with a really stressful job.

Even though he's been out for a while, he still has that prison pallor, that dull cast to the skin around his eyes and deep circles beneath them. A man who doesn't sleep well. Kind of like how I looked not that long ago, when I was sleepless. Comfortless. Kind of like I still sometimes do when I've had a bad night.

"You should get out of here. Find your own place. Why are you still here?"

"It's convenient. That all right with you?"

"Not if it means Bull is tossed out because you get mad at him."

"He snoops."

"He knew you had that bottle. Something tipped him over the edge. He doesn't care what you may keep in your little boyhood room; he just wanted—"

"I know what he wanted."

"What, Jimmy? What?"

"Same thing he always wants." He's speaking in riddles. Jimmy has always had this amazing ability to confound by a mix of prevarication and non sequitur.

"I think that the only thing Bull wants right now is to cling to his suddenly very new sobriety."

"Best place for that is with you."

"Maybe, but he wants to be home."

But then I'd be alone. I know that when my father said that, my response wasn't supposed to be silence, but an offer of hospitality.

"With you."

Jimmy bleats with laughter. "Me? You've been the son they were proud of. Why does he want to live with me?"

"Beats me."

He looks at me with those water-colored eyes. Dead eyes. Jimmy's eyes have been cold fish eyes for decades. I can't think if I've ever seen even a spark of happiness in them. Or joy, or humor that wasn't at someone else's expense, or anything other than malice. Anger. A nurtured anger. It's on the tip of my tongue to ask him, "What happened to you?" We were raised by the same inept parents, but we weren't abused. We were poor, and the town joke because of Bull, but we were clean and had food on the table. Life wasn't so much one of disappointment, as one of no expectations.

And then I think, Maybe I really don't want to know.

It's five miles, mostly uphill, so Cooper is sweating by the time he arrives at Deke's farm. He's going to ask Deke if he can live with him. It's been a bad couple of days and he just can't go home again. He needs a quiet, safe place to be. He'll do chores, anything. Feed the cows, muck the milking parlor. Collect eggs from the henhouse. Shoot, he'll vacuum and dust Deke's place, anything. Just let him stay. Bull won't miss him. He's got his hands full with Jimmy. Cooper just can't take the yelling anymore.

Deke is out back, tinkering with the tractor, pulling spark plugs out and looking at them in the bright sunlight. "What brings you here?"

Deke's collie goes up to Cooper, sniffs, waits for a pat. "Can I stay with you?" He kneels down, presses his cheek against the dog's skull. "Please."

Deke gets down from his perch to stand beside the boy. Puts a hand on the kid's shoulder and squeezes. "I got a cow about to calf. It's her first. I could use some help keeping an eye on her. Someone to let me know when the action starts."

Cooper spends the night in the barn, waking every hour or so to check on the cow, who doesn't calve that night, or the next. By the time she does, in the middle of the afternoon on the third day, Bull has come to fetch him. "Hey, son, I think it's time you left Deke alone. He's a busy man."

"I'm helping him."

"I know, son. You're a good help." Bull's hand on his shoulder is equally directional and affectionate.

"I've got to go. Bull thought I was coming back at noon, but I haven't gotten home yet."

"You tell him hello for me."

"Yeah, right. I'll tell him you can't wait for him to come home. Tomorrow. After work. I'm warning you: Put the rest of your booze in a better hiding place."

Jimmy gives me a smirk.

I think about the little baggie close to my heart and aim a forefinger at him. "See you around."

I get in my truck, figure I'd better get back to the cabin, see what Bull's been up to. Get him cleaned up and make some dinner. Feed the dog. Pretend like we're normal people. Not an off-the wagon drunk and an erstwhile cop with a drug dealer in the family. Tomorrow things will change. I'll take this lovely piece of evidence to Lev. Drop it on his desk like a cat drops a mouse on the kitchen floor. *You maybe want to get a search warrant now?*

I'll go to Nat's after I check on Bull and the dog. I feel a little twinge of excitement and I can't tell if it's because I'm about to see Natalie or because I'm finally about to nail Jimmy.

37

I t's so dry in here. He's dying of thirst. Must be the heat of the
woodstove, which Bull has stoked to the maximum of its safe
limits. Freakin' cold front. He wasn't wearing all that much when
he left home on Friday, just his hooded sweatshirt, so he's helped
himself to one of Cooper's fleece vests. It doesn't zip over his belly,
but it's a little extra layer. Now the cabin is so hot, he's stripped it
and his flannel shirt off, opened the windows. Give him an oil fur-
nace over wood any day.

Not a big fan of water, Bull opens the refrigerator to see if Cooper keeps any Coke. He shoves the bottles of Sam Adams to one
side, then to the other. An open carton of orange juice. Four bottles of Sam. Carton of milk. Four bottles of Sam. Bull swigs the
juice right from the carton, crushes it, and tosses it in the can. Still
thirsty.

The yellow dog sits in the doorway, watching with a nonjudg-
mental look in his brown doggy eye, just hanging out. Coop won't
miss one. Surely he doesn't keep track of the beer in his fridge. Bull
peels a slice of American cheese off the pound, shares it with the

dog. Still thirsty. Still four bottles of beer on the shelf. This strikes him as funny and Bull starts singing "Ninety-nine bottle of beer on the wall . . . " The dog gets up and climbs into his basket.

No TV. What's wrong with that boy? Probably no cable out here in the sticks, so why bother. On the other hand, Cooper must make enough to get one of those dishes. Bull's beginning to feel sorry that he didn't take up Coop's offer to take him home. Even if Jimmy does get mad at him when he finally goes back, he never said Bull should stay away forever. When Jimmy's mad, it's best to stay out of his way, but three days is probably long enough. Boy, was he mad. Maddest Bull's ever seen him, and that's saying a lot. He remembers those tantrums the boy threw as a three-year-old; they were epic. Feet banging, head banging. Making himself sick with screaming. Poor Mona, trying to rein in that kind of fury with her body, getting kicked, scratched.

Still thirsty. Still four bottles of Sam Adams in the refrigerator. Bull remembers a time when he could drink beer as if it were water, with about the same effect. Nothing. Nada. Peed a lot, that's about it. When he was a grunt in Nam, beer fulfilled all his liquid requirements. When he wanted a buzz—and that was pretty much all the time—he used more interesting, less liquid substances. And after coming home, miraculously in one piece—not like these kids today who survive their horrendous wounds because battlefield medicine is so good—those substances were the only thing that kept him sane. Sort of. A good blunt in the middle of the night when the dreams would replay his experiences was about the only thing that could calm him down. The smell of a burning roach filling his nostrils was the only thing to overwhelm the stench of burning flesh that lingered in his memory.

Long time ago. Lot of water under the bridge since then. Those poor kids soldiering in those Muslim countries don't even have the comfort of a glass of beer at the end of a mission. And they still have the scent of burned flesh in their noses.

"You want to go for a walk, dog? Coop said he'd be back for lunch. Let's hope he brings some Coke with him."

The yellow dog is immediately on his feet, nose pointed toward the door, tail wagging.

"Don't know why Coop's being so stubborn about you. You're a good dog. Guess there's just no room in his life for another dog. That K-9 partner of his left some mighty big footprints." Bull manages to zip up the too-small vest and they head out to circle the pond.

It's well past noon when they get back. No Cooper. Bull checks to see if somehow he's missed him, but there's no note. No change in the contents of the refrigerator. Still four bottles of beer. Bull needs to call his sponsor. The four bottles of beer are lying in wait for him, ready to trip him up a mere two, three days back into his sobriety. His sponsor will come and get him, but he needs to get to a phone to make that happen. How far is the main road? Not that far. For a man who bikes to work every day, a mile or two isn't that much. He can thumb a ride into town, maybe get dropped off at Cumbie's, the last place in Harmony Farms to have a pay phone. Bull fishes around in his pants pocket to see if there's a quarter. He finds two. Hopefully, that'll be enough. It makes him laugh, the idea that when he was a kid, phone calls were a dime. And he could fill the Nova with gas for about two bucks, three at most if it was bone-dry. Like he is now. What's one beer? It's not the same as indulging in his friends Jack and Jim. He never even feels the first glass of Jim Beam, just enjoys the bite on his tongue. By the second glass of Jack, if that's what he's drinking, there's only the smooth succor of warmth in his belly. By the next or the next, then he might be feeling a little . . . well, let's call it *content*. Beer hasn't got that power. Beer just goes down easy when you're thirsty. Which is what he is now. It'll take him an hour to get to Cumbie's, at the very least. Plenty of time for one beer to work through his system, even two.

Cooper's organized; Bull will give him that. Bottle opener is in the silverware drawer, right where you'd expect to find it.

When he pops the cap off the third beer, Bull is at the content-ment stage. Life is all right. Maybe not good, but all right. Funny how beer usually does nothing for him. Must be that his resistance is low from being a teetotaler all this time. Bull gets up, amazed to feel the buzz. Amazed to have to reach for the back of the couch to steady himself. The yellow dog looks at him with this extraordinary look of concern. Who knew a dog could look like he thinks you're in trouble. "It's okay, dog. I'm okay."

It wasn't Jimmy's fault that he'd succumbed to temptation on Fri-day. That's one of the things he has to remember, that it's no one else's fault. It's his problem. He has to take ownership of it. Bull lines the three empties neatly on the counter, sticks his hand in his pocket again. Still has fifty cents. Still needs to call his sponsor.

"I gotta leave, boy. You wait here for Coop. I'll leave him a note." Cooper is certainly an organization freak, and he has a dry-erase board on the wall with a grocery list on it. His penmanship is precise, tiny. "Milk. Eggs. Bread. Dog food. Call dentist Tues-day. Truck insurance due 15th." Bull adds: "Thanks for every-thing." The three words are disproportionate, the *thanks* outweighs the preposition, and the *everything* peters away to lie up against the edge of the board.

It's getting colder, but Bull remembers to bank the woodstove. He sure wouldn't want Cooper to come home to a burned-down cabin. He's a good guest, so he fetches an armload of wood off the porch. It's a big armload, so he doesn't shut the door, letting the warm air out and the cold air in for the minute or so it takes him to set four splits around the base of the stove to warm them up. Bull pulls his hood up, heads out. It's a trudge, getting to the main road, and Bull keeps his head down and his hands shoved into his kangaroo pocket. The hood helps against the rising wind, even as it limits his peripheral vision. Eyes on the ground, one foot in front of the other, he's hoping that before long he'll hit pavement. The track is pretty easy to follow, although the subtle rise and fall of the terrain keeps catching at his feet. He stays upright; he's not that drunk. One foot in front of the other. Left, right, left. Just like the army.

Behind him is the yellow dog, happy to get another walk. Happy to follow.

It was pleasant, this second walk of the day. The yellow dog follows Bull as he moves along the two-track dirt road. The deepening cold lifts interesting scents up out of the ground, a rabbit, a vole. A coyote, the big male. The dog adds his own scent, obliterating the coyote's mark. The man he knows is called *Bull* keeps moving, muttering human language as he stumbles. His grumbling doesn't put the dog on alert; it's more like that muttery sound his mother once made. A comfortable complaint.

They reach the end of the track and Bull pauses. The dog sits behind him, patiently awaiting the next thing. He's getting a little hungry—which is to say, his normal state of being—and he thinks that going back would be a good idea. But Bull doesn't. So the dog follows, marking places where other dogs have walked along the verge of the paved road.

Cars go by, bending around the bulky form walking backward along the side of the road, his thumb out and his bleary eyes focused on the faces of the drivers who buzz by. Most don't slow; some do and then speed away.

The dog keeps to the bushes, keeping himself out of reach of strangers. Finally, one car stops completely, and Bull disappears into it.

The dog sits, neatly hidden by a screen of stunted junipers. Alone. Hungry. What's that? The sound of a small creature scurrying beneath the crispy layers of leaf fall? The dog drops his nose, finds the scent, and is at once a hunter. Feral. Gone.

38

When I get home, Bull and the dog are gone. At first, I think that maybe he's just gone to give the dog a walk, but then I notice the scrawled thank-you note on the dry-erase board. Okay, he's apparently walked out of here. But the dog? It seems that Bull has taken the dog with him. I don't even try to figure out why he took the dog, it's such a Bull kind of impulsive decision, but now I've got to go collect him. With Jimmy at the house, there's no way I'm going to trust the dog not to bolt at the sight of him.

It's so cold that I think maybe he went by the lone cab that serves Harmony Farms, he and the dog. Which I quickly realize would be impossible. No phone to call a cab. I can't figure Bull out, so I stop trying. In the words of youth: *whatever*.

I shower and dress in fresh clothes, suitable for an evening in, or an evening out. Text Natalie that I'm on my way. Happily, I get a text back suggesting I stop for pizza. At least this time it'll be warm.

The tiny Baggie is still in my inside coat pocket. I should put this someplace safe. There's a ceramic cookie jar in the shape of a pig on the counter. I never bother to go to the trouble to put cookies in it, so it's empty except for the cookie crumbs left in there by previous tenants. I drop the baggie in, put the pig's head back onto its shoulders. Which is when I notice the neatly lined up and very empty Sam Adams bottles. Oh, Bull.

My fault for leaving the beer in the fridge. His fault for drinking it. I take a deep breath. I just can't worry about him anymore. He's managed to walk out of here, and I didn't see him facedown along the side of the road, so I assume he also managed to hitch a ride. Which means I can spend my evening going from bar to bar until I find him, and, in a fairly accurate reenactment of my teenage years, pull him out, take him home, and sober him up. Or I can stick with my plans and leave him to his own devices. It's kind of a no-brainer. Besides, if he's got the dog with him, maybe he just went home. I'll drop by to retrieve the retriever after my dinner with Natalie.

I wash my hands, grab my keys, and I'm out the door.

The temperature has dropped even more, and as I drive along Lake Shore Drive I think that if this cold front keeps up, the ice may thicken up enough for ice-skating. At the very least, shallow Bartlett's Pond will freeze up and I may have a little more company than I'm used to in my remote location. When I was a kid, we played pickup hockey on Bartlett's Pond, as Lake Harmony was given over to ice fishing and the surface was never smooth enough. I was a pretty good hockey player in my youth and I coached a peewee team as my community volunteer service while I was working—part of the PALS program. I enjoyed it but felt bad for the kids who had never skated on natural ice, with its random clumps of vegetation sticking through to catch a skate, or detour a puck aimed for a teammate; to never learn to avoid the places that were too soft to skate on, cloudy instead of clear.

Rocco's isn't too busy, so I'm in and out in twenty. My text tone beeps—Natalie asking if I would mind picking up some milk at Cumberland Farms. She's so sorry to ask. I text back: *No problem*. And I smile, feeling like a, well, like a husband. It's really the mundane that defines a relationship, isn't it? Errands, chores. The tilt of a chin, a smile. Finding a favorite cookie in the cupboard. Cleaning the frost off a windshield without being asked. I am suddenly nostalgic for the ordinary, and I pull into Cumberland's parking lot with a mild surge of hope.

And there is Bull, leaning against the brick wall beneath the NO LOITERING sign, sucking hard on a cigarette, paper cup of coffee in one hand. No dog in sight.

"Bull, what are you doing here and where's the dog?" I ask when I get out of the truck. I have a horrible image of the dog dead by the side of the road.

He looks at me as if he has no idea who I am. He tosses the cigarette butt onto the ground, plants a big foot on it. "Dog?"

"The dog. The one you left my cabin with."

"I didn't take your dog."

I don't say, again, that he's not my dog. "He's not at the cabin. Did you let him out?"

Bull leans back against the brick wall. I can smell the fumes from where I stand. He's not drinking coffee out of that cup. "I left, but I didn't take your dog."

"You need to go home. Now." I am so pissed. I've got two pizzas rapidly cooling in my truck. I've got plans. I've got a life. But now I have to bundle Bull into my truck, drive him home, find some explanation to give Natalie as to why I'm going to be late. And find the dog. Again. I know. It's not the end of the world. But it is frustrating. If I hadn't spent most of my boyhood doing exactly this, I might be a little more patient, more understanding. But I did spend my youth pulling Bull out of bars, walking him home or, when I got my license, driving him home to sober up. Making sure he didn't choke on his own vomit. Making sure he had aspirin and water by his bed so that when he woke up with his daily hangover, he'd have relief. And then I caught up with my friends, or got to practice, late again. That boyhood resentment simmers so close to the surface.

"Get in the truck."

"No. I'm waiting for someone."

"Get in the truck, Bull."

"Coop, it's okay. I know what I did, and my guy's coming for me." He puts one hand against my chest, pushing me away.

His guy? Then I get it. "Your sponsor?"

"My guy."

"Why don't you wait inside. It's cold out here." I have visions of Bull freezing solid to the bricks, despite the infusion of alcohol.

"Kid behind the counter doesn't like it when I do that."

I yank open the heavy glass and metal door, go in, and grab a gallon of 2 percent milk. As I pay, I catch the kid's eye. "That old man out there?"

"Yeah, what about him?"

"Let him stay inside till his ride comes."

"Can't. He's loitering." He hands me my change. "Besides, he's drunk, and we can't have that in here. Makes the other customers nervous."

"You want a man frozen to death on your premises? That ought to make customers really nervous." I shove a ten-dollar bill at him, "That's enough for him to be a customer." I grab the milk and go back outside.

Bull sees me coming, waves me away. "I told you, he'll be here any minute."

"Go in. You've got ten dollars' worth of time in there. So go in. Get a real coffee."

"Coop, I didn't lose your dog." He looks genuine; he looks sad. "I wouldn't be that careless."

"I know." Intentionally, I think, *intentionally* careless about anything.

By now it's dark, and although it makes no sense to start looking for the dog now, I have to. I hate thinking of him outside on a night like this, whether of his own volition or by accident. I call Natalie before I leave the parking lot, suggesting that I drop the food and milk off, then take a slow turn along the roads that lead to my cabin. I'm hoping that she'll volunteer to go with me.

The truth is, things had kind of gone south when I called Natalie to wish her a Happy New Year, which is why I was so pleased to have gotten her call today. We keep doing this, this strange, cautious dance. I think it was when I mentioned that I wasn't going to renew my contract with the town but that I also wasn't going to apply for reinstatement on the K-9 unit. It was New Year's Day, what else does one talk about except resolutions?

"My resolution is to be out of this job at the end of the fiscal year," I'd told her.

"What will you do? Go back to law enforcement?"

"Possibly. But not the K-9 unit."

"Why not? It's what you love."

"Loved." End of story.

The pizzas are nearly cold when I get to Natalie's, but we each eat a slice before heading out. Natalie climbs into the cab of my truck, reminding me that the dog's bigger now, has a layer of good retriever fat that will help keep him warm. He's experienced out there. That will help.

"I don't know. I hope so." I still believe that Bull, in some careless, inconsiderate, alcohol-blunted way, has somehow lost the dog. But I didn't tell Natalie that. I glossed it over, saying that my father must have left the door open. I certainly didn't tell her about his headlong pitch off the wagon. Some things aren't for public consumption. I just said that Bull had left the cabin and the dog had disappeared.

I take a left out of her driveway. We don't say much, our eyes focused on the road ahead of us, the scrubby verge beside us. I risk a glance in her direction. She looks tired. I recall the despair in her voice earlier today. The frustration. The fact that she reached out. "I'm glad that you called me. I was wondering if you were mad at me."

"No. Yes. Maybe."

"And what are you now?"

"Better."

"If I can ask, what, exactly, did I do that set you off?"

"It's about being honest. Open."

"How have I not been *open* with you?" If my hands weren't occupied with steering, I might have used air quotes over the word. Instead, I grip the wheel. What is so magical about telling every detail, every truth, to a woman?

To my complete surprise, she laughs. "Oh, yeah. You're about as open as a locked door."

"You know the basics—reluctant return of the native; divorced." I take a breath. "My loss."

"I wish you'd tell me about that." Natalie lays her hand on my leg, just above the knee. Has anyone ever acknowledged the power of that not wholly sexual feminine gesture? It's the hand of support. Like the supportive hand on the back from a teammate after a heartbreaker, or the linking of arms that young girls do: *I'm here.*

And so I tell her the whole story.

"I wasn't supposed to fall in love with Argos. By doing so, I was breaking the tacit rules about being a K-9 handler. The dog was supposed to be a tool, like the firearm and the Mace and the handcuffs on my belt. But I did fall in love with him, and his loss crushed me. It wasn't just the tinnitus in my left ear or the dull pain in my back that prevented me from getting another canine; it was the fear of enduring another loss. The relationship between Argos and me was more than the sum of its parts, irreplaceable. He'd saved me, but I couldn't save him. I don't mean pulling me out of a burning building, which he never did; or savaging a man about to fire at me, which he did do, twice. But Argos came into my life at a time when I was unmoored, uncertain, and unfocused. "

He'd do anything Cooper asked. Anything. At his master's command, Argos would streak like a demon, elegant jaws slashing at the air until he tackled his target, taking him down, his jaws slashing at flailing arms. Moving at the speed of a jackal, moving so fast, he appeared elongated, ears flattened, one long furious dragon of a dog.

Cooper was his boss. His commander. His master. Argos looked to him with the devotion and loyalty and trust that defined his legendary breed. One-man dog. One-dog man. Cooper was smitten. He had never had any creature so entirely his. So entirely certain of his infallibility. When Argos was beside him, Cooper caught the admiring eyes of passersby; the approval of strangers who welcomed them, who knew that they were there for their safety, their protection. They were equally goodwill ambassadors and feared. Feared by the felons and fugitives, the drug dealers and convenience-store robbers. If Argos and Cooper were on the trail, there was no hiding. From Argos. From his exquisite nose.

So late one night, a night so deep into winter cold that it seemed like nothing could survive outside, Cooper and Argos got called into work. Reluctantly, Cooper crawled out of his bed, where his wife slept on barely disturbed. He pulled on layers of clothing, long johns, winter pants, two pairs of socks, cotton undershirt, uniform shirt, fleece vest, and heavy jacket. Argos would be fine as he was, his double-thick coat more than enough to withstand the elements. It was a quiet night, no wind to speak of.

This would be an easy collar. All they had to do was pick up the guy's scent and follow him. Although there was no snow on the ground, the cold weather would help Argos track him. There would be no place to hide from Argos's superior nose, unless their quarry had snagged a ride, and then his scent would dead-end. But the reports were that he'd beaten a path into an old, run-down neighborhood. This was a bad guy; this was a guy they all wanted to see brought to justice.

Argos cast around for the scent, sorting it out from the muddle of fellow cops, reporters, bystanders, and within seconds he struck it. It was so cold that it almost hurt to breathe in the air, and made it hard for Cooper to keep up with the dog, who plunged ahead, oblivious to the penetrating cold, happy to be working. Cooper had seen some football routes that were less complicated than the path this fugitive had taken. Up one street, down the next, through an alley, over a hedge. The fugitive must have figured there'd be a dog on his heels. Argos planted his forefeet on the lids of garbage cans, sniffing the empty air for the invisible trail the suspect had left behind, a trail of skin cells and effluvia.

Finally, Cooper and the dog came to a stop outside a small two-family house. No lights, no barrels set out front for tomorrow's trash collection. The screen door was ripped off its hinges and Cooper could see the jagged edges of broken glass in the windows. But there was something very live about the silent, dark, abandoned-looking place. In the cold stillness of the midnight air a subtle sense that a door had just shut, or maybe a tattered shade hanging in a blank window had moved. It was as if the house were breathing. Or holding its breath. Cooper stepped away from the pool of light cast by the one working streetlight on this rough street. Despite the wool scarf wrapped around it, he felt a chill run up the back of his neck.

Cooper radioed their position to the unit. Argos growled, then barked. The fugitive was out the back door, and Cooper instantly decided that they didn't have time for backup, that their quarry would be gone before a squad car could turn the corner. He took out his weapon. "Police!"

For months, the city had been plagued by a nutcase mad bomber. He'd call and say that he'd set up bombs on bridges or in tunnels, or in trash cans in highly trafficked areas. Lots of K-9 hours had been lost searching for the bombs he claimed to have planted, only to have him call back and say that he had planted a real bomb somewhere else. The city was on high alert. Not enough time had passed since the Boston Marathon bombing, and this nutcase was being taken very seriously. His fake bombs were all but real, saving one element or another, so it was clear that he knew how to make a bomb, and unclear why he kept tormenting the city with his series of fakes.

And now they had him, Cooper and Argos, had him corned like the vermin he was. In the dim light of a faulty streetlight, Cooper could see that their fugitive was dressed entirely in black, from the top of his head to the balaclava over his face, his midsection bulky and his legs spindly. He looked like a spider.

It should have been a pretty easy collar. Cooper had him cornered. He had the dog. He had backup coming any minute. He was so anxious to make this arrest that he felt as if he were vibrating. All he had to do was pull the trigger.

And now I'm almost to the end of my story when I will articulate what I have not spoken out loud to anyone. I pause for a moment. Natalie waits, letting me find the words.

"So I shouted, 'Put up your hands!' I leveled my weapon, gripped, as I'd been trained, in two hands. Even so, I felt the adrenaline pulse my aim out of true. I had him in my sights, within range, within protocol. He put his arms out as asked. But then, in a confident, almost casual motion, one hand went in toward his chest.

"I should have shot him, but instead I released the dog. I sent Argos into the arms of a suicide bomber. I sent him to his death. That dog had given me everything and I failed him entirely. I sent him in."

I've long since pulled the truck over to the side of the road. I'm quivering exactly like I was on that other cold January night. My heart is beating with the same tympanic volume.

Natalie's hand gently squeezes my leg. But she stays quiet, and I know that she's trying to find the words to excuse me.

"When I was interviewed after the fact, I told my superiors that I was not confident that I would have hit him. What I implied was that I thought my dog was fast enough that he would down him before he pulled the detonator."

It comes out of me then, the truth that has lodged in my soul like a tumor. "The truth is, I hesitated. I'd never shot to kill before. It was my fault. If I had . . . " I let the sentence hang.

Natalie takes me in her arms and rocks me, patting my back and telling me that it's really all right, to let it out. I try to say that I shouldn't be giving in, that I should be well past the weeping stage, but then I realize that she's quietly weeping, too. I don't know if it's for me, my story of loss, or for her own. It doesn't really matter. She pulls a crumpled tissue out of her jacket pocket and dabs at her eyes, then hands it to me. "Aren't we a pair?" She gives that little laugh that follows a meltdown, and, after a moment, I do, too.

The barn doors are closed, the horses all snug in their stalls, wrapped in their blankets, sipping water from heated buckets and munching the extra hay that will help keep them warm on this very cold night. I've put my inexpert electrical knowledge to work and gotten her tank heaters going again. We haven't found the dog and have come back to her place defeated. It's late, so I don't stay much longer, just long enough to eat a couple of slices of reheated pizza. She knows the worst of me now, but she doesn't flinch. I say good night and promise to let her know as soon as I find the dog. I love that she is so optimistic, saying that I will find the dog.

I have one final truth to share with this woman who loves animals and hasn't condemned me for losing mine; I tell her how Argos saved me. He'd provided me with something that I could love unconditionally without fear of its being taken away from me. He was wholly mine.

The stars are brilliant, diamond specks in the inky sky—just like the night that haunts me. But this night, the deadweight of my grief is gone. Lifted away. Someone has understood the depth of my grief, hasn't mocked it or told me I'll get over it. I should get over it. I must get over it.

It's cold and brilliant and so very clear. And there, waiting for me on the cabin porch, is the yellow dog.

39

His sponsor had sat with Bull for hours, until the soporific effects of the booze had been countered with the buzz of endless cups of coffee. They had talked, and then not talked. Over and over, Bull was reminded that every day was a new start and that he didn't need to think about why he'd succumbed to temptation, only think about not doing it again. His sponsor is someone Bull has known a long time, who has had some of the same troubles as himself, maybe not a dead wife, but a divorce. Vietnam. Maybe not a son quite like Jimmy, but a daughter who got herself in the family way at age sixteen. Everybody has troubles. When his sponsor dropped him off at the Poor Farm Road house, Bull thanked him, truly appreciative of the guy's efforts, a little maudlin at the kindness. He felt sober, and cheered.

"Thought you were staying at Coop's." Jimmy is sitting in the living room, dressed in a bathrobe, bare feet stuck in slippers, flipping channels. A new bottle of Jack Daniel's sits on the low end table.

"I left. Got homesick."

"Join me?" He puts his hand on the bottle. "Good stuff."

"Please don't, Jimmy."

"Hey, Bull, I'm just joking with you. I'm not sharing." Jimmy settles on a nature program.

Bull sits on the other end of the couch. "Coop doesn't have a TV."

Jimmy looks at his father, chuckles. "He always was an odd one."

"Still is."

40

L ev Parker stares at the baggie that I've dropped on his desk.
The little rectangle filled with white is in stark contrast to the
inky black of his professionally uncluttered blotter.

"Think that's enough for a search warrant?"

"Probably."

"Okay."

"The thing is, Jimmy's only one guy."

"With a shitload of heroin stashed in the stovepipe."

"Cooper, we've got the county's drug task force working on this."

"So? I've just dropped fifty dollars' worth of evidence in your
hands."

"And we're grateful."

"But?"

"We want them all. We can bust Jimmy, but then the whole operation disappears out from under us."

"Unless he talks."

"Cooper, he never has before. Why would he now?"

Lev is right. Even as a little kid, Jimmy never ratted out a friend.

As a juvenile, he took six months in juvenile hall rather than give up his Fagin. As an adult, he spent twelve years without parole and never breathed a word against his partners. I could never tell if it was fear of retribution or a curious and misplaced loyalty.

"I've done what I can. It's up to you."

"Hey, thanks, Cooper. It will help. When the time comes. In the meantime . . . "

"I know. I'll pretend like we're the fucking Cleavers."

"Something like that."

Okay, I'm disappointed. Maybe it's colossally unbrotherly, but I spent far too many years of my professional career working to put men like my brother behind bars. I've seen up close and personal the devastating effects of what these bastards peddle. And I'm seeing what he's doing to Bull. The drug task force is a great idea, except that it's more than likely Bull will end up on the receiving end of an arrest warrant. Knowingly harboring drugs and drug activity—that should be good for a long sojourn in prison, and not county jail this time. Bull may be able to carry off playing dumb with a lot of folks, but not those guys. He may piss me off, but I really don't want the old man sent to prison.

I maybe shut Lev's door a little aggressively, but I really don't care.

Polly is grinning at me when I get back to the shelter. "You've got a message!"

She's adjusted to her role as assistant ACO with a vengeance. The place is spit-polish clean; the ancient Mr. Coffee has been discarded and a new Krups coffeemaker that she bought with her first week's pay sits in pride of place, usually with a plate of homemade cookies beside it. The cat room boasts a carpet-covered multiplatform tree, and I never once have to complain about the stink of the litter boxes. As part of her self-defined job description, she's been fielding all my calls instead of letting the answering machine do the hard work. Now she hands me a pink *While You Were Out* slip. "Barkwell Kennels. Mr. Stinson. They'll be at home all day," it says.

"Well, I'll be a son of a bitch."

"Cooper. Language."

I'd like to, but I don't sweep her up and swing her in my arms.

There is only one dog in residence today, the yellow dog. Polly doesn't keep him kenneled while she's here. He is flopped down in the cat room, apparently at home with felines. They ignore him. "Hey, bud, we're going to find you your lost owner today. What do you think of that?"

He gets to his feet, shakes, ambles over. For once, I give him a good solid pat. My determination to find the perpetrator who shot this dog hasn't diminished, but my certainty that his missing owner is the culprit fluctuates. At this point, I'm just hoping that the owner is a nice lady who will be glad to have him back. In my heart of hearts, I know that it will be well nigh impossible to prove abuse. But one thing is for certain: I'll be keeping an eye on whoever his owner is.

I grab a chocolate-chip cookie off the plate, gently close my office door, put my feet up on the desk, and dial the number for Barkwell Kennels, which by this time I have memorized. I am finally rewarded with a human voice. I quickly identify myself and tell an abbreviated version of the story, give the kennel owner the microchip number. Mr. Stinson tells me to hold on for a minute, and I hear him moving papers around. "Yeah, here it is. That number was assigned to a pup we sold to a guy named Boykin. How'd he get to you?"

"Boykin? Are you sure?"

"Yeah. Donald Boykin, Harmony Farms."

Bad year for dogs.

Cynthia Mann and Donald Boykin do not seem the type of people to leave a lost dog unreported. More like the type of folks who would launch a massive search party, post pictures, advertise a reward well out of proportion to the value of the dog. I take another look at the list of Labradors registered in the last year. Neither a Boykin nor a Mann registered a dog at all, and I know that their deceased spaniel should come up in the registry—if she was licensed. A ten-buck dog license. It's not like they can claim hardship. And, as our first selectman, it behooves Cynthia not to be a scofflaw where her dogs are concerned. I go back another year and find the spaniel. I'll give them a pass; it's pretty easy to forget to get an annual dog license, especially given the busy lives they must lead.

It just niggles at me, the fact that they never reported this dog missing. Then I wonder if he was never lost. Adolescent dogs can be pains in the neck. Maybe this yellow dog didn't fit into their busy lifestyle and they gave him away and whoever had him did the damage. Well, I can conjecture all day long; it really doesn't matter. What matters is returning this dog, who is nibbling at something Polly is hand-feeding him. I pick up the phone and punch in the number for the Mann/Boykin residence.

The female voice on the other end of the line bears the same Eastern European accent as the housekeeper at the old Callahan place. "Stacia speaking."

I identify myself and she waits until I state my business.

"We don't have any dog."

"No, I know. I've found a dog that belongs to Mr. Boykin."

"He doesn't have a dog."

"Stacia. Did he have a dog?"

There is a pause. "Yes."

"A Labrador?"

"I don't know. The black-and-white one was hit by a car. I don't know what she was."

"I know that. This is a yellow dog, big. A hunting dog."

Another hesitation. I don't think it has anything to do with English as a second language. "

"When will Mr. Boykin be home?"

"He's on a business trip. Home tomorrow night."

"Tell him I have his dog."

"Yes, sir."

Cynthia Mann doesn't keep regular office hours as selectman, but I've seen her often enough in the town hall around midafternoon, sometime between her ladies-who-lunch date and her afternoon yoga. I pop the yellow dog into the town's SUV and head over. The place is quiet on this Friday afternoon, sleepy almost. I nod to the tax collector, steal a handful of M&Ms from the town clerk's jar. "Cynthia around?"

"Just missed her. I think she said something about going down to Boston. She was dressed to kill, if you know what I mean." In Harmony Farms, any woman spotted wearing panty hose is considered dressed up. "Some big charity event."

"Thanks, Judy. If she should call in, ask her to call me." I have no real expectation that Cynthia will interrupt her philanthropic do-gooding to call the local dogcatcher.

That's about all I can do right now about the critter lounging in the back of the town's Suburban. I guess I'll have to suffer one more night with my roomie.

It is so cold tonight that I begin to wonder how long I can stay in this barely insulated cabin. Even with the Jøtul burning hot, the rest of the place is numbing. I have to leave the bathroom faucet dripping to ensure that the pipes don't freeze, which makes me realize that my hearing is way better, because the *drip drip drip* is driving me crazy. It's almost enough to make me invite the dog into my bed, a one-dog night. But I don't. Instead, I get a mercy call from Natalie.

I don't hesitate, just grab a toothbrush and the dog and head to Second Hope.

41

M ike and Dave are in the house when Bull gets home. Jimmy's
pals. All three of them are sitting around the kitchen table,
like they're looking for a fourth for a game of poker, except that there
are no cards, no chips on the table. The little piles that are in front
of them aren't real nickels.

"What are you doing home?" Jimmy casually places his hands
over the bags in front of him, then looks at his friends, who do the
same, like kids trying to hide something. They *are* trying to hide
something.

"I live here?" Bull gives them a smile, hands palms-up like a cartoon character's.

"Jimmy, I thought you locked the door." One of them, Dave or
Mike, mutters. Bull doesn't remember who is who, just the pair of
them, like conjoined twins MikeandDave. "I told you this wasn't a
good idea."

"You're home a little early." Jimmy's voice is not conversational.

"Yeah. About that."

It was only a matter of time. He was sick of that job anyway. Outside in all weathers, splinters and breathing in sawdust.

"You should go lie down. In your room."

"I'm a little old to be sent to my room." Bull blinkers his eyes with the flats of his hands. "I'm not around, I don't see anything, but I'm thirsty and I'm going to my own fridge."

"I mean it." Jimmy gets to his feet, motioning to his comrades to stay put, that he's got this.

"Jimmy," the other one says. Dave or Mike. "Leave him alone. He's your father."

"He's a pain in the ass."

One of them leans back in his chair. "Hey, Bull, you want to make some money?"

"Supplement my unemployment?"

"Yeah. Something like that. You want to keep your boy happy? Keep Jimmy safe? Do us a favor and I'll make it worth your while."

"Dave, this is not a good idea." Jimmy sits back down. It's weird to see Jimmy in a subordinate position, but clearly he is the low man on this three-man totem pole.

"Would you be interested in taking a package—oh, let's say of books—meeting a guy who's a great reader?"

"You want me to be your mule?"

"I wouldn't call it that. Our bike-delivery guy."

"No."

"Let me put it to you another way. You know a little too much not to be involved. Either work with us or . . . well, I don't think you'd much like the alternative."

"Dave, please. He's not reliable. He'll be fine. I can keep him under control." Jimmy's voice is pitched a little higher than usual. "Come on, Dave. You can't be serious."

It's Dave. That's who this one is. The bigger one. The one with the clean hands. The other guy has prison tats all over his. Mike.

Bull pulls a bottle of water out of the refrigerator. It's not what he wants. He wants a real drink. Something that will muffle the tension that is building here, something to blame when he makes the wrong decision. He knows that Jimmy is going to lose this argument. Jimmy needs to be smarter than that. These guys aren't friends; they're thugs. He takes a swig of the water. Drug dealers. Bull knows that if he doesn't take Dave's offer, take the bait, bad things will happen, not just to him but to Jimmy, too. Some kids admire basketball players or astronauts. Jimmy always admired the fugitives on *America's Most Wanted*. Bull can see him for what he is, a punk trying to be a player.

"I'll do it. How much you offering?"

Cooper has taken the afternoon off to take his old man down to the Social Security office in Leominster. Bull is grateful but nervous. He's afraid that his former law-enforcement officer son will somehow sniff out the big secret that Mike and Dave and Jimmy have forced on him, that he has gone from being willfully ignorant to complicit in their business. He's clean-shaven and freshly showered, old but fresh chinos on, a frayed-at-the-cuffs button-down shirt. His parka still bears the fragrance of lumber, but it's the only winter coat he has, since he never did find the other one. He's wearing the Christmas hat and gloves, but he's still cold, even in Coop's nice truck.

They've signed Bull up for Social Security. See if he can live on that. He's enjoying this, being able to say that he's retired instead of unemployed, retired instead of up and quit. Coop's idea. Smart kid.

"You think I should retire to Florida?"

"Yeah, why not. You can live cheaper, that's for sure."

"I'd miss my friends."

Cooper is kind enough not to point out that Bull doesn't really have any honest-to-God friends. Lots of acquaintances, but that's hardly a reason to stay put. Especially if things get tense with Mike and Dave and Jimmy.

"I'd miss you." Bull says this without looking at Cooper, not wanting to see his reaction. Waits a beat, two. No response. He's not going to ask if Coop would miss him, too.

"I'd come visit. Maybe take a vacation down there. Fish a little." Bull looks out the window, smiling.

When they get back to 179 Poor Farm Road, Jimmy's car is gone, and Bull relaxes a little. He doesn't want Cooper to ask about Jimmy, or, worse, want to go in while he's there. Jimmy has made it clear that shouldn't happen again.

Cooper pulls up beside the derelict Nova, doesn't make noise about going inside. Between them, the dog reaches over the seat back, noses Bull in the ear. Bull reaches back, pats him, and climbs out of the truck. "Hey, thanks, Coop. I appreciate the help."

"No problem."

"See you."

"Hey, Bull. Can I ask you a question?"

"Shoot."

"Why do you still have that car?" He nods in the direction of the Nova. "It's not like you were ever going to restore it."

Bull walks around to stand between Cooper's open truck window and the rusted-out car. He runs a hand over the roof, crusty with tree litter and ice. "I don't know."

"It's been over twenty-five years, Bull."

"It reminds me."

"Of what?"

"Of consequences."

"The consequences of Jimmy's behavior? It didn't help, did it?"

Bull has always known that on some level everyone blamed Jimmy for the accident. If he hadn't been in trouble, Mona wouldn't have driven away, lost control of the car, and crashed into that massive oak at the bottom of the hill. But that wasn't really fair. And it's not fair that Bull has never tried to correct the error. "No. Mine. Didn't you ever know that she hit that tree because the brakes went? That I hadn't put brake fluid in? That if I'd gotten air in her tire, she wouldn't have even taken the Nova."

"Does Jimmy know this?"

"I don't know."

"Bull, you are a piece of work." Cooper closes his window, backs out of the driveway, then stops, pulls back in, and lowers his window again. "I'm sorry, Bull. That was rotten." He didn't look at Bull as he said that, but now he turns his face to look directly at his father. "I know what consequences feel like."

42

A bitterly cold night spent in a centrally heated house did wonders for my spirits and everything for my self-esteem as Natalie, now that I'd let her into my confidence, my trust, welcomed me into hers. We split a bottle of wine and talked. She talked about Marcus and I talked about Argos. She told me about the special challenges of being in an interracial marriage, I told her about the challenges of being the town drunk's kid. And then we stopped talking. Our dogs nested together in Betty's bed and Natalie and I nested in hers. We spent the weekend being as lazy as people responsible for the care and well-being of animals can ever be. We bundled into long johns and polar fleeces to feed horses and muck stalls, peeling off layers as the work heated us up. I made us chili and Natalie baked corn bread. I was as happy as I had been in a very long time.

Then Monday afternoon, Bull laid his revelation on me. It was my own fault; I shouldn't have asked why he had kept that hulk for so many years. I don't know why it's bothered me that he has, but now it's going to bother me more, now that I know he holds himself to blame. And, of course, he is to blame. But that doesn't take the responsibility for what happened off of Jimmy. It was still his action that set everything into motion. At least to my mind.

Well, I can't dwell on it. That's what Nat said when I called her. "Cooper, it doesn't change a thing. But you've got to feel sorry for him."

"Who, Bull or Jimmy?"

"Both of them." A beat. "All of you."

The Eastern European housekeeper at the Mann/Boykin residence is polite but emphatic that neither sir nor madam are available. I glance at the yellow dog, at this moment flat on his back while Polly scratches his belly. "How long have you worked for the family?"

"Six years."

"And you have no recollection of a yellow Labrador retriever being there?"

"A yellow dog?"

"Yes."

I can almost hear the wheels spinning, the internal debate. What mystifies me is the prevarication about such a simple question. Did the Mann/Boykin family ever have a yellow dog? Yes. No. Simple. What's the big deal? There is something decidedly stinky about this. This is not a language barrier. This is someone protecting her job. I think about the kitten that Polly "found" wandering on the old Callahan property, and how happy that housekeeper was to get her back. Maybe there's something in Balkan DNA that is careless when it comes to other people's pets.

I sigh. No point alienating the woman. "When do you expect them?"

"I will give them the message."

"Please do."

The dog heaves his own sigh—this one of contentment.

"Cooper, why don't you try Cynthia on her cell phone?" Polly pushes herself upright, leans on the edge of the desk to get to her feet.

I stick out my hand to help. "I would if I had her number."

"I do."

Why am I not surprised that Polly Schaeffer, recovering animal hoarder, would have the first selectman's cell number?

Polly whips out a recent-vintage iPhone, scrolls down her contacts list, and hands me the phone. I read off the number as I dial it from the shelter's landline.

I'm about to wonder if Cynthia doesn't take "unknown caller" calls, when I get the automated voice-mail message. I leave my name, both numbers, cell and office, but hesitate to tell her that I have her dog. Given her recent loss, that could be cruel. I do add that I've left messages at her residence, the implication being that I'm going to keep doing so until she or Donald Boykin get around to calling me. I'm not going away.

Time for a ride-along. I snap my fingers at the dog, who no longer bolts when I do. He lets me clip the leash to his collar and willingly accompanies me out the door and into the Suburban. We've come a long way. But it's time for this dog to go home.

I wend my slow way around town. It's warmed up a little, and folks are venturing out, doing those errands that they've put off while the extravagantly cold weather made the simplest chores painful to accomplish. I can't say that I'm actively looking for Cynthia, but she's ubiquitous in this town, so it wouldn't be unusual to spot her Volvo with the oval Euro-style window decal: HARFAR, Cynthia's latest bid to put Harmony Farms on the tourism trail. So far, she's the only one sporting it. I roll past the yoga studio and the Country Market, circle around the town hall parking lot. Nada.

A dogfight at the dog park pulls me off task and I give up my quest for the moment, but that's all right, as I plan to drop by the Mann/Boykin residence on my way home. I've been too patient. Besides, at this point it will look odd for me to hang on to this dog when I know where he lives. I really don't have to wait for them to come and collect him. The housekeeper with the faulty memory can just hang on to him till "sir and madam" get home.

I've dealt with the dog incident at the dog park, a fight I'd characterize more as a kerfuffle. No blood drawn, and the pair now gamboling about the park like old pals. It's the owners I have to separate. I suggest that they, both fairly new to dog parenting, learn to identify true aggressive behavior as opposed to posturing. Almost as soon as I return to my SUV, my cell phone barks. Glory hallelujah, it's Donald Boykin.

"My housekeeper said that you wanted to speak to me?"

"Yeah. I have your dog."

"I don't have a dog. You brought our dog home—in a plastic bag."

"A yellow Labrador. He's chipped and Mr. Stinson at Barkwell Kennels said that the number corresponds to a dog you purchased from him in October."

There is enough of a silence that I think that the call has been dropped. "Mr. Boykin? Is Stinson mistaken?" My tone of voice doesn't suggest that I'm giving him an out. It suggests that he damn well better not lie to me. It's a shadow of my former professional voice, but it does the trick.

"Where is it?"

"With me. I'll drop him off."

"No. Not necessary. I'll come to you."

The day had started out overcast, but now I have to fish around for my sunglasses as the midday sun sparkles off the melting snow. The yellow dog puts his head over the back of my seat, his breath tickling my cheek. I give him a pat on his boxy head. "You ready to finally go home, big boy?"

To my surprise, my voice catches a little.

I'm at my desk with a ham and cheese sandwich and a can of V-8 juice when I get an unexpected visit from Chief Lev Parker. He looks equally businesslike and uncomfortable. "I'm just saying, as a friend, you should maybe take your father someplace for a couple of days."

The yellow dog takes one look at the uniformed policeman with the service weapon on his hip and heads into the kennel room, where he sequesters himself with the shinbone I picked up for him at the Country Market.

"I assume that, as an officer of the law, you won't tell me why." I say that, but he really doesn't have to say more. Given his *suggestion*, it's a no-brainer that the drug task force is about to swoop down on my brother and whoever it is he plays with.

"Right."

I take it as a sign of professional respect that Lev is willing to stick his neck out this way—a tacit appreciation for the help that I've given him. I feel pretty good. "I guess I could take a couple of days off. Take him out of town."

"It's for the best, Cooper. And anything he might want to talk about might help in the long run."

If Bull informs on Jimmy and his friends, he might save himself. But I know that he won't do that.

I toss the remains of my sandwich.

He's here. He's here. He's here. The never-forgotten scent of human anger, human temper floats through the building. A particular human's anger and temper. The dog whimpers, a long, drawn-out, anguished whine, and then bolts out the kennel door to the run, where he can go only six feet before coming to the wire. He presses himself against it, as if he can squeeze through the wire diamonds. He begins a frantic digging, scraping toenails against the concrete until they bleed. His trembling threatens to shake him off his feet. He pants, tongue lolling, salivating, sides heaving. It is as afraid as he's ever been. *The man is here.*

━━

Polly appears at my doorway, "Mr. Boykin is here."

I stand to invite the town's leading philanthropist into my small, dim office. Donald Boykin doesn't look like one of those six-foot power brokers with a full head of white hair, a white shirt, and a power tie. He's smallish, almost dainty, balding, wearing fashionable eyeglasses. His suit is well tailored, charcoal gray, and his shirt is crisp and light blue. He's wearing a tie that could almost be called whimsical, with tiny multicolored staplers floating on a field of yellow. His footwear is clearly of the expensive designer variety, but it's soiled now with the gritty slush of the shelter parking lot. Nonetheless, he exudes the authority of one who draws a bonus-inflated seven-figure salary.

"Thank you for coming down. I would have been happy to drop him off." I offer Boykin a seat. He looks like he wants to dust it off before he sits, but he doesn't. He does that thing with his trousers, pinching the fabric at his thighs and lifting it as he sits, a gesture I haven't seen in years, at least not since polyester was introduced.

"Mr. Boykin, let's talk about your dog."

"Well, the thing is, I don't have a dog."

"Microchip says otherwise."

He thinks about this for a moment. "My assistant once purchased a hunting dog for my use. It failed as a hunting dog."

"Last fall?"

"Yes."

"Okay. So what happened to him?"

His eyes are milky blue behind the round lenses. He has a little tick; one eyelid blinks faster than the other. I can't decide if this is a "tell," or not. He's not the nervous type, or maybe it's more accurate to say that he isn't the type to show nerves. "Nothing. I sent it back and fired my assistant."

"Seems a bit harsh."

"Not at all." Boykin pats his knees. "Well, enough said. I suppose I have to take it."

I ask Polly to fetch the yellow dog. It all seems anticlimactic; after months of wondering about this dog's origins, I have his owner, but not his story.

Polly is taking a very long time. Finally, she shows up at the door to my office, empty-handed and flushed. "He won't come out."

I could chalk it up to the yellow dog's usual stranger/danger behavior. He's been cowering in his cell since Lev Parker was here. But the dog will do anything for Polly.

"Give us a minute, will you, Polly?" I get up and shut my door. With all my heart, I wish that I had a one-way mirror and a colleague behind it. "Just to clarify, you sent the dog back. To where? Barkwell didn't have him."

Do I detect a slight flush above that razor-sharp collar? "I found him another owner."

"So you- -I'm sorry—your assistant bought an untrained dog; then you found out it didn't know what to do."

"Something like that."

"And when he wouldn't perform, you got mad."

"No." He clears his throat, considers his next words. "I would characterize it more as being embarrassed. I was hunting, for the first time in decades, with my immediate superior and a very important client. I had sunk a lot of money and time into this junket, the best liquor, the best cigars, the best blind, the best weapons, and the best guide. And this craven dog ruined the day."

"So you shot him."

"No. Never." He looks genuinely shocked. "I would never."

"Who did?"

"We're men who don't tolerate disobedience. Insubordination. We fire whole departments for underperforming. But we don't shoot dogs."

"The way I see it, you literally fired this dog. He was found with bird shot embedded in his hip."

Boykin begins to lose his mild-manneredness. He begins to get angry. "I told you. No one shot that dog. Why do you keep saying that?"

"But you were embarrassed, so maybe you kicked him? His X-rays showed multiple fractures of his ribs. Maybe hit him with your gun stock?"

He says nothing, picks a fleck of something off his lapel, then slides his hand into his inside pocket. "How much do you want?" His checkbook is one of those impressive ones, long and thick.

"We'll get to fines and medical reimbursement in a moment."

"No, I mean, what do you need here? New kennels, computers? Dog food?"

"I'm sorry, I don't understand." Is he bribing me?

"How about you? Is there something on your wish list? Everyone has a wish list."

He *is* bribing me. The first selectman's husband is bribing an officer of the law. It makes my head spin.

"This is inappropriate. Put that away, Mr. Boykin. You don't want that kind of trouble."

Boykin gets to his feet. I can see now that despite the daintiness, he is a formidable man. I'm sure that his staff quakes every time he speaks. He abandons the effort to bribe me. "I can make your life pretty miserable. Give me the fucking dog or enjoy the consequences."

"I've already done miserable. There's hardly anything you can do to improve on it."

"I can have you dismissed."

"I appreciate the favor, but I'm not sure that you can."

Behind him is Polly, who has the yellow dog on the end of a slip-knot leash, and he's straining hard to be anywhere but here. She's got both hands on the leash and is even redder in the face than she was before.

Boykin puts his hand out, fully expecting that Polly will place the leash in it.

43

The hard freeze of the past week has finally let up and a warm front brought rain instead of snow last night. Now the snow that was on the ground has turned to slush, making it a sloppy bike ride. The backpack shifts a little, making Bull's already-awkward pedal up the hill harder. Cars pass him; a jogger waves cordially as she sprints up and over the rise and out of sight. Bull huffs. He's really got to quit smoking. Over the rise is a short path through the state-owned land that leads to a rest stop off the highway. This is Bull's destination. He's to meet a guy there. The rest stop has no facilities; it's just a turnout for weary motorists, a place to catch a few z's, eat a quick picnic, pee behind a tree, or walk a restless dog. He's to wait for a silver car, New York plates. One guy. He's not to approach the car, but wait. Wait for the guy to wave him over to the car. That's what Jimmy said: "Just wait."

This is the part that scares Bull. Like being on patrol in Nam, that feeling that tonight might be your night. That some grunt would sneeze or fart and bring the Vietcong down on them. That a trip line would plunge you facedown into death. Bull tells himself this is different. It's broad daylight; he's just meeting a guy, handing him something he's driven a long way to get. He's just the messenger, just the grunt. Jimmy was so clear this morning when he lifted the backpack onto Bull's shoulders. "Don't do anything to screw this up. Don't get curious; don't say anything. Hand this over and get out of there."

There is a high chain-link fence bordering the perimeter of the rest stop. Bull supposes it's meant to keep hunters from using it as a convenient parking lot. He doesn't see any break in it, no easy place to gain access to the turnout. He's too fat and old to climb over it. It seems to him that Jimmy would have known that there was no easy way to do what it is he wants Bull to do. Unless he walks a half a mile to get around it, this fence is going to make things very difficult. What if the silver car shows up while he's looking for a way around? The only other thing to do is stand here, wait for the car, and then throw the back pack over the top of the fence. Bull leans his back against a tree to wait.

This is his third time running the errand, or, as he likes to think of it, simply doing a favor for a friend. His son's friend.

The first time, he almost blew it. Bull was sitting in a McDonald's on the highway, where Dave had dropped him off. Lo and behold, who should show up but Deke Wilkins. Bull ducked his head behind a post, but Deke, on his way out of the men's room, spotted him. "Bull Harrison, what the hell you doing here?"

"Could say the same to you."

"Dentist. Getting to the age where the teeth are worn-out and the bladder won't hold the twenty miles down to the dentist's office."

"Too much coffee. That's my problem."

"Yeah. You with someone? Got a ride?"

"I do. It's fine." Bull wasn't given much to praying, but he did right then. Prayed first that Deke wouldn't decide to sit down and then that he'd be gone before Bull's contact showed up. On the bench seat beside him was the blue backpack like the kids use. Once the contact showed up, Bull was to go to the men's room and forget the pack on the seat, then head outside and light a cigarette. Although he had no idea what his contact looked like, Bull had been told that the person would signal him to leave by dropping his wallet.

Deke lingered long enough that Bull fretted that his contact had come and gone and that he'd screwed things up. Mike and Dave have made it clear that failure was, as they say, not an option.

"You don't want to be late for your appointment, do you, Deke?"

"I'm all right. I always allow enough time for a stop."

"You don't worry about traffic jams?"

"That's why I always make a midday appointment."

A big black guy in a do-rag stood in line at the counter. He fumbled with his wallet but didn't drop it. Another guy came up to him and said something; they laughed, grabbed the food, and walked out. Bull took a breath.

"Well, I'd better get on the road." Deke buttoned his coat. "You sure you're okay?"

"Fine. Nice seein' you, Deke."

"Been seeing quite of bit of Cooper these days. You know he's been courting that horse-rescue lady?"

"No shit?" Bull had to smile. "That boy keeps things so close to the vest. Maybe a little romance will keep him in town."

"I don't think that's the best thing for him."

"Maybe not. He did love being a cop." Bull felt himself cringe at the word *cop*. Great. What if the contact heard him? "See you, Deke."

Deke finally left, and the next customer in line at the counter did drop his wallet. Bull scrambled out of the booth and fairly ran to the men's room.

An hour goes by. A blue Toyota pulls in, then a white van. Another hour and three black cars in a row come in for a pause in their travels. But no silver car with New York plates. Bull has alternated between pacing the length of the fence like some kind of zoo animal and leaning against a tree, because the ground is too wet to sit on. He's shrugged off the backpack, put it back on, and then taken it off again, relieving his back of the deadweight of the contents. Another hour goes by. He really needs to sit down. It occurs to Bull that maybe the backpack would be a good-enough seat. He's certainly not going to crush the contents, whether it's money or dope, and it's a good sturdy nylon backpack, impervious to the wet. He takes the pack off, sets it gently on the ground, and lowers himself with the help of a handy limb. That's better. Now he's hungry. Jimmy never said how long he should wait. Screw this. He'll call Jimmy and see if he should call it a day. Bull punches his hands into his jacket pockets, looking for his cell phone, hoists himself up, pokes around each of the pockets in his jeans. Nada. He could have sworn that it was in his back pocket, but it's not there. Frustrated, Bull kicks the backpack, which meets his toe with a clunking sound, like there really are books in it.

44

Boykin puts out his hand in that entitled manner of the 1 percent. Polly, clearly confused, puts the leash in it, at which point the dog bolts with enough propulsion that Boykin loses the leash and nearly goes to his knees. I grab his bespoke jacket and keep him upright.

"That dog sure doesn't seem to like you."

"It doesn't really know me. I had possession of it for less than a day."

It is probably my imagination that this dog, who freaks out at the presence of any stranger, is reacting to Boykin with even more panic than usual. I know that I'm reading my own developing dislike for Boykin as proof enough that he has had some part in creating the problem. He's certainly proven himself a bully. As a professional, I can't allow myself to do that. It's facts, not fantasy, that build cases. I have no proof that Boykin did anything more violent than fire his luckless assistant.

But I have one more arrow in my quiver. "You said you had a guide? Who?"

"One of those Haynes men. I can't remember which one."

"Is there any chance your solution was to give the dog to him?"

"He expressed some interest and offered to train him."

"Right then and there?"

Boykin's eyes dart to the left, and I've got his "tell."

"Did Mr. Haynes *discipline* the dog?"

Boykin does look at me now. "Not in front of me."

"Mr. Boykin, if you will tell me the truth, I'll be willing to overlook your indiscretions regarding my wish list and my continued employment." I guide him gently back into my office. "And I'll take the dog off your hands."

Four men and a dog leave the brand-new Range Rover in a safe parking space at the trailhead. It's barely dawn and three of the men are a little hungover from the previous evening's manly bonding over oysters and rare Scotch whiskey. The fourth man is silent, refusing the proffered "hair of the dog" and the Cuban cigar the others are tucking into multipocketed camo vests for the anticipated celebration they'll have once they've bagged their limit of ducks.

The dog, a pedigreed yellow Labrador, is delighted to be outside, and the scents and sights have his tail wagging in a metronomic side-to-side beat. He is young, just an adolescent, and this is all new to him. The sharp odor emanating from the pores of these strangers, the dull chemical scent of the guns is curious, if a little repulsive. Nonetheless, he shows himself eager to join the game, whatever it is. The fourth man, the one who has the scent of dog permeated throughout his clothing—there is another kind of aura about him, one that keeps the dog from approaching him.

The group finally sets off along a path that leads to water. The fourth man is the leader, and the three others follow silently, one of them holding the leash that is attached to the dog's fluorescent orange collar. He jerks the leash periodically, as if trying to tell the dog that he's in charge, that he's the alpha. The dog knows better, knows instinctively that this man is indeed subservient to all the others. He hears it in the way the man speaks to the others. There is a little of the puppy in him, licking the chops of the older, wiser dogs. The adolescent Lab is a submissive pup himself, always ready to take a lesson from an elder. Having this in common, he shoves his cold black nose into the palm of the man holding the leash and is rewarded with a smack. "Quit that."

He's never been struck before, and it startles him into ducking away from the man. He's immediately yanked back to the man's side.

They reach the blind and Len Haynes positions each of the other men in a row, shows them how to keep from shooting one another's brains out accidentally, and then takes the dog's leash, ties him to a ring screwed into the side of the flimsy wall before ensconcing himself behind the blind to take a nap.

The pond is quiet, not a duck in sight. An hour drags by, then another. The sun strikes the placid pond, revealing its shimmering emptiness. Donald Boykin is thinking that maybe this junket was a bad idea. Cynthia didn't like the concept of a boys' weekend at her house, despite the net worth those boys represent, and fled to New York. She also emphatically insisted that he not invest in a dog for a one-off duck hunt. They have a perfectly nice dog and they do not need another. Boykin has no intention of keeping the dog; he isn't defying his wife entirely, but will flip him like a penny stock. The worrying thing is that unless they bag a duck soon, this thousand-dollar mutt is never going to prove his worth in front of two men whose opinion is critical to him and his future with the corporation.

Haynes appears at the blind's opening. Is that an amused smile, or has the man got a bellyache? Haynes lifts a duck call to his lips and sounds it twice.

"Can't get a real duck, maybe we'll shoot this guy. After all, if it sounds like a duck . . ." This from the client. Boykin and his boss, Jonathan Wiley, laugh with desperate appreciation.

Boykin is unaware that he was holding his breath, but he lets it out at the sound of a real duck answering the fake one. The hunters hunker down, the dog somehow caught against them and the short wall of the blind. Len blows on the wooden duck call again. It's a good one, one he bought from that bearded cracker family on television. "That ought to do it."

Sure enough, from the far side of the small pond floats a pair of ducks, effortlessly gliding toward the sound of their phony fellows. Boykin has no idea if they're Mallards or Black Ducks or Muscovy or Daffy. He doesn't want to be the one to shoot first; that honor goes to his guests. But neither one fires. "Go ahead," he whispers. "It's your shot."

Len Haynes, leaning into the side opening of the blind, serves the three would-be hunters with a look that inspires all three to fire at once.

At the explosion of three shotgun barrels blasting over his head, the dog howls. He tries to bolt from the blind, but the fixed leash snaps him back. Wiley fires his second barrel and the dog tries to bury himself under Boykin's legs. Upended by the terrified dog, Boykin kicks out, his booted heels colliding with the dog's ribs. Another yelp.

"I got it!" The client is pointing wildly at the dead duck. Get the dog to retrieve it."

Boykin hauls himself to his feet, unties the dog's leash from the ring, and pulls him outside to the pond edge. Whatever is the command? Fetch? He tries it, but the dog continues his violent shaking, panting and bucking at the end of the leash, so much so that Boykin is afraid to let him go for fear he'll bolt into the surrounding wilderness. "Go get the damned duck." Boykin shoves the dog into the water, points madly.

There is the sound of laughter behind him, Haynes's ugly chuckle. "Looks like that dog won't hunt."

"Haynes. You get him out there." Boykin is furious. How dare this yokel laugh at him? Here, in front of Wiley and the client? At this moment, it is more infuriating than embarrassing. He'll teach him to laugh. "Get the dog out there or go get it yourself. I'm paying you enough."

"I ain't your dog. Get it yourself. Ain't deep." Haynes pockets the duck call, turns on his heel, and walks away.

Boykin immediately regrets paying Haynes the thousand bucks in advance. Highway robbery at that. Thousand bucks for a dog that won't hunt and a thousand bucks to have this moron walk them six hundred feet to a pond that has only two ducks.

"He's got you, Boykin. Never thought I'd see you bested by a hick." Wiley pulls a flask out of his vest. "And a dog." He offers the flask to the client.

Boykin knows that he should laugh, make the joke his own, but he is humiliated. Wiley doesn't offer him the flask.

In the center of Bartlett's Pond, the corpse of a Black Duck floats, motionless in the still water.

"I admit that I was upset with the dog's performance, and when Haynes said he'd take him, it seemed like the best thing for everyone. I was out the cost of the dog, but I didn't care at that point. As I said, I hadn't hunted in years and this was a one-off to impress the client. I didn't need the dog, didn't want it. Haynes did."

With the help of Boykin's testimony, and according to the Massachusetts General Laws, I have Len Haynes on the following violation: "to subject, cause or procure an animal to be tortured or tormented; to be cruelly killed, beaten or mutilated." In this state, those are felonies.

I've called dispatch to request that a patrol car meet me at the Haynes's place in an hour. In the meantime, I'll go pick up Bull.

The deep cold of the past couple of weeks has moderated and the day feels almost balmy. The snow left over after the last storm is nothing but gray slush along the side of the road or gritty mounds in parking lots. The kids have forsaken Bartlett's Pond, leaving behind a net and a lone hockey stick.

I'm in no hurry to collect Bull, but it's already been more than half a day, and Lev was pretty clear that sooner rather than later would be better in getting Bull out of the way. Although I want to bust Len Haynes, it's more important that I do as Lev has asked. Besides, Haynes isn't going anywhere.

I've called Bull's cell phone, but it's going right to voice mail. The only thing left is to run by the house on Poor Farm Road and see if

I can make it look like the most natural thing in the world to drop by and invite him to stay with me. If Jimmy is there, I won't stop. I won't jeopardize the operation by acting out of character. I'll figure something else out.

I'm in luck: Jimmy's car is gone; the only vehicle in the yard is the ancient Nova. I bang on the front door, but no one answers. I rattle the knob and am surprised to find that it's not locked, so I push in, call Bull's name. No answer. I'm not getting a good feeling about this. Just in case, I do a quick search through the house for him. His bedroom looks tossed, but it always does. Jimmy's bedroom door is wide open and, unlike Bull's, his room is fairly neat—no piles of clothes, no cocked-open bureau drawers, the closet door shut tight. A pair of nice oxford-style shoes are, heels out, under the made bed. I walk down the hall to the bathroom. A single toothbrush dangles from the porcelain holder, one disposable razor with beard filings lodged in between the blades, lies on the counter, along with a can of Barbasol shave cream. I happen to know that Jimmy likes Gillette. I also happen to know—after all, he's my brother—that Jimmy takes blood-pressure medication. The only medication in the medicine cabinet is an ancient bottle of Phillips' milk of magnesia and a five-hundred-count bottle of extra-strength Tylenol.

Back in the kitchen, I give the stovepipe a rap with my knuckles. It clangs with a hollow ping. I open the firebox door and find nothing inside by ancient ashes. Jimmy's gone. Bull's gone. And the evidence is gone. Either the drug task force has finally swept in or Jimmy's on the run. I don't know if Bull is with him or if he has been left dead in some ditch by Jimmy's cronies.

I shut the front door behind me and lean on the rusted-out Nova as I call Harmony Farms's chief of police. Either Lev's going to be pissed that the DTF missed Jimmy or he'll tell me that my brother and father are in custody. I'm hoping that's the case. I can bail Bull out, get a good lawyer. I've got a little money from the sale of the condo Gayle and I owned.

Lev is understandably pissed off about my news, but he gathers his professionalism to his breast and thanks me for the info. Then tells me, "You ought to go find your father."

"Yeah, I will. Hey, I asked for a squad car. I've got to do an animal-cruelty arrest today. That going to be okay?" In other words: Will your boys be too busy to help me out?

"I'm sure it'll be fine. Good luck."

If it were the bad old days, I'd start with the local watering holes, checking into each one until I found Bull. But as far as I know, he's stayed sober since that weekend he spent with me. Without drinking and without a job, he's got nowhere to be. Nowhere to go. *And* not answering his phone.

There are bike tracks leading out of the driveway and down Poor Farm Road. I put my truck in park and climb out to see if I can determine which direction Bull might have gone. There is just enough slush to take a print, but more than enough dry pavement that he wouldn't have had to pedal through it, so the trail ends at the stop sign. If he turned left, he was heading for the village of Harmony Farms. A right turn and I have no idea where he might have gone except for a jaunt around the lake. Hardly likely. I take the left and drive like I'm hunting a lost dog, slowly and with my flashers going.

I'm not seeing any sign of Bull. He's not at Cumbie's, his go-to hangout, dragging on a cigarette and slurping coffee, so I pull into a space in front of the market and go in, hoping that he's chewing the fat with Elvin, who's recently back from his Florida vacation. Bull's not there, but Deke is.

"You see Bull around?"

"Not today. Last time I saw him was at the McDonald's rest stop. I was going to the dentist, but he didn't say where he was going."

"Who was he with?" I don't know if the *who* or the *why* is the more important question, but I don't think Deke can supply either answer.

"Didn't say. Didn't see anyone. Seemed like he was preoccupied, though. Wasn't too chatty." We both know that Bull loves to beat his gums.

"When was that?"

"Gosh, must have been a week ago, my appointment was on the sixth."

Elvin pipes up. "He was in here yesterday. But you're right, Deke; he didn't seem himself. Came in, grabbed a Mountain Dew, paid, and left. Not a word out of him." Elvin hefts a tray of freshly ground beef. "Interesting, though, he paid with a fifty."

Oh boy.

"Thanks, guys. If he shows up, let him know I'd like a call from him."

Elvin and Deke nod in an eerily synchronous motion.

I have that hollow feeling you get when something is out of kilter, and although something is very wrong about Bull's appearance at a highway rest stop and his current absence, that's not what's causing it. My limbs feel light, and there is a slight current of vibration flowing through the veins in my hands. But if I'm trembling, it's not from worrying about Bull's whereabouts, but from an adrenaline punch. I'm pumped as I head out of town toward the Haynes's place. I'm going to deal with Len Haynes now.

I'm like a real cop; I've got the law on my side and penalties like jail time and whopping fines. It gets my blood flowing. It's a familiar feeling, this rush, and I wonder why I haven't missed it more. It's a nice safe reminder of the pleasures of law enforcement. Justice will be served. All my life I've wanted justice. To be unfairly equated with my reprobate brother, to be despised for being Bull's son—these were injustices that were only cured the first time I made an arrest.

Now I'm on my way to bring righteousness to bear on behalf of an animal who has suffered the injustice of abuse, and for the first time since I took this job, I'm pumped.

It's probably a mistake, but I've got the yellow dog in the truck with me.

45

H e should have known that something was going on. This was the first time Jimmy had set him up as courier. Before that, it was Mike who made the plans and gave him the loaded backpack and detailed instructions, and Dave who drove him to the site. Bull takes the time to read each title of the sixteen thick paperbacks stuffed in his pack, recognizing a couple of the authors, James Patterson, Dan Brown. He's heard of Jane Austen, but the type is really small and dense, nothing he'd want to read. Bull fishes around in the outside pockets of the pack, hunting for anything that might be what his contact will be looking for, hoping that Jimmy hasn't done what he thinks he has.

Bull lights a cigarette, takes a good drag, deep enough that there's hardly any exhaled plume. The hand that's holding the cigarette is shaking, and he's surprised to find tears in his eyes. It's pretty obvious Jimmy is in trouble, whether of his own making or as a result of someone else's bad planning, Bull doesn't know, but intuition tells him that Jimmy is doing something really stupid. If Jimmy has betrayed Mike and Dave and whoever it is they all work for, he's a dead man. Is Jimmy trying to protect him by sending him on a wild-goose chase of a drop that's never going to happen? Or just making a fool out of him?

Bull drops the cigarette onto the wet leaf mold beneath his feet, stomps on the butt, just to make sure it's extinguished. He shoulders the backpack and heads back to his bicycle. The wind has picked up, making the temperature feel colder than it is. The instinct that suggests Jimmy is in trouble works to keep Bull from simply riding toward home. If Jimmy wanted him away from the house so badly, he'd probably better stay away for a little while longer, long enough that whatever was going to happen already has.

Instead of pointing the Raleigh toward Poor Farm Road, Bull points north, the wind in his face, and sets course for the Lakeside Tavern.

46

It's been an hour and I'm sitting in the town's animal-control vehicle, pulled onto the side of the road in front of the Haynes brothers' stockade fence, right beneath the sign that warns me that I'm awfully close to private and well-defended property. I'm waiting for my cruiser to arrive so that I can take Len Haynes into custody. They're late. Although I have the authority to arrest, only a fool would do this alone. Len and Bob may be all wind when it comes to their views on the right to bear arms, but I don't want to be the test case. Although, as my job falls under the purview of the police department, I have the right to wear a weapon, I don't. I won't. I'm done with that.

Another six minutes tick by. No cruiser. I really don't want to let this go another day, and when Len Haynes's truck draws beside my idling SUV, I really have no choice but to address the issue and hope that my backup won't be much longer.

Len Haynes scrolls down his passenger window, his face wearing his most belligerent expression. Apparently, my pass for being Bull's son is over. "What do you want?"

"Got to talk to you about a dog."

"We talked about dogs. You saw that I did what you said about the kennels."

"This dog." I gesture beside me, where the yellow dog sits.

"What about him?"

I'm not going to have this conversation through car windows. "Pull in." I wait as Len drives up the incline into his ragged yard. I follow, parking my SUV right behind him. A ruckus of riotous barking comes from behind the shed. I get out of the vehicle, leaving the door open. The yellow dog remains where he is, his head cocked in mild interest at the cacophony from the unseen dogs.

Still no squad car. I zip up my jacket. The temperature is above freezing, but a sharp north wind has come up, reminding me that winter is far from over. "I need to ask you a couple of questions."

"You're entitled. I'm entitled to maybe not answer."

"You took a hunting party out last fall?"

"Couple of 'em."

"This one was with a local guy, Donald Boykin, and his coworkers."

"Don't know who they were. Some muckety-mucks with more money than brains, that's for sure." Len has modified his belligerent expression to something not quite as hostile. "Big fancy car, good guns, and a dog that wouldn't hunt. That the dog?"

"Why yes, it is. You recognize it?"

"Seen one yellow Lab, you've seen 'em all. Could be that dog, maybe not."

The dog is framed in the open door. He's sitting in my seat now, his ears perked, his expression alert.

No squad car yet and I have to assume at this point that there won't be one anytime soon. So I square my shoulders. If I don't carry a weapon, neither do I carry the tools for an arrest, but I'm going to take my chances and tell Mr. Haynes exactly why I'm here. If he's willing to come with me peacefully, great. If not, he can wait here for Lev's officers or become a fugitive. I don't really care. I'm that tired of the situation.

"Mr. Haynes, Mr. Boykin has come forward and accused you of willfully mistreating this dog." I begin to list the abuses Boykin told me that Haynes had committed. "And after kicking and beating him with a gun stock, you shot this dog."

Len Haynes is silent for a moment, and I can't help but think of myself as someone who has riled a grizzly. His color darkens and his eyes bulge, until I hope that he'll say something before he explodes. "Damned liar. He beat and shot the dog. His pals walked off and he had one more shell in his gun."

"His word against yours."

"I tell you one thing: If I'd'a shot that dog, I'da killed it."

"Were there witnesses?"

"Yeah, there was. Me. I was walking back to get him. His pals were already in the car and they all wanted to go home. I got back to the pond and there he was, screaming and waling on that dog."

Even with the aggrieved tone, I don't buy his story. "Why didn't you report him?"

"Why should I? His property. None of my business."

From the corner of my eye, I see the dog jump down from the seat, stretch, and shake himself. And then it hits me: The dog isn't afraid of Len Haynes. He was terrified of Boykin. He's not trembling, or panting, or running off. He's ignoring Len Haynes. Haynes is telling the truth.

The dog is a witness and he's just saved me from making a big mistake.

"I'm sorry, Len. Would you be willing to testify?"

Len's face slowly returns to a more normal color, but his hostile expression remains. He takes a good look at the yellow dog, and I can see that he's noted the scar on his hip. "Yeah, I will."

As I head back to the shelter to write my report, I continue my fruitless search for Bull.

47

The ice that looked so substantial from the shore creaks under his weight, but Jimmy keeps moving. He's struggling to walk against a stiff north wind. Each time the ice creaks, his heart, already beating hard from the exertion, jolts him with intimations of mortality. He hasn't been afraid before, but now he is. He had planned this all so perfectly: leave Harmony Farms and his coconspirators, his sad-sack father, his lawman brother, disappear forever on a fake passport and the proceeds of his deal with a rival dealer. The months of trying to keep Bull safe and Mike and Dave ignorant of his duplicity have been exhausting. He's just so tired.

When he left the Poor Farm Road house, all of the heroin and cash tucked neatly into a backpack similar to the one that Bull has been using for the small drops orchestrated by Mike and Dave, Jimmy decided to take the longer and more scenic route. He was to meet his man in a parking lot on the north side of the lake, at the man-made beach he and Cooper used to go to back when they were kids. No one would be there this time of year. The exchange would be swift and efficient and, like a movie cowboy, he'd drive off into the sunset. By this time tomorrow, he figured, he'd be sipping piña coladas in the Caymans.

Jimmy has planned for every contingency, but who could have planned on a deer? When the doe jumped into his lane, Jimmy jerked the wheel and the Honda skittered sideways, its front tires hitting a patch of black ice. Forgetting to turn in the direction of the skid, Jimmy overcorrected and the Honda ended up in the ditch. The seat belt kept Jimmy from bashing his head on the windshield, but he was momentarily stunned by the surprise of it. He sat there for a moment, collecting himself, then unbuckled and climbed out.

There was no hope of extricating this car without a tow truck. Before some do-gooder could pull up and offer help, Jimmy popped the trunk, shouldered the heavy backpack, and faced the expanse of the lake. The shortest distance between him and his destination, his future waiting for him on the opposite shore, was to go across it.

Now Jimmy pauses in his struggle across the ice and pulls out the cell phone he liberated from Bull's back pocket as he put the backpack filled with paperback books on his father's shoulders. He flips it open, sees that Cooper has called Bull several times. Cooper never calls. That bodes ill. Jimmy can never forget that Cooper is a cop. Oh, he may have demoted himself to ACO, but at heart, he's a suspicious, nosy, lousy cop. He thumbs in the memorized cell number of the man he is supposed to meet. "I had a little car trouble. I'm on foot." Jimmy hopes that his new best friend won't get nervous, think this is a trap of some kind. "I'm really sorry. I hit ice and my car went off the road. Yeah, I've got everything with me. Maybe you can give me a lift out of town?"

Jimmy never learned to swim. The most he'd ever do was paddle around near shore, clinging to a boogie board or an inner tube. He never imagined that one day he'd owe this lake for his escape, or owe it his life. Jimmy has forgotten the treachery of lake ice; he's forgotten about Stevie Bonner, who died when they were kids, crossing the ice on a dare. Or the ice fisherman from downstate who wasn't found until May. Or the heroic rescue performed by the brave passerby who hauled those two duck hunters out of the freezing water. He doesn't notice that there are no ice-fishing shacks arrayed at various distances along the deepest part of the lake because the ice is no longer sufficient to support them.

All he knows is that on that opposite shore lies his salvation, his way out of a life that has become fraught with blood pressure–elevating events. When Carlos approached him, on neutral ground, quietly, the germ of the idea of a new life began to take hold. Carlos has arranged everything, from the passport to the bank account in the Caymans. All he wants in return is the dope and the turf. Jimmy is putting his trust in him. He doesn't hate his own handler, but he knows that the boss will never let him go. He will always have the whip hand. It's been that way since he was a kid, just learning the business. Right from the get-go, the boss treated him like a son—pats on the cheek, an extra hundred for a good job. But the boss will never let him go, not even out of gratefulness that Jimmy never took the plea bargain, never gave him up to the authorities. "You're too good a man, Jimmy. I need you." End of conversation.

Jimmy's boots are beginning to weigh him down, each sticky step a battle against the burning ache in the small of his back and the increasing sharpness of the wind. The sky is mouse gray, the snow on the ice absorbing the color until it, too, is more gray than white. Where the snow has blown off the ice, it's a pale silver gray, just the color of his own eyes, and Cooper's. Cooper, who hates him so much. It's a tough thing to be hated by your only brother. What Cooper can't know is that he pretty much hates himself, too. That's why it's been so easy to follow the path of least resistance, to cling to a life that has been lived on the edges, in the world of big bucks and no conscience.

Jimmy takes another dogged step; he's halfway across now. The rest should be easy. The creaking is almost a comfort now, an accompaniment to each step, telling him that he's making progress, even if he feels like his frozen feet in their rubber boots are dead-weight. He can't tell what time it is by the dull gray of the sky; the winter sun is diffused behind the scrim. His hands are too cold to pull out the phone to check the time, his fingers too numb to press the tiny buttons to let Carlos know he's still coming. His gloves are wet from taking hard falls onto the ice. He thinks that he's been out here an hour, but it could be two hours, or maybe only fifteen min-utes. He needs to stop, catch his breath, rest for a minute, but he's terrified Carlos will leave, imagining that Jimmy has bailed. But he's got to stop, if only for a second. He turns in a slow circle to make sure there's no one out there to see him, a black figure against the gray-white scene.

Once when they were kids, way before Mona died, Bull brought them out here to the lake to fish. Somehow, Jimmy fell into the wa-ter, and he can still recall the terrifying moment when he thought he would drown. Bull's big hand grabbed him by the shirt, hauling him to his feet. "You're okay, boy," he said.

They'd all had a good laugh; the water was only waist-deep.

So, when the ice gives way beneath his feet, Jimmy plunges down-ward, hoping that it's only waist-deep.

48

I 've put arresting Boykin on hold; my sense that Bull is in big
trouble has only grown in the time I've spent trying to find him.
I'm on my way to the Lakeside, my last hope. It's only by chance that
I've come this way, the shore route. I'm actively looking for Bull,
not Jimmy, but it's Jimmy's Honda I find wedged into the ditch.
When I spot the vehicle, I pull up and climb out of my town SUV.
I'm sure it's Jimmy's car, although one black Honda looks pretty
much like another. I crawl inside, pop the glove compartment, and
read the registration, which confirms that Jimmy's and my felon
brother is around here somewhere. I examine the muddle of footprints, hoping to find two sets, but I'm able to discern only one type
and size of clear tread. The trunk has been left wide open, gaping.
It's empty.

The yellow dog has invited himself out of the SUV and has his
nose pointed toward the lake. He barks, getting my attention. And
then I see him, eking his way across the lake, a backpack against
his shoulders, head down, persevering. Jimmy. Is he nuts? Walking
across the lake? I have a small pair of binoculars in the Suburban

and I reach in to get them. I have to be mistaken; this must be some fisherman checking a pole. This can't be my older brother, intent on reaching the other side of the lake, but it is. I lift the binoculars to see what he's heading for. The town beach. There's a car parked in the lot, an ordinary-enough car, midsize, American-made. Just the one car.

Jimmy pauses, bends from the waist, and I'm sure he's winded. He's in lousy condition and the ice has the consistency of sludge. Pulling himself upright, he makes a slow pirouette, and I figure that he's spotted me, because, he suddenly drops, like he thinks that he can hide from me. Then, with real horror, I realize that the ice has given way beneath him. I'm watching my brother die.

I frantically hit 911 and shout my stats to the communications center. Seconds are precious. The fire rescue team can't possibly get here fast enough. This is what I'm thinking as I grab my ice cleats out of the truck and tug them over my boots. Calling to Jimmy to hang on, I head out onto the ice.

My dreams are all too often the kind where I can't move fast enough, or at all. And that's just exactly how I feel right now. I'm really grateful that I at least have the legs and the lungs to run, even more grateful that I have my Yaktrax on and can make headway without falling. But I seem to be making no progress at all. I hear the crack of strained ice and hold up long enough to wonder what I'm doing out here, trying to save a brother whose whole life has been a cluster fuck.

The yellow dog moves ahead of me, cheerfully bounding in an erratic but forward direction, and I realize that he has some animal instinct about the safest route. I follow him, repeating uselessly "Find him, find him" at gasping intervals. I can't see Jimmy. I'm not even sure at this point if I'm heading in the right direction or will overshoot his location. Then I see a head, arms on the edge of the hole as he hauls himself up high enough that he can grab a breath. I drop flat to the surface of the ice, my emergency training kicking in. Just like a commando, I crawl toward my brother. The dog, seeing this new game, comes over to me, and I realize that he's putting me in danger by adding extra weight to the ice. "Sit. Stay."

God is with me, and he does.

I hear the sound of sirens in the distance. In the best of my dreams, backup does arrive. But in the worst of my nightmares, it doesn't reach me in time. I can hear them, but I don't see the rescue vehicles, and the American-made car in the beach parking lot is gone. I press myself flatter and creep a little faster, digging the cleats of my Yaktrax in deeper, impelling myself forward. They're not going to get here in time. It's my rescue now.

"Cooper!" Jimmy's terrified face rises from the hole in the ice like a pale apparition. His dark hair is slicked back, his gray eyes filled with panic. "Get me!" His teeth are chattering, and ice crystals decorate his eyebrows.

"Don't waste breath; just try to relax. I'm getting there." I have nothing to work with, no ladder, no rope, nothing except my superior position of being on the ice and not in the water, and my upper-body strength. And I don't think that's enough. The best I can do, the very best, is to hang on to him until help arrives.

I stretch out my right hand. "Take it, Jimmy. Take it."

The dog is barking. It could be encouragement, or it could be warning. I don't know. I'm in that zone where my only focus is on reaching my quarry. "Reach for me, Jimmy. Reach." I stretch out my arms as far as I can and waggle my fingers, as if I'm coaxing a baby to walk. Finally, I feel his icy hand in mine, and suddenly I'm in the water, too. The ice has caved in and I'm sinking under the weight of my clothes and my brother, who has panicked and is working against me, pushing me deeper under the water. I duck his flailing arms, grabbing for the best purchase on him, the backpack, which is adding to the saturated weight of him.

I start to pull on the straps, but he starts screaming. "No. I can't." His face is a mask of sheer panic; he's equally afraid of the water and losing the damned backpack. "I can't." With that, he kicks and twists around, dunking me back under the water.

I shove him aside, kick myself to the surface, and launch myself as far as I can to grasp at the bumpy ice. The dog is barking furiously. Clinging tenuously to the fast-failing edge of solid ice, I look up, to see the impossible image of Bull Harrison riding his bicycle across the surface of the lake, the yellow dog racing to meet him.

"Stop!" I think that I'm yelling, but I'm not sure. He's got to stop. I'm underwater again.

"Stay calm! Stay calm! I'm coming!" Bull Harrison drops his bike on the ice. Over his shoulder is the orange life ring that he's grabbed from the on-shore lifeguard stand. Attached to the ring is a twelve-foot line. Not a lot, but enough if he can get closer.

Bull had biked past the Lakeside Tavern. Kept his eyes on the road in front of him and kept going, finally arriving at the private pier at Upper Lake Estates. Warm from his uphill and downhill exertion, he'd been mulling over his situation, when he caught sight of two men out on the ice. At first, he thought they were a couple of nutcases skating on the soft ice. Then, to his horror, Bull figured out who the two men on the ice were, and what was happening.

Both his sons are in the water. Two boys he loves, even though they haven't been model children. Maybe they even, in their own fashion, love him back. Jimmy sent him on a wild-goose chase, sixteen paperback books loaded into the backpack instead of drugs. Cooper brought him home night after night, paid that clerk to let him stay inside Cumbie's. That's love. Sure it is.

The bike skitters away and Bull drops to his knees, makes his prayer to the Higher Power: *Let me save them and I'll stay sober forever.*

Don't let me lose both of them. Bull skates the life ring toward the open water, clings to the end of the line with both hands, keeping his sons afloat.

The yellow dog hunkers down beside Bull.

In the distance, drawing nearer but not close enough, sirens.

Two heads rise above the water; one hand finds the life ring. Cooper embraces his brother around the neck with one arm, furiously treading water to keep Jimmy's face up. There's no way Bull has the strength to pull them both up. Jimmy is barely conscious now, a deadweight, and Cooper is weakening fast in the cold water. "Give me some slack," he calls out to his father, and is rewarded with enough looseness that he thinks he can fit the ring over his brother's shoulders. But he can't. The backpack is in the way. Cooper's hands are almost too numb to work, but he manages to slide one strap off, then the other. The heavy pack disappears to the bottom of the lake. He still can't maneuver the ring over Jimmy, so Cooper links his arm through it, grasping Jimmy's coat collar in his other hand.

"Dad! Don't let go!"

The slack tightens, but they remain in the water. Cooper knows he's got to get out, help Bull on the other end of the line. But he can't. He can't feel anything anymore. Not fear, or adrenaline. He knows that he's giving in to hypothermia, but he kind of doesn't care. He hangs on to Jimmy's inert form, his treading water slowing down, his grip on Jimmy's jacket frozen into permanence. Cooper realizes that his brother is dead. His pale gray eyes are glazed over; all the fight in him is gone.

The yellow dog is barking furiously. Funny, he sounds just like Argos. That deep, proud, challenging bark. It's a comfort, that sound.

49

I have little memory of when the fire department pulled me out of the water. I remember that they wrapped one of those metallic space blankets over my shoulders. Jimmy's, too. Even though I knew that he was dead, they worked on him in the ambulance, where I lay beside him, and in the ER, where they took him behind a different curtain. With utter clarity, I heard the order from the attending doc: "Call it. Sixteen ten hours."

I am tethered to an IV drip, so maybe it's the warm saline coursing too fast into my veins, thawing me, but the warm fluid leaks out of my tear ducts.

A few minutes later, Bull comes into the unit, his Fu Manchu mustache still sparkling with droplets of lake water, his eyes red. "He's dead, Coop. Your brother's dead." He collapses into the side chair, covers his face in those great big mitts of his.

I pull my free hand out from under the heated blanket they've swaddled me in. I pull his hands away from his face. "I know, Dad. I'm so sorry." There is something else I need to say to him. "Thank you for trying to save us. You did all you could."

He squeezes my hand. "We both did."

The warm blanket begins to cool and the nurse comes in to replace it with a newly heated one. Bull keeps my hand in his. I'm just so sleepy.

We don't say much more. What is there to say? And then I think of something and startle myself awake. "Where's the dog?"

"Polly's got him. He's fine. Do you know, he pulled on the rope with me. Not like it was a game, but like he knew I needed the help. Planted his hind legs in and gripped that line with all his strength so we could keep it tight. Without him, I might not have been able to do it."

It sounds like something my Argos would have done.

I fall asleep, and when I wake again, Lev Parker is here and Bull is gone.

He's out of uniform and looks a lot like that kid I used to hang out with, my old teammate. He's wearing an untucked polo shirt, and I can see that he's a little thicker around the middle. His hair is prematurely shot through with gray, but he's still got the taut jaw with the five o'clock shadow he's battled since he hit puberty. "How you doing, Coop?"

"Guess I'm okay." I push myself upright. "Yeah, I'm okay."

"I'm sorry about Jimmy." He's not looking at me when he says it. "But I'm really glad you made it." He does look at me then. I see an old fondness, like he's just remembered that we were once friends.

"Tell me something, Lev."

He's on his feet, a tattered ball cap with our high school logo on it clutched in his hand. "If I can."

"Why didn't the drug task force act sooner? Why the delay when you had the proof on your desk? Proof that I gave you."

Lev Parker is a man of consummate integrity and devotion to his job. I watch the inner debate ride across his face as he weighs how much the truth will cost. We are in a public place, despite the privacy curtains. I can hear the relentless beeping of medical machinery, the incessant ringing of telephones at the nurses' station, and the squeak of rubber-soled shoes on the linoleum of the treatment rooms. Finally, Lev reaches a decision. He sits down in the side chair, pulling it up close to the edge of my bed. He leans in. "It was a mistake. Bad timing. The DTF was supposed to sweep in tomorrow because our inside man said that they would all be there for a meeting, everyone, including the ringleader. It was our opportunity to get them all."

"But he ran instead. Jimmy bolted."

"Looks like it."

"You think he got wind of it, the raid?"

"I don't know." I can see in his eyes that this failure is going to haunt my old friend for a while. He sits back, pats his knees like he's getting ready to leave, then leans forward again. "I hear you're planning on bringing Donald Boykin in."

"That's right."

"Can I ask you not to do it that way? I'll call him and have him come down to the station."

"Why?"

"His wife is our first selectman."

"That's hardly a reason. Are you suggesting that we can do this under the public radar?"

"Yes."

"It won't stay under the radar. It can't."

"It'll be more dignified for a man of his stature in the community."

"Dignified? Do you know what he did to that dog?" The warm saline drip is finished and the cold seeps back into my body. The heated blanket is barely warm. I am shivering again. "How does dressing well and handing out money here and there absolve you of cruelty? Do you know what he does to his employees? Fires them if they screw up. That's it, no mercy. And when this dog failed to perform, he beat him. Then, when the dog managed to get loose, he shot him. And you want me to treat Boykin with dignity?"

"Settle down, Cooper." Lev's voice isn't calming, but commanding. "I sincerely hope that you have the proof you need to make this stick, because if you don't, well, I don't need to tell you what will happen."

The implication is clear: One of us will be out of a job, most likely me. And that's just fine. "I've got a witness."

"Haynes?"

"Yes. You read my report." I don't tell him that the dog himself is a witness, although I've said something to that effect in my hastily written report: "Reactive in Boykin's presence."

"I did. And, Cooper, it's Len's word against Boykin's." Meaning, the redneck versus the philanthropist. Old Harmony Farms versus the new.

"That may be, but if I have to, I'll subpoena his boss."

"I won't tell you not to do what you have to; just be careful. That's all I'm asking. Really think about it."

The shivering is becoming uncontrollable; my teeth are chattering. I need more warm saline; I need another blanket.

Lev stands up, pats my shoulder. "You take care now."

A nurse starts a new saline drip, brings a freshly warmed blanket, and I doze off again, waking only when I feel the weight of another body slide in next to mine, the sweet weight of Natalie's arm over my side. Her cheek rests against my back. I am warm finally, well and truly warm.

I'm discharged from the ER just before midnight and Natalie drives Bull and me home to the Poor Farm Road house. The yellow dog is there waiting for us, courtesy of Polly Schaeffer. He greets Bull like a returning hero, all bounce and wag. I desperately want to go home with Natalie, but I can't leave Bull alone now. Even if I'm still numb to it, Bull has lost one of his sons. Natalie fries up some eggs and bacon for us, sees that we eat, and then strips and changes Jimmy's bed so that I have a place to sleep. I don't think that I can sleep anymore, but I do, and when I dream, it's of my mother. Her face floats under the water, her crystal gray eyes open and looking into mine.

When I woke this morning to bright sunshine, the yellow dog was staring at me, his muzzle planted on the edge of the bed, his brown eyes clear and bright. I'm not going to think about how much that reminded me of the way Argos would wake me in the morning. I'm not going to let myself slide backward into that abyss of grief. This is another dog, one who's finally healed from his wounds. Polly thinks she has a foster home for him, so he'll be out of my life soon. I'll put all of this to rest, happy enough with a successful outcome. That will have to do.

Bull is in the kitchen, making the day's first pot of coffee. I let him pour me a cup, then climb into my still-damp clothes. I have business to attend to— Mr. Donald Boykin to arrest.

Polly picks me up and drives me to where I'd left the SUV yesterday, pulled off the road behind Jimmy's abandoned Honda. The Honda is gone, impounded no doubt, and the Suburban is alone.

"Are you sure you don't need my help?" Polly would dearly love to accompany me to this event, but I'm not going to let her talk me into taking her along. I've called once again for a cruiser, and this time I'm assured that one will meet me at the Boykin residence. The dispatcher tells me that there was a bad accident out on the highway yesterday, hence the failure of my backup to arrive at the Haynes's.

Upper Lake Estates at Harmony Farms is lovely on this bright morning. The artfully winding road is impeccably clear of slush, and the only snow left is a gritty pile lodged near the maintenance building. From the top of the highest point in the neighborhood, I can see Lake Harmony, opaque with the dull pewter of its softened, treacherous ice.

Suburban moms are out in force, ferrying their kids to music lessons, dance lessons, hockey lessons, Saturday play dates. I'm passed by a phalanx of mom cars, all big, all with highest safety ratings, all tricked out with those little family stick-figure decals representing parents, children, and the family dog. I spot one HARFAR Euro decal on a Mercedes SUV. Good for Cynthia: They're catching on.

I glance in my rearview mirror and spot the cruiser slowly following me. Good. Now I just have to hope that Donald Boykin will be at home on this lovely Saturday morning. I signal and pull into the circular drive belonging to the town's first couple. Unlike the last time I was here, bearing the body of their deceased spaniel, I have not called ahead, so no one greets me in the front yard.

The cruiser pulls in behind me and, much to my surprise, it's Lev Parker who gets out. My first reaction is that he's going to try again to convince me not to do the job I am here to do, but he doesn't. "Officer Harrison, I've got your back." He gets in step beside me and together we walk up to the front door.

"Thank you, Chief. I appreciate it."

The housekeeper is a lot prettier than I had imagined. Twenties, blond, Slavic cheekbones. She doesn't wear a uniform, just a simple outfit of khaki trousers and white polo shirt. She takes one look at the town's chief of police and steps back, flushing. Probably in her country, the appearance of a police officer on your front step isn't a good thing. "Can I help you?"

We ask for Boykin and she invites us into the foyer, where we wait in silence for Donald Boykin.

I have failed before, in small ways and in large. I failed as a husband. Long before Gayle declared me unredeemable, I wasn't a good husband, a loving husband. I failed certainly as a son, estranging myself from my only parent out of a decades old resentment, a childish grudge. And I failed as a cop, failed my K-9 partner and thus lost him. My failures have brought me here to this moment, a dog warden; an unarmed, two-bit quasi–police officer.

On that deeply cold night, when the yellow dog and Cooper are invited to stay with Natalie, they are cozy on her sofa, a handmade afghan covering their legs, while the dogs are nested together in Betty's round bed. Natalie links her fingers with Cooper's. He playfully holds their hands up, examining the way that they look, ten fingers interlocked, hers neatly coupled with his.

"Marcus would do that; he loved the degree of difference in our skin."

Cooper gently extricates her hand from his. "I'm sorry."

"Why? You shouldn't be sorry to trigger a memory from time to time. I'm not going to not talk about him. He was a part of my life. But that doesn't mean that my life is fixed in amber. I don't mean my life; I mean my feelings. Just because I will always love Marcus, that doesn't mean that I can't move on. That I can't have a future."

I will not fail now. "Donald Boykin, you are under arrest for subjecting an animal to be beaten and attempting to kill said animal." I am a cop once more.

Epilogue

Three Months Later

I swear, this is the last time I'm going to bring the Bollens' miniature donkey back to his donkey-stubborn parents. Cutie-Pie is placidly strolling beside me down Main Street, carrot by carrot, as I hold them out for him, encouraging each hard-won step one at a time. A pair of tourists dressed in hideous floral shorts stop and ask if they can snap our picture. I put on my best duty face and stop short of telling them where they can put their iPhones. I'm pretty sure they take our picture from behind anyway. But it really is the last time I'm doing this. Cutie-Pie will become the problem of the next ACO for Harmony Farms. Next week, I'm back on the job.

I pull into the driveway of the Poor Farm house. The yellow dog hops out of the truck, his tail swashbuckling behind him, bounding over to Bull, who's sitting in a lawn chair, smoking and sipping Mountain Dew.

"I've got a favor to ask, Bull. A kind of permanent favor."

"Shoot."

"Can you keep him for me?" I point to the dog, who is sitting by Bull's side, looking up at him with adoring eyes.

"You got it." Bull bends over and ruffles the dog's fur between his shoulders.

"I mean permanently."

I'm heading downstate to train with my new dog. Lev Parker has secured some grant money and I'll be back soon enough to take up my new position in the Harmony Farms police department as the resident K-9 unit. He says he got the idea when the DTF had to borrow a sniffer dog from another community to finally bust the drug ring, which was enough to convince Lev Parker that a dog on the force will be a useful thing. If they'd had a dog in the first place . . . Well, as they say, hindsight is 20/20.

Bull lifts his rumpled-paper-bag face to me, grins, and nods furiously. "Sure, sure. I'd love to have him."

I'll be back in a few weeks, but I've given up the Bartlett's Pond camp. We're moving in with Natalie; me and my new K-9. I've been assigned, at my request, a Labrador. A black one. Her name is Zeena.

"Hey, what'd you do with the Nova?" I've just noticed the empty rectangle of barren dirt, bare from decades under the car.

"Got it hauled away. The guy gave me a hundred bucks for scrap." Bull pushes himself to his feet. "Hey, you gonna name this dog before you go?"

I turn and look at him, the yellow dog pressing himself against Bull's side. "You do it, Dad."

I walk away quickly, not wanting to see the pleasure writ so large in my father's big baby face. Not wanting him to see me misty-eyed.

Acknowledgments

When I count my blessings, Jennifer Enderlin, Andrea Cirillo, and Annelise Robey are top of the list. None of this could have happened without the support, guidance, and belief in the work that this trio provides me. I am honored and humbled to be one of your authors.

I am also blessed with the fantastic team at JRA: Don W. Cleary and Don Cleary, Christina Prestia, Julianne Tinari, Michael Conroy, Danielle Sickles, Peggy Boulos Smith, Liz Van Buren, and of course, Jane Rotrosen Berkey. Much gratitude to the savvy, smart, and dedicated folks at St. Martin's Press, who take care of the nuts and bolts of getting a book from mind to market, including Ervin Serrano, who has given this book yet another of his amazing covers. Thank you Jeanne-Marie Hudson and Joan Higgins, Sara Goodman, Chris Holder, John Murphy, Kerry Nordling, Sally Richardson, Anne Marie Tallberg, Stephanie Davis, Caitlin Dareff, and Lisa Davis—and Carol Edwards, who has, on more than one occasion, saved me from myself. Thanks also to the wonderful folks at Macmillan who bring the written word to the voiced, Brant

Janeway, Samantha Beerman, Mary Beth Roche, and Robert Allen.

For insights into the work of a small town ACO, I am indebted to Barbara Prada, Animal Control Officer and Inspector of Animals in Edgartown, Massachusetts.

Finally, I am grateful for the loving support of my family, friends, and legions of readers. I do it for you.

For Alexander and Hadley,
my Wish Givers

Chapter

1

✳ ✳ ✳

Griffin Penshine had three freckles under her left eye that sometimes looked like stars. This was a good thing, as Griffin was always wishing. She wished when a ladybug landed on a windowsill, she wished on dandelion dust, and she even wished on tumbling eyelashes. In fact, she often rescued the eyelash of a friend and reminded her to wish. But then again, Griffin always noticed the smallest of details. She could track her way out of a forest, spotted everything from worms to woodbeetles, and giggled at absurd words on menus like "jumbo shrimp." Griffin also liked certain things a certain way. She loved peanut butter on brownies, hated wearing turtlenecks,

and insisted her mom buy cool mint toothpaste.

On the last Sunday of a hot Kansas summer, a ladybug flew in through Griffin's bedroom window and landed on her arm. Griffin smiled and opened her new blue-lined notebook and scribbled her next few wishes.

I wish all vegetables had cool names like bok choy, alfalfa, and parsnip.

I wish to become an amazing bass guitarist.

Griffin thought for a moment and then crossed off her first wish. She didn't want to waste a wish on vegetables. As for being a great bass guitarist, she wished for that every chance she got. Too bad she hadn't wished for protection. But how could she know that within one hour the most horrible curse would fling itself at her and coil through her long, beautiful shiny red hair?

"Griffin!" called her mom from downstairs. "We're going to be late." Griffin's mother, an astronomer, loved to calculate the time it would take to reach Saturn, Neptune, the Andromeda galaxy, and even the center of town. She knew if they didn't leave in five minutes they would not make their afternoon appointments. Dr. Penshine hated being late,

and she loved to wear her huge collection of inspirational T-shirts that said things like SAVE THE EARTH. Only now that Dr. Penshine was pregnant, the words stretched over her huge bump and read SAVE THE EAR.

Griffin giggled from the top of the stairs. "I like your shirt, Mom."

Dr. Penshine looked down at her bulging tummy. "Ears need saving too!" she said, laughing.

Griffin grabbed her bass guitar, ran down the stairs, and slid into the car.

"Before I drop you off at your music lesson, I need to make a fifteen-minute stop at Mr. Schmidt's shop," said her mom. "He received a shipment of artifacts from Egypt—ancient clay scarab beetles—and an antique model of the solar system from an English castle. He's saving them for me."

"Okay," said Griffin. She didn't mind stopping. Mr. Schmidt, their neighbor, had the strangest objects at his store. Maybe she would find something for her pet turtle, Charlemagne's, terrarium or a good luck charm for tomorrow—the first day of sixth grade at her new middle school—or some cool object for her Mysterium Collection Box that she hid under her bed.

Although it was only a shoe box with a rectangle of midnight blue felt lining the bottom, inside the box were two

eagle feathers passed down by her great-grandfather before they became illegal to keep, half of a heart from her best-friend-forever necklace she shared with Libby Barrett, an old lace valentine her grandma Penshine had made as a girl, and three smooth stones.

Her grandma had given her the three lucky stones: a moonstone thought to have the power to grant wishes, a tigereye for courage, and a piece of purple amethyst. Her grandma said Leonardo da Vinci believed amethyst could protect people from evil and make them smarter.

Too bad she didn't take her purple stone in her pocket that morning. But she wouldn't think of that until it was too late.

A COLLECTIBLES, ANTIQUES, AND WONDERS sign hung above the door to Mr. Schmidt's tiny shop.

Griffin pushed open the door. Rusted bells jingled, and smells of dust, must, and exotic spices twisted up her nose. Long rows of glass shelves with faded lace fans, heavy silver hand mirrors, ladies' hair combs made of bone and shell, and stained decks of old maid cards glowed under the dim cabinet light.

At the back of the store, from behind a velvet curtain, Mr. Schmidt poked his head out. "Good morning, Dr. Penshine

and Griffin," he said. "Let me get that prized antique I was telling you about." He shuffled away.

Griffin bent her head over a glass case, looking at the lapis eye of a peacock feather and a mirror made of pitch-black polished stone. A handwritten card attached to the exotic feather read: *From India 1913. Believed to make wishes come true.* Under the circular black stone the card read: *Obsidian mirror—used by the ancient Alchemists, passed down from Aztec priests. See your future!*

A chill blasted through the room, and Griffin looked up. Behind the counter appeared the oldest woman she had ever seen, wearing a long black dress with a wilting red lily pinned to it. With her greasy gray hair pulled tightly into a bun, the woman's face resembled a shriveled apple. Wicked wrinkles gouged in her skin, and a grid of purple veins looked like a grotesque spiderweb covering her face.

Griffin stared.

The woman's eyes drank in Griffin. Then in a low, crackly voice she said, "Only once before in my life have I seen that shiny liquid red color woven into a girl's hair—half autumn leaves and caramel kisses, half blazing sunset."

"Griff?" said her mom, coming from behind her. "Find anything?"

"Dr. Penshine and Griffin, forgive me," said Mr. Schmidt,

returning from the back room. "I need to introduce my great-aunt Mariah Weatherby Schmidt, who has come from Topeka to visit for a few weeks. She offered to help me today at the store."

A sinister smile curled on Mariah's cracked lips. "What a pleasure to meet you, Griffin Penshine. What are you looking for today?"

"Something for my turtle's terrarium or something lucky for the first day of school," Griffin said.

"I see," said Mariah, her yellow eyes narrowing. "I have just the thing for you. One moment."

Griffin looked at her mom, but she was too busy examining the antique model of the solar system.

Mariah disappeared through the heavy curtain. Griffin's head spun. The scent of spices, mandarin orange, dried lavender, cloves, and incense pounded in her brain. "Mom, I have a headache. I'm going to wait outside."

"Okay. I'll be five more minutes," she said.

Just as Griffin's hand touched the doorknob to leave, Mariah's cold hand brushed hers. "Where are you going, dear?" She held out a ring box. "This is for you."

"What is it?" asked Griffin, not moving from the door.

"Open it," the old woman said, beckoning with her long, spindly fingers.

Griffin slowly took the box from Mariah's bony hand and looked inside. Beams of light shot out all over the ceiling like lasers, illuminating the store. Carefully Griffin removed a single Indian Head penny.

It bounced in her hand.

"That's the shiniest penny I've ever seen," said Dr. Penshine.

"I'm sure it is," said Mariah. "I never forget to . . . polish it. It is priceless. An Indian Head penny from 1897. Very rare, very valuable, and shall we say . . . very lucky."

"Wow," said Griffin, mesmerized by the pulsing glow. Droplets of light sprinkled all over the room.

"It must be yours!" said Mariah, her eyes flashing.

The strangest sensation knotted inside Griffin, part repulsion, part desire. "How much is it?" she asked.

"It is my special gift to you." Mariah smiled wickedly. For a moment Griffin swore Mariah looked younger, luminescent, something wild and alive in her eyes.

"I can't take something priceless for free," said Griffin, now blinded by the magnificent penny.

"Just promise you'll keep it shiny, and it will be . . . worth it to me. You will accept my gift, won't you?"

Every cell in Griffin's body fought to say, "No. No, thank you!" But the Indian Head penny shined so hypnotically

that Griffin could hardly speak. Her pupils dilated from the beams shooting off the penny. She tried to shake her head, stop the odd breeze that whirled around her body. *No,* she mouthed, but no sound came out. Instead "Yes" exhaled from her lips.

Mariah froze. Then very deliberately she said, "It is done. Let me get a box of polishing cloths from the back for you. Give me a few moments to find it."

Griffin tucked the penny into her pocket, and it burned against her skin.

Penny, penny bring me luck,
'cause I'm the one who picked you up.

Chapter

2

H ow neat to have a lucky penny for the first day of school, Griff," said her mom, carrying her own prized antique back to their car.

"Yeah, but why do you think Mariah said 'It is done'?" asked Griffin. Goose bumps sprouted on her arms when she repeated the words.

"Probably just an old-fashioned saying. She *really* is ancient," said her mom.

Suddenly a cloud above them smothered the light in the sky. Both Griffin and her mom looked up and at the exact same time said, "It looks like it's going to rain!"

"WISH!" Griffin said, smiling. She believed that

whenever two people said the exact same thing at the exact same time, a wish would be granted. Griffin counted quickly on her fingers. "It looks like it's going to rain" had seven words in it. "Seven wishes!" she said to her mom.

"You already know what I wish for seven times," said Dr. Penshine with a dreamy smile on her face. Griffin knew she wished for a healthy baby. Griffin climbed into the car as raindrops started falling in giant plops. Her mom carefully set the antique in the backseat.

Griffin looked at the darkening sky outside the car window. Silently she thought of her wishes . . .

I wish to become an amazing bass guitarist.

Griffin had been studying bass for the last four years with her guitar teacher, Mr. Castanara.

I wish my new school smells like warm chocolate chip cookies!

She smiled. Her old school smelled like erasers, floor cleaner, and sharpened number two pencils. Maybe her new school would be different.

I wish for a baby sister.

She loved the girl names Janis, D'Arcy, and Michelle, after her favorite female rock stars.

I wish for Grandma Penshine to get well soon.

For the last year her grandma had been having unexplainable dizzy spells and horrible headaches.

I wish the dentist will not have to pull my two back molars for braces.

I wish no kid in the world has nasty green food caught in his teeth and no one tells him.

I wish when it stops raining that no soggy worms will fry on the sidewalk the next sunny day.

Just as she made her last wish, the sky turned a greenish hue, the air hung still and deadly, and heavy moisture weighed upon her skin. Suddenly thunder roared and needles of rain unleashed from the sky.

"Summer storm!" said her mom, starting the engine.

Thunder clapped as javelins of lightning flew through the sky and bounded over the rooftops. Rain, wind, and leaves swooshed violently all around the car.

"This is unbelievable!" said her mom, fiddling with the

radio. "It's like a warm and cold air mass just collided in front of us."

"Attention, Dadesville citizens. This is from the National Weather Service." A series of high-pitched beeps blasted through the speakers. "A tornado warning has been issued for Dadesville. Please take immediate shelter in your basements. A tornado is headed directly toward Dadesville."

Tornado sirens posted on poles throughout town suddenly screeched out a steady alarm, which vibrated the car's windows.

"We've got five minutes to get home!" said her mom, swerving the car around in a fierce crazy eight.

Griffin shuddered. An ominous emerald sky now cloaked the town. When a tornado circled its prey, the sky turned green. Outside the car window, the wind raged.

"Hang on, Griff!" said her mom, speeding the car through the street toward their home. Trees swayed like toothpicks, and the roofs of houses cringed from the heavy rain attacking them.

Finally they made it to their garage. Dr. Penshine took a deep breath and rubbed her big belly. "I'm going to go get our portable radio and a flashlight. Run down to the base-

ment and wait for me. I'll call Dad on my cell phone and see how far away he is from home."

Griffin ran through the door. With her bass guitar swinging on her shoulder, she grabbed Charlemagne from his kitchen terrarium and leapt down a flight of creaky stairs to their basement. The single lightbulb hanging from the ceiling hardly lit up the dank room. Her family never used their basement except to store potatoes, onions, and sports equipment. Griffin shivered and sat on the cold cement floor. She realized she was still clutching in her left hand the small box of polishing cloths Mariah had given her.

"Dad is stuck at Grandma's house," called her mom from the top of the stairs. "He can't drive home now. He's going to stay in Grandma's basement with her. I need to grab some blankets for cover."

"Can I help?" called Griffin.

"No! Stay downstairs! The tornado is moving closer!" yelled her mom.

The penny that Mariah had given her felt hot in her pocket.

Does copper attract heat? Griffin wondered. She hoped her best friend, Libby, was safe in her basement with her family. She tried to call to see if she was okay, but her cell phone was dead.

"Mom, can I run upstairs and use the kitchen phone to call Libby?" Griffin yelled.

"No! Stay off the phone! With all this lightning, that's how you get electrocuted!"

Right when her mom said the word "electrocuted," thunder crashed so deafeningly that the entire house shook, and the clasp on the box of polishing cloths sprang open. A few soft cotton rags toppled out. Griffin scooped up the cloths, and a burst of light exploded out of the box. A massive glow lit up her face. Concealed beneath the polishing cloths rested ten radiant pennies in a thick black velvet pad. One slot was empty. "WOW!" gasped Griffin.

After pulling the penny from her pocket, Griffin placed it in the unfilled slot. It fit perfectly. A box of eleven perfect pennies! Gently she pulled the first penny out of its slot. Attached to it was a narrow faded yellow label stuck across the width of the coin. One word was written on the label with a black pen. In the most precise handwriting, the letters spelled "puppy."

She pulled out the next penny. The narrow label attached to it read "no homework." The next one read "STOP" in all uppercase letters. Another one read in tiny, tiny letters "change the world." The next penny: "popular."

Griffin pulled out the second row of pennies. This one read "a baby." The next read "a dad," another one "success."

Another one read "most beautiful." Griffin held the dullest penny. It read "world peace."

"Huh?" said Griffin aloud.

Are these people's wishes? she thought. A powerful thunder blast pounded the sky and jolted her house to its foundation.

Copper light zigzagged on the ceiling from the pennies' glow. Griffin slipped her fingers around the inside edge of the box and discovered the slotted velvet lining was loose. Peeling back the velvet, she felt the bottom of the box and found an old, yellowed envelope. Across the front, in that same strange handwriting, it read:

To: Griffin Penshine, the girl who accepted my "lucky penny"

From: Mariah Weatherby Schmidt

When I saw you, a memory sprang into my head. Only once before in my life have I seen hair the color red like yours, like a gussied-up copper penny. I am very, very old. Some people might call me ancient. Right, my dear? But the curse must live on. All that work for nothing would be such a waste. You are the one. Inside the envelope is my story.

A horrible feeling tossed in Griffin's stomach. Gingerly she opened the envelope and spread the fragile typed letter on the floor.

Long ago, when I was hardly done being a girl, I accepted my first job as a secretary at an inn. The inn stood at the crossroads of Topeka, Kansas, and a bubbling fountain graced the center courtyard.

The first time it happened, it was an accident. On a hot Kansas day I heard a plunk-splash in the water. I pushed away the white lace curtain to see a little boy and his mom standing before the fountain. The boy said, "I wish for a boat." From high up in my office I saw exactly where his penny landed. That's how it began.

At night, after working late, I would dip my hand into the fountain, scoop up the wet pennies, and toss people's wishes around in my palm. A person's penny could be a wish for a pony, but it bought me a pretty silk ribbon instead. For years I swept up the change,

buying myself sweets, eating people's wishes. I loved to twist their dreams in my hair with the fancy ribbons I bought for myself. I heard a lot of wishes in those years, as people stood alone before the fountain, not thinking.

I could hear the plunks and pings of the coins diving through the water. And the things they wished for! Silly things, sad things, important things.

Sometimes people were really desperate and would throw dimes into the fountain. Dimes could buy you something really nice back then. Dimes didn't plunk in the water like a penny. A dime was like a little ping. Ping. Ping. Like a silver raindrop. It was a beautiful sound. I'd wait a few minutes till the people were inside fiddling with their bags and I'd rush out, pretend I was cooling my fingers, trailing them in the water. But when I pulled my hand out, a wish was captured in my palm.

✳ ✳ ✳

I am 92 years old. After all these years, these eleven pennies never lost their glow. Sometimes they even felt hot in my hand. They are all Indian Head pennies, much more potent and valuable than regular pennies. I saw exactly where they landed, heard the secret wishes aloud. I labeled them so I wouldn't forget. I never felt a drop of guilt either. Like my father told me when I was a young girl, I wasn't going to amount to much so I should just stop dreaming and wishing and filling my head with silly thoughts.

You are the new guardian of the eleven stolen wishes. You are the new Wish Stealer.

There are three rules to wish stealing:

1) A Wish Stealer's good wishes will not come true.

2) A Wish Stealer's evil wishes will come true.

3) If a Wish Stealer tells anyone about the

curse, he or she will be cursed for life, and the person he or she tells will never have any of his or her wishes come true.

P.S. Once you've accepted the wishes, they are yours. IT IS DONE. You can't dump them into the garbage, or toss the whole box into a fountain and forget about them.

In that same strange handwriting as on the envelope, she had written in pen at the bottom:

P.P.S. You could trick someone into accepting the box, but you don't seem like that kind of girl—yet. The penny I gave you at the shop flew like a leaping ballerina vaulting into the water. That person didn't say her wish out loud, but her penny was as dazzling as her long red hair.

Griffin stood in shock. *A Wish Stealer.* She pulled a penny from its slot. "STOP" was written on its label. *Stop what?* she wondered. Her head pounded. Mariah Weatherby Schmidt had tricked her! Furiously she stuffed the box of pennies into the side pocket of her guitar case, and clenched Mariah's letter in her hands.

Griffin's mom clunked into the basement. "The tornado is getting closer. Are you okay?"

"I . . . ," said Griffin, staring at her mom and her big belly.

"Griff, what's in your hand?"

Mariah's letter flopped like a limp fish in her palm. "Uhh, a letter I was writing to . . ." She gulped. "Grandma." Just as she said the word "grandma," a bolt of lightning struck the house.

Penny for your thoughts,
nickel for your dreams.

Chapter

3

The next morning rain dribbled outside the Penshines' kitchen. Dr. Penshine set three hot blueberry pancakes on Griffin's plate and three on Griffin's dad's plate. "Pancakes to celebrate the first day of school," said Dr. Penshine.

"You can say that again!" said Griffin's dad, reading the morning paper before heading to Eastern Kansas University, where he taught law. "It says here that Dadesville hasn't experienced such erratic weather in the last hundred years. One minute it's a summer day; the next minute a tornado nearly destroys the town."

"I can't believe our house was struck by lightning! Thank goodness you weren't near water or on the phone, Griff!" said Dr. Penshine.

Griffin chewed the mountain of pancakes and nodded with her mouth full. Last night, when the announcer on the portable radio had said the tornado had diverted its course and she was allowed upstairs, she hid the box of pennies under her bed. Would none of her good wishes come true? Could she really ruin other people's wishes if she told them about the pennies? she wondered. She knew her dad wished for wars to end and to get tenure. Griffin shook her head. She believed in wishes, but not in Wish Stealers. Mariah had to be totally bonkers, a senile old lady, *ancient*, like her mom had said. Griffin refused to believe in curses. There was no way a box of Indian Head pennies could hurt her.

She decided to just enjoy her mom's blueberry pancakes.

"Griff, I forgot to tell you. When you were upstairs getting dressed, the dentist called. It turns out that she is going to have to pull your back molars for braces. There's an opening next week."

The pancakes morphed into a lumpy ball in her throat. Wasn't that one of her wishes? *I wish the dentist will not have to pull my two back molars for braces.*

If you are a Wish Stealer, none of your good wishes will come true blasted through her head.

Probably just a coincidence, Griffin reassured herself, but she lost her appetite anyway.

✳   ✳   ✳

Coincidence . . . or . . .
COIN-incidence?

Chapter

4

riffin slid into the car. Charlemagne had acted strangely all morning, afraid to come out of his shell. Griffin thought it had to be the weather. She refused to think about Mariah or the curse. After all, it was the first day of school. She and her best friend, Libby, had planned their outfits a week before and had promised to wear their gold heart best-friends-forever necklaces today.

She wore her new canvas Converse sneakers that she'd spent all summer decorating with permanent colored pens. One side of each sneaker was blue, and the other side sported purple paisleys. "Go Green" was written on the white rubber rim. A peace sign swirled on the tops. She'd even sat on

her bedroom floor coloring her shoelaces in tiny multicolored stripes. That had left little marks like an outlined centipede on her hardwood floor that she thought looked supercool (a feeling her mom didn't share).

Dr. Penshine parked the car in front of Griffin's new school and read, "George Washington LeGrange Middle School. You're growing up so fast, Griff." Her mom's eyes moistened.

"I love you, Mom," said Griffin, hugging her. Lately her mom cried over Hallmark card commercials, a dead goldfish, and every time someone mentioned that the planet Pluto had gotten demoted.

"Pregnancy hormones," explained Griffin's dad each week. He also stocked the freezer with Häagen-Dazs mint chip and butter pecan ice cream for Dr. Penshine's cravings, which made Griffin love it even more that her mom was pregnant.

"Have a great day!" called her mom.

Griffin dashed toward the school lobby, where she planned to meet Libby. Giddy in her raincoat, with her hood flying off, she splashed through the puddles, forgetting all about stolen wishes. Looking up at the rain, she hoped each and every drop would either turn to chocolate or grant a year of good luck for the person it fell on.

Griffin did not notice Mariah across the street, drenched in her long black raincoat, staring at her like a waiting crow. An evil smile curled on Mariah's cracked lips. Through the cold, misty rain Mariah crept closer to the school.

✳   ✳   ✳

Beware the person with
the Buddha smile and snake's heart.
—Chinese proverb

Chapter

5

✳ ✳
✳

Mariah pounced across the flooding street. Her shoes slapped over the sidewalk, and her cold palm pushed open the school doors. Inside the school lobby she smoothed her hair and opened her black bag. After pulling out a delicate flowered scarf, she tied it over her hair, removed her black coat, and pinned a bright red flower, a lily, the same color as Griffin's hair, onto her dress. Mariah chanted under her breath, "Stars, hide your fires. Let not light see my black and deep desires." She cackled in the hallway and slithered toward the front office.

Locker doors slammed, and the buzz of students swarmed

through the polished halls. So many kids jammed the corridors that it was hard to walk and not get smacked by a giant backpack or an oncoming slew of kids. Griffin and Libby tried to push their way toward room 13, first period English class. Middle school was nothing like fifth grade, where students stayed in one classroom.

"Come on, Libbs," said Griffin.

"I'm trying!" said Libby when some towering eighth graders cut in front of her.

Libby had a cute upturned nose, warm brown eyes, and shoulder-length blond curls that bobbed as she walked. Today she wore a superbright pink, yellow, and green striped sweater that looked like it spent its free time keeping ships from crashing into the shore.

"Room 13, " said Griffin, reading her schedule and leading Libby toward the opposite side of the school building. Libby had no sense of direction, loved garlic mashed potatoes, and dreamed of being a famous artist like Frida Kahlo one day. She loved to tape pictures from magazines all over her bedroom wall and make origami out of silver bubble gum wrappers. Most of all she loved hanging around Griffin's grandma, who was a painter and gave them lessons on the weekends when she felt well enough.

Griffin, on the other hand, wanted to be a rocket scien-

tist or a rock star. She was also very proud of her sneakers. They entered the classroom and grabbed two desks toward the front. Both of their BFF heart necklaces glowed from the raindrops that had fallen on them.

Just as Griffin sat in the seat, "Griffin Penshine, Griffin Penshine, please come downstairs to the front office" blasted over the loudspeaker.

"Huh?" said Griffin. "That's weird. Did I forget something? Be right back. Can you save my seat?" For a moment a strange feeling crept over Griffin. *Could this have anything to do with Mariah?* she thought. But she shook her head and told herself she was being silly.

"Sure," said Libby.

Griffin powered through the emptying halls to the front office.

The strong scent of lilies wafted through the stairwell. Like cloying perfume or a dying bouquet in a funeral home, the smell shot up Griffin's nose and gave her a headache. Griffin walked into the office.

Sitting behind the administrator's desk stacked with unopened mail, a jolly woman with a ruddy face and a booming voice said, "You must be Griffin Penshine."

"Yes," said Griffin.

"I'm Mrs. Davis, and you have the nicest, sweetest grandma in the whole world," she said.

"How do you know?" Griffin asked.

"She just came in from that nasty rain to give you something she forgot—a first-day-of-school gift! Said she'd been waiting *years* to give it to you. Isn't that so sweet?" said Mrs. Davis, leaning her weight over her desk and handing a small box to Griffin.

Griffin beamed. Even in this terrible weather, with her grandma not feeling well, she'd still taken the time to drive to school. She adored her grandma Penshine. Dropping off a special gift for her was just like something her grandmother would do. While Griffin's mom used to write notes with a nontoxic black pen on a banana like *I'm bananas over you!* and stick it in her lunch bag, her grandma gave magical gifts like a hand-knit bag with lucky stones and a four leaf clover inside. (Charlemagne ate the clover by accident, but Grandma Penshine said not to worry, it just made Charlemagne a very lucky turtle.) Griffin opened the box. A tiny golden key lay inside with a note: *Good luck. From Mariah.*

All the color drained from Griffin's face.

✳   ✳   ✳

Good luck or bad luck can flip on a dime . . . or a penny.

Chapter

6

D ashing back to first period English class, Griffin couldn't stop sneezing. The smell of dying lilies barreled through the hall. *Mariah pretended to be my grandma!* The thought enraged her. *What is this key for?* She sneezed five more times.

Griffin clenched the key in her hand and darted into a bathroom. She stuffed her pocket with toilet paper for her runny nose. Finally she made it back to room 13. She quietly opened the door and scanned the sea of heads for Libby's blond hair and striped sweater. But the seat next to Libby, the one she'd asked her to save, was taken. A beautiful girl with long brown hair as silky as mink, and with the high preppie

collar of her shirt turned up, sat there. Griffin walked to the one empty desk in the back corner of the classroom.

That smell. She couldn't get that sickly sweet smell out of her nose. "Haaaaachuuuuuuu! Haaaachuuu! Haaachuuuuuuu!" Griffin sneezed uncontrollably.

"Ewww," said a boy in front of her.

"Excuse me," said Griffin.

"Gesundheit!" said the teacher.

Libby turned around and mouthed *I'm sorry* and tipped her head toward the girl who'd taken Griffin's seat.

Rain hit the classroom windows, and the sky darkened.

"Whoa! Look at the sky!" a boy exclaimed.

"Creepy!" said a girl.

"'By the clock 'tis day / And yet dark night strangles the travelling lamp,'" quoted Mrs. Gideon, the English teacher. She had short silver-gray hair and wore a long skirt and a necklace made from chunky, colorfully glazed pottery pieces. "What perfect weather to begin our study of Shakespeare's condensed *Macbeth*!" Mrs. Gideon clapped her hands together. "Some people think this play is a bit advanced for sixth graders, but I say nonsense. It's about desires, greedy rulers, and betrayal— themes found in most of your computer games."

On the board Mrs. Gideon wrote, *Lilies that fester smell far worse than weeds*, and drew a witch's hat next to the

sentence. "Everyone has three minutes to write down on a piece of paper what they think this quote means."

Is this why the school smells so bad? Griffin wondered. *Was it part of the lesson?* Griffin stared at her paper. Suddenly her hand felt possessed and she scrawled out a sentence.

"Okay, class. Time's up! Pass up your papers so I can read some aloud," said Mrs. Gideon. She flipped through some of the answers and stopped on one paper. "Who is David Hunt?" called the teacher.

David raised his hand.

"You wrote 'This quote means weeds really stink, but beautiful flowers stink worse,'" read Mrs. Gideon. "Interesting." She rustled through more papers. "Who is Griffin Penshine?"

Griffin raised her hand.

Mrs. Gideon smiled and read Griffin's paper, "'This quote is really about people. Some bad people are like weeds, ugly on the inside and outside. But what's worse is to be a good person who turns bad, does cruel things, and rots on the inside.'"

"Very good. Very good, Griffin," said Mrs. Gideon. "Maybe you'll be my new English star this year."

Griffin blushed. Libby turned around and smiled at her. The gorgeous girl next to Libby swiveled her head at Griffin. She narrowed her swampy green eyes. Griffin stared back. She

had never seen eyes like that, green cold slits like a reptile's.

Just then the intercom blasted through the school. "Attention, students. This is your school principal, Dr. Yeldah. Please walk to the auditorium with your class for our welcome assembly."

All the kids packed up their bags. Griffin slid the tiny gold key in a side pocket of her backpack. *What awful thing does it open?* she thought, shivering.

Libby ran up to her. "Griff, I'm sorry. I told that girl I was saving that seat for you, but she just ignored me and sat there with her two friends."

"It's okay, Libby. It's not your fault. Maybe she got confused," she said.

"Why did you get called downstairs?" asked Libby.

Anger surged through Griffin. She couldn't believe Mariah had come to her new school!

"Griff?" said Libby.

"Uhh, my grandma"—Griffin gulped—"gave me a present."

"Students, stay in your group, line up on the far left of the auditorium, and file into the first three rows of seats," said Mrs. Gideon.

Libby and Griffin scanned the auditorium for some of

their friends from their old school and looked at all the new kids from different schools. Already they'd heard whispers about the cutest boy in sixth grade, Garrett Forester, whom they spotted on the opposite side of the auditorium.

While Griffin and Libby stood waiting to enter the row of seats, the girl who'd stolen Griffin's seat talked with her two friends. On her left stood a tall girl with long flat-ironed blond hair. She wore a necklace with the name Sasha sparkling in silver letters. On her right a girl with shoulder-length brown hair wore a pink headband with the name Martha embroidered on it in green. She wore a beige plaid designer skirt. Martha was saying, "Samantha, I just know you're going to win the Fresh Face! Prettiest New Face Contest. The whole school has already seen you model on your dad's infomercials. Everybody knows he's the best dermatologist with the *best* skin products in Kansas."

Samantha smiled, glad that Martha was talking so loudly. She turned around and looked Griffin and Libby up and down. "What school are you guys from?" she demanded.

"We went to Dadesville Elementary," said Libby.

"We went to Westminster *Private* School," said Samantha. Sasha and Martha did not move or smile.

"Isn't that the school with its own planetarium? My mom said the planetarium is really cool," said Griffin.

"It's totally lame. I hate planetariums," said Samantha. "Wait, is your mom the town astronomer, Dr. Penshine, the one who always wears those stupid T-shirts?"

Red flames shot up Griffin's face. Lilies. That horrible smell of putrefied lilies crept up her nostrils. She sneezed five times.

"Disgusting!" snarled Samantha. "Use a Kleenex! You almost ruined my cashmere sweater!"

Griffin reached into her pocket for a tissue and blew her nose loudly. "I *love* my mom's T-shirts," said Griffin. She did not notice that a long piece of toilet paper fell out of her pocket and onto the auditorium floor.

"Samantha Sloane," called the gym teacher. "Please go sit up on the stage. The principal chose your name out of a hat to welcome your class."

Samantha flipped her hair and walked away.

"I've seen her on her dad's infomercials. She's rich, beautiful, and mean—like a queen lizard," said Libby.

Somehow the image of a lizard queen walking around school cracked Griffin and Libby up, and they couldn't stop laughing.

Students finally settled into their seats. The principal walked onstage. "Welcome, students. Before I speak, I'd like to call up the three class representatives I randomly picked

this morning to read our state motto in unison, 'To the Stars Through Difficulty! *Ad Astra Per Aspera*,' and tell me how he or she thinks this motto applies to our exciting school year!"

Samantha and the seventh- and eighth-grade representatives moved toward the microphone. Suddenly a group of boys roared with laughter. Griffin and Libby stared. The boys pointed at Samantha as she pranced in front of the whole school. A long piece of toilet paper was stuck to the heel of her designer shoe.

Samantha looked down, ripped the toilet paper off her shoe, and glared across the auditorium at Griffin.

What a strange illusion it is
to suppose that beauty is goodness.
—Tolstoy

Chapter

G riffin's foot tapped under her desk in third period math class. A queasy feeling sloshed around inside her. Maybe she was just nervous; after all, it was the first day of school. But the stench of rotting lilies still coated the school from floor to ceiling, and she had already made an enemy.

"It reeks in this school!" kids cried in the hallways. Griffin spied a group of janitors searching for the source of the odor. "It's the oddest thing," she overheard one of them say. "We don't have a clue where this smell is coming from. We scoured the place from top to bottom only two days ago."

She thought back to her last seven wishes. Two had evaporated in the last 24 hours.

X   *I wish the dentist will not have to pull my two back molars for braces.*

X   *I wish my new school smells like warm chocolate chip cookies.*

She told herself she was being silly. It was all just coincidence. Wasn't it?

"Fifteen more minutes on these last math problems," said her teacher, Mrs. Sato. "Concentrate! I'm assessing your math skills from this quiz."

Was Griffin going crazy, imagining things? A tightness wrapped itself around her throat. She remembered her two most important wishes: *I wish for a baby sister. I wish for Grandma Penshine to get well soon.*

Chills, like sharpened fingernails, crept up her back. In case there was even the tiniest bit of bad luck stuck with Mariah's wishes, and these weren't coincidences, Griffin had to get rid of them.

"Griffin?" called Mrs. Sato.

"Yes?" she said.

"Are you okay?" the teacher asked, bending over her desk. "You've been very distracted ever since class began."

"I—I'm sorry, Mrs. Sato. I didn't get much sleep last night," said Griffin, gazing down at her paper. On it she had written her name, had numbered from one to eleven, and had drawn a large penny.

When Mrs. Sato walked away, Griffin wrote down Mariah Weatherby Schmidt's age, ninety-two, and the sentence from Mariah's letter—*hardly done being a girl*. What age would that be? Most people consider someone done being a girl or boy at eighteen, the official adult age. So if Mariah wrote that her first job was around this time, she was probably eighteen or a little younger. Griffin wrote $92 - 18 = 74$.

Seventy-four years ago, give or take a few years, Mariah Weatherby Schmidt had started stealing wish pennies from the fountain. All sorts of people of all ages made wishes. Griffin clasped her hand over her mouth. Griffin guessed a lot of the people whose wishes Mariah had stolen were probably dead!

Mrs. Burns leaned over Griffin's desk as she scribbled numbers fiercely on her notebook. "Much better, Griffin!"

Griffin smiled at her teacher, but her thoughts were flying. She was determined to make Mariah take back her box
of stolen wishes after school.

Refuse to take on other people's bad luck.

Chapter

8

Late afternoon sunshine beat mercilessly down upon the asphalt. *It's as if the storm and rain never happened,* thought Griffin. She moved closer to Mr. Schmidt's house carrying Mariah's black box. Every drop of water had evaporated. On the sidewalk worms writhed, frying in the sun. Griffin grabbed a broken branch and tried to gently move worm after worm to the safety of the grass, but there were too many.

I wish when it stops raining that no soggy worms will fry on the sidewalk the next sunny day, ran through her head.

"This is awful," said Griffin. Crows circled above. "I wish . . . ," she began, but she stopped herself. For the first

time in her life she had lost her confidence in wishing.

Up ahead of her was Mr. Schmidt's house. All the shades were drawn, and it looked sealed like a tomb. Griffin walked up to the front door and knocked three times. "Mr. Schmidt!" Griffin shouted, and knocked even harder. "Mr. Schmidt!"

"Griffin?" called a neighbor from next door.

"Hi, Mrs. Jasper," she answered.

"I heard all the commotion out here. I thought someone was knocking on my door," she said.

"I'm looking for Mr. Schmidt and his great-aunt. Do you know when they'll be back?" asked Griffin.

"Your family hasn't heard?"

Griffin shook her head.

"It happened around ten this morning," said Mrs. Jasper. "I'm sure it was pneumonia. The evening the tornado passed by I saw Mariah out on the front porch in the rain! Imagine sitting in a rocking chair in weather like that! I was about to call Mr. Schmidt to get his aunt out from that awful weather, I thought maybe she wasn't quite right in the head. She was very old, you know. Anyway, when I looked out again, she was gone. Mr. Schmidt said she lay down to take a nap this morning and died in her sleep. He said there was the strangest smile on her face. He's gone back to Topeka to arrange the funeral."

Griffin gasped.

"I know, dear," said Mrs. Jasper, coming closer to her. "These things can be very sad, but what a long life! Did you know his aunt?"

"Not really," she whispered.

"Nice lady, very old. Only been here a week. Imagine that," said Mrs. Jasper. "Mr. Schmidt asked me to get the mail. Was it something important you needed?"

"No, I . . . did his great-aunt have any children?"

"As far as I know she never married, and Mr. Schmidt was her only relative. But she wanted to be buried back in Topeka."

Griffin trudged home, now feeling the horrible heaviness of the box of stolen wishes in her hands.

The best way out is always through.

—Robert Frost

Chapter

9

Samantha's long hair swayed like a sheet of perfectly smooth silk. In English class the next day not one strand dared disobey her. She wore a designer dress with horseshoe logos all over it, bead bangle bracelets all up her right arm, leather riding boots, and a scarf knotted into a headband. Instead of a backpack she carried an Italian handbag her mom had handed down to her when she'd gotten bored with it. Some of the boys feared her, others had crushes on her, and the rest had a little bit of both. Girls chimed throughout the hall, "Hi, Samantha. You look amazing!" or "Oh, my gosh, Samantha. I *love* your dress!"

"What a wonderful start we had with *Macbeth*! A storm

to set our stage!" said Mrs. Gideon. "Now we will dive into the play, which opens with three witches telling Macbeth his fortune. Not what *will* happen, but what *could* happen as painted in the stars."

Griffin sat in the back row, stuck in that lonesome seat from the first day of class. Scanning the heads in front of her, she saw Samantha surrounded by new girls who wanted to be friends with her.

Her grandma always said, *To have a friend you must be a friend.* Griffin thought Samantha didn't seem like she'd be a kind friend, but it didn't seem to matter. Everything felt upside down, and Griffin hated not telling her parents, Libby, or any of her old friends at her lunch table about the way Mariah had tricked her. But what if something bad did happen, and everybody's wishes started unraveling if she told? She would never trick someone like Mariah had tricked her into accepting the box of wishes. If only there were a way to return the wishes. She sunk her head onto her folded hands and looked out the window at the shifting clouds.

"Macbeth and Banquo ask the witches to tell them their fortune," said Mrs. Gideon. She read from the play, "'If you can look into the seeds of time, / And say which grain will grow and which will not, Speak then to me . . .'

"It is only the second day of school, but I already have a surprise for you. The Shakespeare Is Not Dead Traveling Globe Theatre Company. They just arrived in town! Please welcome the three witches from *Macbeth*!" Mrs. Gideon clapped ecstatically.

From outside the hallway a wretched cackling echoed. Three stooped hags with straggly hair, dressed in black shredded rags, moth-bitten shawls, and pointy hats shuffled into the room.

Every student sat straight in his or her seat. Although everyone knew the witches were just actors, the women's faces looked wildly aged, bumpy with warts, and lined with a million creases. One of the witches carried a spell book under her arm, with the title *The Future, Fate & Mortal Wishes.*

"They look real!" whispered a student in front of Griffin. Chills ran up and down her spine. They did look real. Impossibly real. Horribly real.

"Double, double toil and trouble; / Fire burn, and cauldron bubble . . . Eye of newt and toe of frog, / Wool of bat and tongue of dog . . ." they crowed, hovering in a coven in front of the room. Griffin couldn't take her eyes off the spell book. *It's just a prop,* she reminded herself.

The three witches finished their lines and stood like

vultures, with their beady eyes scanning the classroom.

"Beyond lifelike!" said Mrs. Gideon. "Students, do you have any questions?"

Griffin's hand shot up. "What's in your spell book?"

The first witch answered, "Would you like to take a look, my dear?"

Griffin nodded, mesmerized by the witch's yellow eyes. Just like Mariah's.

The witch hobbled over to Griffin and dropped the spell book onto her desk. "Be quick, my dear. Time is almost up," she whispered.

Her face, so close to Griffin's own, looked familiar. Those pinched lips, sunken hollow cheeks, rotted skin, and dried desert of wrinkles . . .

"Next question for these otherworldly actors!" said Mrs. Gideon.

Griffin bent her head over the book and opened to the table of contents. Ancient mildew wafted up at her. She traced her finger down the page, feeling a covering of sticky cobwebs. *Chapter 4: Stealing and Returning Mortal Wishes.* Griffin turned to Chapter 4. Her heart raced as she read:

If one possesses a stolen wish, the best way to break its curse is to return the wish to

its rightful owner. That is the most powerful magic. Be advised it takes some time for the magic to work.

If that is impossible, one can return the wish to a person who is on the same journey as the original wisher. The magic is not as strong, but if the intention is sincere, it may work.

Griffin memorized each and every word. Then she read the final sentence on the page.

If a stolen wish or wishes are not returned, they corrupt the new owner, and all that is good and full of light inside that person will be destroyed. Evil will infest its host, and tendrils of darkness soon will overtake him or her.

Griffin's face lost all color.

"I'll be needing that back now, my dear. Did you find it . . . *lucky*?" asked the witch, suddenly hovering over Griffin.

"Uh, yes," said Griffin, looking deep into the witch's swirling eyes.

"Enchanted!" said Mrs. Gideon. "Let's give the three actors a huge round of applause."

Evil smiles set on the three crones' faces, their black teeth bared to all the students.

Bringgg rang the bell.

Libby waited for Griffin outside class. "Mrs. Gideon is really into this play!" said Libby, and she mimicked the teacher, "'Fair is foul, and foul is fair!' Those witches were freaky!"

"Yeah," said Griffin. Her head pounded.

Together they walked toward their bright orange lockers. Earlier that morning they had decorated them. Griffin had brought photos of her family, her grandma and her, Libby and Griffin river rafting on a giant inner tube, Charlemagne, a shooting star, Griffin jamming on her bass guitar, and Janis Joplin singing.

"Griff, look, is there something on your locker?" said Libby as they came closer.

Toilet paper streamed out from the locker vents, trailing all the way down to the floor.

"Samantha!" said Libby.

Griffin opened her locker. Toilet paper twisted inside like paper snakes. Just then Garrett Forester walked by. His dirty blond hair flopped over his bright blue eyes, and his jeans hung loose and baggy. "Whoa," he said, smiling at Griffin, who was now standing in a pool of toilet paper. "Cool photos," he added. "Is that you playing bass?"

"Yeah," she said.

"Awesome," he said, smiling again.

Griffin blushed as red as a fire engine.

Genuine gold fears no fire.

—Chinese proverb

Chapter
10

E arly the next morning Griffin opened the box of
pennies and scooped up one for each pocket, and
then tucked the box into her backpack. All night
she had debated about what she should do. Mariah Weatherby
Schmidt was dead. There was no returning the stolen wishes
to her. Even if she gave the box back to Mr. Schmidt, he
would probably stick it on a sagging shelf in his overstuffed
garage or just dump it into the garbage. Then she might still
be stuck with bad luck. She decided she would *try* to return
some of the wishes to "a person who is on the same journey as
the original wisher," whatever that meant. Maybe that would
help stop these "coincidences."

X   *I wish the dentist will not have to pull my two back molars for braces.*

X   *I wish my new school smells like warm chocolate chip cookies.*

X   *I wish when it stops raining that no soggy worms will fry on the sidewalk the next sunny day.*

?   *I wish to become an amazing bass guitarist.*

?   *I wish for a baby sister.*

?   *I wish for Grandma Penshine to get well soon.*

?   *I wish no kid in the world has nasty green food caught in his teeth and no one tells him.*

In her left pocket was the "no homework" penny, and in her right pocket was the "world peace" penny.

Griffin couldn't stop touching the pennies. The natural oil from her palms was making them glow. No homework and world peace seemed nearly impossible, so she decided to start with them. Even on math tests Griffin always attacked the hardest problems first.

"See you after science. We'll save a seat for you at lunch," said Libby, with Maggie Hart and Madison James, friends from elementary school, heading toward their social studies class. Griffin continued walking alone down the long science wing, past bulletin boards of colored paper, past the stingy

water fountain that doled out a droplet at a time, and into the huge science room with cardboard planets dangling from the ceiling.

A few kids sat in their seats, staring at the planets slowly swaying back and forth as if they were on a hypnotist's chain. Griffin took her seat.

"Good morning, my bright and amazing students, the future scientists of the universe! We are here to understand THE WORLD! THE ENTIRE SOLAR SYSTEM! THE UNIVERSE!" said Mr. Luckner, the sixth-grade science teacher. He wore yellow pants and a black shirt with puffy planets dancing all over it. "Can you all believe at this very minute that at the equator our planet is spinning one thousand thirty-eight miles per *hour*? The average speed for a car on the highway is fifty-five miles per hour! Think about how fast the earth is moving right now! Dizzy, anyone?"

The boys in the back row kept staring at the cardboard planets, heads swaying.

"We all should be dizzy just thinking about it!"

A few kids yawned as some others quickly tried to finish their homework while Mr. Luckner wasn't looking.

"All-righty! How many minutes would it take a rocket to travel from Earth into space?"

Griffin's hand shot up. "Nine minutes!" she blurted out.

"Very good, Griffin, very good," said Mr. Luckner. Griffin knew this because her mom always said, when stuck in holiday traffic, "I can't believe this! In a rocket we could reach *outer space* in nine minutes and we're stuck in Dadesville County traffic for thirty minutes!"

Griffin smiled, thinking about her mom. A boy she didn't know, Zeke, at the desk next to her smiled back. Giant chunks of green spinach snarled in his braces. A girl sitting to her left, Ashley, smiled. Green goop stuck in her front braces too.

Griffin's eyes grew huge. That was another of her wishes: *I wish no kid in the world has nasty green food caught in his braces and no one tells him.*

I have to tell them! she thought. "Zeke!" she whispered. "Zeke!"

Mr. Luckner called, "Griffin, would you come to the board and try to estimate how long it would take to travel from Earth to Jupiter if I gave you some facts?"

"Okay," said Griffin, distracted by the spinach.

She walked toward the front of the class. Mr. Luckner handed her a dry erase marker, and she climbed up on one of the high stools to write the formula on the whiteboard. Just as she placed her foot on the inner rim of the stool, her penny tumbled out of her pocket and rolled on the floor

like a wobbly planet, in front of the whole class.

Mr. Luckner swooped down to pick it up before she could climb off the stool. "Find a penny, pick it up, all day long you'll have good luck," sang Mr. Luckner, turning the penny over in his hand.

"'No homework,'" he read.

Griffin stood in front of him. The whole class hushed.

"Griffin, are you trying to send me a message?" he asked.

"No. It's just a penny I found," she answered.

A strange look washed over Mr. Luckner's face. "A penny that has 'no homework' taped on it!" said Mr. Luckner. A stillness engulfed the room, and even the swinging planets stopped. The science room snake flicked its tongue against the glass wall of its terrarium. Its yellow eyes lit up, glaring at Griffin. Mr. Luckner stared, mesmerized by the penny. Light from the penny blinded the entire class.

Mr. Luckner exploded, "THIS IS A MARVELOUS idea! A stupendous idea! NO HOMEWORK!"

Every kid in the room sat up, electrified.

"Instead . . . ," said Mr. Luckner. A strange glow emanated from the penny and scattered light off the hanging planets. A copper radiance swirled in Mr. Luckner's eyes. Mr. Luckner spoke again. "Instead of nightly homework for

the next month, I'm assigning all of you participation in our school's science night. In the past, science night was voluntary for sixth graders, but it is now *mandatory* for all of you! You will create a booth, display materials, and write a six-page paper to present at science night. You must work on this using books and the Internet. You have a little less than one month to get ready for science night.

"My whole life I've been wishing for no homework to correct!" said Mr. Luckner, and he tossed the penny back to Griffin—but just then a gust of air swept through the room, flinging the penny into the tropical fish tank.

Griffin watched the penny sink through the aquarium water, past the sharp red coral, and disappear into a plastic sunken ship. All the fish bulged their fish eyeballs, circling around and around in pursuit of the lost penny.

"Your first quarter science grade will depend on your science night booth and your oral reports on a famous scientist, due next week," said Mr. Luckner.

He wrote on the board:

Wednesday, September 10, ORAL REPORTS (on famous scientists)

Wednesday, September 24, SCIENCE NIGHT (booth and paper)

"That's all folks. No homework! Just two projects this month. No more nightly correcting for me! Brilliant idea, Griffin!"

"Now look at all the work we have to do!" said Zeke. Green vegetables stuck in his braces.

"I'm excited!" said Audree Stein, who had long chocolate brown hair that fell in soft waves around her pretty heart-shaped face.

"I'm not! Thanks for ruining the first month of school!" said Michael Janis.

Griffin bit down hard on her lower lip. She thought, *This is how the first wish begins.*

Be careful what you wish for.

Chapter

11

"How's school going, Griff?" asked her dad when he picked her up at car pool.

"Fine," she said, but school had been anything but fine the last three days. Kids in Mr. Luckner's class were angry at having to do a science project, and she'd found more and more pieces of toilet paper stuck in her locker. She slid the "world peace" penny deep into her pocket for the whole world's safety.

"Really?" said her dad, knowing her too well. He pulled onto the main road headed to the bakery in the center of town.

"I guess it's just getting used to a new school," said Griffin.

* * *

When they entered the bakery, smells of cupcakes and melting chocolate greeted them. "Would you like a sample?" asked the lady behind the counter, holding out a frosted double chocolate brownie to Griffin and her dad.

"Just what I was wishing for, Griff!" said her dad, licking the chocolate from his fingers like a little boy.

"Yeah," Griffin said, and she smiled sadly. She wanted to tell her dad so badly about Mariah.

"We're here to pick up a cake for my wife's baby shower," he said.

"Oh, yes, we're almost done frosting Saturn's rings. Can you give us five minutes?" asked the clerk.

"Sure," said her dad, spying the newspaper rack.

"Dad, I'm going to go outside and look at the cakes in the window."

"Okay, Griff."

In the large refrigerated bakery window, rose petals were scattered on the floor of the case. Three cakes of different shapes rested on stands. One was shaped like a race car, another heart-shaped with strawberries and raspberries on top, and the largest cake of all frosted a perfect pink. A beautiful porcelain figure of a ballerina twirled on top of it.

A few feet from Griffin a tall, willowy girl, whom Griffin recognized from gym class, stopped with her mother to look

in the bakery window. "Look, Mom," said the girl. "Look at the cake with the ballerina! She's beautiful! Can I please, please, *please* take ballet lessons?"

"Kristina, I told you, it's a waste of money," said her mom.

"How do you know?" Kristina asked.

"Only one percent of ballet dancers can even get a job or make a living."

"What if I'm the one percent?" asked Kristina.

"Most people aren't meant to be dancers; they're meant to watch. Lessons are a lot of money, and then for what?"

"Mom—"

"The answer is no!" said her mom. "Come on. I'm going to get a parking ticket!" Kristina's mom walked away.

"I know I could be the most beautiful dancer if I took lessons, Mom," called Kristina to her mother's back.

Griffin froze.

Most beautiful rang in Griffin's ears. *That's one of the wishes,* she thought. She turned to look at Kristina.

Kristina slunk a few paces behind her mother.

Griffin went back inside the bakery. A giant cake was set on the counter in the shape of Saturn, its rings frosted in yellow, orange, and red. The frosted letters on top read, *Congratulations! We're over the moon (s) for you!*

Griffin smiled. Saturn had more than sixty moons, so

the writing was a special joke for the people who worked at the observatory. "It's not every woman who would want a Saturn-shaped cake," said her dad, laughing.

The bakery door flung open behind them. Samantha, Sasha, and Martha strutted right past Griffin, pretending not to see her. At the counter Samantha said to the saleswoman, "I'm here to pick up my forty chocolate chip cookie invitations to my birthday party."

Glancing down at the Saturn cake, Samantha whispered to her friends, "Nerd cake! Maybe they should serve it with *toilet paper*."

Sasha and Martha laughed.

Griffin stared at the three girls and mumbled under her breath, "I wish Samantha looked like a queen lizard with warts all over her face!" Griffin gasped. What a horrible thing to wish . . . even on Samantha! Her chest felt tight, her throat went dry . . . as if dark tentacles coiled inside her.

"We'd better hurry, Griffin," said her dad.

"I know," she said.

Inside Dadesville's domed planetarium a galaxy of millions of stars was projected against the darkening blue sky. The Pleiades, Betelgeuse, Sirius, Pegasus, Orion's Belt, Ursa Major, and Hercules all shined in the dimming heavens. Even

Cygnus, the swan, soared on the giant ceiling above them.

Griffin sat alone in one of the reclining chairs looking up at the universe. From the bottom of her backpack she took out the box of pennies and hid them under her coat. Penny number one, "no homework," had not gone well at all. How had it fallen out of her pocket when she had stuck it deep inside the cotton lining?

Griffin peered into Mariah's black box. Slowly she studied the different pennies. She had slid the "world peace" penny back into its slot. Griffin held a penny up to the faded ceiling starlight. The label was curling off. It said "success." "Success?" she whispered. Griffin's grandma said she had a great success every time her garden bloomed in the spring. Was success qualifying for the Olympic team, having a true friend, or being a great parent?

"Please, please, please," she whispered, "to all my old and favorite stars my mom taught me, help guide me to return these stolen wishes."

When it is dark enough, men see stars.

—Ralph Waldo Emerson

Chapter
12

T he next day in Mr. Luckner's class, Griffin
watched the planets swish on the wire above her
desk. Mr. Luckner gave the class some time to
work on their projects in class, but kids just slumped in their
seats and chatted. Griffin tried to cheer herself up. She had
returned the "no homework" wish, and maybe something
good would come of it. David Hunt tugged a strand of
Griffin's hair from his desk behind her. He teased, "Girls go
to Jupiter . . ."

Griffin whirled around. "David, you're saying it all wrong.
It's 'Girls go to Mars to become rock stars.'"

"Yeah, right. Girl rock stars stink," said David.

"Dude, there are some amazing girl rock stars: Janis Joplin, Michelle Shocked, Tina Weymouth," said Garrett, flipping his moppy bangs as he walked past their desks.

How can he see under all that hair? Griffin wondered.

"How do you know so much about music?" she asked.

"I'm in a band," he said proudly.

"Really? That's so cool. What's the name of your band?"

"Excuse me," said Mr. Luckner. "This is work time, not social hour. Everybody is so busy chitchatting that it seems you all prefer partners. Okay, class, it's TEAM PROJECTS, then! You all must earn a grade together! My two As, Audree and Aiden—a team! Brian and Brent . . . Garrett and Griffin . . ."

"Come on, no, Mr. Luckner, please!" some students begged if they were unhappy with their partners. On the other hand, people who got hardworking partners couldn't stop smiling.

Garrett beamed.

Griffin cringed.

She couldn't imagine working with Garrett for the next month. Although half the girls already had crushes on him, with his crazy hair and twinkling blue eyes, Griffin noticed how he doodled nonstop in every class they were in together.

Garrett stood over her desk.

"Have you started a project or picked an idea?" asked Griffin.

"Yeah. It's practically finished." Garrett shrugged and tossed his hair out of his face.

"Really?" said Griffin, shocked. She hadn't even decided on a topic yet. Trying to concentrate on anything was difficult with the weight of those wishes upon her.

"What have you done?"

"It's done in my head," he said.

The bell rang.

After ripping off a piece of her notebook paper, she wrote down her number. "Can you call me tonight? We can decide on a project, divide up the work, and set some times to meet at the library. Science night is a huge grade, Garrett. It's really important to me. My mom's a scientist and . . ."

"Yeah," said Garrett, smiling like he'd just won the lottery. "It's *way* important to me, too!" He walked out of class and hummed, "Girls go to Mars . . ."

On the way to lunch after gym class, Griffin noticed a slumped figure hunched by the water fountain in the hallway. It was the girl Griffin had seen in front of the bakery the day before. "Kristina?" called Griffin.

When Kristina turned around, her face was swollen like she had been crying all night. "Are you okay?" asked Griffin.

"Yeah," she said, not meeting Griffin's eyes.

"I'm Griffin. You were amazing during the fitness tests today!"

A tiny smile pulled on Kristina's lips.

"You know, I saw you at the town bakery yesterday," said Griffin.

"Oh, yeah?" she said, shrinking with embarrassment.

"I heard you say you loved ballet." Now Griffin blushed at what she was about to say.

Just then Mr. Luckner walked past them, whistling to himself. Griffin wondered if she was doing the right thing at all. Taking a deep breath, she continued. "I have something for you," said Griffin, digging into her backpack.

"Really?" said Kristina.

"This is a very old lucky penny. Maybe you could be the most beautiful dancer if you wished on it," said Griffin in one hurried, embarrassed breath.

Kristina took the penny and read, "most beautiful" on the tiny tag glued across the penny.

Quickly Griffin swiveled her head to see if anyone was watching.

"What do I do with it?" asked Kristina.

Gurgling water surging inside the water fountain pipes gave Griffin an idea. Griffin knew water conducted electricity. Maybe if the penny were dunked in water it could reenergize its original wish. "You should wash it off, *recharge* it, and make a 'most beautiful' something wish. Be specific, then wait until it comes true."

Kristina probably would have thought it silly, holding the penny under the trickling water fountain, if it weren't such a miraculous-looking penny. "This penny is psychedelic!" She swished the dripping wet penny in her palm, squeezed her fingers around it, and mumbled her wish. Light surged out between Kristina's fingers.

BAAANGGGG!

Griffin jumped.

Kristina's hand jerked open. A locker slammed in a distant hallway.

"Oh, no!" Kristina cried.

"What?" said Griffin, looking down the empty hallway.

"The penny! I just dropped the penny down the water fountain drain!" Kristina's face started to turn blotchy.

Griffin stared at the water fountain. "That's okay, Kristina. Uhh, it's exactly what was supposed to happen! How could I have forgotten to tell you?" said Griffin, thinking fast. "After

you wish, you need to throw the penny into water for the magic to travel. Usually it's a well, but the school water fountain is just fine." Griffin wiped her sweaty palms on her jeans.

A second locker door slammed and Samantha Sloane, carrying a stack of huge chocolate chip cookie invitations, slunk toward Griffin and Kristina.

"What are you guys doing? Why did you just give Kristina that penny?" demanded Samantha. "Are you *paying* kids to be friends with you?"

"What?" said Griffin.

"Griffin was just—," said Kristina.

"NO! Don't tell, Kristina!" said Griffin.

"Thanks. Gotta go!" Kristina said, and she ran down the hall.

Griffin stood face-to-face with Samantha. "Don't tell me what?" asked Samantha, her teeth glinting in the fluorescent hall light.

"None of your business," said Griffin, meeting her stare.

"Hey, Griffin!" said Garrett, walking up to them. "What's your number again? I lost it, but I'll call tonight," he said. "Here, I'll write it on my arm so I don't forget."

Samantha's eyes grew narrower and narrower as Griffin told her number to Garrett.

"Passing out pennies and your number, *Griff*?" she said.

"Science project, *Sam*," Griffin shot right back.

Suddenly Samantha swirled around and flashed her eyes like a lit-up slot machine at Garrett. "Hey, Garrett," she purred. "I wanted to give you one of my chocolate chip cookie invitations to my birthday party this Saturday." She handed over the frosted cookie with her address and the time of the party.

Samantha's B-day

Sat. 9/6

1:00 PM

408 Rosmell Court

"Cool cookie!" he said, taking a bite out of the time and address. Now it read:

Samantha's B-day!

at. 9/6

00 PM

smell Court

Griffin read the mangled cookie and smiled.

"I hope you come," Samantha flirted.

"Thanks," said Garrett, taking another bite of the cookie as he walked away. "Later."

Samantha whirled back to face Griffin. Just then Samantha's two best friends ran up to her. Martha, who always looked like she stepped out of a designer accessory catalog, said, "We just passed out another twelve cookies, and so far everyone is saying *yes!*" They high-fived and giggled.

"Your party is going to be amazing!" said Sasha.

"With only the coolest people invited," said Martha, ignoring Griffin.

"I know," said Samantha, and they strutted down the hall with smirks on their faces.

No pessimist ever discovered the secret of the stars
or sailed an uncharted land,
or opened a new doorway for the human spirit.
—Helen Keller

Chapter
13

Jamming on her bass guitar in her bedroom after
school, with her headphones on, Griffin slashed
at the strings and pounded her head to the raging
music. She hated Samantha's clique. *Did it really look like
I was paying kids to be friends with me, bringing presents for
people I'd just met?* thought Griffin. Griffin's back hurt. Her
head hurt. Everything hurt.

"GRIFF! GRIFF!" yelled her mother outside her room.
"GRIFFIN!" Her mom knocked on her door.

Griffin jumped down from her bed and opened her door.

Her mother put her hand on her hip and stared. "What's
going on? Didn't you hear me?"

"Sorry, Mom. My music was too loud."

"Is everything okay?" she asked.

"Yeah," Griffin said with a shrug, avoiding her mom's eyes.

"I've been calling you. The phone has been ringing off the hook," said her mom, holding the phone in her hand. "Libby called and said call her right back. She has to tell you something really important. Also the dentist called and said she made a mistake. She said she was looking at the wrong X-rays. She doesn't have to pull your back molars after all, and a Garrett Forester called."

Did Griffin just hear her mother right? The dentist didn't have to pull her molars? Her wish had come true! Maybe giving the "no homework" penny to Mr. Luckner had done something good! Maybe she could do it. Maybe there was a way to stop the curse. Griffin jumped up and down, ran up to her bed, and cartwheeled off. "NO WAY!" she shouted. "I CAN'T BELIEVE IT! I AM SOOOO HAPPY!"

Griffin's mother stared. "Is this because that Garrett boy called?"

"WHAT?" said Griffin, stopping mid-cartwheel. "No! Oh, my gosh, Mom, no! I just can't believe that the dentist said she doesn't have to pull my molars. You don't understand!" Griffin twirled around the room again.

"I guess not," said her mom, staring at Griffin oddly. "Who is this boy?"

"Mom, please! Garrett is my science partner for science night. We got assigned to work together."

"Okay," said her mom, still staring.

"I better call Libby back! Thanks, Mom!" said Griffin, now dancing around her room. *It worked!* She didn't have to have her back molars pulled! Maybe giving Mr. Luckner the penny counted! Her intention had been sincere to help Kristina, too. Maybe Kristina could be the "most beautiful" dancer and another of Griffin's own wishes would come true! She couldn't believe how Kristina's mom had talked to her about dancing— just like a Wish Stealer. She could never imagine her parents talking to her like that, stomping on her dreams.

I'm on a roll! she thought. Griffin cartwheeled off her bed again. *I refuse to be a Wish Stealer! Take that, Mariah!* Another cartwheel made her dizzy. *Then again,* Griffin thought, *if it's working, that means I need to return more wishes so the opposite of my other wishes won't come true!* Griffin remembered her wish for her grandma to get well. She thought of the new baby on the way. She had to work even faster to return the wishes.

"You're growing up, Griff," said her mom, all teary-eyed, watching her from the doorway.

"Mom, please!"

Just then the telephone rang.

"Forester Garrett," read Griffin's mom off the caller ID. "He's calling again?"

"Mom, it's a science project! I gotta take this." Griffin took the phone from her mom's hand, waved good-bye, closed the door, and flopped onto her bed.

"Hello?"

"Griffin, hi, it's Garrett. Sorry, I was going to leave a message 'cause my mom and I are going out for pizza."

"Yeah, thanks for calling. We need to pick a science project idea. I have a couple ideas."

"Maybe we could blow something up, show how explosions work, or grow something really gnarly," said Garrett.

"Huh," said Griffin, thinking. *Maybe we could make a force field against Samantha?* she thought. But instead she said, "Can you meet me at the town library after school tomorrow? We can look at some books and decide on a topic. I can talk more with my parents tonight about it, okay?"

"Okay," he said, "but I gotta be quick. Band practice."

"Cool," said Griffin, feeling her face getting warm.

"Griffin, are you coming? Dinner's ready," called her mom.

"Garrett, I gotta go eat dinner," she said.

"All right," he said. "Bye."

"Bye," she said, surprised her heart was beating so fast.

Quickly Griffin dialed Libby. "Hey, Libbs, what's up?"

"I have the most unbelievable news ever! But first, I think Garrett Forester totally likes you. Audree agrees with me. She said he totally flirted with you in science class."

"What?" said Griffin, blushing again alone in her room.

"He smiled at you twice by your locker! I know he thought the picture of you playing bass was supercool," said Libby.

"Libby, I was standing in a puddle of toilet paper! Who wouldn't be smiling?" said Griffin.

"Trust me," said Libby.

Griffin shook her head. Just as she was about to tell Libby that Garrett had called, Libby said, "Anyway, I just heard that Samantha did *not* win the Fresh Face contest because she broke out in an unexplained rash on her face right before the finals! She has bumps all over her face that look like lizard skin!"

Griffin's heart plunged. Suddenly she remembered the horrible wish that had popped into her head at the bakery when Samantha had called her mom's cake a "nerd cake." *I wish Samantha looked like a queen lizard with warts all over her face!*

Oh, no! thought Griffin, sinking into her bed. Samantha

was cruel, but Griffin hadn't really meant for her to break out in warts. Had she? Griffin ran to the mirror and looked at herself. Her eyes had an odd yellow tint . . . like Mariah's.

"Griffin, are you there?" said Libby.

"Yeah. Sorry, Libbs, my mom's calling me for dinner."

"Okay. But isn't this just like in English class? *Something wicked this way comes!*"

"Yeah. Something wicked. See you tomorrow."

Griffin clutched herself. Had one of her hurtful wishes come true? She thought back to Mariah's letter. *If you are a Wish Stealer, only your evil wishes will come true.*

Griffin lurched under her bed, scooped up the amethyst stone for protection, put it into her pocket, and went downstairs for dinner.

"Is everything all right, Griff?" asked her mom when she sat at the table.

"Yeah," she said.

"Who is this Garrett?" asked her dad.

"Mr. Luckner made Garrett and me partners for our science night project. The only problem is that I get the feeling that Garrett doesn't do any homework. Is it okay if I walk next door to the town library after school tomorrow to meet him? Then can you pick me up when I'm done?"

"Okay. Just call when you want me to get you. Do you have any science project ideas? I used to love science fairs when I was in school," said her mom, smiling.

"That's because you won them all," her dad said with a laugh.

"I really want to do something about the environment," said Griffin. "Garrett wants to grow something weird or blow something up."

Across the table Griffin's parents raised their eyebrows at each other.

Make a wish together
and change the world.

Chapter

14

At school the next day Samantha came in with a thick coat of makeup on her face, looking deeply tan or orange, depending on the light. Griffin gulped.

Samantha, Martha, and Sasha passed out reminders for her birthday party, sticking chocolate chip cookie magnets on the invited kids' lockers.

Walking by Kristina, Griffin heard her mumble under her breath, "I'm never invited to cool things."

Another girl cried when every locker surrounding hers had a chocolate chip cookie magnet on it except hers. "Whoa,"

said Robert Winbell, passing by Samantha, "you wear more makeup than my grandma."

"It's called a tanning bed," said Samantha. "You are so not invited to my party."

Griffin narrowed her eyes. She started to wish the party was ruined or no one showed up—*NO, NO, NO, I DO NOT WISH THAT! Do I?* thought Griffin.

How easy it was to wish awful things when she was upset.

Griffin tried to focus on making it through the school day and meeting Garrett at the town library instead.

Griffin spread five books across the library table. Garrett was nowhere in sight. She checked her watch. For fifteen minutes she had been waiting, and she wondered if he'd remember, even though she'd reminded him in science class. Walking toward the library computers, Griffin spotted Garrett sitting on the floor between two bookshelves, reading a guitar magazine.

"Garrett," she said. "I thought you forgot."

"Hey, Griffin," he said. "No, I got here twenty minutes ago. Just getting some ideas. Never been here before. It's pretty neat. I mean, man, I found some wild stuff."

"*Band Magazine?*" she read aloud, standing over him. "What's that?"

"Just reading about this band called the Austin Alchemists—got their name from wizards or something," he said.

"Can I see?" Griffin asked. Garrett stood up and gave her the magazine.

She read aloud from the article interviewing the lead singer. "'We got our band's name after the ancient alchemists who were, like, radical wizard scientists, man. They tried to find a secret formula to turn lead into gold. Just like we're gonna get a gold record when our CD sells a million copies!'"

"Cool," said Garrett. "If I could make gold, I'd buy my mom all the stuff she ever wanted."

Griffin continued reading the interview, "'Alchemy was like the bridge, this awesomely long bridge between superstitions and modern science. Our band is, like, modern, man.' I never heard of their band. But maybe Mr. Luckner would let us do our project about turning ordinary metals into gold."

"This could be so cool!" said Garrett. "Maybe we could do an experiment at the science fair. Blow all the kids away! Like take a penny and turn it into gold!"

Like turning a penny into a wish, thought Griffin, but she didn't say that aloud.

"Let's ask a librarian for help, okay?" she said, leading Garrett to the information desk.

Mrs. Eve, the nicest librarian in the library, happened to be at the help desk. With her huge smile, sparkling eyes, and framed photo of her new baby on the counter, kids felt like they could ask her anything.

"Hi, Mrs. Eve," Griffin said.

"Hi, Griff. Great to see you. Looks like you brought a friend," she said smiling.

"This is my science partner, Garrett."

"Hi, Garrett. Nice to meet you," said Mrs. Eve.

"Hi," said Garrett.

"We're looking for info about the ancient alchemists," said Griffin. "It might be a totally weird topic . . ."

Mrs. Eve said, "Weird? Not at all! Ancient alchemy is one of the most fascinating topics you could research. Turning lead into gold, the transmutation of ugly things into beauty— the study of alchemy is a great choice! Let's go to the ancient books section. All of our oldest and most valuable books are locked up down there."

She reached for a huge loop of keys behind the counter. Down two creaky flights of stairs, Garrett and Griffin followed behind Mrs. Eve. Underground caverns of books appeared in long rows stretching like a silent city beneath the library.

"I never knew this existed," said Griffin. Sounds of a metal door being unlocked echoed through the crypt of books.

"Ancient Alchemy," said Mrs. Eve, pointing to the last row of books by the wall. "Amazing things inside. You two may never want to leave!"

"Thanks," said Garrett and Griffin at the same time.

WISH! she wanted to shout, but bit her tongue instead. She didn't even want to think about that.

Just then the phone rang inside the ancient book vault. Mrs. Eve reached to answer it. "Hello?" she said. "I'll be right there." She hung up the receiver and said to Garrett and Griffin, "I have to run. We usually don't let people unsupervised down here, but, Griffin, I've known you and your family for years." She smiled at them. "I'll be back in ten minutes, okay?"

Griffin nodded her head. "Thank you so much." Mrs. Eve's footsteps echoed through the silent underground room as she walked up the stairs.

Griffin stared at Garrett when the door slammed. They were left alone.

"Cool," said Garrett. He pulled a giant book from the shelf. "*The Dictionary of Ancient Alchemy, 1785.*"

The book weighed a ton. Dust flew off it like a poisonous cloud. Garrett opened the antique book and placed it on a reading stand set up at the end of a bookcase. Griffin and Garrett stood side by side in front of the book. Garrett read,

"'We start with *Z*. Zosimos of Panopolis.'" His voice bounced off the walls of the tomblike room.

"It's kinda creepy down here, don't you think?" said Griffin.

"Not really. I stay at home by myself all the time," replied Garrett, shrugging. "Look at this!" He continued reading. "'Zosimos, called the father of alchemy, believed only *four* metals could be changed into gold.'"

"What are the four metals?" asked Griffin, now centimeters away from Garrett.

"'Lead, tin, silver, and copper,'" read Garrett.

"Copper!" said Griffin, leaning her head over the book. Her long, shiny hair brushed the page.

"'Maria Prophetissa, the most famous woman alchemist, made the first laboratory equipment. It was called a *tribikos*, to make gold,'" she read excitedly.

"Your hair smells like strawberries," said Garrett.

"Really?" said Griffin, jerking her head away.

Garret and Griffin stared at each other across the book, and they both blushed at the same time.

"I—I guess it's my shampoo," she said, her face now bright red like a giant strawberry.

Do I have green food stuck in my teeth? thought Griffin, and she suddenly became self-conscious. Quickly she looked

down and continued reading. "'Basil Valentine, said to have lived in Paris in 1394, believed in the properties of a metal called antimony. This strange, poisonous metal fascinated Isaac Newton.'"

"Look at that," said Garrett, pointing to a picture. A black shiny circle was drawn on the next page. He read, "'This circular black ob-sid-i-an mirror can be seen today in the British Museum. It was believed to have been stolen from Aztec priests by the conquistadors, who transported it to Europe. This magic mirror was used by the ancient alchemists to see the future.'"

Griffin glued her eyes to the page. The magic mirror was just like the one she'd seen in Mr. Schmidt's shop.

Turn something ordinary
into something extraordinary.

Chapter

15

Six times the town bell rang outside, reminding Garrett and Griffin they had been researching for two hours. "Wow! That went by fast," he said. Pushing through the heavy wooden doors, they emerged into the library's front courtyard, each with a stack of books.

"CDs! Buy your violin CD here," called a sad-looking sidewalk musician standing by the flagpole. In one hand he clutched his violin and bow, in the other he held up his self-produced CD for sale. Before him lay a stack of unsold CDs and an open violin case. Not a single coin had been tossed inside. People walked in and out of the library and passed by

him as if he were a lamppost. With his head bowed to the ground, he picked up his violin. Slowly he played a haunting, melancholy song. Griffin stared.

"Griffin?" said Garrett. "You okay?"

"Yeah. His violin case is empty," she said.

"What are you going to do?" Garrett said. "Give him some leftover lunch money?"

When the violinist stopped playing, Griffin walked up to the forlorn man. Although he wasn't that old, his face sagged. "You play really great."

"Thanks," he said, not meeting her eyes.

"I play bass guitar."

"Good for you. Hope you don't end up a failure like me."

Griffin's mouth fell open. "You're not a failure," she said. "Your music sounds incredible!"

The man smiled sadly.

"Griff! I'm parked right here," called Dr. Penshine from the open car window.

"I gotta go," she said, turning to Garrett. "That's my mom. Do you need a ride home?"

"No, I'm gonna walk," he said.

"Don't you have band practice like you said on the phone?" asked Griffin.

"Nah, we bailed," said Garrett.

"Okay. Well, we got a lot done. Thanks. See you tomorrow," she said.

"Tomorrow's Saturday," he said, and smiled.

"Oh, yeah." She blushed.

"Hey, are you going to Samantha's party?" he asked.

"Uh, no. I . . . ," she said.

"Yeah, it will probably be lame. I ate that cookie anyway." Griffin laughed.

Garrett smiled at her again.

"Griffin!" called her mom.

"Gotta go," she said, running to the car and slipping into the front seat.

"Hi," said her mom. "Is that Garrett over there?" Her mom pointed to Garrett, who was talking to the sidewalk musician.

"Yes," Griffin said.

"Does he want to have dinner with us?" her mom asked.

"Who?" Griffin said.

"Garrett," said her mom.

"I don't think so."

"How is he getting home?" asked her mom.

"He said he's walking," said Griffin, staring out the window.

"At night? By himself? I don't think so!" said her mom.

"Why don't we eat across the street at Friendly's? Dad's working late. Maybe Garrett would like to have dinner with us? I can drop him off afterward."

"It's okay, really," Griffin said.

"He shouldn't be walking home in the dark," her mom persisted.

"All right," Griffin said. She got out of the car and walked up to Garrett. "Hey, Garrett. Do you want to go to Friendly's with us? Then my mom can drop you off."

"Friendly's?" he said with a huge smile. "I love their Reese's Pieces sundae."

"Yeah," said Griffin.

"Okay," he said.

Settled into the restaurant booth, Dr. Penshine asked Garrett, "Do you want to call your parents and let them know you're eating with us?"

"It's okay. My mom works late most nights, so she won't even know the difference."

"Does your dad work late too?" said Griffin.

"He doesn't live with us," said Garrett, studying the menu.

"Where does he live?" asked Griffin.

Garrett shrugged his shoulders and shifted uneasily.

"Alaska. He's a fisherman. Hey, the double-decker looks awesome!"

Clanking dishes and clinking glasses spun circles around Griffin.

"What can I get you all?" asked the waitress, chewing gum.

"A double-decker and Reese's Pieces sundae," said Garrett.

"All-righty," said the waitress. "And you, young lady?"

But Griffin just stared at Garrett.

"Griffin, the waitress is talking to you," said her mom, raising an eyebrow.

"Sorry. A veggie burger, please," she said, returning her focus to Garrett. "Have you ever *wished* for your dad to come back, Garrett?"

"Griffin!" said her mom. "That's a very personal question!"

"It's okay," said Garrett. "I don't care. He left two years ago. I was ten. I used to wish on my birthday cake for him to come back. But now that I'm older, I don't wish for such stupid things."

"I don't think it's a stupid wish at all, Garrett. I know lots of people who have wished for amazing things! Crazy things!" said Griffin, leaning across the table.

Cackling laughter caught Griffin's ear from a few booths

away. In full costume the three witches from *Macbeth* gnawed on chicken bones, with spinach and chicken flapping in their teeth.

"Oh, my gosh," gasped Griffin, spotting them. "It's the witches!"

"Who?" said her mom.

"What?" said Garrett.

Griffin's heart raced.

One of the witches noticed Griffin staring at her. She waved her bony fingers and called to her, "'In the cauldron boil and bake . . . *Lizard's* leg and owlet's wing . . .' Right, my dear? 'For a charm of powerful trouble.'"

"My goodness, they look lifelike," said Griffin's mom.

"They performed for my English class. Actors from some traveling theater company doing *Macbeth*," Griffin said, and gulped.

"Gnarly!" said Garrett.

"I'd love to hear what you two picked for your science night project," said Dr. Penshine, changing the subject.

"Alchemy! Turning lead into gold!" said Garrett.

Just then the three witches left their table, heading for the exit. As they passed Griffin's table, one of the hags leaned over and whispered, "'When the hurlyburly's done, / When the battle's lost and won,' ehh, my dear?"

The crone's eyes swirled yellow.

When the three weird witches exited the restaurant, a cold gust of wind snuck through the doors.

"What does that mean?" Griffin asked her mom, shivering.

"I think it's a line from the play. 'Hurlyburly' means everything's upside down, lots of confusion. My goodness, those are either the oddest or most committed actors I have ever seen! They must be in character rehearsing their parts," she said.

"What does the second line mean?" asked Garrett.

"'When the battle's lost and won'? I think it means someone emerges victorious from a battle between good and evil."

Turn a single penny into gold.

Chapter

16

R ight here," said Garrett as the Penshines' car pulled
up in front of a small, dark house without a single
light on.

"Good night, Garrett. It was nice to meet you," said
Dr. Penshine. "Quite an evening, a real dinner theater experience with those actors!"

"Bye," said Griffin, her eyes scanning the darkness
around his house. *Why did the witch say that to me?* she
thought.

"Yeah, thanks for dinner," said Garrett, shutting the car
door.

They waved through the window and watched as Garrett

traipsed down the broken cement path to his house, netted in shadows.

"You know, Griff, when I was at the counter paying for dinner, the clerk gave me back a bunch of pennies."

"Yeah?" Griffin said. She couldn't stop thinking about the witches. What did they mean "when the battle's lost and won"? *What will I lose if I fail?*

"Are you okay?" asked her mom, studying her in the passing streetlights.

"What were you saying about pennies?" Griffin asked, eyes darting. *Did my mom find Mariah's note under my bed?*

"They reminded me of something that might help your alchemy project. There's a charity called Pennies for the Planet." Dr. Penshine rounded the corner, and a streetlight flickered on. "This charity helps protect the environment. Every year the projects change, but this year I think kids are collecting pennies to buy an acre of the rain forest. This saves it from being destroyed.

"All those ordinary pennies turn into something extraordinary when they're added together, like the alchemists turning lead into gold."

"That's a really cool idea, Mom. I'll text Garrett about it," said Griffin.

The car hovered at a red light.

When the hurlyburly's done, when the battle's lost and won screeched in Griffin's head. *Can I return all these wishes?*

✳ ✳ ✳

Courage is . . . mastery of fear, not absence of fear.

—Mark Twain

Chapter 17

The art store on Saturday morning glowed with sunlight streaming in its windows. Neat rows of paints in silver tubes waited like dignified soldiers to be purchased. Brushes in every shape and size tickled the shelves above them. Griffin and Libby loved to come here to buy a few new supplies before heading to Grandma Penshine's house for their art lesson. In the afternoon, when the weatherman predicted the temperature would hit eighty-five degrees, they'd meet Audree, Maggie, and Madison to swim in Maggie's grandpa's pool.

"My grandma says today she's teaching us about the Venetian painters, so we should pick out our favorite blues

and yellows to paint an amazing sky," said Griffin as they looked through the rack of paint colors.

"Cobalt blue, azure mist, lapis lazuli, Caspian Sea blue, aquamarine, cerulean swirl," read Libby as she carefully examined each tube. "How many blues can there be in the world?"

Just then a breeze blew through the store, and five girls, babbling loudly, some on their cell phones, others laughing, burst through the art store's doors.

"Grab every color. My father said he'd pay for everything. We want my birthday party banner to be huge! We'll drape it across my house so everyone will know which house to come to!" said a familiar voice.

Griffin turned as Samantha and her followers surged around the paint rack, trying to bump her and Libby out of the way.

"Excuse you," said Griffin, refusing to be pushed.

"What are you two doing here?" Samantha snickered.

"We're buying paints for our art lesson," said Libby.

"Do you guys think you're going to be famous artists one day? Now, that's hilarious!"

"They are so not invited to Samantha's party," Martha whispered loudly as she ripped paint tubes from the metal shelves and put them into a basket.

"Totally," said Sasha. "They're probably here because they heard we were coming to the art store and they're hoping to be invited. Desperate!"

"We only have three hours before my party. Come on. We want my sign to be gigantic!" Like a writhing octopus with groping arms on all sides of the paint display, the girls grabbed at the lapis, cobalt, and aquamarine. Soon the Caspian Sea blue, cerulean swirl, and azure mist were all snatched away too.

"Hey, you guys can't take them all!" said Griffin, reaching to protect some paints.

A windmill of arms slapped the space in front of her. Griffin's eyes narrowed in disgust. The entire rack of paint was stripped, except for one fallen soldier of *triste bleu*, and that was only because no one in Samantha's clique could read French.

"Hurry, girls! My older sister is going to take us to drop off some extra chocolate chip cookie invitations at the boys' houses. Boys always need to be reminded."

Then, looking right at Griffin, Samantha said, "First stop, Garrett Forester's house."

A tube of paint fell onto the floor. As Samantha's followers stampeded to the checkout, they trampled on the abandoned tube, squirting paint all over Griffin's sneakers that had taken her all summer to design.

"I wish your party is a total bomb!" blurted Griffin aloud. But Samantha had already sashayed to the cash register. *Oh, my gosh! What have I just wished!* thought Griffin, eyes bulging. Then she looked down at her favorite sneakers, totally ruined. "Come on, Libbs. Let's go. My grandma has some awesome paints we can use."

Griffin could hardly contain her anger as they walked the seven blocks to her grandma's house. She clenched her teeth the entire way there.

"Griff, who cares? Who'd want to go to their stupid party anyway?" said Libby.

"It's not that. It's the way Samantha tries to make people feel bad and rubs it in their faces about her party."

"Did you see Samantha's skin, Griff? It's really looking lizardlike. I think her friends are afraid to tell her, but it's getting worse."

"Really?" Griffin smiled. Then she gulped. The witches' chant rang in her head, *In the cauldron boil and bake . . . Lizard's leg and owlet's wing . . .* She wondered, *Did I cast a wish of powerful trouble?*

That wish had been an accident. But what had she wished now—that Samantha's party would be a total bomb? What did that even mean? Griffin felt sick to her stomach.

Libby pressed the doorbell. Classical music trilled. Libby smiled. "I even love your grandma's doorbell!"

"Yeah," said Griffin, still in a terrible mood, though she knew it was hard to stay angry when at her grandma's house. Crystal candy jars jammed with jelly beans rested on tables for visitors. Fresh flowers, including blooming orchids, stretched in every room in every color all year round. Grandma called her flowers "A sunrise in a vase!" It was impossible to sit in a chair without sinking into feather cushions. On the couch Grandma's needlepoint pillows were handcrafted with quotes from her favorite artists, like Matisse: "There are always flowers for those who want to see them."

Grandma Penshine, neat and trim in her gray slacks, black ballet flat shoes, and a hand-knit shawl, greeted them at the door. "If it isn't two of my favorite people in the whole world!" Her soft white hair framed her still-pretty face, and her warm brown eyes twinkled like a mischievous teenager's. Besides laugh lines, she had very few wrinkles. At eighty-five years old, Grandma Penshine looked like most sixty-five-year-olds.

"Hi, Grandma," said Griffin.

"Hi, GP," said Libby, calling Grandma Penshine by her nickname.

Grandma Penshine moved to hug them. "You two seem upset. What's the matter? Did something happen?"

"Nothing, Grandma," said Griffin, still furious, clutching the triste bleu paint.

"We only got one tube of paint," said Libby sadly.

"That's okay. I just thought you two might want a dab of a new special color."

"I wished Samantha's birthday would be a total disaster!" said Griffin.

"Griffin, what's the matter?" asked her grandma.

"The most awful girl in the entire school bought all the paint in the store just as Libby and I were picking ours out."

"How insensitive of her," said Grandma Penshine.

"I wished horrible things on her," said Griffin.

"That's not right either, Griff," she said. "Don't stoop to her level. You're better than that."

"I don't care," said Griffin, with an odd feeling in her stomach. "I hate her," she said, and her eyes glowed yellow.

"Griffin! Your eyes!" said Libby.

"They look a bit yellow," said her grandma.

Griffin ran into the bathroom and stared in the mirror. A yellowish glint reflected in her eyes. Slowly she walked back to Libby and her grandma. "I think I'm tired."

"Libby, why don't you start practicing before our lesson?

Your easels are set up on the back porch. It's such a lovely day! Griffin, can you please help me reach some paintbrushes in my guest room closet?"

"Okay," said Griffin, following her grandma down the hall.

"Griffin, whenever I've seen yellow eyes before it's because a person wasn't eating enough fruit or getting enough sweetness in life. What's the matter?"

"Nothing," said Griffin. She and her grandma stared at each other. Then Griffin asked, "Have you ever wished horrible things on people?"

"Well," she started, and then paused. "I can't say that I haven't wanted to when I got boiling mad, but no, I never did. Wishing horrible things, doing horrible things, saying horrible things—it all twists into your face, making it droop with cruel words and then pinching it up tight. Treat yourself with respect and ignore people who don't treat you with dignity," said her grandma.

Griffin's hands shot up to her face, and her cheeks felt warm. Her eyes grew huge.

"What's the matter?" asked her grandma.

Griffin plopped onto the guest bed. Mariah's face came jutting into her mind, wearing a wicked sneer, each wrinkle pulling tighter and tighter into an evil circus clown smile.

"I just remembered a ninety-two-year-old lady with the most creased face I've ever seen," said Griffin. "Do you think people can *steal* wishes?"

Grandma Penshine quieted. Griffin heard the clock tick and the cotton curtains rustle, and she shivered from a cold breeze that shot straight through the bedroom. Both Griffin and her grandma caught the chills.

"Yes, I believe people can steal wishes. Those people—Wish Stealers is what we used to call them back when I was a girl in Topeka—are the worst kind of people in the world."

Griffin's heart beat out of control.

"Wish Stealers are filled with fear. They are the first people to spit on a dream." Grandma Penshine sneezed and moved to grab a tissue. "Wish Stealers make people ashamed for trying, eat up people's courage, and stomp on their enthusiasm. Do you know why? Because they're afraid. Jealous they can't do it themselves. Wish Stealers are afraid to dream."

Flashes of Mariah's face seared into Griffin's head.

"Wishes are a bit like snowflakes: powerful and fragile at the same time," said Grandma Penshine. "They can melt at any minute but are magnificent just the same. They are filled with nature's *most fierce and wild power*. That's what's in a wish, *a fierce and wild power.*"

Suddenly Grandma Penshine couldn't stop coughing.

Hacking. Gasping for air. Her fragile chest heaved for breath.

"Grandma!" shouted Griffin.

Her grandma coughed until her chest looked like it might collapse. "Grandma!" shrieked Griffin, and she ran to grab a glass of water.

✳ ✳ ✳

Nothing happens unless first a dream.
—Carl Sandburg

Chapter

18

First thing Monday morning Griffin slumped down the school hallway. Shadows and bags hung under her eyes. All weekend she'd worried about her grandma. Her coughing attack had been so severe she'd had to lie down and cancel their lesson. *I wish for Grandma Penshine to get well soon* rattled through Griffin's head. Right before school, she slipped the "change the world" penny into her shoe. She figured so much in her world needed changing. Including herself.

"Griffin, did you hear?" said Libby, running up to her.

"Hear what?"

"At Samantha's party! Her dad bought paintball guns as

a surprise so everyone could play in their huge backyard, but the paint cartridges overheated and exploded—a giant paint bomb splattered everywhere!"

Every hair on Griffin's arms stood up. "Really?" she said, bug-eyed. *Did I wish that?* she thought. *A paint bomb!*

"Hey, Griffin! Hi, Libby," said Garrett, coming up to them.

"Hi, Garrett," said Griffin.

"How was Samantha's party? Did you go?" said Libby.

"Yeah, she and some girls came to my house and practically dragged me to the party. Then her parents freaked when paintballs exploded and grafittied their lawn furniture. All the food was ruined and everyone just went home covered in paint. I had to take, like, three showers to get the paint off."

Griffin stared.

"Wow!" said Libby.

Griffin's heart plummeted. Had her wish caused the paint to explode on all the kids? Were tendrils of darkness overtaking her, winding their way around her soul as she stood there? *I need to work faster, try harder, and return these wishes,* she thought.

"Griffin?" said Libby and Garrett at the same time. Her face had turned white.

"Yeah, sorry. I spaced," she said.

"Bye. See you at lunch," Libby said, running off.

"Bye," she said. "Garrett, do you still want to do our project on alchemy and the Pennies for the Planet fund-raiser I texted you about?"

"Yeah," he said.

"We have to ask Mr. Blackwell at lunch. He's the science coordinator and has to give final approval for all the projects at science night."

"Okay," he said.

"Meet you in the teacher's section of the cafeteria," she said.

"Cool," he said, walking off.

Griffin did not notice Samantha in a velvet minidress and knee-high crisscross fur boots lurking by the lockers. "Lunch date?" snarled Samantha.

"It's for the science project, Samantha," said Griffin, willing herself not to wish anything bad on her.

"The one you're going to bomb?" taunted Samantha.

Griffin thought of her grandma. "Our project is gonna rock," said Griffin, and she walked away.

At the start of lunch period Garrett, eating a bag of Fritos, was hovering by the water fountain. "Hey," he said.

"Hi," said Griffin.

"Fritos really make you thirsty," he said. "You want some? They're way better than school lunch!"

Griffin smiled. "No, thanks."

Garrett crunched harder.

Walking over to the teachers' table, Garrett wiped his greasy Fritos hands on his pants. He smelled like a giant corn chip.

"Excuse me, Mr. Blackwell?" said Griffin.

Mr. Blackwell turned to face them. Gooey crumbs stuck to his mustache. "Yes? Is this important enough to disturb my lunch?"

"Sorry to interrupt," said Griffin, "but Mr. Luckner said we had to get your approval for our science night project. We wanted to do our report on the alchemists and their contributions to modern-day science. We also wanted to do a fundraiser that would turn pennies into gold—kinda like the alchemists. A charity called Pennies for the Planet helps kids collect tons of pennies and uses them to stop the destruction of the Amazon rain forest."

Still chewing his food, Mr. Blackwell looked at them. "Do you two really think *pennies* will help save the Amazon rain forest? It's not worth your effort."

Suddenly Griffin felt the "change the world" penny in

her shoe start to burn. "We thought we'd try," she said.

"Actually, my rock band volunteered to play at science night as free entertainment to try to get donations for the planet."

"Really?" said Griffin, looking at Garrett.

"Yeah, my band is awesome. We could totally raise money!"

Food dribbled on Mr. Blackwell's tie. "I had a band once. Every kid thinks he can be in a band. But ninety-nine percent of bands fail. No one shows up to rehearse. Everyone wants it his own way. How long have you had this band of yours, Mr. Forester?"

"Since last summer," said Garrett.

"You'll see."

Griffin reached for her shoe. The sole of her foot was on fire. She took out the labeled penny, and it burned her palm. "Actually, Garrett's band is amazing. They're really talented," she said, even though she had never heard them. "Plus, we already have our first donation: a lucky penny that is worth much more than one cent." She held out her palm, revealing a coin that shot light like a laser.

Mr. Blackwell read the label stuck on the penny, and said, "A little penny to *change the world*. How sweet. Are you two *numismatists* now?"

"What?" said Garrett and Griffin at the same time.

"A new-miss-ma-tist, kiddos. A coin collector of rare and special coins. Look at that! An 1872 Indian Head penny!" His eyebrows scrunched together.

The coin was on fire, shining streaks of light on the cafeteria ceiling.

Walking toward the table, Mr. Reasoner, the metalworks teacher, said, "What is that beautiful radiance? Flash anything shiny at a fish or a metalworks teacher, and both will get lured right in!"

He stooped over and examined the penny in Griffin's hand. "I know an awful lot about coins. Any kind of metal is my specialty. A 1872 Indian Head penny! What a lovely label." Mr. Reasoner sighed and said, "I certainly do wish we could change the world!"

"What's so great about an 1872 Indian Head penny?" asked Garrett.

"Most old pennies aren't worth much, usually one cent or maybe a few dollars. If you're *really* fortunate, every once in a while, you might find an old penny worth ten dollars. If a penny is unpolished and hasn't been touched for hundreds of years, it can actually be worth thousands of dollars, but this penny is probably worth about a hundred and fifty dollars."

"A hundred and fifty dollars!" said Mr. Blackwell, Garrett, and Griffin in unison.

"That's a great start for our fund-raiser!" said Griffin.

"Maybe you'd like me to keep it safe for you?" said Mr. Blackwell. He reached to scoop the penny out of Griffin's hand, but his fingers accidently flicked it instead. A burst of copper shot though the air and landed in the custodian's dirty mop bucket nearby.

SPLASH! sang out, and the penny sank to the bottom of the dark swirling pail. Water swooshed up at the custodian, Mr. Newoski. "Was that a rocket? I was almost blinded!" said the janitor, wiping his eyes.

Garrett and Griffin rushed toward Mr. Newoski. "Are you okay?"

"Yup. I didn't know I'd have to watch for missiles while I mopped!"

Mr. Reasoner and Mr. Blackwell gathered around the container. The mop bucket slopped filthy water everywhere. A sneer seeped out of Mr. Blackwell as he peered into the black bucket. "Well, better get your penny, kids."

Griffin glared at him. "Can we do our project or not?"

"Go right ahead. Let the band play!" He went back to his table. "But don't be disappointed with the results. Being realistic is important."

Mr. Reasoner turned toward the janitor. "Mr. Newoski, there is a valuable penny in this bucket. Do you think we can dump the water so that the kids can get back their coin?"

"Not a problem," he said, plunging his hand straight into the bucket. After fishing on the bottom for the penny for a few seconds, he grabbed it and wiped it dry on his rag. "Little dirt never hurt anybody!" He placed the penny in Griffin's hand. It was now even more spectacular, immaculately clean from the detergent.

"Come by the metal shop at afternoon recess, Griffin," said Mr. Reasoner. "I can give you an empty ring box to keep your penny in."

"Thanks, Mr. Reasoner," she said as she tucked the penny into her pocket.

Garrett and Griffin walked back to the kids' side of the cafeteria. Griffin said, "So you'll play at science night?"

"Yeah. We're great. We're rehearsing tomorrow in my garage. You wanna hear us? Bring your bass so I can hear it. I'm gonna tell the guys we should rename our band the Alchemists."

"What's your band's name now?"

"Five Cool Guys," he said.

She laughed. "I thought we could work on our project tomorrow."

"We already worked on it Friday," said Garrett.

"Yeah, *once*. We have so much more to do," reminded Griffin.

"Fine," said Garrett. "Come to my house tomorrow and see my band, and we'll work after. I'll talk to my friends about the rock concert."

"What rock concert?" she said.

"For the planet," he said.

"Oh, yeah, cool," said Griffin. She hoped his band was good.

At the start of recess Griffin headed to Mr. Reasoner's huge metal shop.

"Hello. Come in, Griffin," he said. "I have this box that will be perfect for your penny. What's this I hear about a fund-raiser?"

"It's for science night. We're collecting pennies for Pennies for the Planet to help save the Amazon rain forest," she said.

"Count me in. I have two huge mayonnaise jars of pennies that I've been waiting to donate to a good cause."

A boy with a goofy grin, reddish hair parted down the middle, and a sprinkling of freckles all over his face was working in the back of the metal shop. He listened to every word. Griffin noticed him eavesdropping but didn't think anything of it.

✳ ✳ ✳

Keep away from people who try to belittle your ambitions. Small people always do that, but the really great make you feel that you, too, can become great.

—Mark Twain

Chapter

19

At afternoon recess Garrett ran up to Griffin in the yard where she stood in line for basketball shots. "Hey, Griffin," said Garrett, "you'll never believe the stuff I read on the Internet during computer class. These alchemists were so cool! Basil Valentine, Zosimos, and Nicolas Flamel. They all turned lead into gold!"

"That's awesome! I wonder where all that gold went," said Griffin.

"They probably buried it or something," said Garrett.

"Probably." Griffin felt the first raindrop plop onto her head. "Uh-oh. It's gonna pour any second," she said, scanning the gray sky. "Hey, Garrett, I brought you something."

Griffin reached into her pocket for a penny. The previous period she'd rummaged through her backpack, peeked inside Mariah's black case, and studied the remaining pennies. She'd pulled out a penny for Garrett and jammed it in her pocket.

"Really? What?" he said, facing her.

Griffin dug into her pocket, pulled out the coin, and held out her palm.

"I found a few lucky pennies at a shop." She didn't want to tell him much more.

He took it from her, and a few more raindrops drizzled on their heads.

"WATCH OUT!" A spinning rubber ball bounced into a puddle, squirting water all over them.

"Sorry!" called the players.

Garrett's eyes narrowed. "This penny says 'a dad'! Why would I want this stupid penny, Griffin? I never want to see my dad!"

Hail began pelting the kids on the playground. Mrs. Gideon yelled, "Come inside, everybody! Come inside. 'Fair is foul, and foul is fair: / Hover through the fog and filthy air!'" Hoards of kids raced indoors. Griffin didn't know if it was rain or a teardrop in Garrett's eye, but before she could look again, Garrett hurled the penny out of his hand like a

hockey puck and yelled, "Like I wish for a dad!" There was a brilliant streak as a disc of shining light skimmed across the wet asphalt and disappeared into the overflowing gutter. Staring at Garrett, Griffin knew he'd seen that strange light too, but before she could speak, he tore through the yard and stomped in a puddle, splashing water all over her.

Wishes travel in strange ways.

Chapter
20

"Doorbell!" called Griffin's mom from the laundry room in the basement. "Can you see who it is?"

"Sure," said Griffin. She had just texted Garrett after dinner:

Hi. I'm really sorry 4 giving u the penny. Do u still want me 2 come over tom. and see ur band after school?

He texted back:

OK. Can u bring ur bass guitar?

* * *

She texted:

OK, but I can only stay a ½ hr then my mom wants to pick us up and drive us to the library to work.

He texted:

OK.

Relieved that Garrett was not mad at her, she put her phone down. Eight fifteen p.m. Her dad was working late, and she couldn't imagine who would ring their doorbell. Peeking through the peephole, Griffin saw a man wrapped in a dark coat. Shivers shot through her. "Mom, it's Mr. Schmidt!" called Griffin.

"I'll be right up. Let him in," she called.

Cautiously Griffin opened the door. Mr. Schmidt never came over. *Did Mariah tell him about the pennies before she died?* she wondered.

"Hi, Mr. Schmidt," said Griffin. The eerie night hovered outside, casting long shadows behind him.

"Good evening, Griffin. Sorry to come by so late, but there was something I needed to bring over."

Just then Dr. Penshine came up from the basement. "Hi,

Mike. Please come in. We were so sorry to hear about your great-aunt."

"Thank you," he said, but he did not look at Dr. Penshine. Instead he stared at Griffin. "Actually, I stopped over because of Mariah."

Griffin's throat went dry.

"Although my aunt only met you once, Griffin, she must have been quite taken with you. Maybe you reminded her of herself when she was young. She had long red hair as a girl too."

Griffin cringed.

"Mariah never married or had children, but when I was going through her things in my guest room, I found this box that she left for Griffin. I guess the very afternoon my aunt met her, she wrote this letter. It was taped to it."

Mr. Schmidt read Mariah's note aloud.

Dear Mike,

Please be sure to give this box to that sweet young girl, Griffin Penshine, whom we met at your shop. I have some old memorabilia, not worth anything really, but which may be fun for a young girl.

Mariah W. S.

Mr. Schmidt held out Mariah's box, which had a golden lock on it. Mariah W.S. Did her initials stand for Weatherby Schmidt or *Wish Stealer*? The golden key. Now it made sense. Griffin stared at the menacing gift, afraid of what was inside. More stolen wishes? Hideous, horrible things? Things Mariah had bought with people's wishes?

"Well, Griff. It's flattering that you met Mariah only once and she remembered you like this," said her mom.

"Mariah was meticulous—a memory like a steel trap. Never forgot anything or anybody," said Mr. Schmidt. "Always kept wonderful records."

Griffin still did not come forward. "Griff, what's the matter?" asked her mom.

"Well, it has a lock on it," Griffin said, and gulped, hoping Mr. Schmidt would take it away.

"That's easy. Any pair of pliers could take it off. I couldn't find the key, and I didn't want to damage it before giving it to you as my aunt wished."

Griffin's stomach twisted into knots.

"Would you like me to cut the lock for you?" he said.

Griffin leapt forward. "No. It's okay. I, uh, like surprises." She snatched the box from him. What if it was something that could hurt her mom if she saw it. The box was heavy. Her face drained to white again.

"Thanks," said Griffin.

"Thank *you*," he said. "I better get going. Good night."

Griffin spied through the peephole as Mr. Schmidt disappeared into the darkness.

"Do you want to open the box and see what she left you?" asked her mom.

"I think I'll wait," said Griffin. She didn't want her mom involved with the wishes. *What if the contents of the box are wicked?* she wondered.

"If that isn't discipline!" said her mom, laughing.

Griffin put the box down and hugged her mom tightly, hugged her maybe even for protection. Then she heaved the box up the stairs to her bedroom.

Griffin lay on her bed, staring at the box. "Hi, Charlemagne," Griffin whispered as she picked him up from his upstairs terrarium. He crawled toward her on the bed. "I guess I should open it. It can't get much worse, right?" Griffin got up, locked her door, and moved to pull down her bedroom shades. Through the window she peered out at the murky night. She could see the top of Mr. Schmidt's house. Lights were on in his attic. She yanked down the shade and knelt before her bed. Heart racing, hands trembling, she took the golden key out from the side pocket of her

backpack where he'd left it, and put it in the keyhole.

The box sprang open. Charlemagne shot his head inside his so quickly, he lost his balance and almost toppled the bed. Gently Griffin picked him up, placed him by side, and peered into the box. Inside were four things: Topeka Inn guest book register with a cracked leather cover, a large bloodred garnet ring, a skein of old gray yarn, and the black obsidian disc from Mr. Schmidt's shop with the card that read *Obsidian mirror—used by the ancient alchemists, passed down from Aztec priests. See your future!*

Griffin inhaled ancient dust from the leather book and its mildewing pages.

The old yarn smelled stale and musty. It looked like a coiled spiderweb. She didn't want to touch it. As bright as molten lava, the ring flashed red light all over her ceiling. She averted her eyes. The shiny black stone disc reflected only darkness. The guest book gazed up at her with a helpless, lost look. Picking it up, she blew dust off the cover and opened the first faded page.

* * *

Best wishes.

Chapter

21

✳ ✳

✳

Griffin's eyes raced up and down the first page of the guest book. Three different columns listed the names of guests, the dates they stayed at the inn, and their room numbers. Some names were funny. Some were old-fashioned. Ethel, Mabel, and Selma stayed in room 9. Mr. Leroy Simmons and Annabelle Lee Simmons stayed in room 8. Penciled next to some of the names were tiny words, hardly legible. Griffin zoomed in on the pencil scratches. Next to Annabelle Lee Simmons's name were the words "best friend." Next to Selma's name was "a husband." To the left of Hatter Bloom's name was "money." Beside Georgina Pironi's name read "go home to Italy."

Did Mariah write down the wishes she stole from these guests? wondered Griffin.

Scanning each and every column, Griffin looked for a penciled word that would match even one of the eleven pennies she had under her bed. Suddenly her finger stopped dead next to Florence L. Daniellson: "puppy." *Puppy.* "PUPPY!" screamed Griffin.

Furiously flipping through the rest of the pages, Griffin searched for more matches, but there were no others. "PUPPY!" she yelled again.

"Griffin? Are you okay!" called her mom through the door. "What are you shouting about?"

After slipping the guest book and Mariah's box under her bed, Griffin opened her bedroom door. "Hi," said Griffin.

"Did I hear you say, 'puppy'?" Her mom sat down on her bed. "Why are you talking about a puppy?"

"No reason," she said.

"No reason? Do you want a puppy because the baby is coming and you feel left out?"

"Mom, I can't wait to meet the baby! I just had an idea about a puppy for a project. That's all," Griffin said while crossing her fingers. Charlemagne crawled on Griffin's lap. "Plus, I don't know if Charlemagne would feel too safe with a puppy. A puppy might think Charlemagne's a football."

Charlemagne ducked his head inside his shell again. Dr. Penshine rubbed Charlemagne's belly.

"Have you decided what you and Dad are going to name the baby?" asked Griffin, wanting to change the subject.

"Why don't we go up to the roof and I'll tell you."

Griffin's mom had installed a mini-observatory on their roof years ago. Three telescopes stood ready during the spring, summer, and fall. The roof looked like any ordinary roof from the front, but on the back her mom had built a platform for stargazing. Dr. Penshine had named her three telescopes Galileo, Sir Isaac, and Copernicus. Griffin's mom knew all eighty-eight constellations in the sky.

Together they walked to the rooftop. The cool breeze brushed against Griffin's cheeks. She was relieved they couldn't see Mr. Schmidt's house and its creepy shadows from the roof. Thankfully the platform faced only their backyard and the deep night sky beyond it.

"Here, Griff, look through that telescope and tell me what you see."

Griffin looked through the telescope and saw Polaris, the planet Jupiter, the constellation Sagittarius, and the swirling spiral galaxies M81 and M82.

"I see stars that must be millions of light-years away," said Griffin.

"In one of those distant and deep parts of space is a hidden and beautiful constellation called Caelum. It can only be seen at the equator or in the southern hemisphere, where your dad and I gazed at it on our honeymoon. We want to name the new baby Caelum if he's a boy and Caela is she's a girl."

"What does Caelum mean?" asked Griffin.

"It's a constellation named in 1754 by my favorite astronomer, Lacaille. Caelum means 'the heavens.' Its second meaning is '*les burins*,' which is an old instrument for engraving on copper."

"Engraving on copper? Like a penny!" said Griffin.

"A *burin* probably helped engrave the models for the first pennies."

"Wow!" said Griffin as she drank up the night sky filled with millions of bright stars. I can't wait to meet Caelum or Caela!" Then she had an idea. "Mom, wait here!"

Griffin ran downstairs and lunged under her bed. She took the label off the "baby" penny so her mom wouldn't become suspicious. Bounding back up the stairs, Griffin held out the penny to her mother. It glowed wildly under the canopy of stars. "This is a lucky penny I found."

"Really?" said her mom.

"Yeah," said Griffin. "Do you want to make a wish about the baby?" she asked.

"Okay," said her mom, smiling. She put the penny in her left palm, closing her fingers tightly around it. In her right hand she held Griffin's hand.

A meteor whizzed by overhead.

"A shooting star!" exclaimed Griffin. At that exact moment her mother made a wish and gently placed the penny down on the railing.

The door to the roof swung open. "Hello, everybody. What are you doing up here?" asked Griffin's dad.

"Hi, Dad! Mom and I just saw a shooting star!" said Griffin.

"You know what Mom says about shooting stars, right?"

"They're lucky!" said Griffin, feeling better for the first time in a while.

"Griffin gave me a lucky penny to make a wish for the baby," said her mom to her dad. Then Dr. Penshine scooped the penny off the railing. It was wet, now covered in dew. It sparkled even more like a star that had landed.

"Mom, we need to save this and give it to the baby when she or he is born."

"Good idea. Where should we keep it?" asked Dr. Penshine.

"I know," said Griffin, taking the penny from her mom. "Good night!"

"Good night, Griff," called her parents, smiling.

Griffin raced downstairs, but before turning into her own bedroom, she tiptoed into the guest room that had been converted into a nursery. The penny felt warm in her palm. Very carefully she placed the penny in a keepsake box on a high shelf next to the crib. The "baby" penny glowed.

Starlight, star bright,
first star I see tonight.
I wish I may, I wish I might,
have the wish I wish tonight.

Chapter

Louder!" shouted Garrett over the cacophony of banging drums inside his garage. Griffin forced a smile. Her mom had dropped her off after school and had gone to run an errand. "In thirty minutes I'll be back to pick you both up," she'd said.

"Louder, guys!" Garrett yelled again as he pounded on his drums.

Covering her ears was what Griffin really wanted to do. She had a splitting headache from thinking about Mariah's gifts. *What did Mariah use that creepy yarn for? Why did she have that bloodred ring?* Mariah's antique black mirror gave Griffin the chills. Did it reflect only the dark side of things?

Did it show the sadness people felt when their stolen wishes never came true? The song ended, but no one finished at the same time.

"Hey, Griffin," called Jason Scott. "Garrett wants our band to play for science night. We usually charge for our gigs, but because this is Garrett's science project, we're going to play for free."

"Thanks," said Griffin, swallowing the lump in her throat.

"What do you think, Griffin?" asked Garrett as he stepped out of the open garage onto the driveway, where Griffin stood. Griffin didn't know what to say.

"Cool." She gulped. "It's really nice your mom lets you have the garage to practice in."

"It's mostly our hangout. We just practice here when we feel like it," said Garrett.

"Oh," said Griffin.

Garrett looked at Griffin funny. "Hey, where's your bass? Did you bring it?" he asked.

Griffin was so afraid that she wouldn't be able to play because of the curse that she hadn't brought her bass guitar. "I totally forgot it, but I have some video of me playing bass this summer. I was in a band at the music conservatory where I take lessons."

"Cool," said the guys, passing around Griffin's phone and watching her play her bass guitar.

"You're amazing!" said Todd Wherry, who played electric keyboard.

"Cool stuff," said Ethan Bergwein, the lead singer.

"Thanks," said Griffin. Inside she shrank. *Maybe I'm not a good player anymore because of the curse. I wish to become an amazing bass guitarist* sirened through her head.

"Hey, guys. Let's break for today," Garrett called.

Griffin looked at her watch. They had five minutes until her mom picked them up.

"We've been jamming hard. Let's meet the same time next Tuesday. I gotta go work on that stupid science project."

All the guys started high-fiving one another. Two of the boys besides Garrett went to their school: the lead singer, Ethan, and the guitar player, Jason, who Griffin recognized from classes at Dadesville's music center. Todd Wherry and Kurt Keene, who were packing their instruments, went to the rival middle school.

"Mom! We're done!" screamed Garrett to the dark upstairs windows.

Nothing happened.

"She must be asleep." Garrett shrugged.

Jason's older brother, whose car was at the end of the

driveway, blasted the horn. "Come on, kiddies, jump in the Batmobile!" he yelled. The four boys lugged their instruments down the driveway.

"Later," they called.

"Later," said Garrett, banging some final beats and fills on his drums. "I'm just gonna put some of these speakers away."

"Okay," said Griffin, who sat down at a broken piano in the front of the garage.

"Do you think my band is bad?" Garrett said.

"No," she said, not meeting his eyes.

"Come on, tell me the truth. You think my band stinks, don't you?" said Garrett.

"No, I think you guys could be amazing—"

"Could be? Like we're *not* or something?" he said, sounding defensive.

"No, I didn't mean it like that—"

"You sound like Mr. Blackwell," he said with a sharp tone.

"No, I don't! He's a Wish Stealer!" Griffin blurted out.

"A what?" said Garrett, staring at her.

"He just makes fun of people for trying," said Griffin.

"Whatever," said Garrett, turning away from her. He beat loudly on his drum.

"What's going on in here?" asked Garrett's mom,

sticking her head into the garage. She looked very tired.

"Nothing," said Garrett.

"Hi. You must be Griffin," said Garrett's mom.

"Hi, Mrs. Forester," Griffin said, standing up from the piano bench to shake her hand. "Nice to meet you."

"Were you about to play the piano?" she asked.

"No. I play bass guitar," she said.

Mrs. Forester had the same dancing, kind blue eyes as Garrett.

"Mom, my band's going to play a concert for science night."

"I'll make sure to get out of work early so that I can be there."

"But Griffin said my band stinks. I don't go to the music center like *she* does."

Griffin's mouth flew open. "Garrett! I didn't say that!"

"I would love to send you to the music center, Garrett." The saddest sigh deflated out of Mrs. Forester. "We just can't afford it right now. I better let you kids do your work. Nice to meet you, Griffin." She headed inside.

Just then Dr. Penshine honked the car horn. Griffin swiveled her head toward the car and then back to Garrett.

"I don't feel like working on our project tonight," said Garrett angrily.

"I have more stuff to do on my part," said Griffin, her eyes now moist. "I guess I'll just work on that."

"Yeah," he said, not looking at her.

"Bye, Garrett," she said.

But Garrett had already bolted inside his house and slammed the door.

People's dreams are fragile—be gentle.

Chapter
23

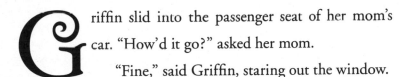

Griffin slid into the passenger seat of her mom's car. "How'd it go?" asked her mom.

"Fine," said Griffin, staring out the window.

"How's his band?" asked her mom.

"Fine," she said unconvincingly.

"So they weren't very good?"

"I don't know." She shrugged.

"I see," said Griffin's mom. "Where's Garrett? Is he coming with us?"

"He's not coming," said Griffin.

"Why not?" she said.

"Garrett's mad at me. Garrett's mom said they couldn't

afford to send Garrett to the music center for lessons, he thinks I think his band stinks, and now he doesn't want to come to the library," said Griffin in a single breath. "I really am a Wish Stealer." She bit down on her trembling lip.

"What's a *Wish Stealer*?"

"Someone who makes people afraid to try. That's what Grandma told me."

"I see," said her mom as she backed the car out of the driveway. "I have to agree with Grandma. Wish Stealers are awful, the worst kind of people."

Griffin stared at her mom. Tears filled her eyes. *Does my own mom think I'm awful?*

The car stopped at the stop sign at the end of Garrett's street. "But you are far from a Wish Stealer."

Griffin couldn't look her mom in the eyes. How little her mom knew.

A group of pigeons congested the road, and the car slowed again. "Remember when we saw that beautiful duck on Fern Lake?" asked her mom.

"Yes," said Griffin as she watched the pigeons flap to the curb.

"It seems like a duck is just gliding along like magic. But do you know that underwater it's kicking and paddling,

moving its little webbed feet so fast, working hard to move through that water?"

"Yeah," said Griffin.

"I think that's how wishes work. Like when astronauts walked on the moon, someone made a wish and dared to dream something impossible at the time. But then someone dared to work for the wish. I'm sorry Garrett is sensitive about his band right now, but with a little practice I bet they could be great."

Griffin stared out the window.

"What timing!" said Dr. Penshine, and she pulled into the ice cream store's parking lot and got the best parking spot.

"Mom, what are we doing?" asked Griffin.

"The very first way to approach a problem is to relax and get a scoop of rocky road ice cream!" said her mom, laughing.

"What?" said Griffin, laughing too.

"I just remembered I got an e-mail that the music center is holding open auditions for reduced rates for really good students. I can forward the e-mail to Garrett's mom if you like. I have her e-mail from the school directory."

"Okay," said Griffin.

"There are always a couple ways to solve a problem."

Griffin laughed. "Mom, after our ice cream cones, can you drop me off at the library?"

"Sure. How about I pick you up in an hour? Is that enough time?"

"Thanks, " said Griffin. Her mom's words ran through Griffin's mind. *There are always a couple ways to solve a problem.* But the new idea she had just might get her into big trouble.

Even magic has a secret.

Chapter

F ingers steady on the keyboard, Griffin typed in her new password, WISH.

Kids were allowed thirty minutes on library computers for research. Griffin clicked on Google. She ripped a scrap of paper out of her notebook. Two names were written on it:

Florence L. Daniellson: puppy.
Garrett Forester: a dad.

She entered the first name. Florence L. Daniellson, Topeka, Kansas.

A recent obituary popped up:

```
August 4
Busby, Elmer Bingham. Ninety-two, Topeka,
Kansas. Survivors: Wife: Florence L. Daniellson
Busby. Children: Lorraine, Henry, and Paul.
Grandchildren: Lucy and Roger. Funeral home
address ...
```

Could this be the same Florence L. Daniellson who'd wished for a puppy long ago? August 4 was only a few weeks ago. There was a good chance that Florence L. Daniellson Busby was still alive . . . and about the right age for a wish if she were close to her husband's age. Griffin copied down the funeral home address.

Next she typed in the words "Forester, Alaska, fisherman." An Alaskan newspaper came up: the *Nome Nugget*, the oldest Alaskan newspaper. Griffin clicked on the link. The article was titled BIG FISH! A grainy picture of a man standing proudly next to a giant fish filled the screen. Under the picture a caption read:

```
Brian Patterson Forester, of Nome, Alaska,
catches a 59 lb. 52 inch king salmon! Looks like
```

this former landlubber from Topeka, Kansas, has really learned to fish in the rough waters of Alaska! Brian said he is dedicating this catch to his son, Garrett.

Griffin looked up the address for the *Nome Nugget* and wrote that down too.

"Griffin!" someone called.

Rotating her seat, she spotted Garrett walking toward her. Quickly she closed her notebook and the window on the computer screen. "Garrett! What are you doing here?"

"I wanted to get some more alchemy books, and my mom said she won't let me get a dog if I didn't come," he said.

"Garrett, I'm really sorry if I hurt your feelings about your band. I didn't mean to at all," said Griffin.

He said nothing.

"I didn't know you wanted a dog. That's so cool," said Griffin.

"Whatever," he said. They walked to a long table, sat on opposite ends, and worked on their project in silence. Garrett did not look at Griffin once.

Garrett and Griffin walked outside at five thirty.

Beautiful violin music floated through the dark court-

yard in front of the library. "That music is so incredible," said Griffin, spotting the lonely, sad musician again.

"Yeah, I bet he practices a lot," shot Garrett, skimming a rock down the sidewalk.

The large town clock rang, drowning out the musician's Tchaikovsky violin concerto. The man stopped playing, hung his head, and waited for the clock to cease chiming.

Griffin wiggled off her left shoe. Lately she'd been keeping a few pennies in each shoe just in case.

"Not another penny!" said Garrett, watching her.

But Griffin just stared straight ahead at the musician, flipping the penny in her hand. "Excuse me, sir?" called Griffin to the violinist.

The musician looked up, surprised, like no one had ever called him "sir" in his whole life. "Your violin sounds amazing. What's your name?" Griffin asked.

"Stanley," he said.

"I'm Griffin."

"Hi," he said.

He plucked the gloomiest notes on his violin. "Stick to your studies, kids, so you don't end up like me!" This time he played an angry chord. His violin strings screeched in pain as he sawed against them with his bow.

"Stanley, I have a lucky penny for you to wish on," said Griffin, opening her hand.

Stanley stopped his violin and looked at the shiny penny in Griffin's palm. "That is very kind of you," he said, bowing his head. "But I'm gonna need more than a penny after quitting my job and pouring my life savings into a dream!"

"You can't give up," said Griffin. "Here, make a wish. Just try!"

"Not everyone has a perfect life like you, Griffin," said Garrett.

"Believe me, my life is far from perfect," said Griffin sadly.

For the first time Garrett's and Griffin's eyes met. Tears brimmed in Griffin's eyes.

Stanley gently took the penny from her. Taped across it was the word "success."

"Success!" he read, and started to laugh bitterly. "To make a living doing what I love would be the greatest success to me."

Holding the penny tightly, he closed his eyes as if seeing a strange and faraway dream. Then he shouted, "I wish to be a success!" He rocketed the penny high up in the dark sky. Upward it streaked like a fiery comet. At that same instant the night sprinklers burst on. The blazing penny, already in

the air, became engulfed in one of the water jets and began dancing. It bobbed gloriously on the shooting water.

Craning their necks, the three of them gasped as the penny pranced high in the air, sparkling light everywhere, like fluorescent fireworks. "Wow!" said Stanley, smiling for the first time. He grabbed his bow and began playing the most beautiful music, the *Paganini Etudes,* to accompany the shooting water.

"Griffin!" yelled her mom from the car window.

Griffin scooped up her backpack. "My mom can drive you home if you want, Garrett."

"No, thanks. I got a ride."

"Okay," said Griffin, trying to make eye contact, but Garrett had already turned his back.

"Bye, Stanley. Good luck," called Griffin.

Stanley bowed and continued playing as the water waltzed.

The future belongs to those who
believe in the beauty of their dreams.
—Eleanor Roosevelt

Chapter

B
edroom door: locked. Shades: drawn. Griffin tiptoed to her desk and switched on a tiny desk light. The hands of her clock arched toward midnight. Carefully she unfolded the piece of notebook paper.

FloRence L. DanieLLson: puppy.
GaRReTT ForesteR: a dad.

Griffin stared at the paper. She grabbed a pen and began the first sentence.

Dear MRs. FloRence L. DanieLLson Busby,

I am very sorry to hear about your husband. I am sending my condolences. I wanted you to know that, by accident, I may have something that once belonged to you. If you wished for a puppy and threw a coin into a fountain in front of the Topeka Inn when you were a girl, please contact me at the address below. If not, please ignore this letter.

Sincerely,

G. Penshine

Griffin stuffed the letter into an envelope and licked the envelope shut. On the outside of the envelope she wrote:

To: The funeral director

Please forward this letter to Mrs. Florence L. Daniellson Busby. Thank you.

From: A well-wisher.

Sticking that envelope inside a bigger envelope, she wrote the address of the funeral home where Florence's husband's funeral had been held. Griffin slumped back into her desk chair. She was trying her best to return these wishes, but she wasn't sure she was doing anything right. Taking another deep breath, she ripped off a second piece of paper. She was more determined than ever to help Garrett. Maybe if she helped him, he would not be mad at her anymore. With her pen poised, she began:

Dear Mr. Brian Patterson Forester,

I'm a friend of your son, Garrett. I Googled you and found out you lived in Nome. I hope I'm writing to the right person. If I am, please write back. There is something I need to tell you. Thank you.

Sincerely,

G. Penshine

* * *

She enclosed this letter in an envelope, sealed it, and wrote on the front:

PLease forward mail to MR. BRian Patterson Forester of Nome, ALaska, catcher of the big fish. Thank you.

FRom: G. Penshine.

In very neat cursive letters Griffin wrote the address to the *Nome Nugget*, care of the fishing department, on the outside of the second envelope.

Griffin thought she would mail these letters from the mailbox by the school yard. If her mom found out she was sending letters to strangers, she'd *really* get in trouble. Maybe she shouldn't even sign her name? Maybe she should use a fake address? *Wait a minute!* thought Griffin. Maybe she should use her grandma's address? Griffin decided to use her own address on Florence's letter, and her grandmother's address on Garrett's dad's envelope. Two strange letters coming to her house would be too obvious. The grandfather clock chimed again. Griffin's parents were fast asleep.

She reached under her bed and removed the ring, black mirror, and yarn from Mariah's box. Griffin placed the ring on

top of the mirror. *Why did Mariah give these to me?*

"Owwww!" Griffin's hand shot up to cover her eyes from a blaring light. The garnet ring and mirror threw a violent glow onto the ceiling, bathing the whole room a bloody red. Steadying herself, Griffin squinted her eyes and examined the ring again. She picked up the black disc, the strange stone polished like a smooth lake. She gazed into its pools of darkness. Her reflection was distorted. In the blackness she looked like an old lady. *Is that my future? A rotted Wish Stealer like Mariah?* thought Griffin. She flung the black disc under the bed, where it shattered into shards. "Oh, no!" Then she jumped into bed and, tunneling under the covers, she gathered the blankets tight all around her.

Hold fast to dreams
For if dreams die
Life is a broken-winged bird
That cannot fly.
—Langston Hughes

Chapter

26

✳ ✳ ✳

Griffin lumbered her way through the hallways toward the science room. Today the oral reports on famous scientists were due. Carrying her clumsy poster board made it difficult to walk. The board caught currents in the hallway as if a wind were blowing against her.

"Hi, Libby. Can't wait to see you at my sleepover party on Saturday!" called Samantha as Libby and Griffin walked down the hall. "It's going to be so much fun! Free makeup and my dad's products for all of us."

Griffin could hardly move with all her books and the poster flapping against her body, but she turned in time to

look at Samantha. The girls surrounding Samantha shot Griffin nasty looks as she passed them. "Libby?" said Griffin, confused.

"She e-mailed me really late last night. I'll tell you about it later. I'm so not going," she whispered. "I can't believe her parents let her have a party, like, every weekend!"

Griffin's heart whirled. She'd talked to Libby late last night on the phone. Why hadn't Libby told her about Samantha's invitation? Would Libby change her mind and go to Samantha's party?

A new feeling twisted in her stomach.

"Bye, Griff," said Libby as they parted for different hallways. Griffin continued alone to the science room.

"Okay. Let's see how the projects turned out," said Mr. Luckner as kids shuffled into the classroom. "Put your posters on the back counter and then take a seat." Griffin dropped her books onto her desk.

"Hey, Griffin. If I don't finish my stupid science night project, I'm going to fail because of your no homework idea!" said David Hunt.

"You'd fail because you didn't do your project. Don't blame me!" she said.

"Collie Redmond, a report on Albert Einstein," called Mr. Luckner.

"I, uh, was working so hard on science night that I got behind," said Collie.

"No excuses. Next. Harrison Slovis, Sir Isaac Newton. Come on up . . ."

"Mr. Luckner, the science night thing has really—"

"Are you ready to give your report today or not?" boomed Mr. Luckner from the back of the room, where he sat to grade the presentations.

"Nope."

"Next: Griffin Penshine," called Mr. Luckner. "Have you completed your Marie Curie report?"

Griffin stood up. Hard, mean stares sliced through her. The closer the science night deadline, the madder everyone became. "Yes," said Griffin as she walked to the front of the class. David Hunt's and Michael Janis's faces snarled with hostility. Even the skeleton in the back of the room seemed to grin an evil smile. Garrett's desk was empty. *Where was he?* Looking out at the class, Griffin felt nauseous. "Marie Curie was one of the most famous scientists in the world."

"We don't care!" whispered Michael Janis, sitting in the front row.

Griffin cleared her throat and continued. "Marie was born in Poland in 1867, studied in France, and won two Nobel Prizes, in physics and in chemistry."

"Doesn't matter. She's dead!" mumbled David Hunt, also sitting in the front.

Griffin narrowed her eyes at him. "For four years, night and day, she worked in an unheated shed to discover the element radium."

"Nerd!" heckled Michael.

Gritting her teeth, clenching her jaw, and planting her feet on the tiled floor, Griffin said the next few lines of her report staring at Michael and David. "Many people made fun of Marie Curie, told her she was crazy, said she couldn't be a scientist, that she was just a woman, that she was reaching too high. People were cruel, stupid, and mean to her, but Marie Curie never gave up. She never let people's ignorance, jealousy, or fear stop her."

David and Michael stared back.

"Marie Curie said if she ever was lucky enough to find radium, she hoped it would have a beautiful color. When she did finally find it, radium was more than a beautiful color, it had *spontaneous luminosity,* which meant it was bright and glowing like a star. Marie Curie is one of the most respected and famous scientists to ever live."

"Thank you, Griffin," said Mr. Luckner. "I like how you focused on her persistence. Overall, great job. Though I

would have liked to hear more about her daily dedication and routine. Nice poster."

Griffin sat in her seat, her face as red as her hair and almost as red as the cardboard Mars whirling over her head.

We must have perseverance
and above all confidence in ourselves.
—Marie Curie

Chapter

27

After class Griffin trudged back to her locker. A yellow Post-it note stuck on it read:

NOT INVITED

Griffin flicked the sticker off and jammed it into her backpack. Stacking her books on the cold linoleum floor, she turned her head in time to see that freckled boy who had been working in the back of the metal shop the other day. He passed by her locker, stared, but didn't say a word. Then from the corner of her eye she noticed Kristina headed toward her.

"Hey, Griffin," said Kristina.

"Hi, Kristina," Griffin said sadly. If only someone would give *her* a real lucky penny right then.

"Griffin, I want you to know nothing has happened since I made that wish on the penny you gave me! 'Most beautiful'— what a joke! I tried out for the tap-dancing team, the drill team, and the cheerleading team and messed up in all of them."

"I'm sorry, Kristina."

"You said the penny was lucky, but I just looked really dumb."

"You didn't look dumb, Kristina. You tried."

"I wish I could get that stupid penny back from the water fountain and undo my wish, because I think that penny was unlucky." Kristina's face began turning a blotchy red color. "Actually, I think *you're* unlucky, Griffin!"

Griffin slammed her locker hard. "No, Kristina, I'm not. Maybe your mom was right about you!"

"You're mean!" said Kristina, turning and running down the hall.

Why did I say that? I'm becoming a Wish Stealer! thought Griffin. "Kristina!" called Griffin, but her voice just echoed in the empty hallway.

After school Griffin slunk toward the sidewalk mailbox. Would Libby, her best friend since first grade when they'd

both accidently worn matching socks three days in a row, want to become friends with Samantha? Could Samantha bewitch even Libby? Griffin's heart plummeted. Would Samantha convince Libby to go to her party?

A creak let out when Griffin opened the slot and dropped the two letters in. "Good luck," she muttered, and shuffled away, head bowed. Griffin looked at her watch. The first raindrop splattered on her head.

Honk! Honk! sounded from her father's car.

Her dad rolled down his window. "Hurry, Griff. It's going to pour!"

Griffin slid into the passenger seat.

"Hi. A big storm is coming to Dadesville. Weatherman predicts six inches of rain—thunder, lightning, the whole shebang. We have to go to Grandma's house and stock her up with food before your music lesson. She's not feeling so well."

Griffin's insides contorted into a thousand knots. "Do you think Grandma will be okay?" she whispered. She watched as the rain spit arrows onto the windshield.

"She's one strong lady. I think she'll be fine. How was school today?"

"Okay," she mumbled, and thought of the cruel boys in science class as she gave her Marie Curie report.

"Just okay?" he said.

"Yeah, okay." Griffin felt her stomach tighten again. She couldn't flush the image of Mariah out of her head. Her pinched face lurched into Griffin's head so fast that Griffin shot up her hand to hold her forehead.

"Griffin, what's the matter?" said her dad.

"Headache. A *real bad* headache, Dad," whispered Griffin.

Don't let today's disappointments cast a shadow on tomorrow's dreams.

Chapter

28

A jumble of trumpets, oboes, bassoons, and drums being played, along with the rain pelting outside the music center, sounded like the whole world was coming undone. Griffin's head pounded. She couldn't wait for her bass guitar lesson to be over. Then she could go home and sink into her own bed. Pull the covers over her head. Try to make sense of so many things going wrong.

She walked toward music room 3. Her lesson started in ten minutes. Chiming in unison with the raindrops, the most soothing music rippled down the hall. Griffin followed the heavenly sounds and peeked inside the open auditorium door. A woman with pitch-black hair in a long braid sat

onstage playing a golden harp. After trilling the last notes, the woman stopped, bowed her head, and then smiled at Griffin. "Hello," she called.

"You're so good," said Griffin.

"Thanks from me and my golden harp. Would you like to see it?"

"Sure," said Griffin, walking up onto the stage.

"I'm Aurora," said the lady, holding out her hand.

"I'm Griffin. How long have you played?"

"Since I was a little girl. I'm on a national tour giving concerts, but when we pulled into Kansas, I had to see my old music teacher on the way through Dadesville."

"Wow!" The harp was as tall as Griffin. "This must be hard to move."

"Nothing that can't be done if you just go slow and be careful," said Aurora, smiling.

"Yeah," said Griffin, transfixed on Aurora's aquamarine eyes. They looked like crystals.

"Griffin Penshine, next!" called her bass guitar teacher's voice from the hallway.

"I gotta go," said Griffin. "Bye, Aurora." She walked off the stage back toward her lesson in room 3. She wondered what she would do if Florence and Garrett's dad wrote her back.

* * *

Griffin's fingers felt numb on the four stainless steel strings of her bass guitar. Over and over again she fumbled her scales. Her left hand plucked, but her fingers cramped, and none of the sounds blended. Her teacher exhaled a long, frustrated breath.

Griffin clutched the neck and fret board of her guitar with her right hand, but her palm was so sweaty that the soft cushions of her fingers slipped over the strings and messed up the walking bass line.

"Griffin," said Mr. Castanara. He removed his glasses and stared at her. "Have you practiced?"

"No, I . . ." *I wish to become an amazing bass guitarist* rang in her head like a sad joke.

"Please stay here by yourself and use this time to practice."

"Okay," said Griffin, staring at the four steel strings. She was afraid if she looked up she might cry.

Mr. Castanara left the room, but kept the door ajar. Griffin's eyes clouded over with tears.

"Griffin? Is that you?" It was Jason Scott, thrusting his head into the room, carrying his guitar.

"Hi," she said, sucking in her breath trying to stop any tears from falling.

"What are you doing here?" he asked.

"My teacher wanted me to work on some scales."

"I just wanted to say *thanks a lot* for saying our band stinks!" he said.

"What do you mean?" she asked. Her heart began to drum.

"Garrett wasn't in school today," he said.

"Yeah," she answered.

"Do you know why?"

"Why?" Her back tightened.

"'Cause he said you said our band *stinks*! He skipped school to stay home all day to solo practice his drums."

"WHAT?" said Griffin. "I never said that!"

"*We* aren't the ones who stink!" he said.

The aroma of hot chicken soup tantalized Griffin as she trudged through the front door. "Nothing better than soup on a cold, wet night!" said her mom.

Griffin slumped right past the kitchen.

"Hey," called her mom. "Best bowl of soup in Kansas! Grandma's own recipe."

All Griffin wanted to do was cry into her pillow. But the soup smelled so good.

"Hot bowl ready for you, Griff."

"Okay," said Griffin, pulling off her boots and raincoat. She walked into the kitchen.

"Hi," said her mom, studying her face. "You look tired."

"Yeah," said Griffin, taking a seat. She dragged her spoon through the clear broth. Bobbing in the liquid were celery floats and carrot cushions.

"So how'd your lesson go?" asked her mom.

"Not so great," she said. "I haven't really practiced. I've had a lot of schoolwork."

"It's been a busy week for you. It happens to all of us. How'd your Marie Curie report go in school today?"

"Fine," said Griffin. "Mom, I think I'm getting sick. Can I stay home from school tomorrow?"

Her mom spun around. "Hmm," she said, feeling Griffin's forehead with her palm. "You don't feel hot at all. Eat your soup. You could be coming down with something. Let's see how you feel in a little bit, okay? Oh, and Libby called."

Maybe she's decided to go to Samantha's party after all, thought Griffin.

"Do you want to see an amazing constellation with my telescope? Now that the rain has stopped, the sky is oddly bright."

"Which constellation?"

"Draco is lit up tonight, brighter than I've seen him in a long time."

"Who's Draco?"

"The dragon, remember?"

How could I forget the dragon? she thought. The whole world was bursting with wicked dragons . . . the kids in her science class, Kristina, Jason at the music center. Was she even losing Libby, too?

"Do you want to take a look?" asked her mom.

Holding her bowl up to her mouth, Griffin slurped her soup to consume the final golden droplets. "Sure."

They climbed the stairs. On the roof, adjusting the telescope, her mom said, "There he is! The dragon. Ancient Greeks believed dragons were the guardians of temples and treasures."

Griffin looked through the telescope, scanning the five stars that composed the constellation. The flickering stars hurt her eyes, so she turned the telescope away from her.

"What? What is it, Griff?"

"Nothing. My eyes hurt from squinting."

"Did you see something?" asked her mom, and she took another look. "It's just Draco waiting." Reaching out her palm, Dr. Penshine felt Griffin's head again. "You know, you are warm. Why don't you go to sleep."

"Good night, Mom," said Griffin, and she walked down the stairs to her bedroom. Diving into bed with her clothes on, she sunk into a deep sleep—dreaming of dragons with the faces of the kids at school.

Dragons guard the temples
of transformation.

Chapter
29

For the first time in her life Griffin dreaded going to school. Dreaded what horrible thing might happen next. She had hoped for a high fever, hoped she'd wake up hacking. But when she woke up, her mom was already by her bed feeling her forehead. "Your temperature is just fine. Are you feeling better?"

Griffin took a deep breath. She did feel fine, just not in her heart. It was stuck in a sunk position. "Yeah, I'll be okay," she said, sighing as she got up to prepare for school. Clutching her books to her chest like armor, Griffin slogged through the school. All over the hallways posters hung that read:

HELP RAISE PENNIES FOR THE PLANET!

Bring your donations to Science Night

Starring the band:

THE ALCHEMISTS

WE ROCK!

See Garrett Forester, Jason Scott,

or Griffin Penshine for early donations.

"WHAT!" Griffin couldn't believe it. Dashing down the hallway, she looked for Garrett.

Garrett turned around just as he was finished hanging another poster.

"Hey, Garrett," she said.

Garrett shrugged. "Hey."

"I'm really sorry," said Griffin.

"Apology accepted, because my band is gonna rock. I practiced all day yesterday. We're gonna be great. You'll see. I'm auditioning this Friday at the music center too. My mom called for me."

"Cool," said Griffin.

"I'm gonna be like U2 and Bono. They rock out and help the planet."

Griffin stared at him. "The posters are really nice."

"We need to make, like, twenty more. If kids come up to you, take their donations and save them in an envelope, okay? We'll add it all together later. Some of the guys from my band came over last night to help make posters. We should put a penny donation jug, like a Sparkletts container or something, in the front lobby to start collecting."

"Yeah, okay," said Griffin.

"Hi, Griff. Hi, Garrett," said Libby, waving as she came up to them in the hall. "Your posters are so cool! I can donate a ton of pennies for Pennies for the Planet. Griff, why didn't you call me back yesterday? My mom said I could have a sleepover on Saturday night for our friends. I would never, ever go to Samantha's party. Yuck! Mine will be a blast! We so won't look at skin products!" Libby giggled.

Garrett smiled.

Relief flooded through Griffin. Libby wasn't going to Samantha's party.

"I'm sorry, Libby. I wasn't feeling great last night."

"No worries. Text you later," she said, hurrying off to class.

"Griffin, I have an idea to make our booth totally awesome," said Garrett. "If we win, it's a five-hundred-dollar prize, you know. Can you meet Friday afternoon at the library?"

"Sure."

"Cool," he said.

"I'll see you there tomorrow, then," she said.

He turned the corner to put up some more posters.

Griffin's heart climbed up a notch. Pennies for the Planet was a great idea. If Garrett's band did practice, they had a shot at raising some money after all. Just then, Samantha, Martha, and Sasha slithered up to Griffin in the hallway.

"Hey, Griffin, are you meeting Garrett on *Friday night*? Is this a date? Is he your *boyfriend* or something?" taunted Samantha.

"No. He's not my boyfriend, Samantha," said Griffin. "We're doing our project together."

"Are you in the band? We saw your name on some of the posters," said Sasha.

"I'm collecting money," said Griffin.

"What? *Pennies?* That's not going to work!" The girls giggled. "Plus, we hear Garrett's band stinks!"

"Garrett's band doesn't stink, Samantha. They're amazing!" said Griffin, just as Garrett came up from behind them.

"It's all your fault we have to do this stupid project," said Samantha.

"It's not her fault," said Garrett. "All you have to do is find a cool topic."

"Puh-leez!" said Martha.

"Why are you guys so nasty?" asked Garrett.

Griffin had an urge to wish something nasty right back at the three girls with their spiteful, pinched faces. It took every ounce of her willpower not to.

"I'm not nasty, Garrett! I'm a model in my dad's commercials!" called Samantha, and the three girls huffed off.

True beauty is a light from within.

Chapter

30

✳   ✳
✳

I t seemed impossible that the town library could be so busy on a Friday afternoon. But with science night around the corner, most of Mr. Luckner's students were there working on their projects. Griffin, busy reading about alchemists at the study tables, was waiting for Garrett. After his music center audition he was supposed to meet her, and then her mom would drive them home. But it was hard for her to concentrate. Were the kids in the library mad at her? Did they think having to participate in science night was all her fault? Maggie, Madison, and Libby all had Mrs. Wilkens for science and didn't have to participate in science night.

Keeping her eyes and hands steady, Griffin continued to take notes about the alchemist Basil Valentine and his laboratory equipment: silver eggs, ancient shells, peacocks' tails, chunks of gold, and dragons' scales.

Eden Snyder, a classmate, came up to her table. "Hey, Griffin. Can I ask you something?"

"Yeah," she said.

"Do you know how to use the library's science database on this computer to find an old magazine article?"

Griffin knew this from her mom, who accessed the science database at home all the time.

"See, Eden, first you enter in . . ." Now three more kids gathered around her as she showed Eden.

"Hey, Griffin, did your mom ever say anything about black holes?" asked Robert Winbell.

"Yeah, they're collapsed stars. She says they're like a giant vacuum pit in space where everything gets sucked in. Even light can't escape. It gets suctioned down into the blackness."

"Cool. My partner and I gotta change topics."

"Would Griffin Penshine please come to the front desk? Would Griffin Penshine please come to the front library desk?" boomed the loudspeaker.

"Wait, Griffin!" called Caden Nosam, tapping on

Griffin's backpack. "Do you have any project ideas? My partner and I are switching topics too."

"You could research how to survive a bear attack. Some hikers who survived a bear attack said their backpacks saved them."

"Wow!" Caden said.

"I better go," said Griffin.

Eden, Robert, and Caden all thanked her. Griffin walked to the front desk toward the librarian. "Griffin, your mom is waiting outside," said the woman.

Griffin looked at her watch: five fifteen. Garrett hadn't shown up, and her mom had been waiting fifteen minutes for her. Walking to the car, she looked around for Stanley, the sad violinist.

"Stanley?" she called out. The sidewalk was desolate, filled with wet newspapers floating in puddles.

"Who's Stanley? Your *other* boyfriend?" Samantha snickered, heading into the library with Sasha.

"No one," said Griffin.

"You're friends with imaginary people?" Samantha said.

"You wouldn't understand," said Griffin.

"We don't want to!" they said, breaking into laughter.

Griffin gritted her teeth. *I wish . . . I wish . . .* She bit down hard on her lower lip. Desperately she wanted to

wish something wicked on them. . . . *I wish* . . .

Don't stoop to their level, she heard her grandma's voice say in her head. *You are better than that.* Griffin took a deep breath. She hoped Stanley was okay.

Kristina carried a stack of books up the sidewalk toward the library. "Hey, Griffin!" said Kristina, stopping in front of her.

"Hi, Kristina," said Griffin.

"I'm really sorry I said that you and that penny were unlucky. I was really upset and didn't mean it. I finally convinced my mom to let me take ballet lessons, and my teacher thinks I have a lot of talent. I know it won't happen overnight, but who knows, maybe I can be an incredible dancer!"

"That's great," said Griffin. "I'm sorry I said what I did too. I didn't mean it either. I was really having a bad day."

They smiled at each other.

"Good luck on your project," called Kristina.

"You too," called Griffin, smiling. *Has the "most beautiful" wish been returned? Did something work after all?* she wondered.

Her mom honked.

Griffin got into the front car seat.

"Hi, Griff. Garrett's mom called and said she was sorry that Garrett's drum audition ran over so he couldn't get to the

library. She asked if she could bring Garrett over to our house tonight so you two could work for a few hours instead. I invited her and Garrett over to dinner with us to celebrate."

"Celebrate what?" she asked. *That another wish just maybe was returned!* she thought.

"Garrett passed the drum audition! The drum teacher, Mr. Sanchez, was really impressed. He said Garrett has gobs of natural talent that needs to be tapped. He's going to take him on for free."

"That's awesome! What are we having for dinner?"

"A turkey."

"A turkey?"

"You've been talking an awful lot about wishes lately, so I decided to surprise you with a special dinner. I thought maybe you'd like a wishbone from a turkey."

Griffin stared at her mom. "A wishbone?" she said.

"Your very own. Well, to share with Garrett, too."

Griffin couldn't stop smiling.

✳ ✳ ✳

Follow your bliss.
—Joseph Campbell

Chapter

31

Okay, are we ready?" asked Griffin's dad. Griffin's face glowed as she looked around the messy dinner table. Dinner had been delicious. Everyone had gobbled up the turkey, stuffing, and sweet potatoes. Griffin's mom presented the turkey's cleaned wishbone on a plate and brought it to the table.

"Here we are. The famous wishbone!" said her dad.

Garrett's mom laughed. "I used to do this as a kid. Haven't seen a wishbone in years!"

"Griffin, you grab one side of the wishbone," said her dad. "Garrett, you get the other one, and on the count of three, pull as hard as you can. One . . . two . . . three!"

Garrett stepped back, holding the larger piece of the wishbone over his head.

"Got it!" he shouted.

"Double congratulations today, Garrett! Since you pulled the larger piece of the wishbone, you get to make a wish," said Dr. Penshine.

"But it already came true," said Garrett, beating imaginary drumsticks in the air.

Everyone smiled.

"Well," said Griffin's dad, "if your first wish already came true, then you must be on a roll for a second one."

Griffin smiled. *If my own wishes can't come true, at least Garrett's can,* she thought.

Garrett made his second wish, but he wouldn't tell anyone what he had wished for.

"Hey, before you kids get to work, does anyone want a tour of my observatory? The sky is perfect for stargazing tonight," said Dr. Penshine.

Garrett, Griffin, Mrs. Forester, and Griffin's dad ventured up to the rooftop, with Griffin's mom leading the way. The night was cool and clear. "Let's see what's bright in the sky tonight. Well, we can all see the Little Dipper, or Ursa Minor, and look, there's the Pleiades rising in the East. Over there is one of my favorites: Cassiopeia."

"Cassio *what*?" asked Garrett.

"Here, Garrett, look through my telescope. Do you see those five stars?"

"Five stars in that giant zigzag in the sky?" he said.

"Yes, that's Cassiopeia. She was a beautiful yet wicked Greek queen. She claimed to be more beautiful than Poseidon's daughters. Poseidon, the king of the sea, was so offended that he sent a sea monster to destroy the city where she ruled. The only way to stop the monster was to sacrifice Cassiopeia's own daughter, Andromeda."

"What happened?" asked Garrett.

"Well, the brave hero, Perseus, discovered an ingenious way to kill the gigantic monster and rescue Andromeda. They lived happily ever after, and when they died, Andromeda and Perseus ended up as beautiful constellations."

"Cool," said Garrett.

Griffin smiled at her mom.

Until nine thirty that night Garrett and Griffin worked at the kitchen table, making clay models of the alchemists' tools and more posters for Garrett's band. With science night less than two weeks away, they were completely prepared. "I don't think I've ever finished a project early in my entire life!" said Garrett.

"Takes the pressure off," said Griffin.

"Yeah. Now I can jam with my band to get ready for the concert. Hey, could you give Kurt bass lessons? He really needs help. Come to our next rehearsal. I'll e-mail you the music."

"Sure," said Griffin. For a moment she longed to be in the band too, but she didn't dare wish that.

The doorbell rang. Mrs. Forester was back to pick up Garrett.

"Thanks for dinner. Bye, Griffin," said Garrett, smiling at her.

Griffin was glad it was dark, because for some reason she couldn't stop blushing. "Bye," she said.

"See you all soon at science night!" said Mrs. Forester.

"We look forward to it," said Griffin's mom.

Griffin ran to look at Andromeda and Perseus one more time.

* * *

Shoot for the moon.
Even if you miss,
you'll land among the stars.
—Les Brown

Chapter

32

S aturday morning a gray sky domed over Dadesville. Griffin and Libby poured bright-colored paint into ice cube trays in Grandma Penshine's kitchen for their art lesson. Suddenly a cackling sound came from Grandma Penshine's living room. The noise did not sound like rain, or lightning, or anything natural. In fact, it sounded hideously unnatural.

"Did you hear that?" asked Libby.

"Yeah," whispered Griffin.

"Sounds exactly like —," said Libby.

"DON'T SAY IT!" said Griffin, jostling the tray of colors. They slopped all over her grandma's kitchen counter.

"Grandma? Is everything okay?" called Griffin. Her grandma was searching for some art books in the living room.

"Girls, you have to come see this," she answered.

Griffin and Libby ran to the living room. In front of the large bay window Grandma Penshine stood watching as three witches hobbled toward her front door carrying a sign that read, SHAKESPEARE IS NOT DEAD! COME SEE US AT THE TRAVELING GLOBE THEATRE CO. FESTIVAL.

"Freaky! It's like adult Halloween," said Libby.

"If that isn't impressive. Actors going door to door to promote their play. I really admire dedicated artists," said Grandma.

The doorbell rang.

"Grandma!" said Griffin. "Libby and I saw those actors in class already. Can we just not answer the door and do our lesson?"

"We can't dishearten other artists, even if they are in the dramatic arts," she said.

"Please, Grandma!" said Griffin.

"One minute only. I promise," said Grandma Penshine.

"Grandma, we really want to learn about . . . Who did you say we're learning about today . . . George?"

"Giorgione, the great Venetian painter from fifteenth-

century Italy who changed the world with how he painted light and color—changed art forever, really. A true master."

The doorbell rang again.

"Let's just wish them well with their play," said Grandma. She opened the front door of her home, still in her art smock covered in shocks of color.

Griffin's head spun. The scent of spices, mandarin orange, dried lavender, cloves, and incense pounded in her head. She knew she had smelled that odor somewhere before.

"Hello," said Grandma Penshine. "What an inspiring sign you are all carrying."

"Thank you, my lady," cackled one of the witches.

"This is for you, my dame," said another. With her bony hand the hag passed her a brochure about the traveling festival.

"Shakespeare lives!" cackled the third witch.

"I couldn't agree more! The importance of keeping Shakespeare's great works alive is a responsibility of all artists," said Grandma Penshine. "Do you three know that my favorite line from Shakespeare is from *Hamlet*, act 1, scene 4: 'Angels and ministers of grace defend us!'"

Just then the sun burst through clouds, and glorious light beamed down. The three witches shielded their eyes, snatched back the brochure, and whirled their black shawls

over their heads. Without a word they retreated down the walkway out into the street.

Griffin couldn't move. Her grandma and Libby watched until the witches had moved far down the road.

"Weird," said Libby.

"Those actors certainly are committed to their roles," said Grandma Penshine, shutting her door and locking it. "Can anyone believe this heavenly weather! The sky has shifted and is wild with joy!"

"Should we paint outside now?" asked Libby.

"On days like this the sky demands to be painted!" said Grandma, setting up an easel on the back porch. "If this were my last hour on earth, I could think of no better way to spend it than with you two wonderful girls, feeling the sun on my face, painting my flowers, and cherishing each and every whirl of color."

Tears sprung to Griffin's eyes. She watched as her grandma mixed paints as if mixing sacred medicine. She realized how much she'd miss her grandma if anything happened to her. Her voice always felt like a giant hug.

"We must paint the sun breaking through the cotton clouds just like Giorgione," said Grandma.

Griffin looked up at the sky and imagined she could jump into the clouds, float away on sunshine, forget witches,

forget wishes, and forget all things gray and black.

"Grandma, were people nice to Giorgione?" asked Griffin.

"That's hard to say since he lived in the late 1400s, but I do know at first that people laughed at him. They said he didn't know the rules, his work was strange—too much color, too much magical light. Clouds were not *supposed* to be painted that way." Her grandma swirled some sapphire and crystal blues together on the canvas.

"Did he give up?" asked Libby.

"Certainly not!" she said. "How do you think I even know the name Giorgione more than five hundred years later? Personally, I think I know his secret."

"What?" asked Libby.

"I think he took some of those beautiful clouds he painted and stuffed them right into his ears. Then he couldn't listen to all the doubters who told him his stuff was too strange."

"Cool," said Libby.

"Griff, can you do me a favor?" called Grandma Penshine. "Could you please get my shawl in my bedroom? I just caught a chill."

"Sure," said Griffin, leaping up and going into her grandma's lavender bedroom. On the bureau, lilacs tucked in white

porcelain vases swept perfumed shadows through the room. A blushing pink orchid rested languidly in a pot. The soft bed looked like a velvet pincushion. Grandma's shawl was flung over the rocking chair in the corner of her room. Suddenly Griffin noticed a wooden box inlaid with mother-of-pearl on her grandmother's dresser. Sticking out of the box was a skein of yarn. It looked exactly like the yarn in Mariah's box. Griffin froze.

White cotton curtains rustled in the breeze. Through the blinds, across the street, Griffin saw the witches holding hands in a circle.

"Griffin!" called Grandma Penshine. "Libby!"

Grabbing the shawl, Griffin dashed out of the room back to the kitchen patio. "Here, Grandma," she said.

"Girls, look!" said Grandma Penshine, pointing above her.

A dark cloud was marching head-on into the blue sky. "The sky is shifting! Right before our eyes. Quick!" Sinister, dark, heavy clouds were smothering the light. Libby and Griffin helped Grandma Penshine carry the canvases and tubes of paint inside. In one instant everything had shifted to gray. "Quick, girls! Please, shut my windows!" said Grandma. Griffin and Libby dashed through the house closing windows as rain pelted the house.

"What is with this weather?" said Grandma. "Downright

mystifying. One minute the most glorious sun, the next minute as gray as the storm's evil eye."

Lying in her bed Sunday night, Griffin thought about the phrase "as gray as the storm's evil eye." All weekend it rolled through her head. Even at Libby's superfun sleepover party the night before, she couldn't help thinking that those gray clouds had brought something strange to town. Something wicked. *Why did those actors come to my grandma's house?* In the rush of shutting all the windows, Griffin had forgotten to ask her grandma about the yarn. *Why does she have the same yarn as Mariah? The sky is shifting.* Griffin thought of Stanley. Was he out there in the rain with his violin? When would the witches leave town and go far, far away? Then she thought about Giorgione staring at the clouds five hundred years ago.

Stuff your ears with clouds.

Chapter

Monday afternoon at school, Samantha and her friends had slipped notes into Griffin's locker. In Samantha's curly cursive writing the notes said: *Hi, Griff. I think I love you. From your new boyfriend, Garrett.*

Griffin stuffed these at the bottom of her backpack to dump into the garbage. Only one thing could make Griffin forget Samantha—a letter, which arrived in the mail after school. It was addressed to G. Penshine, and the return address read:

Mrs. Florence L. Daniellson Busby

"Hi, Griff," called her mom from upstairs. She was decorating the nursery. "I'll be down in a minute. There's a letter for you on the table."

Griffin grabbed the letter and leapt up the stairs two at a time. After locking her door, she threw her backpack down and carefully opened the letter. Shaky words appeared on blue-lined notebook paper:

Dear G.,

I don't know who you are, but you must know me because I once threw a penny in the Topeka Inn fountain when I was an eleven-year-old girl. I held my penny so high and shouted with all my breath, "I wish for a puppy!" I still remember that summer day like it was yesterday, the warm Kansas sun on my face. It's funny, I can hardly remember what I ate for breakfast today, but I remember that day as clearly as

church bells chime on Easter Sunday. I never did get a puppy. My little brother was allergic to dogs, and then I married a wonderful man, but he was allergic to dog hair too. I wonder what in the world you could have of mine all these years later? Please contact me at my return address.

Sincerely,

Florence Lorraine Daniellson Busby

"Griffin?" called her mom through her bedroom door.

"I'll be right out," she answered.

"Who's the letter from?"

Griffin hesitated. She never lied to her mom, but she couldn't risk having her hurt by Mariah's curse. Griffin crossed her fingers and said, "An old lady. Part of a community service pen pal thing." She tucked the letter back into the envelope and slid it under her bed before she opened her door.

"I'm going to the store," said her mom. "Do you want to come? I'm having serious pregnancy cravings for mustard, orange juice, avocado, and barbeque potato chips!"

"Sounds really gross, Mom!" Griffin laughed.

"Doesn't it?" Her mom smiled and rubbed her big belly.

"I'm okay. I'm just gonna start my homework," said Griffin.

When Griffin heard the front door close behind her mother, she grabbed the phone and dialed information.

"City and state, please," said an operator.

"Topeka, Kansas. The Sunflower Assisted Living Home, please," said Griffin. She copied down the number and dialed.

"Hello, Sunflower. How may I help you?"

"Hello, my name is Griffin Penshine and uh . . . I'm a friend of Mrs. Florence Daniellson Busby. I'm thinking of getting her a top secret present, and I was wondering if your home allows pets."

"Yes, we do. Cats, small dogs, and certain kinds of birds are allowed. What kind of pet were you thinking of?"

"A small puppy."

"That sounds very nice."

"Thank you," said Griffin, and she hung up the phone.

"Griffin?" said her mom in her bedroom doorway.

"HUH!" Griffin jumped. She hadn't even heard her mom come in.

"What are you doing?" asked her mom with her hands on her hips.

"You're back already!" said Griffin.

"I forgot my wallet," said her mom. "Now, who in the world are you calling? Who is Mrs. Busby? What's this about a *puppy*?"

"Well, see . . ." Griffin just stopped. "Mom, before I tell you, I have two questions: How far is Dadesville to Topeka? And how much would a puppy cost?"

"It is a twenty-minute drive to Topeka from here, and a puppy rescued from the pound would probably be about seventy-five dollars."

"Mom, you know how you asked if I wanted a puppy a week ago?"

"Yes."

"Can I get one and then give it as a present to someone?"

"Griffin, *what is going on*?" said her mom.

She crossed her fingers behind her back again. "Mom, I was just trying to make an old lady's wish for a puppy come true. Kinda like a service project. Is that okay?" Griffin began to sweat.

"I need to think about this one. Let me talk it over with your dad," said her mother.

Griffin uncrossed her fingers.

At midnight Griffin jingled the last few pennies in her hand: "STOP," "popular," "world peace," and the unlabeled penny

were still complete mysteries. Clasping two pennies in one hand and two pennies in the other, Griffin paced around her dark bedroom. *I've given away more than half the pennies, and I think a few wishes have come true,* she thought. The nightlight in her room cast strange shadows on the walls, mocking the faded stars on her ceiling. *I need to put new stars up,* Griffin thought. New sticker stars that glowed, shimmered, and shone to replace the dull ones. Her mom would help her with that; they'd probably replicate the real night sky. Griffin slowly parted her curtains, scanning the inky night roofs.

Don't let your stars fade.

Chapter 34

"If this isn't a first!" called Dr. Penshine from the kitchen after school. "Mr. Castanara called from the music center and had to cancel your lesson. It seems he's caught a terrible cold."

"Really?" said Griffin. *My wish of becoming an amazing bass guitarist is definitely not coming true,* she thought.

"Since I thought you were going to be at your lesson, I made a doctor's appointment, and Dad won't be home until late tonight. Do you want to go over to Grandma's and hang out with her so you're not all alone in the house?" asked her mom.

"Sure," said Griffin. She wanted to ask her grandma about the yarn she'd seen in her box. After they played a

few games of cards, she would ask her why it was just like Mariah's yarn.

Grandma Penshine was in her bed, covers tucked high all around her, when Griffin came over. "Hi, Grandma, how are you feeling?" asked Griffin. It didn't seem possible that her grandma could look so tired. What had happened to Giorgione and his soft clouds?

"Come here, my love." Grandma Penshine clasped her warm hands around Griffin's hand. "I've felt so tired the past few days. Like those dark clouds sapped some of my energy."

"Can I get you something, Grandma?"

"A glass of water, please. Oh, and in the kitchen on the table is a FedEx package that came for you today," said Grandma. "Why is it coming here for you, Griff?"

"I'll go get your water!" Griffin darted into the kitchen, where a thin FedEx envelope waited. Return address: Nome, Alaska. Griffin took a deep breath and pulled on the perforated cardboard strip.

Dear G. Penshine,

What do you have to tell me? I'm often on my boat, the Internet rarely works, and

mail takes forever here. Please use the
FedEx envelope and pre-addressed slip
I enclosed in this package. Just seal it
and drop the envelope in a FedEx bin.
Thank you.

Sincerely,

Brian Patterson Forester

Griffin's stomach tightened. *What* do *I have to tell Garrett's dad about him?* That Garrett used to wish for a dad, but he doesn't wish for such "stupid things" anymore? *What have I done?* She slammed the letter down, filled a tall glass of water, and trudged toward her grandma's room.

"Why such the long face?" asked her grandma, sitting up in bed.

"It's nothing, Grandma."

"Really? In my experience 'nothing' doesn't look like *that* on someone's face, especially not on yours. Do you want to tell me about that FedEx package? Did you open it?"

"Yes."

"And?"

"Well, see . . . Grandma, I'm not sure if I did something good or bad. I kinda wrote to someone and they wrote back," said Griffin.

"Maybe I can help?" said her grandma.

Griffin slumped on the side of her grandma's bed. "What if someone wished for something, and you wanted to help them get it. But then, when you thought about it, maybe they don't really want that wish to come true, and you've just made things worse for them."

"That's a tough one," said her grandma. "You know, that makes me think of a story. Can you see that bush outside my window?"

Griffin strained her neck to see out her grandma's bedroom window.

"The butterflies like it there because it's protected by the house, and the leaves give them lots of nourishing food to eat while they grow. Every spring I watch the butterflies struggle and struggle to break free from their caterpillar cocoons, and every spring I want to get my garden gloves and help them out of their cocoons, but that would be the wrong thing to do. Because if they don't do it themselves, they won't be strong butterflies. Actually, they might not

even be able to fly if I help them. So, to answer your question, sometimes it's wrong to help people do things. They might not *want* help or even be *ready* for new things to happen. But there are always exceptions.

"One spring we had the oddest weather; one minute it was cool, the next minute hot as the desert, and this little half butterfly, half caterpillar didn't know whether to come out or stay in. Then he was almost gobbled up by a crow, so I shooed the bird away, picked up the cocoon, and nestled the little guy in the shoulder of a tree. So I did help him. I interfered right down to jingling bells at the crow. But when he finally broke free, he was one of the most beautiful butterflies I've ever set my eyes on. All summer he kept me company, fluttering his rainbow wings and visiting my windowsill. So sometimes it's best to leave things alone, and sometimes your heart tells you to jingle bells at the crows!"

"I'm not quite sure which one this is."

"When in doubt, trust your heart. How about we take a break and play a game of pistachio poker?"

They played eight games of pistachio poker until Grandma's eyelids flickered like two falling stars, and Griffin knew it was time for her nap. She realized she'd

forgotten to ask her about the yarn. Carefully she gathered the deck of cards and placed them in a neat stack. Then she returned to the kitchen to read Mr. Forester's letter one more time.

✳ ✳ ✳

The heart has its reasons,
of which reason knows nothing.
—Blaise Pascal

Chapter

35

Midnight again, and Griffin fiddled at her desk, her eyes glued on Garrett's father's handwriting. Dark bags hung under her eyes from staying up so late the past few nights. Slowly Griffin began to write to Mr. Forester.

Dear Mr. Forester,

My name is Griffin Penshine and I'm twelve. Garrett and I are in the same science class in Dadesville, Kansas. I'm very sorry to have bothered you with a

letter. Garrett and I were assigned by
our science teacher to do a huge project
together for science night. When my mom
took us out to dinner after working on
our project, Garrett told us he used to
wish on his birthday for a dad. So I gave
him a lucky penny and secretly wrote to
you for extra luck to happen. I think he
would be mad if he knew I wrote to you.
I'm very sorry to have touched a cocoon I
shouldn't have touched.

Sincerely,

Griffin Penshine

Griffin slid her letter inside the FedEx envelope and zipped it inside her backpack. The only FedEx drop she knew of was at the front office at school by Mrs. Davis's desk. During lunch tomorrow she would quietly place the envelope in the bin.

"Good morning, Miss Penshine," said Mrs. Davis from behind the desk in the front office.

"Hi, Mrs. Davis," said Griffin.

"What are you doing here? Certainly *you* can't be in trouble?"

"Can I put this in the FedEx bin?" she asked, holding the packet.

"Sure. They pick up at three o'clock. Whatcha dropping off?" she said.

"Just, uhh—a note," Griffin said.

Mrs. Davis swooped around her desk and peered into the FedEx bin. "'Brian Patterson Forester,'" she read aloud. "'Sender: G. Penshine.' Hmmm. Forester? I remember that name from entering school records. Is that Garrett Forester's dad?"

"Uhh, maybe. I'm just dropping something off for my grandma." *Brrrringggg,* screeched the school bell.

"Oh, that wonderful lady I met the first day of school? Why is your grandma writing to Garrett's dad, sunshine? Are they acquainted?"

"It's about science night, that's all," said Griffin, through her clenched jaw.

"Look here! On the address line! Nome, Alaska! Garrett's dad lives in Nome, Alaska? Ain't that a hoot! Bear country! You know what they say about Nome, don't ya?"

Griffin shook her head, now dizzy, as the floor became quicksand sucking her down.

"They say," Mrs. Davis said, and started choking on her laughter, "there's no place like Nome!" Her laugh boomed all over the front office.

Griffin left the office and hoped Mrs. Davis wouldn't say anything.

To keep your secret is wisdom;
but to expect others to keep it is folly.
—Samuel Johnson

Chapter

36

S cience Night was only a week away, and Samantha
and her friends were panicking, and panicking
meant supervenom. It took every ounce of strength
for Griffin not to wish wretched things on Samantha's
clique. Like maybe Samantha's, Martha's, and Sasha's
teeth would turn black and fall out, or they would all
grow bushy beards. But darkness filling Griffin's soul in
exchange for Samantha's sprouting a beard was not worth
it. And some of the kids were excited about science for the
first time. Audree constantly doodled blue-footed birds of
the Galápagos. Photos of black holes plastered the inside
of Robert Winbell's locker. Caden Nosam was bumping

around the hallway with a stack of books, discussing bears with Mr. Luckner.

"Hey, Griffin," whispered Jason, a few desks down from her in social studies class. "Are you coming to band rehearsal today at Garrett's? Kurt really needs help."

"Yeah, I'll be there." For the past week she had learned all the songs for Garrett's band.

Trying to concentrate in class was becoming harder and harder for Griffin. Something was definitely wrong. The tingling-sinking feeling returned, and she'd had it ever since she'd left the front office.

A cold breeze swept through the hallway and throttled Griffin by the throat. As she unloaded books out of her locker, every hair on her neck shot straight up. She knew with one word what had happened.

"GRIFFIN!" yelled Garrett, rushing toward her, his face blistering red. "GRIFFIN," he said again, and now he was right in front of her. "DID YOU WRITE TO MY DAD?"

Her eyes grew large. "What?"

"I just bumped into Mrs. Davis, who said, 'Garrett, how neat that your dad lives in Alaska. There's no place like Nome!' I asked, 'How do you know that?'"

Griffin felt a steel rod zoom straight up her back.

"Mrs. Davis said, 'Well, your friend Griffin Penshine just sent him a letter.'"

"Can I talk to you after school?" she asked, looking down at her shoes as students passed by them in the hallway on the way to class.

"NO! I don't care if I'm late for class. I don't care if I never go to another class EVER!" Garrett was an erupting volcano.

Samantha and her group paraded by in a line, eyeing both Griffin and Garrett, who were standing, red-faced, inches apart from each other. "Look! Look! They're having a fight!" she heard the girls whisper as they passed them.

Griffin bit down hard on her lower lip and looked straight at Garrett. "Garrett," she said, and took a deep breath. "I'll tell you everything, but could we please talk after school?"

"NO! TELL ME RIGHT NOW!"

"Fine." The class bell rang, but Griffin didn't budge. "Garrett, you once said you wished for a dad. I wanted to help out your wish, so I Googled your dad and found out he lived in Nome. Then I asked him to please write me back.

I never thought anything would happen, *ever*. Then he sent me a FedEx package to put my next letter in. In my second letter I said I'm sorry, this is none of my business. I should not have written."

"I never want to see my dad! I hate you for writing to him! I'm not doing my science project with you, Griffin! I don't care if I fail! Do the stupid project yourself!" Garrett punched three lockers in a row and exploded out the school doors.

Griffin looked up from the swirling floor in time to see Samantha and her mean friends' faces pressed against the window of the classroom door, their shiny eyes like wolves'.

"Griffin Penshine! What are you doing out here? The class bell has already rung, and you're LATE!" shouted Mr. Blackwell, patrolling for tardy students.

"I—I—I was just getting my books," stammered Griffin.

"You're tardy. That means a thirty-minute detention after school in room 201."

"But, Mr. Blackwell . . . I . . . ," pleaded Griffin, holding back tears.

She didn't hear anything for the last two periods of

school; only a giant blur and drone of buzzing surrounded her: "Did you and Garrett break up?" "Did Garrett dump you?"

Griffin knew she was lost inside one of Giorgione's inside-out clouds.

*   *   *

Ride out the storms when clouds hide the face of the sun in your life, remembering that even if you lose sight of the sun for a moment, the sun is still there.

—Blessing of the Apaches

Chapter
37

Mrs. Forester called that evening, after Griffin had come home late from detention. From her bedroom Griffin could hear her mom talking. "We're so sorry, Mary Beth. So sorry. I know this must be very hard for Garrett and you. We can assure you Griffin had no idea what this meant to both of you. She was trying to be helpful."

Dr. Penshine clicked off the phone and knocked on Griffin's door. "Griffin, please open the door," said her mom.

But Griffin locked the door and buried herself under the blankets. She never wanted to go to school again. She never

wanted to help another person again. She swore she would never write another letter or use another penny again in her whole life.

"Dad and I want to talk to you downstairs. Take fifteen minutes for yourself, but then we want you downstairs in Dad's office. No ifs, ands, or buts."

After Griffin heard her mom's footsteps go down the stairs, she took out Mariah's two boxes and put them on her bed. The "puppy," "STOP," "popular," "world peace," and the unlabeled penny remained. Griffin slowly took out Mariah's red ring, its huge garnet stone resembling trapped blood. Tears dribbling from her eyes, Griffin tried to see her reflection in the stone. But tonight there was no glow, just a dull red. One of Griffin's teardrops smacked the middle of Mariah's ring. Griffin brushed away the tear, leaving a smudge. Setting the ring back in the box, she scanned the remaining pennies. "Popular" looked dull and tarnished. Carefully she slid that penny out of the ring slit.

Long ago someone wished to be popular. Griffin wondered why that person had made that wish. Did he or she have that same suffocating feeling that Griffin did right now? Like the whole world was against her?

The grandfather clock chimed. Time to go downstairs and face her parents. The small desk light was glowing on her

father's desk. Her parents sat on the couch together. Griffin slumped into the leather chair across from them.

"Griffin, it's time you told us what's going on," said her mom. "Garrett's mom is beside herself. She said Garrett is so upset. What made you write a letter like that?"

Griffin took a deep breath. She remembered what Mariah had said: *If you tell anyone about the curse, you are cursed for generations, and the person you tell will never have any of his or her wishes come true.*

Griffin chose her words carefully. "Remember when I met that lady, Mariah Weatherby Schmidt, at Mr. Schmidt's shop?"

Her mom nodded.

"She gave me a penny and a box of polishing cloths. But actually, in the box of cloths were some other lucky pennies. I was only trying to help make Garrett's wish for a dad come true. I gave him a lucky penny and wrote that letter to speed up his luck. Mariah also gave me a ring and a leather guest record book from the inn."

"May we see the ring and guest book Mariah gave you?" asked her dad.

"Okay." Griffin nodded and dashed upstairs to retrieve the box. When she returned, her mom examined the ring. "This stone is a garnet. It looks about six carats—worth quite

a lot. They are never this large. The gold band is thick, too."

Together her parents opened the guest book and studied it, like careful archeologists. "An odd and interesting bequeathal," said her dad. "Reminds me of a quote from Ben Franklin. He said, 'If a man could have half of his wishes, he would double his troubles.'"

"I made a huge mistake. I just wanted to try to help Garrett."

"We know your intentions were good, but when you make a decision that affects someone else's privacy, you need to be respectful and really consider how the other person might feel."

Griffin nodded her head, as tears spilled from her eyes.

"I see here the name Florence L. Daniellson and the tiny word 'puppy.' Is this what the puppy thing is about?" said her mom. "This woman wished for a puppy?"

"I just thought it might be nice to make her wish come true."

"I see," said her mom.

"Garrett refuses to do the science project with me now. After all the work we did together, he'll totally get marked down if he's not there. He hates me too."

"First, I think you should write apology notes to Garrett and his mother. Try to explain what you meant to do."

"I told him already!" cried Griffin.

"Giving people time to calm down is best," said her mom. "Science night is still a week away. Maybe Garrett will change his mind. If not, you need to honor his choice, and we'll help you set up your booth. What do you want to do with Mariah's stuff?"

"Throw it in the garbage."

"Do you want to keep the ring?"

"No, it scares me," answered Griffin.

"I have an idea. Let's sell the ring, and any money you make we'll donate to Pennies for the Planet. I'll take care of it for you, okay?"

"Okay," said Griffin, tears still streaming down her face.

"Griffin," said her mom, "everybody makes mistakes or uses poor judgment once in a while, but it's what you do *next* that counts. Now, why don't you write those apology notes and get a good night's sleep."

Her mom stood up, kissed Griffin on the forehead, and went to make some tea. Her mom's warm kiss made her feel like crying even harder. Griffin turned to her dad. Between sniffles she said, "Dad, would you ever wish to be popular?"

"I'm sure a lot of people would like to be popular. It can make things easier or more pleasant, but popularity changes, grows, and can even get silly. The more honest and kind you

are, the more the *right* kind of popularity comes to you."

"Yeah," said Griffin, wiping her wet eyes.

"Griffin, we love you—popular, unpopular, around the moon, and back again," said her dad.

Back in her bedroom Griffin dangled the "popular" penny in her hand and stood by her dark bedroom window. In the swirling moonlight she stared at the copper coin. Tomorrow she'd take the "popular" penny to school.

✳ ✳ ✳

Popularity?
It is glory's small change.
—Victor Hugo

Chapter

38

✳ ✴ ✳

D r. Penshine dropped Griffin off at school fifteen
minutes early. In the lobby of the school well-
lit display cases held trophies and notices for
science night. In front of the cases was a water jug Garrett
and Griffin had placed there for donated pennies.

The jug looked sad. Empty. Forgotten. Inside the jug two
inches of pennies nestled at the bottom of the container, most
of which Griffin and Garrett had donated themselves.

The halls were clear of kids, but a stampede of rushing
students would burst through the doors in ten minutes.
Griffin dug into her pocket and removed the "popular"
penny. She wanted Pennies for the Planet to be the most

popular charity, raising tons of money for the environment. Then, at least, this mess could count for something. Griffin was sure Garrett wished the same thing. But there was no way she could give it to him now. Griffin held the penny in her hand.

Samantha, Martha, and Sasha barged through the front doors of school. Huge designer bags were slung over their left shoulders, and they clutched chilled bottles of designer mineral water in their right hands.

Griffin's and Samantha's eyes locked.

Swiveling their heads, the girls looked at the pathetic almost-empty water jug. They laughed. "Checking on your project?" said Samantha. "We heard Garrett refuses to work with you. Too bad about *your grade.*"

The penny started to burn into Griffin's palm. Round edges of copper pressed against her flesh, singeing her skin. Griffin took a deep breath. *Treat yourself with respect and ignore people who don't treat you with dignity* ran through her mind. The penny was scorching her palm, burning to be set free. Heat surged through Griffin's entire body. *Popular! Popular!* chanted through her head. Griffin fought to not throw the penny at Samantha's face. Her fingers could hardly contain the penny, now a hot coal.

"What's in your hand, Griffin? A frog?" said Samantha.

"Nothing," said Griffin.

"*Nothing* doesn't make your hand jump like that. Show us!"

"No," said Griffin.

"Show us!" said Samantha, moving closer.

"No, Samantha. You're such a bully," said Griffin, fighting to keep her hold on the burning penny. But it burned so badly that she lost her grip and the penny tumbled out along the cold floor.

Sasha ran for it, scooped it up, and placed it in Samantha's palm.

Griffin stood in front of her. Anger surged through her entire body.

"Look at this! This is too cute!" said Samantha, mocking. "A penny with 'popular' taped across it. Are you wishing to be popular? Do you carry around lucky pennies with labels on them for yourself?" The three girls howled with laughter.

Griffin bit her lip.

"You know what I think of you and your stupid penny?" said Samantha.

"I think this penny must be *nasty* being inside *your* pocket." She dumped some of her designer water on it, and the ink on the label began to bleed. The word "popular" spread in all directions.

Griffin glared.

"Oh, look at this, girls," said Samantha. "Her penny is ruined!" The girls laughed. "Maybe I should make a wish before it fades away . . ." In a baby voice, with her lips in a snarl, she mocked, "I wish Griffin becomes *superpopular.*"

The three girls cracked up. Sasha laughed so hard she snorted. She added, "Don't forget her dork charity, too."

"And her dork charity, too."

"Here, Griffin, better take back your *lucky* penny!" said Samantha. But just as she threw it, the school bell blasted, and a charge of kids burst through the front doors along with a gust of wind. The penny flew through the air like a smoldering comet. In a ribbon of light the penny landed inside the water jug on top of the heap. The container lit up from within.

Samantha glared at Griffin. "Why did that penny light up? What kind of penny was that, anyway?"

"A lucky one," said Griffin.

All appears to change when we change.
—Henri Frédéric Amiel

Chapter

39

On science night, rubber sneakers squeaked over the gym floor that reeked of sweat and salt. Griffin had transformed the splatters and paint smudges Samantha's friends had squirted onto her sneakers by turning them into a cool design. She'd made the paint blobs look like a van Gogh–inspired rain forest.

While Dr. Penshine parked the car, Griffin dragged her bags through the gym in search of her booth. Passing Samantha's and Sasha's booth, number 23, Griffin locked eyes with Samantha. An electric sign over her booth blinked: THE SCIENCE AND JOY OF MY DAD'S DERMATOLOGY PRODUCTS. Samantha's father had donated the sign. When Griffin

looked closer, she noticed Samantha still had large warts all over her face.

"This lighting is unbearable!" screeched Mrs. Sloane. "Look at you! This is so bad for your father's business." Pulling more cover-up out of her purse, Mrs. Sloane slapped at Samantha's skin. The gold bracelets up and down Mrs. Sloane's arm jangled, calling even more attention to Samantha. "This is disgusting! I'm so embarrassed!"

Samantha glared at Griffin.

Griffin stared back. Mrs. Sloane made Samantha look kind. For the first time Griffin actually felt sorry for Samantha. Maybe there was a reason Samantha was so mean.

"Hi, Griffin!" said Audree, who was setting up her display table with facts about Darwin, the Galápagos Islands, and blue-footed birds.

"Wow, your booth looks great, Audree. Did you make that picture?"

"Yeah, my whole family. We spread out a giant sheet of paper on the living room floor and colored in the blue-footed birds. It really looks like a duck with powder blue feet."

"It's amazing. Good luck tonight," said Griffin.

"Thanks. You too. My mom said I worked so hard on this project that I can have a huge sleepover party! I'm calling everybody tomorrow!"

"Cool. Thanks," said Griffin, and she slid her heavy bags through the aisles, stopping at booth 17, which was assigned to Garrett and her. Doors opened to the public at six p.m., but Garrett was nowhere to be found.

Sighing, Griffin started to unpack all the things she and Garrett had made for their booth: poster boards, fact booklets, and clay models of alchemists' equipment. First she hung the huge poster board: THE ALCHEMISTS: GOLD, WISHES, AND FUTURE SCIENTISTS. She set up the models of the equipment the alchemists had used in hopes of turning ordinary metals into gold. Griffin put out a tray of gold sprinkled cookies she had baked with her mom.

"You doing okay, Griff?" asked Dr. Penshine, hauling more bags for the booth.

"Yup," she said.

"Looking really good!" said her mom. Carefully her mother took out a jar of pennies. Inside the jar, she and Griffin had displayed the "change the world" penny in a ring case. It was surrounded by a moat of pennies. Also displayed in the jar was a money order for eleven hundred dollars from the sale of Mariah's ring, made out to Pennies for the Planet.

Griffin smiled looking at this. When her mom had told her the ring was worth so much, Griffin had jumped up and

down. She bet Mariah had never known her ring would one day help the environment.

Behind this jar Griffin and her mom tacked up poster boards that explained how pennies can be turned into gold, how when enough people give, each penny can help save the rain forest. *Saving the Amazon rain forest from being cut down is so important because trees supply most of the Earth's clear air and oxygen,* read her poster. Griffin had drawn the Earth with lungs in the middle and trees circling the planet.

Every time the gym doors opened, Griffin thought maybe Garrett had changed his mind and was showing up after all. Maybe he'd even forgive her.

"The booth looks great," said Mrs. Forester, walking over from the locker rooms.

"Mary Beth!" said Dr. Penshine.

"Nice to see you both," said Garrett's mom, smiling. "Hello, Griffin."

"Hi, Mrs. Forester." Griffin gulped.

"Thank you for your cards to me and Garrett. It meant a lot to both of us," said Mrs. Forester.

Griffin nodded. "Is Garrett coming tonight?"

"He's in the locker room practicing. The guys have been rehearsing night and day at my house. I was counting down to science night, just so I could get some sleep! I told him he

has to come over to the booth and help as well. I don't want him marked down either, but he's being very stubborn."

"Okay," said Griffin with a sad smile.

Taking a deep breath, Mrs. Forester said, "I want you both to know something. Garrett doesn't know this yet. I plan to tell him at the end of science night. His dad flew into town late last night from Alaska. Ever since he received Griffin's letter, we've talked every day. He wanted to come support Garrett for science night. Maybe even stay awhile. I told him he can watch, but he should only talk to Garrett when the night is over so Garrett doesn't get nervous or upset."

Griffin froze. Garrett's dad was *here*? From Alaska?

"It's okay, Griffin," said Mrs. Forester, looking at her ashen face. "It might be very good for Garrett to have his dad around if we can all forgive one another. None of us ever stopped loving one another."

Griffin and her mom stared at each other. Then Dr. Penshine turned to Mrs. Forester and spoke. "Mary Beth, that sounds like big news. Congratulations."

"Thank you," she said. "I'd like you to meet Garrett's dad, Griffin. I want to show him the booth you both worked so hard on. One minute, okay?"

Griffin turned toward the back of the room. Sitting on the bleachers was a tall, handsome man with a brown beard.

Just like his picture, thought Griffin. Mrs. Forester waved him over, and he walked back to booth 17.

"Griffin?" he said in a deep voice.

"Hello," she said.

"Hi, I'm Garrett's dad," he said, and shook her hand. "I wanted to thank you for writing to me. I wouldn't want to miss this. I've missed so much already."

"I wasn't sure I should have written to you," whispered Griffin.

"I'm so glad you did. I hope one day Garrett is too. I'll be rooting for your booth and for The Alchemists tonight."

"Thank you," she said.

"You guys need any help?" he asked.

"I think things are under control, right, Griff?" said Dr. Penshine.

Griffin nodded.

How does one become a butterfly?
You must want to fly so much that
you are willing to give up being a caterpillar.
—Trina Paulus

Chapter
40

"Griffin! Griffin!" called Jason, out of breath and running toward her booth.

"Griffin, I have to talk to you!"

"What's the matter?"

"We need your help!" he said, panting. "Kurt got really sick, stage fright or something. He started to hyperventilate and then threw up everywhere! His mom's taking him home."

"Oh, no!" she said.

"We really want to play tonight. We've been practicing for hours every day. Do you think you could play his bass? We have all the music here."

Griffin looked at her mom.

"Up to you, Griff," said Dr. Penshine.

"We're on in twenty minutes!"

Griffin looked at the stage set up at the front of the gym. What if she couldn't play? *I wish to become an amazing bass guitarist. Did I return enough of the wishes so I'm not cursed with that wish too? Will I mess up onstage? Can I even do it?*

Slowly she turned to Jason. "You know, Garrett refused to do the booth with me tonight. If he'll come to our booth when the judges are here, then I'll play in your band."

"Awesome! I'll go tell him! Be right back!"

He darted away. "Twenty minutes?" said her mom. "Can you do it, Griff?"

"I know the music. I was supposed to teach Kurt, so I learned it."

"Go for it! I was in a band, you know," said her mom.

"You were?" said Griffin.

"Yeah. In college. The Rocket Girls."

They burst out laughing.

Jason came running back. "Garrett said okay. Come back to the locker room."

"Mom?" said Griffin.

"I'll watch the booth until you take over," she said.

Maneuvering through the booths about black holes,

electricity experiments, and jungle animals, Griffin located the locker room. Garrett stepped out from the door. Half his face was painted gold like a rock star.

"Hey," he said.

"Hey," said Griffin.

"Thanks for playing in the band," he said.

"Yeah," she said. "You'll come help with the booth when the judges arrive?"

"Yeah," he said.

They both smiled.

"We go up onstage in fifteen minutes. Here." He tossed her a tube.

"What's this?" said Griffin.

"Our costume," said Garrett. "We're The Alchemists, so you gotta paint half your face gold."

"Really?" she said.

The other three guys poked their heads out the door, one stacked on top of the other like circus clowns.

"Hey, Griffin. Thanks a lot!" they all said.

A big smile spread across her face. The boys looked so funny painted half gold—foolish, even. But Griffin shrugged and went to paint her face too. In the girls' locker room she stared at herself in the mirror. Her eyes glowed and her hair was shiny. Griffin peered into the mirror and thought about

all those pennies, how she had tried so hard to give them back, break the curse, and help people. Griffin drew a long golden line down her face and painted the right side gold. On the left side of her face, around her three freckles, she drew shooting stars.

✳ ✳ ✳

If you don't risk anything,
you risk everything.

Chapter

41

L adies and gentleman, your attention, please!" called Principal Yeldah from the gym's stage. "We are so proud to welcome you to science night!"

Clapping echoed through the gym and crackled through the stage microphones. "Before the judges make their rounds to evaluate each student's booth, Garrett Forester and his band, The Alchemists, will be playing. They'll kick off our evening to help raise money for Pennies for the Planet. This fine charity helps turn pennies into gold for the environment. You all may notice there are five empty water jugs in front of the stage. Please donate your change. Students, dump out your mayonnaise jars of coins you brought from

home, and let's fill these containers! All proceeds go toward protecting our environment. Now, it is my great pleasure to introduce . . . The Alchemists!"

The lights dimmed except for a few spotlights hovering overhead. Applause inside the cavernous gym sounded like thunder. Griffin's heart was pounding louder than any drum she'd ever heard. *Why did I say yes?* she thought.

"One, two, three!" shouted Garrett, and the first song boomed through the speakers. Garrett's drums and Griffin's bass made up the rhythm section and set the base and anchor for the whole band. Kids cheered and started dancing. It was good the lights onstage were so bright and the audience so dark, because Griffin could hardly see anything. At first her fingers moved too slow. She messed up a few notes, but she recovered. Music and energy swirled around her. The Alchemists played three fabulous songs.

Out of the corner of her eye she saw what looked like shooting stars soaring in front of the stage. Turning her head, Griffin saw pennies being flung into the plastic containers. *Pings, plops,* and *whooshes* flew in electric zigzags as people threw money into the jugs. *Ping. Ping.* A dime bounced in too. *This is a different kind of ping!* thought Griffin. *Nothing stolen, just given. A silver raindrop. A shooting penny. A copper missile defending the rain forest.*

"Thank you! Thank you, everybody!" shouted Ethan and Garrett, both breathless as the lights flashed on. Roaring applause sounded like a jungle downpour through the gym. "Thank you. Please make your donations to Pennies for the Planet."

Mr. Reasoner and Principal Yeldah walked together onstage. "Folks," said the principal, taking the center microphone. "First, another big round of applause for The Alchemists!" Griffin could now see all the faces in the bright gym lights. Hundreds of faces! Libby, Audree, Maggie, Madison, the kids in her science class, and Garrett's mom all beaming with pride. Griffin's father was there holding her mother's hand, smiling at her. Everyone else was passionately clapping. Except Samantha. And Martha and Sasha. They just scowled. But no one noticed. In fact, everyone was having such a good time that no one paid much attention to them.

"We have a special announcement this evening. Tonight we will witness how small things can add up to very big things! Mr. Reasoner, " said Principal Yeldah, handing him the microphone.

Mr. Reasoner stood before the crowd. "Good evening, everyone. Tonight I would like to introduce one of my most dedicated metal shop workers, Alfred Coombs."

Griffin gasped. It was the silent boy from the back of the metal shop. Griffin held her breath.

"Alfred has been collecting pennies since he was five years old. One day in class, after Alfred heard about Griffin Penshine and Garrett Forester's fund-raiser idea, Alfred whispered a little something to me."

Alfred wheeled up on the stage two huge water jugs filled with glittering pennies packed to the top. "Each full jug of pennies is worth three hundred and fifty dollars. Alfred is donating two full containers to Pennies for the Planet!"

The audience erupted in applause. Griffin jumped up and down.

"That leaves the rest of the night to fill the five containers in front of the stage.

Also, Principal Yeldah informed me that we also have a donation from Nome, Alaska, for two hundred and fifty dollars."

Both Garrett and Griffin froze, looking out at the audience.

"Let's hear it for Alfred and for The Alchemists!" More clapping. Griffin looked at Alfred Coombs and smiled. He smiled his goofy grin back. He wasn't strange at all. He was fantastic.

"How about one more song from The Alchemists!" shouted Mr. Reasoner.

Thankfully they had one more song to play. It was called "Celebration."

✳   ✳   ✳

Never doubt that a small group of thoughtful,
committed citizens can change the world.
Indeed, it's the only thing that ever has.
—Margaret Mead

Chapter

42

When Griffin walked into science class the next day, the entire school smelled like warm chocolate chip cookies. The home economics teacher and her students had baked cookies for every student in the school to promote their department.

Griffin smiled, inhaling the scent that wafted in every corner of the building. *I wish my new school smells like warm chocolate chip cookies!* Maybe she was on track after all! She hoped things had gone well for Garrett—meeting his dad last night. She wondered if he'd even show up to school today, with his dad in town. Maybe he would be mad at her until the end of school, or even mad at her forever.

"Did you hear, Griffin?" asked Audree.

"Hear what?" asked Griffin, and she sat down in her seat.

"The newspaper is coming!" she said.

"What?" said Griffin.

"Shhhhh. Here comes Mr. Luckner," Audree whispered as the class bell rang. Just then Garrett darted in from the hallway and plunked into his seat.

"Well, class. I am humbled and amazed," said Mr. Luckner. "Your projects last night were out of this world. I'm so proud of all the hard work and *learning* that you've accomplished! Of course, the biggest winner of all last night was our own Earth. Now, Principal Yeldah has a special announcement."

BZZZZZZZZzzzz. The loudspeaker broadcast Principal Yeldah's voice through the school into each and every classroom. "Good morning, students. Congratulations on your stupendous work at science night. I'm so proud of all of you. A gigantic congratulations to last night's two team winners, Audree Stein and Aury Laww and Caden Nosam and Carol Peters. A huge thank you to both teams for their incredible generosity in donating their prize money to Pennies for the Planet. I need to say a special thanks to Griffin Penshine, Garrett Forester, Alfred Coombs, and The Alchemists for all their hard

work protecting our Earth. In fact, in addition to Alfred's donation of two jugs of pennies, the remaining five jugs were filled last night, making the grand total for Pennies for the Planet five thousand fifty-three dollars and eleven cents!"

Applause erupted throughout the school. "Five thousand dollars!" kids shouted in classrooms. Griffin looked down at her desk and scribbled the math in her notebook:

- Seven jars of pennies (around $350.00 each) = $2,553.11
- An 1872 Indian Head penny (in a ring case) worth: $150.00
- Mariah's garnet and gold ring: $1,100.00
- An anonymous donation of $250.00 from Nome, Alaska
- Two $500.00 science night winner donations.
  TOTAL: $5,053.11 for Earth!

"Some of the most exciting news is that the *Kansas Tribune* called the school early this morning and wants to do a huge front page article about how young students can protect and help our planet. Next Saturday at eleven o'clock in front of the town hall Mayor Alexander will be giving an

award to Griffin Penshine and Garrett Forester for starting the campaign. Television news channels are coming as well, and Dr. Fonda, a representative from Pennies for the Planet, is traveling from Washington, D.C., to accept a giant check representing the entire donation."

Applause exploded from the entire school, and Griffin and Garrett blushed simultaneously. When Griffin looked up, a note was on her desk.

Carefully, under her desk, she opened it:

Hey, great job last night. Amazing bass guitar.

I saw my dad last night. He's really cool. He's a champion fisherman. Sorry for the things I said.

G.

Griffin turned around in her seat.
Garrett smiled at her.

✳   ✳   ✳

Help others achieve their dreams,
and you will achieve yours.
—Les Brown

Chapter

43

"om?" called Griffin from her bedroom before school.

"Yes?" said her mom from the couch. Sweat beaded on her mother's forehead. Her breathing was heavy.

"Mom, are you okay?" asked Griffin, walking down a few steps.

"I'm fine. The baby is coming soon. I can feel it. Maybe she or he is coming early for your award! We are all so proud of you." She laughed and wiped her damp face with a cloth.

"You sure you're okay?" asked Griffin. All the wishes except four had been returned. Returning seven wishes had

to count for something. "Puppy," "world peace," the unlabeled penny, and the "STOP" penny were left.

"Mom, before the ceremony next week, there's one more thing I have to do. Could we get a puppy for Florence Daniellson Busby, the lady who wished for one? When I called the assisted living home, they said pets are allowed there."

"Hmm," said her mom, and rubbed her belly. "I'll tell you what, let me make a few calls while you're at school. Can you give me the name of the assisted living home?"

"Sure."

When Griffin came home from school, her mom didn't move from the couch.

"Mom?" whispered Griffin. *I wish for a baby sister* sprang into Griffin's head. *Have I not tried hard enough? Will my mom and the baby be okay?*

"Griff," she said, waking up. "I have some good news." Her mom struggled to get off the couch. "I made a few calls, spoke to the Sunflower Home director, Mrs. Regan, and explained things. She was charmed by the puppy wish and said it's just what Florence needs. Dad can't drive you there on Saturday—he's got a morning appointment—and I think I should stick pretty close to home with the baby kicking

so much. Garrett's dad agreed to take you and Garrett to pick out a puppy for Garrett and another one for Florence. I guess Garrett has been begging his mom for a dog for a year! I called ahead and paid for Florence's puppy, so you just choose one that would be best for an elderly lady, okay?"

"Thanks!" said Griffin, throwing her arms around her mom.

"It seems Mr. Forester is a big believer in wishes lately," said Dr. Penshine.

No dreamer is ever too small;
no dream is ever too big.

Chapter 44

At exactly ten o'clock Saturday morning Garrett rang Griffin's doorbell. Griffin's heart raced. The sky had never been so clear, like a blue birthday streamer floating free above them.

"Hi, Garrett," said Griffin, opening the front door. She had checked her teeth three times for anything green. Libby had come over the night before and helped her pick out her outfit too.

"Hi," said Garrett. "Are you ready?"

"Yup," she said. *Did Garrett just blush? Could he be nervous too?* she thought.

Dr. Penshine called from the couch. "Have fun! I'm so proud of you both!"

Griffin slid into the backseat of the car.

"Good morning, Griffin," said Garrett's dad, smiling. They drove straight to the Dadesville Humane Society.

Puppies, cats, and rabbits were all up for adoption. Animals of all shapes and sizes were poking pink noses out of rows and rows of cages. Garrett bent down and looked into one. Tiny whimpers came from within. "Griffin, look!" There was a litter of five puppies bouncing around inside.

"Their mom got hit by a car, and they need good homes," said the volunteer.

"Look at that one!" said Garrett. One of the puppies was rolling over on her back, her tiny white paws wiggling in the air.

"Can I hold her?" asked Griffin. The volunteer placed the puppy in Griffin's arms. A pink tongue slurped all over her face. She giggled. Another one of the puppies was tugging hard on a piece of rope, wagging his tail.

"That's my dog!" said Garrett.

Garrett's dad bent down to look. "They both look great," he said.

At the front desk they filled out all the registration papers. Mr. Forester explained to the woman at the desk that they were taking Griffin's puppy straight to Florence; Garrett and his dad would come back for Garrett's puppy in the afternoon.

In the backseat of the car Mr. Forester carefully placed the puppy's cage between Garrett and Griffin so they could sit on either side of her. Her little paw kept shooting through the cage trying to touch them. Griffin giggled.

"What are you naming your puppy, Garrett?" asked Griffin.

"Nick, after Nicolas Flamel, or maybe Zosimos," said Garrett.

"Cool," said Griffin.

"How about you?" he asked.

"I think Florence should name her, you know?"

"Shhhhhh," Griffin said to the puppy as she bounced up and down in the parking lot of the assisted living home. "Don't ruin the surprise, silly!" Griffin dug her fingers in her pocket. The "puppy" penny was still there.

"Good morning. You must be Griffin and Garrett," said Director Regan, meeting them at the front door.

"Hi," they said in unison.

"I'm Garrett's dad, Brian Forester," he said. "The kids are so excited about this."

"We are too. Florence will be so happy. Who do we have here?"

The director bent down to pet the new puppy through the cage. "Girl or boy?"

"Girl," said Griffin.

"She's perfect. Right this way. I told Florence she had some visitors today. A certain G. Penshine who wrote her a letter and her friend Garrett Forester. Florence got all dressed up, even put rouge on her cheeks!"

Garrett's dad waited outside Florence's room with the puppy to keep her a surprise until just the right moment.

"Knock, knock," said the director, tapping on the door. "Florence, your visitors are here."

"Come in," said Florence.

Garrett and Griffin walked into her room. Florence looked very old and soft sitting in a chair by the window. She held out her hand to welcome them. "Welcome, welcome! Visitors to see me? What an exciting day. The real G. Penshine who wrote me a letter!"

Griffin said, "Nice to meet you, Mrs. Busby."

"Nice to meet you. Such a pretty and polite young lady. And who is this handsome young man?" said Florence.

"I'm Garrett," he said.

"What a beautiful couple," she said.

Griffin and Garrett both blushed a deep crimson.

"I don't get a lot of young visitors. I was so excited when I was told you were both coming to visit me today."

"Mrs. Busby, I was the one who wrote you that letter a few weeks ago."

"Yes, yes, if I recollect correctly, you said you had something of mine? What could you possibly have that might belong to an old lady like me?" she asked.

"Someone gave me something that once belonged to you," said Griffin, reaching into her pocket and pulling out the penny. Gently she placed it in Florence's tender hand.

"A penny?" said Florence, and she studied it.

"I met a very, very old lady before she died," said Griffin. "She said she overheard you make a wish for a puppy. She wrote down the wish in a guest book next to your name. She labeled your penny: 'puppy.'"

"NO!" gasped Florence. She held the penny tight in her hand and closed her eyes. "I remember that summer day clearly, that scorching Kansas sun on my cheeks. I threw that penny high into the air. With all my heart I called out, 'I wish for a puppy!'"

A long sad pause penetrated the room. "My very own

penny *returned*. My very own wish taken out of the fountain and returned to me after all these years. What a beautiful thing to make something right even after so many years have passed." From her faded-blue eyes a single tear tumbled onto the penny.

A glow crescendoed through the entire room as if the sun had charged on full blast and poured the brightest rays into Florence's room. "Well, that's not all," said Garrett. "Dad!"

Mr. Forester walked into the room holding the puppy. "Good morning, Mrs. Busby. I'm Garrett's dad. The kids have brought you a present. A surprise just for you!"

Mrs. Busby's eyes lit up like a child's. Jumping up from her seat, her arms flew into the air, springing the penny like metallic confetti. "A puppy! A puppy!" she shouted, clapping her hands together.

"Do you want to hold her? She's a gift for you," said Griffin.

"A puppy for me?" She cried even harder now, her shiny eyes crinkling. "A puppy to keep me company! It's hard to feel lonely with a bouncing pup! My first puppy in my whole life!" She held out her old hands to the dog. Florence giggled like a girl as the puppy licked her wrinkled cheek. Laughter and tears came at the same time. "What's the puppy's name?"

"It's up to you," said Griffin.

"Penny! That's her name!" said Florence. "This is a wish worth waiting for!"

Never give up on a dream just because it takes time.
The time will pass anyway.

Chapter

45

Griffin waved as Garrett and his dad backed out of her driveway. Griffin couldn't wait to call Libby and tell her everything! Garrett was so nice and cute and kind to Florence and funny and smart and great at drums. Also seeing Florence so happy made this one of the best Saturdays that Griffin had ever had. Smiling and giddy, Griffin couldn't wait to tell her mom about the puppy, too. She pushed on the front door, but it was locked.

"Mom, I'm home!" she called. She rang the front doorbell. But no one came. Three times she rang the bell. "Mom! Dad! Hello!"

Nothing.

Griffin checked her cell phone. She had turned it off at the Sunflower Home. Her message box was full. "Griff, it's Dad. Everything is okay. I'm taking Mom to the hospital because the baby is on the way! Hang tight. When you get this message, please go to Mrs. Jasper's house. I called her, and she is going to stay with you until I can come pick you up. I love you."

"Griffin!" called Mrs. Jasper, running toward her. "I've been looking out my window for you ever since your dad called me!"

"Did the baby come yet?" asked Griffin.

"I don't know. I just know your mom is in the hospital, and your grandma, too."

"Grandma, too?" Griffin's heart started racing. "They're both at the hospital?"

"Yes," she answered.

Griffin trembled. *This is my fault,* she thought. She still had three pennies. Although she had given away "no homework," "most beautiful," "change the world," "a dad," "baby," "success," "popular," and "puppy," the "STOP" penny, "world peace" penny, and the unlabeled penny remained in Mariah's black box.

"Your dad said it would be best if you stayed with me until he calls, and then I can drive you to the hospital to be with him. Okay?" she said.

"Okay," said Griffin slowly, finding it hard to breath. "Both Mom and Grandma in the hospital," she whispered to herself. *Why is my grandma there? Will the baby be okay?*

They walked over to Mrs. Jasper's house. Eight times Griffin called her dad on his cell phone, but he did not pick up.

Griffin sat at Mrs. Jasper's table, pushing noodles around on her plate. When the phone finally rang, it sounded like a fire alarm and a rushing ambulance to her ears. Mrs. Jasper grabbed for the phone. "Hello. Yes, she's fine. We're eating some dinner. Is everything okay?" There was a long pause and Griffin gripped the sides of her chair. "Here's Griffin!"

"Hi, Griff," said her father, sounding exhausted.

"Hi, Dad."

"You doing okay?" he asked.

"Yeah," she said. "Are Mom and Grandma okay?"

"Your mom is doing just fine. I'm so sorry you had to come home to a locked house. My cell phone ran out of battery in the hospital and I was with your mom in the delivery room. But . . . dun, dun, dun . . . drumroll, please. . . . You have a new happy, healthy baby brother!

A baby brother! The opposite of what I wished for! thought Griffin. *A healthy baby brother is fine with me!*

"Caelum came a week early. We were worried he might be born in the car! We almost changed his name to CAR-lum!"

Griffin laughed so hard tears filled her eyes. "Caelum's here! I have a brother!"

"Yes, a healthy, happy baby brother. Ten pounds! As big as a turkey! A giant baby! He and Mom are doing great."

"Can I come see him?"

"Yes. Mrs. Jasper is going to bring you to the hospital."

"And Grandma?" she asked.

"Grandma had a fall this morning. Hit her head on the floor, Griff," said her dad softly.

"Is she okay?" asked Griffin, her stomach squeezing up into her throat.

"She goes in and out of sleep, in and out of making sense."

"Can I see her?" asked Griffin, starting to shake.

"Yes, we'll see her together, okay? Hang tight, kiddo. I love you."

"I love you, too, Dad." Griffin sat down and couldn't stop crying. *Grandma.*

Don't let the teardrops rust your shining heart.
—Holly Cole Trio

Chapter

46

"Dad!" called Griffin, running to her father in the hospital corridor, hugging him close. With a crumpled shirt and matted hair, he looked like he hadn't slept in a week. "Are you okay?"

"I'm great. Do you want to see your new baby brother?"

"Dad, is Grandma okay too?" she asked.

"She's sleeping right now. We'll go see her after you meet your brother, okay?"

"Okay," she said.

Together they walked down the long antiseptic-smelling corridor. "This is it. The east wing. New arrivals!" he said. "Room 302." She walked faster and faster. Poking her head

inside the room, Griffin gazed at her mom sleeping with a bundle in a crib next to her.

"Mom!" said Griffin.

"Griff," said her mom, lifting her head from the pillow, smiling. "Come here," she said, reaching out her hand.

"Are you okay?"

"Couldn't be happier! It seems Caelum was ready to come into the world, *immediately*!" She laughed and kissed Griffin on the forehead, smoothing back her hair.

"Can I look at him?" she asked.

"Of course," said her mom.

Leaning over the plastic box next to her mother's bed, Griffin whispered, "Hi, Caelum." She touched his tiny pink hand, five velvet fingers. "He's so soft!"

"Like when you were born," said her mom.

"Really?"

"Really," said her mom, smiling and leaning back against the pillows.

"Do you need anything?" asked Griffin's dad, holding his wife's hand.

"Just rest," she said.

"Of course," he said, kissing her. "Griff, let's let Mom sleep a little. It's not every day your mom gives birth to a ten-pound baby almost in the middle of Main Street!"

Dr. Penshine giggled.

"Let's see Grandma and then have some dessert together in the cafeteria. Then we'll come back, say goodnight again to mom, and go home, okay?"

"How long will Mom and Caelum be in the hospital?" she asked.

"Two nights," said her dad. "Standard procedure."

"And Grandma?" asked Griffin.

"I don't know," said her dad.

"Oh," said Griffin, holding back tears.

He put his arm around her as they tiptoed away from Dr. Penshine and Caelum, who were now both sound asleep.

A good parent is the greatest treasure.

Chapter

W here's Grandma's room?" asked Griffin.

"On the eighth floor," said her father. "The doctor made an exception to let you see her in intensive care when I told him how close you two are."

They rode the elevator to the eighth floor and walked to room 807. Unlike her mom's room, this room was very dark. Grandma Penshine was not propped up in bed, but looked shrunken under the white sheets. Up and down went her chest, IVs taped to her arms. Griffin shuffled to the side of the bed.

"Grandma?" Griffin whispered, taking her grandma's soft hand in hers. "We love you."

Suddenly Griffin felt her grandma's palm press inside hers. A nurse talked quietly with her dad in the doorway. "Griff, I want to look at Grandma's X-rays with the doctor. Stay with her, okay? I'll be right back." He left the room.

"Grandma," Griffin whispered, "did you see the sky today?"

"Yes," she whispered. "I still see it."

"Yes!" said Griffin, squeezing her grandma's hand harder.

"It was perfect blue, like satin streamers," breathed Grandma Penshine, and slowly her soft brown eyes opened.

Griffin hugged her.

A peaceful smile spread over Grandma Penshine's face, and she looked at Griffin. "Come closer," she whispered.

Griffin bent her head down so she was cheek to cheek with her grandma.

"In my bedroom," her grandma said, and took a deep breath, "there is a box on my bureau. Look inside it."

"What's in it?" asked Griffin.

"You look and see. I love you," she said, her chest heaving another breath.

"Grandma?" said Griffin.

She squeezed Griffin's hand.

"Will you get well?" asked Griffin. She tried not to cry,

but her tears started falling, like raindrops dotting her grandma's sheets.

"I am well, Griff. Just old. Half as old as a Galápagos turtle," she said, taking a deep breath. "My bones are getting fragile, but I can't complain. They've done such a good job all these years. Plus, it's almost time to see your grandpa and all our flowers again. I've been having the most beautiful dreams about two white doves; at night they land on my windowsill, singing so sweetly. Don't you waste one wish for me to get well when my heart feels so good. It's your turn to make wishes for yourself. I already made all my wishes, and they all came true. I love you forever, my wish giver." She closed her eyes and fell asleep.

Go confidently in the direction of your dreams!
Live the life you imagined.
—Henry David Thoreau

Chapter
48

D r. Penshine and Caelum came home from the hospital on Monday, but Grandma Penshine was still in intensive care. *Why did Grandma call me a wish giver? Why did she want me to look in the box on her bureau?* thought Griffin as she folded baby clothes in Caelum's nursery. Griffin's mom placed the "baby" penny in a silver baby cup that had once belonged to Griffin's dad. "A lucky penny! What a nice way to start life, don't you think?" said her mom, bending over Caelum cooing in his crib.

"Yes," said Griffin, inhaling the sweet scents of the nursery. Everything smelled like baby powder, lotion, and

new things. Griffin's parents let her take the day off from school to welcome Caelum and her mom home. In the afternoon she'd visit Grandma Penshine at the hospital.

"Griff, could you help Dad pack some of Grandma's things to take to her at the hospital? She really wants her favorite socks and a deck of cards," said her mom.

"Sure," she said.

Griffin's dad grabbed a duffel bag before driving to Grandma Penshine's house. Griffin could not wait to look in the box on her grandma's bureau.

Carrying a bag, Griffin went with her dad down the hall into her grandmother's bedroom. The floor creaked. Griffin turned on the lamp in the bedroom, illuminating the flowered wallpaper and cozy blankets on the bed. She wanted nothing more than to curl up next to her grandma and play pistachio poker. But the bed was empty. Inside the room, while her father packed some things, Griffin spied the inlaid mother-of-pearl box on top of the bureau. She picked up the box and brought it to her grandma's bed. Slowly she opened the box. Inside were four things: a blue sapphire ring, the skein of old yarn, a large flat white stone, and one supershiny Indian Head penny.

Griffin heart raced. The ring looked identical to Mariah's ring except that the stone was blue. The yarn was exactly like

Mariah's gray spool. The smooth white stone was the same shape and size as Mariah's black stone mirror.

"What do you have there?" asked her dad.

"Nothing," she said, and gulped.

"Can you help me over here?"

"Yeah. Dad, I want to bring Grandma's favorite box to the hospital to show her, okay?"

"Okay," said her dad. "We'll drive straight there."

In the car Griffin kept the box sealed closed on her lap. *Why does Grandma Penshine have the same yarn as Mariah? Why does she have a ring just like Mariah's, except it's blue? Why does she have a stone just like Mariah's except it's white? Why did she save one supershiny penny?* The penny was as bright as the first one Mariah had given her.

Once they arrived at the hospital, Griffin and her dad took the elevator to intensive care. Griffin hurried in front of her father, clutching the box, until she reached room 807. Griffin stopped dead inside the room. It was empty. She gasped, and tears welled in her eyes. The hospital bed was perfectly made with an ugly mustard-colored blanket tucked tightly between the white sheets. The room had a plastic sterile smell. Griffin didn't move. Her father came in behind her. "Huh?" he said.

"Dad?" whispered Griffin. Chills shot up her spine.

"Maybe they've moved her. Surely we would have been called if anything had happened."

Just then a nurse bumped into them. "Mr. Penshine?"

"Yes. My mother was here in room 807."

"We just moved her to the second floor. She's doing so much better. She woke up, talked a bit, nibbled some toast, even told a joke."

"Good news," said her dad with a deep sigh.

Griffin reached for her dad's hand.

"What room is she in?" asked Mr. Penshine.

"Follow me. She now has a full river view. The staff here call the rooms on this side of the hospital the riviera!" said the nurse. They followed her to the other side of the building. "I'll go get her doctor for you folks."

In her new room Grandma's chest billowed up and down. She dozed in a deep slumber. Griffin's dad bent over and kissed her on the cheek.

Relief flooded through Griffin as she ran to her grandma's bedside.

"I need to go talk to the doctor. You stay here with Grandma."

Griffin took her grandma's hand. "They put you in the riviera rooms," she said. "They knew you'd want to hear the river."

Griffin walked to the window and slid it open. A light breeze blew through the room, and Grandma whispered from her bed, "Griff."

"Grandma!" She ran to her side again. "Are you okay?"

Grandma Penshine did not raise her head from the pillow, but she smiled. Her cheeks had a healthy pink glow for the first time since she'd been taken to the hospital. "Sky is bright blue, isn't it?" she said. "The breeze always feels different when it's clear."

"Yes, it's blue. Grandma, I brought your box for you."

Grandma Penshine smiled and propped herself up a bit in bed. She looked like a flower, soft and delicate. She took Griffin's hand. "I have something to tell you."

Griffin nodded, standing by the bed holding Grandma Penshine's hand. "On Saturday morning your parents told me you were bringing an old lady a puppy, fulfilling a wish for her." She adjusted two hospital pillows behind her lower back. "They told me about that woman Mariah Weatherby Schmidt, who had given you a box of these so-called lucky pennies. I have something very strange to tell you." Then Grandma Penshine leaned forward, looking straight into Griffin's eyes, and whispered: "I met her once when I was a girl."

Griffin stared. Her mouth hung open.

"That's the only time my life ever crossed paths with Mariah, but it was enough."

"You met Mariah!" gasped Griffin.

"Right before my daddy and mama bought their farm, we were traveling through Kansas and stopped at an inn at the crossroads of Topeka."

"The same inn!"

"That inn was a sparkling oasis with a beautiful fountain bubbling in the scorching Kansas heat. I begged my daddy for a coin to throw in the water to make a wish. I must have been around eleven years old. I had the most glorious red hair, like you do now."

Griffin stared at her grandma's thick white hair.

"I wasn't born with white hair, you know," she said, laughing. Grandma Penshine sat straight up in bed now. "We only stayed one night at the inn, and it was some of the hottest weather I have felt in all my life. I kept hearing these plunks and pings coming from the courtyard."

Griffin thought, *Of course my grandma heard plunks and pings!*

"I looked out my window, and people were throwing coins in the fountain wishing for things: bicycles, money, blocks of ice, wheat to grow. I smiled, hoping those people's wishes all came true."

Griffin stared at her grandma with huge eyes.

"But then late that night, when it was still so hot and I could hardly sleep, I looked out my window and saw the young lady from the front desk, Mariah Weatherby Schmidt, swooping up coins in the blue moonlight. I hid in the darkness and watched. Every wild knot in my stomach signaled that *I was witnessing a real live Wish Stealer*!"

"What did you do?"

"The next morning when we were leaving the inn, I begged my daddy for *three coins*. He said, 'Didn't I give you a coin yesterday?' I told him, 'Yes, sir. But I was only practicing then. Today is something different.' He gave me *three new coins* and said, 'Make your wishes, but don't forget—the *real luck* is inside you.' But you see, I knew what I had to do. On that hot Kansas morning, I held my *first penny* high in the sky. Right before I threw it into the fountain, I yelled at the top of my lungs 'STOP!' I think everyone in the whole inn could hear me! I only meant for Mariah to hear. I wished for her to stop stealing people's wishes."

Griffin gasped.

"I saw Mariah rustle the curtains in the office window. Her dark silhouette stood behind the white cotton." Grandma Penshine was getting excited, remembering what she had done. She threw off the hospital sheets and leaned

forward. "The *second penny* wish I did not say out loud. Silently I wished and tossed my coin high like a leaping ballerina. It hit the water, making a million sparks." Grandma Penshine clapped her hands and looked up as if she could see the shooting sparkles.

"What was your second wish, Grandma?" whispered Griffin, tensing her whole body. She remembered what Mariah had written in her letter. *The penny I gave you at the shop flew like a leaping ballerina vaulting into the water. That person didn't say her wish out loud, but her penny was as dazzling as her long red hair.*

"What was it? What was your second wish, Grandma!" said Griffin, her heartbeat going mad.

"For lost wishes everywhere to be returned," she said, smiling.

Griffin clutched the side of the hospital bed.

"The *third penny* that my father gave me I put deep inside my pocket to keep. I decided then and there that I was going to make my own luck in this life. That's what the penny in my old box is for, to remind me that we all make our own luck and to keep my dreams and wishes safe."

"Then you don't believe in luck or curses?" asked Griffin.

"I only believe in love, hard work, and a little bit of magic." A beautiful smile lit up Grandma Penshine's face.

Griffin grabbed her grandma's box on the side table and opened it. She held that old penny in her hand. It bounced.

Griffin broke into a magnificent smile. When she caught her breath, she explained to her grandma what Mariah had said about the unlabeled penny. The unlabeled penny was indeed Grandma Penshine's second wish, made when she was a little girl with hair the color of autumn leaves, caramel kisses, and blazing sunsets.

"I hadn't thought about Mariah for ages, but it all made sense. Mariah stole my 'STOP' stealing penny. What a journey for that penny to land with you!" Reaching out both her arms, Grandma Penshine said, "Griffin, I think you've become the best thing any human can ever be. You're a brave, brave wish giver. I love you."

What lies behind us, and what lies before us,
are tiny matters compared to what lies within us.
—Ralph Waldo Emerson

Chapter

G randma, I have the three last stolen wishes here in my pocket." Griffin reached into her pocket and read the labels. "'STOP,' the unlabeled penny, and 'world peace.' What should I do with them?"

"'World peace' is a mighty big one, but not impossible. That one is for you to decide, but 'STOP' and my unlabeled penny have been returned to me, thanks to you, Griffin!"

Griffin smiled. She had returned three pennies to their original owners. Griffin placed the unlabeled penny and "STOP" in Grandma Penshine's hands. At that exact moment the river sounded loud and clear in both their ears. Grandma Penshine winked. She got out of bed and walked

over to the window with the river below. Slowly she closed her fingers around her two returned pennies and made the exact same wishes. Then she pitched the two pennies into the river.

Plunk! Plunk! rippled and rang out.

"Such a beautiful sound!" said Grandma Penshine.

Griffin's dad walked back into the room. "Mom, you're up!" He hugged her. "You look as healthy as a young girl!"

"I feel like a young girl when I'm with Griffin," said Grandma. "Griffin, can you please bring me my box?"

Griffin placed the mother-of-pearl box on her grandma's lap. Carefully her grandma opened it and removed the large sapphire ring.

"What's the ring for? Mariah had one just like this, but it was red."

"Your grandfather gave this to me long, long ago. He bought it in the fanciest jewelry shop in Topeka. If I recall correctly, I remember him saying it was a very old sapphire, an antique from England. It was once part of a large garnet and sapphire ring. But the jeweler separated the two stones, made them into two different rings. Grandpa bought the blue stone instead of the red one. Blue is the color of the sky and ocean, two things that will always help you remember joy. The ring is now a gift for you."

Griffin slipped the ring onto every finger. It fit best on her thumb.

"We should probably save the ring until you grow up," said her dad.

"Yeah," said Griffin, smiling. She stared at the ring. It looked like a piece of the sky set still and clear behind glass. *Could Mariah's ring once have been attached to my grandma's ring? Mariah and my grandma entwined?*

"And the yarn? What's that for?" Griffin held up the yarn by one end as if it were a dead opossum's tail.

"I bought that yarn more than seventy years ago!"

No wonder it smells so bad! thought Griffin.

"That yarn is from a carnival that passed through Topeka. The man selling it said it was magic yarn. Said the skein of yarn was the thread of life, and if you saved it and didn't cut it, you would live a long, long life. All I know is that he sold it for way more than regular yarn ever cost! Oh, and the yarn salesman was very handsome!"

"You fell for that?" teased Griffin's dad.

"It was worth every penny. Even back then I liked the idea of a long thread of life—made me happy just thinking about it. I think every young girl in Topeka that summer bought some of the magic yarn!"

"Is it magic, then?" said Griffin.

"It must have been magic to the man who sold it for more than plain old yarn is worth!" said her dad, laughing.

"Can I have it?" asked Griffin.

"It's yours," said Grandma Penshine.

Even though it was musty, Griffin planned to keep it in her Mysterium Collection Box.

"What is the white stone for?" asked Griffin.

"I found it by the river bank when I was a girl. I thought it looked so polished and pretty, like a giant pearl. Must have been washed by the water for at least a hundred years to be so smooth. I never found a use for it, but always thought I would one day."

"Can I give it to Charlemagne?" asked Griffin. "I've been looking for something special for his terrarium for the longest time."

"What a great idea! I bet it was once a throne for a turtle king. He'll love it!"

Griffin smiled. Then suddenly a shadow crossed her face. "Grandma, Mariah gave me a black polished stone, said it was a mirror to see the future, but it scared me and I broke it by accident."

"That's a lucky accident. Don't go looking into objects to tell yourself the future, look only in your heart. What did you do with all the black broken pieces?" she said.

"I forgot to clean them up. They're under my bed."

"If you don't mind, I'd love to have them to use to pot my orchids," said Grandma Penshine. "Orchids are some of the most lovely, graceful flowers in all of nature, but the funny thing is they bloom best in tiny jagged rocks and coarse bark. Somehow they can use ugly things to create incredible beauty."

"I'll sweep the pieces up for you," said Griffin, smiling. She thought of all the pink, orange, and yellow orchids that filled her grandma's house. "What will you do with your last lucky penny, the one you always kept in your box?"

"That is also for you. I made many wishes on that penny long ago, and they all came true."

"They did?" said Griffin.

"Yup. You know what was the best wish of all?" said her grandma.

"What?" said Griffin and her father at the same time. Griffin smiled.

"A long, healthy life full of love," said Grandma Penshine. "If you've got that, you've got everything."

The best wish of all.

Chapter
50

T he sounds of drums, horns, trumpets, and whistles electrified the air. A marching band, reporters, and news cameras gathered in the sunshine in front of the town hall. Dr. Fonda, the representative for Pennies for the Planet, had traveled to Dadesville to collect the check the bank had written after counting all the coins.

Griffin, Garrett, and Alfred had been invited to stand on the platform set up in front of the town hall next to the bubbling town fountain, where in half an hour they would present the giant check to Pennies for the Planet. Mayor Alexander of Dadesville would speak first and introduce them. Thousands of people packed onto the town green. Hot dog

vendors, potters, artists, and local clubs all set up booths.

Griffin was supposed to meet Garrett by the information booth at ten thirty a.m.

"Griffin!" called Garrett.

"Hi," she said, smiling. She carried a bag of *Go Green*, *Save the Earth*, and *Peace* rubber wristbands in a bag to hand out to kids.

"Hi. This is pretty cool," said Garrett, looking around at the huge crowd gathered to celebrate something they had started. Griffin gave him a Save the Earth band. They wove their way through the booths.

"Griff!" called Libby, running up to her and hugging her. Maggie, Madison, Audree, and a few other girls were right behind Libby. "This is so awesome. Congratulations!"

"Thanks," said Griffin. She hugged her friends, each wearing a different wristband. Everywhere people munched on organic popcorn and licked raspberry clouds of cotton candy. People kept stopping to congratulate her and Garrett as they made their way to the stage. Garrett stopped to talk to some of his friends.

Passing Mr. Luckner, Griffin saw him eating a huge cotton candy cone like a little kid. "Hi, Mr. Luckner," she said.

"Hi, Griffin. I'm thinking I should assign a big science project every year!"

"Maybe," said Griffin, still smiling. She gave him a *Go Green* wristband.

Mrs. Gideon came up to Griffin. She wore a colorful velvet patchwork skirt and a necklace of small clay squares with Chinese symbols for good luck on each one. "I'm so proud of you! I hand-copied one of Shakespeare's sonnets for you as a gift for all your work to help our planet. It's Sonnet XCIV. The one we talked about in class."

Griffin accepted the beautiful poem written in calligraphy. When she read it, the lines that meant the most to her were: *"They that have power to hurt and will do none . . . and to temptation slow . . . They are the lords and owners of their faces."*

"Thank you so much, Mrs. Gideon. I will save this forever," said Griffin. She gave her a *Save the Earth* wristband and rolled the poem into a scroll to keep in her Mysterium Collection Box. With Mariah's curse she could have hurt a lot of people, and she had been tempted. But she'd refused to end up a rotted lily with cruelty twisted in her face. She now knew: She owned the light inside her.

"Griffin," said Mrs. Gideon, "the Traveling Globe Theatre Company left town early. Some kind of date mix-up. Such a shame. I'd hoped our class would get to see them perform."

"We could always do *Hamlet* and act out some scenes. My grandma taught me the best line from that play. 'Angels and

ministers of grace defend us always against curses, evil wishes, and witches!' Or something like that," she said, smiling.

"*Hamlet?* What a wonderful idea! Maybe we will! I could still use my Festering Lily Perfume too," she said, and winked.

"It's your perfume?" said Griffin.

"I bought it at a Shakespeare festival at Stratford-upon-Avon in England. I thought it would be perfect for a lesson on sonnets!"

Griffin laughed. So that was Mrs. Gideon's secret!

Samantha, Martha, and Sasha—overdressed with giant bags with nothing inside them, and high-heel shoes that kept sinking into the mud—stood a few feet in front of her. No one noticed them. People were more interested in celebrating saving the planet and listening to the music than talking about Samantha's new clothes. Samantha called to her, "Griffin, what are you handing out?"

Griffin said, "Wristbands to remind people about what's important. Do you three want one?"

"Okay," said the girls.

To Martha, Griffin gave a *Go Green* band; to Sasha, *Save the Earth*; and to Samantha, *Peace*.

The three girls studied the bracelets like they were reading a foreign language.

"Uh, thanks," said Samantha and her gang, trying on the bracelets.

"They look good on all of you," said Griffin, and she kept walking.

Garrett called out, "Griffin, over here!" He waited for her at the platform base. Mayor Alexander was ready to go up and speak. Principal Yeldah was one step behind him.

Griffin waved and ran toward Garrett.

"Look!" gasped Griffin as she approached the stage. "Look! It's Stanley! And Aurora!"

"Who?" said Garrett, looking up at the two musicians onstage ready to play.

"Stanley from the library and Aurora the harpist from the music center. Aurora!" called Griffin. "Stanley!"

They both waved. Stanley, smiling, came to the edge of the steps to greet them.

"Hello!" he said, bending down to talk to them. "Thanks to you and that lucky penny, my life has done a flip-flop."

"Really?" said Griffin.

"That old penny you gave me was magic! While I was walking down the street, I accidently dropped it. The penny rolled away, and I thought, 'Just like my life, things rolling away.' But for some reason I chased that penny, and when

I scooped it up, I stood face-to-face with a poster on a telephone pole. It was a picture of Aurora playing in town! Well, I scrounged some money to buy a ticket to her concert, and on the way out I bumped into her. I gave her my CD, and the rest is history!"

Aurora came to the edge of the platform. "Hello, Griffin and Garrett. Congratulations."

"Thank you," said Griffin.

"Thank *you* for helping me find Stanley. Talent like his doesn't come along very often. When I listened to his CD, I knew he was the accompanist I needed! I invited him to come on tour with me."

"Cool!" said Garrett.

Griffin beamed.

"Attention, please. Your attention, please!" said Principal Yeldah through the microphone.

"We're really proud of you both!" said Aurora.

The surging crowd shifted their attention to the stage. Griffin's heart pounded. From the raised steps she observed people pushing closer to the platform. Garrett's dad and mom held hands in the crowd close to the stage. Libby cheered nonstop.

Griffin's head spun when she noticed the top of a Sunflower Assisted Living Home van. Painted on the van's

windows in bubble letters were the words "Thanks, Griffin! Thanks, Garrett! Yay, Penny!" Had Florence and her friends come to the ceremony?

Griffin's heart hammered harder.

"Are you ready?" whispered Principal Yeldah from the stage.

"Yep," said Garrett and Griffin. Alfred from the metal shop arrived on the platform steps.

"Hi, Alfred," she whispered.

"Hi," he whispered back, and blushed. Griffin guessed he was nervous too.

"Ladies and gentlemen," said the principal, "may I have your attention please on this beautiful Saturday in Dadesville!"

Everybody cheered.

"Today we celebrate the remarkable efforts of some of our young citizens who want to make a difference in our world, want to make changes and help our planet. By starting small but thinking big they raised awareness and collected pennies for the charity Pennies for the Planet. From the incredible support of fellow students and the town community, more than five thousand dollars was raised for our planet! I am also thrilled to announce that the Bank of Dadesville has matched that sum, making the grand total for Pennies for the Planet ten thousand dollars!"

Wild applause erupted from the audience.

Griffin, Garrett, and Alfred all high-fived.

"Here today is Dr. Fonda to accept a check that will be used to prevent deforestation of our Earth. But before we present the check, would Griffin Penshine, Garrett Forester, and Alfred Coombs come up onstage and share a few words?"

Alfred spoke first. "Hi, I'm Alfred Coombs, and my grandpa always told me two things: He said, in the words of Benjamin Franklin, 'A penny saved is a penny earned.' I've been saving pennies all my life. But the second thing my grandpa always said to me was, 'Never be penny wise and pound foolish,' which means know what's really valuable and don't skimp on the important things! I'm so proud to give all these years of saved pennies to help our planet."

Applause again rang through the audience.

Garrett took the microphone and spoke next. "I'm Garrett Forester. Doing your part for the planet is cool! Helping out is like being an alchemist—you can turn regular old things like pennies into gold! Peace out!"

Cheers rolled in giant waves across the town green.

Griffin unfolded her speech and scanned the sea of faces. Her mom, her dad, and Caelum were smiling like bright stars in the crowd.

"Good morning, everyone. My name is Griffin Penshine, and I would like to thank all the students of GWL and the citizens of Dadesville for everything you have done to help support our Earth by donating to Pennies for the Planet. It is so important to donate, but it is also important to do little things that add up to big things, like planting a tree every year, not littering, or taking the time to campaign against something you believe is hurting our environment. A lot of little efforts can add up to giant efforts.

"If you look very, very closely at a penny, in supersmall letters you'll see a phrase on each and every one. It reads *e pluribus unum*, which means 'out of many, one.' Just think, if *many* small groups all over the *whole world* did their part—and we combined all those caring groups into *one group*—think how much we could accomplish to stop the destruction of the rain forest! To stop pollution! To promote peace!

"Out of all the pennies that were donated, I have one very old penny that I have been saving for a long time." Digging into her pocket, Griffin pulled out the "world peace" penny. "Some people believe that if you wish on a penny, your wish just might come true if you don't let anybody say, 'It's impossible! Give up! Don't be silly!' Never let Wish Stealers steal your dreams and make you ashamed for trying. I was

hoping all of you out there today could make a wish for world peace on this penny."

The townspeople roared applause in response.

Griffin counted, "One! Two! Three!"

The audience hushed, and everyone made a silent wish for world peace.

Holding the penny high over her head, Griffin tossed the penny into the town fountain. It arced in the sky, sparkling like the most brilliant beacon.

You must be the change
you wish to see in the world.
—Gandhi

Acknowledgments

My first thanks goes to the Wish Givers in my life who helped make this book possible. A profound thanks to my editors: Ellen Krieger, whose extraordinary notes and brilliance helped refine this book and take it to another level; and to Fiona Simpson, whose wisdom and astute guidance helped give form to its finished shape. A heartfelt thanks to my manager, Fonda Snyder, who understands the secret labyrinth of a story like no other and whose intelligence and warmth make working with her a joy and honor.

An incredible thanks to my husband, Alexander Trivas, who read this book a gazillion times, offering priceless feedback and who cut any and all of Garrett's dialogue that sounded like a forty-seven-year-old man in a tweed jacket. Alexander's love, brilliance, support, and kindness are appreciated more than words can express. To our daughter, Hadley, whose intelligence, humor, and empathy shine through already. May you always be filled with courage and grace to pursue and fulfill your wishes, whatever they may be.

Thanks to my mother for her optimism, and to my father for his quiet and deep love of art. They have been Wish Givers in my life, championing writing, art, teaching, and creating as great ways to spend one's time. A huge cheer for my brothers, who refused to hear from any Wish Stealers and pursued their dreams:

Scott as an airplane and helicopter pilot and Todd as an innovator in technology. An incredible thank-you to my in-laws, Sam and Stephanie, whose love and strong arms surround our family every day.

To the great teachers of my life who were true Wish Givers: Dr. Anderson, Mrs. Burns, Mrs. Skripol, and Professor Gelfant, I am grateful. Thank you to the sparkly eyed librarians: Mrs. Fournier, who let me hide out at recess in the Duffy Elementary School library to read; and Linda Clancy, the West Hartford town librarian who saved the *Anne of Green Gables* books for me. A huge thank-you to the great team at Simon & Schuster, especially Bess Braswell, Paul Crichton, Andrea Kempfer, and Alyson Heller. To the friends who read drafts or sections of this book, offering insights, support, or expert information, I am grateful: Aury, Lauren, Robert, Jake, Jennie, Regan, Todd, Elaine, Jyoti, Sarah, Jonathan, Stephanie, Benny, Ilana, Sara, Dennis, McCabe's Guitar Store, Dr. Thomas, Griffin, Audree, Lily, Gabrielle, Yapha, Elisabeth, Jared, Michelle, Nicole, Madison, Bob, Maggie, Ketaki, Eileen, and Eden. A very special thanks to Merly, as always, and to Maria and Crystal, too.

To the readers of this book, I wish you so much luck, love, and happiness as you navigate the Wish Stealers of the world, keep company with the hearty Wish Givers you encounter, and pursue, protect, and believe in your wishes.

Check out

PENNIES FOR THE PLANET

to see how you can make a change!

www.penniesfortheplanet.org

Check out

THE
WORLD WISH
PROJECT

www.worldwishproject.com

This is a website to make kids' wishes come true
and create a forum for kids to inspire kids all over the planet
to change the world! Peace, clean water and air,
and saving the Amazon rain forest are all possible!